A NOTE ON THE AUTHOR

MICHELLE LOVRIC is the author of several novels – *Carnevale*, *The Remedy* (longlisted for the 2005 Orange Prize for Fiction) and *The Book of Human Skin* (a TV Book Club pick in 2011) as well as four children's books. Her most recent novel is *The True and Splendid History of the Harristown Sisters*. Her book *Love Letters: An Anthology of Passion* was a *New York Times* bestseller. She lives in London and Venice.

www.michellelovric.com

Bloomsbury Paperbacks
An imprint of Bloomsbury Publishing Plc

50 Bedford Square
London
WC1B 3DP
UK

1385 Broadway
New York
NY 10018
USA

www.bloomsbury.com

BLOOMSBURY and the Diana logo are trademarks of Bloomsbury Publishing Plc

First published in Great Britain in 2003 by Virago Press
This paperback edition first published in 2015

British Library Cataloguing-in-Publication Data
A catalogue record for this book is available from the British Library.

ISBN: PB: 978-1-4088-4383-3
ePub: 978-1-4088-4284-3

2 4 6 8 10 9 7 5 3 1

Typeset in Jenson by M Rules
Printed and bound in Great Britain by CPI Group (UK) Ltd, Croydon CR0 4YY

FSC
www.fsc.org
MIX
Paper from
responsible sources
FSC® C020471

To find out more about our authors and books visit www.bloomsbury.com.
Here you will find extracts, author interviews, details of forthcoming
events and the option to sign up for our newsletters.

The Floating Book

Michelle Lovric

BLOOMSBURY

LONDON · NEW DELHI · NEW YORK · SYDNEY

A poet is like the birds of passage . . .
They pass singing in the distance, the world
Knows nothing of them except their voice . . .

I was singing, my friends, as a man breathes,
As a bird mourns, as the wind sighs,
As murmurs float on flowing water.

Lamartine, *Le Poète Mourant*

PART ONE

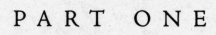

Prologue

She came to me in the secret night,
all the spice of Araby on her skin, to give me
the priceless gift of herself, prised from her husband's lap.
No, it's fine; I'll be satisfied if
she notches on her belt the days she spends with me.

June 63 BC

Greetings, my brother,

On what forsaken crag of Asia Minor does this find you, soldier-boy?

How little we know of one another these days! Reading your letters, nostalgia slings its warm arm around my shoulder and I'm hungering for your laugh, for that reproving look in your fond eye, and I cannot believe our childhood intimacy at all fractured by your absence.

How do you recall that childhood of ours, Lucius? It seems drowsily happy to me. Perhaps it's always so to the younger son.

Perhaps it's necessarily so to a poet.

Is it not strange that *you* can remember my infancy, my first word, when I do not?

In fact I envy you all your memories; unlike me, you also have an image of our mother's face, and of her eyes fixed upon you with adoration. I read recently that the mother-ostrich kindles life in her chicks merely by the loving intensity of her gaze upon the eggs. Those eggs that miss her eyes grow addled and never hatch. I hope

3

to evade such a fate, though our mother died pushing me into this world, leaving me to your tender ministrations.

So – can you guess what has brought on this touching bout of nostalgia? Or where I sit as I write this letter?

Yes! Our father has at last given in to my intolerable pestering and agreed to send me to Rome. In case you've forgotten, I'm eighteen years old this month. It's time for me to take my place at the centre of the empire.

The ten-day journey was uneventful. Our father ensured I travelled in every comfort at the mildest time of the year, for the sake of my mythical weak chest. (Yes, that same damned birdcage always cited when disallowing any robust games.)

Cocooned like a precious jewel in a casket, I arrived in Rome intact. But from the moment I entered the city my sense of self cracked open like a trodden insect.

At the city gate we were obliged to leave the carriage and I myself had to help carry the ignominious straw baskets of my possessions as we proceeded lowly on foot. Little lord of Sirmione, no one turned to salute me here among the impossible palaces and closed-fist faces that stubbed down my pride like a vicious thumb.

Husked of all my pretensions, I was rendered a nothing creature, transparent, absorbent, leaky as a good secret. The innocence dripped off my sweat-sponged forehead and my veins distended in new appetites fed by the stinks and uproar of the streets and the marble eyes of women haughty as balconies.

My new home – rented from Marcus Crassus – turned out to be a fine villa within a shallow sniff of the livid juices of the Tiber. The first thing I did was to despatch back to our father the Veronese servants who had accompanied me on the journey from Sirmione. They were quite possibly his spies, but worse, they had witnessed my sudden degradation to back-street nobody.

Waving them off, I lifted my head and sniffed the tangled salty air. It was late spring, the cooking fires were burning in rich men's houses, and already I had a stack of invitations to attend to. Our father's friends in town were determined to be generous.

4

Caesar himself bestowed his company and his patronage. His house was among the first I visited. (I took care not to be visibly awestruck by its luxuries.) He showed me (our *pater*, rather) the honour of stepping forth to greet me so that all might see how I was esteemed. He held my hand for a moment after he first pressed it, looking into my eyes until I was forced to look away, blushing.

'What are you for?' he asked me, a strange question, I thought. Now I know him better, I realise that it was entirely characteristic. Caesar always seeks the essence, disregarding anything ephemeral, including youth, good looks or humour. He finds no poetry in the little things, but a great lyrical epic in shaping the future. Look at *his* ambitions – praetor-elect and his sights set even higher – compare them to my little poems!

Still, he had the grace not to laugh when I told him that I was a poet, and would be a great one. Instead he put his head to one side and considered me for a long time. The glass of those large grey eyes cooled my spirits, but when I was gently dismissed a few seconds later I put Caesar out of my mind. I went to join the drinkers and the jokers and show them what I was made of, on both counts.

I'm never homesick, well rarely. I've taken to urban life as naturally as rosemary to pork crackling. Yet I still feel myself an outsider. I know we're all Roman citizens now. No matter that our Verona estate rolls into the horizon, or that there's old money in the family, and good blood. I still feel myself irretrievably provincial.

I confess I've also made the occasional *faux pas*, like the sweltering night at Caelius's house when I dropped a lump of ice in my red wine and six of the other dinner guests went home early. Romans! I'm still prickling at the memory. Mind, I myself was so saturated at the time that I needed to be told about it the next day. Then I clapped my hand on my forehead and fretted, for such idiocies breed nicknames that stick for ever in Rome. I was tormented by the thought that my only immortality might be as 'Ice-man' or 'Cooler'. If anything, I think the incident set me scribbling more earnestly, to make sure that I would be known for something much better, *infinitely* better.

Yes, I still dream of writing a book. Meanwhile, I've made my mark in other ways. Our youthful tomfoolery on the banks of Lake Benacus has served me well. Only recently arrived in Rome, I became the star of the Aemilian Draughts and Swimming Club, and performed prodigious feats of swinging from beams and swimming the Tiber with a cat aloft in one hand. The beast scratched my wrists raw and my blood flowed into the river. At last I felt that Rome had taken me in, suckled on me, as it were. So I told everyone who'd listen and they roared at the piquancy of my blasphemy, and then spread it around.

There's worse, too.

A good team of well-bred young men can send any town, even Rome, to hide under its bed. Just yesterday – one of those extraordinary nights when excitement sifts like powder on the skin – when everyone else had scattered, I remember me and Cinna catching a nightsoilman and putting him down a drain. But then everything I do these days is just a bit larger than life; the way I screw up my entire face at a bad smell, the complexity and filthiness of my oaths when I lose at draughts, the delicacy with which I place my drained cup down on the table. I make sure everyone's looking at me, and that it's worth their while to do so. ('No change there then, Gaius,' I hear you say.)

And I've made other friends, Lucius.

People are writing roasting letters to our *pater* to tell him: *Young Catullus has fallen in with the worst company in Rome.*

The gossips are right (I told the old boy they lied, of course). I have become intimate – and I use the word advisedly – with Clodia Metelli and her brother Publius Clodius Pulcher.

Between them those siblings can show the world what's wild and burning bad at the heart of Rome. This much I knew before I even met them: that the brother's a ruffian (his armed escort is smellier and more vicious even than Caesar's); the sister a notorious libertine. She's connected vertically and horizontally (the pun is

6

intended, dear Lucius) with half of Rome's nobility. And Clodia's more than ornamental. She's powerful.

At her house on the lordly Palatine Hill, she entertains the elite of Rome in more ways than are respectable even for a highborn Roman matron with a husband conveniently serving in the provinces these twenty years past. There's a spindly little daughter somewhere, an heiress, but she's of no account. It's the mother who draws the crowds and lights them up. Her dinner parties, at which she reclines in transparent muslins and dances with immoderate suppleness, are famous for their lewd late-night entertainments, and what happens after them.

So yes of course, brother, when I first expressed an interest at the Club, out sauntered all the stale and rancid jokes. 'A Cold Proposition,' they called her, 'But anyone may Go There. Even her . . .'

'Is she not rather gifted, though?' I ventured, flame-faced, gauche as a veal-calf. 'I heard she writes plays.'

'Her wittiest part's between her legs,' someone hooted and I laughed along with the rest.

I finally met her for myself at a dinner in the house of Allius.

Caelius had laid me a bait to the door – of dancing girls, not to mention plates of gilded flamingo tongue and peacock brains seethed in wine. And the company of poets. Caelius styles himself one such, notwithstanding that his verses droop like the eyelids of a drugged prostitute. Meanwhile, though, he's winning fame at the bar, flirting with the old men, unpacking his handsome grin at the right parties.

This was one of those.

So she was there.

In the torch-shimmered threshold he introduced us. 'Gaius Valerius Catullus . . . Clodia, daughter of Appius, wife of Quintus Metellus.' I bowed, wondering if she had heard of me yet.

I remember the sidelong pivot of an eye, of red-brown rich as resin that seemed for a moment to glisten, a flighty black pupil, a heavy thrall of lashes. Clinking emerald earrings, she murmured something inaudible in a low, deep voice, which had the effect of making me lean closer to her.

My heart shot backwards in my breast like a heavy bolt. In the rafters of my ribcage something warm and fragile batflapped through the darkness. I suddenly smelled lightning in the leaden air (and indeed it sliced the sky within an hour, and all the guests splashed home through the pooled and dog-loping streets).

But the storm as yet lay secret in my senses and for a moment I shared breaths with Clodia. Already slightly turning on her heel, she looked me slowly up and down, and moved swiftly on, her breasts shifting minnowlike beneath the tunic pinioned by a magnificent sardonyx cameo. I noticed then that the hem was already stained with the juices of the gutter.

She turned back once to nod at me, and then she was gone, swallowed into a huddle of important men at the kernel of the party. I saw her brother – the likeness was unmistakable – pull her to him and nuzzle a whisper into her ear. I stood simmering, gooseskinned and wisp-tongued in the milk of the moonlight, until the douse of rain chased me into the prattling shadows of the portico, where I listened to my poet friends declaim as if through a cup pressed to a door. I paced her name all the way home through ribbed curtains of water. Above me rose-coloured lightning embroidered the drowning sky with hectic stitches.

Love is only worth what you pay for it, I told myself at the start. I, just like the rest, chose not to sit in the counting house, doling out my feelings only for just returns. When she sent a messenger two days after that dinner at Allius's, I raced up the still-steaming hill to her house in the exclusive Clivus Victoriae on the western side of the Palatine, panting for my climb, panting for her attention, just like all the others, running as if each step pressed pins into my feet, nosing blindly into the white-hot light, my head spiced with holiday oils and all the hairs on my wrists stiffly at attention.

On the way I passed the temple of the Cybele, vibrating with the usual high-pitched howls and febrile drumbeats. No, Lucius, I did not hear a warning in that din! *You* must be steeped in Her myth, living as you do in the Magna Mater's native Asia Minor. But here in sophisticated Rome the cult of Cybele is something of a joke. We find it rather distasteful that there are still men ready to emulate Her disciple Attis and cut off their pricks with stone knives. Anyway, I assure you that self-mutilation was the last thing on my mind as I trotted past the noisy temple towards Clodia's house.

I forced myself to slow my pace when I arrived at her rain-rotted garden and walked slowly past the smoking flowers. When I reached her threshold another manservant greeted me with lowered eyes and led me silently to the room where his mistress awaited me. At first, stupefied by the view, I did not see her reclining on a divan. All Rome's power teemed in miniature beneath me. Clodia's house overlooks the forum, where her brother Clodius was no doubt busy conducting his intrigues even as I stood there. High above the courts and temples, none of their clamour reached her terrace. I heard nothing but insect-song and the quiet scurrying of servants. From that lofty viewpoint Rome seemed like a model displayed for Clodia's regal manipulations.

'Ah, the poet is arrived.' Her voice, cool and amused, turned me around. I started: she was *sparingly* dressed. My eye fell on a terracotta oil lamp on a table beside her. It was intricately carved in the shape of a winged phallus.

'Against bad luck?' I asked boldly.

'That's the conventional meaning,' she murmured evasively. She did not rise to greet me, but fingered a cushion beside her, and smiled. As I walked towards her I saw hyenas carved on the head-rests of her divan.

There were a few preliminaries and then, surprisingly, she gave herself to me without ceremony, as if the act meant nothing to her.

Yet I shall never forget that divan in the porch of her house and the thrum of the cicadas as I kissed her for the first time and fumbled with the cord of her robe, and the puffs of air which came from her pet sparrow's beating wings. The bird circled around us the whole time, trying to alight if we were still for a second. I

9

remember the lisp of wings in my ears, little claws scraping on my back. The scratches I found there that night must have been the result.

It seems that it all happened slowly, for I play it back in my mind slowly, the first afternoon I spent naked and alone with Clodia. It was like a long meal, with perhaps nine or ten courses; some were deeply satisfying; others seemed merely to whet my appetite for what would come next. After a while I stopped worrying if we might be interrupted. I realised from her deliberate style of lovemaking that she had arranged things so as to enjoy me for as long as she wanted, to test my stamina, to audition me. There were moments when the divan felt like a trough in which she was trying to drown me; others when it seemed to float over the ground. She kept me until a wan and wasted moon swung above us. The blind night watched me shamble home.

Her embrace was vigorous; she is of course nearly as tall as I am, and expensively well fed. Her breath was sweet and mingled with the scent of perfumed oil in her hair and eyebrows. I choked on that scent while her hands went everywhere, weighing and pulling rather than caressing. Her breasts were heavier and less responsive than I had hoped, but the joy of fingering what I had passed forty-eight hours feverishly imagining was enough reward for me. I was conscious that she was older than me, perhaps fifteen years older, but instead of disgusting me, that merely made me feel more grown-up myself, as if this were my true arrival not just in adult life, but also in the adult life of Rome and therefore the world. Suddenly all my adolescent desires and flirtations were transformed into earthy male lust.

Her coolness was . . . alluring. From the start I was drunk as a wineshop fly on the challenge of it. It was on this premise that I fell in love with every part of her, just as all the others had done. And just like all the others before me, and after, I'm embarrassed to think of how garrulous I was with it. I could barely wait to tell the world that I had bedded her, and, more eloquently still, how I had already begun to suffer for it. I wrote the first poem that very evening.

But was I ever happy, even then? Even for a second? Perhaps when I first burst inside her? I think not. You will notice that I've talked only of her body, not of her words. There were no intimate exchanges, despite the brawling of our lips. It was quite impersonal. Even the frenzy of our lovemaking was numbed by her rigorous silence. Not a groan did she utter; the only sign that I had perforated the shield of her *froideur* was a single droplet of sweat on the left side of her upper lip. Even that could have been mine, sprayed from my tearful face; each time I wept in the last moments, you see. Prescient tears, though I was too busy and too exhausted to understand what I was crying about.

She decided when she'd had her fill of me, and pushed me off the divan in a peremptory fashion. I giggled weakly: it was less humiliating to read that gesture as a playful one. Once she'd smoothed down her robe, she talked to me in a normal voice of everyday things: the scandals of the town and the Baths. I fancied that her laugh was a little throatier, a little more intimate than hitherto. Very little was said of what had just passed between us, and most of it by me. I was too intimidated by her poise to say what I wanted to, which was, of course, that I had fallen irredeemably in love.

I only know I pleased her because further appointments have been made. Many other appointments. She's never more friendly than on the first occasion; she does not acknowledge our relations in public. A woman who loves cannot help but betray her affections: Clodia has no difficulties with discretion.

I could not flatter myself that I'd taken her heart by storm. Still, well, you know – I'd *had* her. I was so impressed with myself. I was the lover of the most sought-after woman in Rome!

Now I had something to write about.

I immediately christened her 'Lesbia', in my poetry. The way a child gives a name to something it wants, as if that makes possession of it official. Like the sun, or the reflection of the moon in the water. My possession of 'Lesbia' was as substantial as that. This name was the greatest compliment I could bestow. The women of the isle of Lesbia are thought the most exquisite in the world; also, as personified in their ancient poetess, Sappho, the most refined, poetic and delicately passionate. That other meaning, the fellatory one, is not what I mean at all . . . Forgive me if I seem to patronise you by explaining the allusion. I know not if they talk of such things in the provinces and the camps.

Lesbia's sparrow, Lesbia's sandal, Lesbia's kisses . . . Our kisses, I promised, would be more than the grains of sand on the spicy shores of Cyrene. The white heat of the sun, the power of Rome, would all melt before our passion. I boasted that the docility of that sparrow of hers and its gentle assaults on her finger would be nothing to the animal pleasures I offered.

So I'm a soldier too, Lucius. Writing poems about Clodia has turned me into a commander of words!

I'm a veteran now. First I marshal my words and dispose them in formation. Then I say, 'Now, words, do your duty and serve!' Off they go, sometimes hitting the mark straight away, sometimes splitting off into innuendo or meaningless, merely rhythmic, sequences.

At the beginning I thought I was inventing new senses, like 'constriction-sense around the heart', or 'whirring wings around my naked back', but all these images are merely foot-soldiers of the old senses. And so I always come back to those five great generals.

Each new poem, I summon them up and say, 'Mouth! Nose! Eyes! Skin! Ears! Tell me what Clodia has done to you! Consider and report back for duty forthwith!'

They shuffle off to their deliberations and come back with their accounts. I ready my wax tablet and raise my stylus.

'Mouth first!' I say, 'What's she done to you?'

'Ravished me, sir.'

'Nose?'

'Ravished . . . the perfume . . .'

'OK,' I interrupt, 'Skin?'

'Ravished, utterly.'

'Ears, you too?'

'That voice . . .'

'Boring!' I tell them. 'Tell me something original about ravishment.'

Eventually, they do. My mouth fetches me the memory of a kiss; my nose a recollection of an unguent, and eventually something melds together. I keep writing and erasing words on wax until I have a sense of recognition, until I can see my feelings in that pearly mirror making their own steam.

I don't cast a poem off till I can come to it anew, creep up on it by surprise. If I can still say, on re-reading, 'Aha! Got it!' then the poem is ready. It's already fighting on its own account. It rebuffs me and goes out into the world on its own.

To make me famous, to get me talked about.

To let everybody know that this overpraised slut of a city has one more poet's mouth to feed now.

Chapter One

. . . For I will give you such an unguent
distilled upon my lover via Venus and Cupid
that when you smell it
you'll be on your knees,
begging the Gods to make you
All nose.

In certain light-suffused mists, Venice deconstructs herself. One sees faint smears of silhouettes, and in these the architect's early sketches: the skeletons of the *palazzi* as he saw them on paper when they were only dreams. When the haze lifts, those buildings swell again with substance, as if freshly built. But until that happens the Venetians *nose* their way around their city.

In the thickened air every stink and every fragrance is unbearably intensified. The canals smell of billy goat and grass-clippings, the ever-present steam of sea-louse soup smells of dark sea caves, the babies smell of mouse holes, and the women smell of what they desire.

When the sea vapour blanked the town in those days, the streets were dark; only the *cesendoli*, little shrines to the Madonna, remained perpetually lit, and a few lamps under the arcades until the fourth hour of the night. The unpaved streets lurched rutted and holed; the wooden bridges were prone to collapse unexpectedly, rendering the mist, already churning with possibilities of dangerous and wonderful encounters, more threatening and more exciting.

The fog swallowed noises, belching soft echoes of them. Rocking like a sleeping crib on the water, the city cocked a blind ear, sniffed like a mole. On days like that, men and women shuffled through their town like sleepwalkers, their nostrils flared, their toes splayed and all their animal senses acutely alert.

14

The fog created intimate pockets, making impromptu couples of people who merely passed in the street, uniting for brief moments lantern sellers, fried food hawkers, wool beaters, mask makers, fabric stretchers, caulkers. It parted to reveal instantaneous tableaux which soon disappeared again in the vapour – a fat flute player who looked like a constipated but hopeful baby puckering up his lips for the spoon; *scuole* of *battuti* – flagellants who, veiled and bare-backed, perambulated the city scourging themselves with iron chains and birch branches; a cat and her husband in the business of procreation.

Or, out of the mist might loom the face of a large, grinning pig. It was not long since the Senate had outlawed the vagrant Tantony boars that still caused havoc in the streets. The pigs, supposed to be fed by the charity of the faithful, were but loosely tended by the monks of San Antonio. The beasts had grown fat and fierce by merely helping themselves to whatever food they wanted. When the mist soused their bristles they grew skittish, knocking unsuspecting passers-by into the freezing canals.

On days like that, the men who loved Sosia Simeon wondered what she was about, because they knew her. They knew that on a whim, she would betray them all without a thought. And so she was doing, in the first thick autumn mist of 1467, with a middle-aged nobleman she had just passed in the fogbound ghost of a back street in the Misericordia.

She had seen a needy cast in his green eyes and the tell-tale hollow of his breast as he wove out of the fog: he himself might not know it, but Nicolò Malipiero, it was plain to Sosia, was in need of a woman. Instantly, she had opened her cloak just a little so that her warm and somewhat feral smell could visit his nose. Her scent travelled through the soft white vapour, tangible as a prodding finger.

Sosia's nobleman was bulky as a boar himself and awkward with his weight. As Sosia approached him, he gasped. She slowed her pace, lingering on her left foot, looking into his eyes. The nobleman made a whimpering noise, then an unaccustomed swift move, turning around to pull at her wrist. His red senatorial robe spun round them like a wave of blood.

'Who are you?'

'I am Sosia.'

'Are you . . . ? Do you . . . ?'

'Are you Venetian?'

15

'Yes.'

Sosia smiled.

'H-h-how . . . much?'

She said nothing, but drew him into an alleyway, and parted her cloak. The mist isolated them in an instant. He shuddered between her legs, staring into her eyes, which she then closed briefly, twisting on his stalk as if trying to pinch a wildflower from its grasses. He cried out, biting his tongue, but it was the most pleasure he had ever experienced. Tears transpired on his cheeks.

He felt no relief, having had her. Nicolò Malipiero was still asking, again, *When? How much?* as the liquid cooled on her thighs and they stood breath-close together in the doorway, cocooned in the mist.

Sosia said: 'Decide what I'm worth, you do that.'

'I cannot do this. I must know you. This is . . . important.' The tone of his voice rose in an uncertain shameful whine.

Silently, she moved to go, restless as a squirrel in his arms. She was as foreign a woman as he had seen or heard. The Venetian courtesans were many and various in their styles but he had not been with such a one before. Her accent disturbed him; she disturbed him. She had no grace or tenderness to her; none of the motherly kindness of some whores, not even an eye on the commercial possibilities of another encounter.

'When will I see you again?'

'How can I know that?'

'Come to my *studiolo* tomorrow. It will be empty.'

He fastened his hand on her wrist and whispered the directions in her ear.

'Here's the key.' She reached out for it, revealing the yellow badge fastened to her elbow. He gasped but she had slipped the key under a wing of her cloak without looking at it, and was gone.

Of course she did not arrive the next day, when Nicolò Malipiero lay shivering under the blankets of ermine and bear that he had bought to examine and love her upon. He lay alone, sick with fear that he would never see her again, his fists balled up like dead roses.

Nor did she come the day after, by which time a midnight storm had at last erased the mist, and Venice sparkled like malice in iridescent sunlight. He waited for her. He poured wine in splashes and waited till the tiny bubbles at the edge of the glass evaporated, promising himself that she would be there when the red liquid lay perfectly quiescent. By the end of the second day he had not yet left the studio, in terror that she would appear at that moment and be lost to him. The room had started to smell, metallically, of fear and the stale trapped breath of hopeless need. He sent a messenger to his wife: *I am ill; I don't want to infect the children, stay away.*

At the dawn of the third day Sosia pushed the unclosed door open with her foot, and stood profiled in the doorway, the cut of her waist and the slant panniers of her haunches in black silhouette, the key dangling in her hand.

She said: 'So do you have some red wine, Mister Nobleman? That's what I like.'

He was naked, still waiting under the ermine. Now he leapt from the bed, clumsy with joy, the tiny blades of the fur embossed on his plump flesh as if he were a flagellant. Reaching for the pitcher, instead he knocked it to the floor. He turned to face her, humiliated to the darkest core of his soul. He was painfully aware of the splashes of wine sidling down his knees, the ignominious teardrop on the end of his nose, and the aching erection unfurling slowly in front of her.

Sosia thought momentarily of elegant Domenico Zorzi, whose thin lips were infinitely flexible and whose facial skin was pitted like a cucumber. He was no doubt waiting for her, as arranged, in the sumptuous gloom of his *palazzo*. He would have a new book for her, today, he had promised. Well, he would wait. He might even become lost in the book, scholar that he was, and forget about her for an hour or two. Felice Feliciano, she banished forcibly from her mind. Her husband Rabino did not enter it at all.

The cold weather had broken, she was twenty-seven years old, and Sosia Simeon was in the mood and good appetite for a new Venetian nobleman. That morning she had opened a fresh page of her ledger and added the name: 'Nicolò Malipiero' to the Golden Book column.

It looked good, she thought, under all the rest.

Chapter Two

. . . He's married a green girl
who's not even come into bud,
tender-playful as a kid.
She needs kid-glove treatment.
You must touch her as delicately
as you'd pull the skin off a grape.
But he lets her do what she likes,
and you can guess what she likes to do!

Rabino Simeon, discreetly watching her hide the book in its habitual cleft in the scullery wall, saw that his wife had lost substance in the days since he last beheld her. He noted how a strand of dark hair, caught up in her mouth, seemed to draw the corner of her lip towards her unusually complicated ear. Against the eggshell pallor of her face, the black hair looked like a crack in her skin.

He suspected the worst as to the nature of her illness. Mortification cast his eyes down to the floor as she passed him on the stairs on her way up to their bedroom.

Sadly, he noted her thin wrists and the rasp of her breath, but his pity was veined with darker feelings.

As if to dislodge the unsavoury visions conjured by the ledger, Rabino shook his head violently, dislodging flakes of skin that sifted on his robe, uneasy as maggots. He drew his cloak around him, obscuring the yellow circle on his sleeve, and slipped out into the gelid depths of the night. If Sosia planned to spend a rare evening in their home, then he was happier to be out of it.

On the day Sosia Simeon met Nicolò Malipiero, it was exactly twelve years since Rabino had taken Sosia from a wretched family of Dalmatian Jews, initially as a maid and clerk. It had been another moist and frigid day, he recalled, another December, when he himself had not yet reached his fortieth year. She was then twelve, or so he was told, still a *puella*, an innocent and immature girl in the eyes of the law. He soon realised that she was at least two years older. Days after she arrived in his home she had asked him, unblushingly, for rags for her personal use.

He made a nest for her in the attic, and explained her duties as kindly as he could. She edged past him into the room, brushing him with her breast and then looked pointedly down the stairs by which they had ascended. Rabino realised that her privacy was important to her. *She's had none till now, poor little creature*, he thought.

Her grasp of Italian was astonishing, given her background and the limits of her experience in the world. Her schoolteacher father had taught her the language, she informed him. But there was more sophistication in her vocabulary than Rabino had heard in her father's and her grammar was better. More disturbingly, she never stumbled over words.

She rarely spoke more than a sentence, but he found that her eyes were always upon him, no matter when he looked up. Her gaze, that never actually met his own eyes, was neither grateful nor subservient. Sosia appeared to be intensely interested in his every movement. She seemed to study the lines of his limbs, to see through his robes, more like a libidinous widow than a little girl. Rabino was trapped in her gaze like a fly drowning slowly in a bowl of sugar water. Its effect upon him was distorting: he quickly came to think of Sosia as an older woman than she was, mature in her desires and forthright in the expression of them.

Rabino could not decide if the girl was beautiful or ugly. Different moments saw her features gilded with a sensuous light or hard and sullen as if coarsely carved in granite. This conundrum drew his own eyes to her again and again, until watching Sosia intently became an involuntary and chronic act of shame.

She did not seem oppressed by his gaze; on the contrary she absorbed it as if it were her right. He could have sworn that there were times she deliberately placed herself in the way of his eyes. She made a compelling ritual of extracting the seeds of an apple with her tongue. When they ate, she would let the spoon linger in her mouth so that he grew breathless waiting for her to withdraw it. It was hard to believe she was innocent of the effect on him when she splashed her clothes while washing linen so that her chemise grew transparent, revealing her arms and the delicate furrow of her collarbone.

She spoke so rarely that Rabino could not enter her mind. Soon it became convenient to think of her as merely physical, the embodiment of forbidden appetites.

She had lived in his home three months, her shameless gaze devouring his composure, when lust overtook him in the pantry one winter's night. He found himself holding her hips while he entered her. She did not flinch as he put his hands upon her; did not resist as he raised her skirt. She was completely compliant, cool and passive in his arms. As he toiled and blushed, she turned her neck slowly to glance back at him for just a moment. Afterwards she had not looked at him again, but continued scraping the plates with her thin fingers. She touched neither herself nor him.

Watching her from the corner of the room, feeling himself not just violator but voyeur, Rabino found it impossible to believe he had just committed this brutish act in his own home, and that there were no apparent consequences. In the candlelight a splash of foamy liquid glittered suddenly on the flagstone. He turned away, stricken. He, of all people, a doctor . . . he could not bear to think what he had done. The rasp of her nails on the earthenware drove him from the room.

He married her. He knew he did not love her, that she was not the companion of his soul he had always longed to find, but he thought this sacrifice the most honourable way to expiate his sin. He could not admit, even to himself, that he was also afraid that the girl would become pregnant. There had been just that one brief lapse, and he had managed to spill his seed on the floor – however he knew, because the first instance had been involuntary, that it could happen again. He had become, in his own eyes, a monstrous slave to a reprehensible incontinence.

It was not that Rabino had never desired a woman before. But until now he had found it possible to subdue such thoughts with kindness for the object of his love. He knew that he was ungainly, his beard coarse, his eyes over-moist. He had never dared to wish himself upon the kind of woman he himself might want. Sosia was different. Her erotic presence perfumed the air he breathed inside the house, and every oyster, every artichoke she served reminded him of his moments inside her soft body.

He knew from the moment of the act that he was not the first. The initial shock of that realisation only dishonoured him more; instead of saving her, he had joined the rank of those who had apparently brutalised the girl to the point where she saw nothing wrong or even unusual in loveless congress with her employer.

Perhaps she has been trained to offer this service to anyone who pays her? He wondered, but cast the thought aside as too sordid to be true. She was only fourteen, perhaps fifteen; he had taken her straight from her parents, who, despite their wretched state, were respectable in the extreme. Until then she had lived her entire life under their protection. He had been assured of this. Moreover, her gauche manner and her lack of charm forfended any possibility that she might have been reared as a courtesan.

Other times he contrived to see himself as the victim of Sosia's debauchery. His profession had taught him that people who were damaged, whether physically or mentally, manifested the worst behaviours, and that they would drag innocent souls into the abyss with them, for company or to avenge their own wrongs.

Rabino was too good and too intelligent a man to let such justifications deafen the cries of his conscience for long. It soon became his obsession to make up to Sosia what had been robbed from her. He would be good to her. Her life would become good; he would spend the rest of his own redeeming it. She would become his familiar and helper. She would come to trust him and shed the cool furtiveness of aspect that hardened her features now. Kindness she would acquire; all who dealt with sick people did so, in his experience.

And so he persuaded himself, in continual silent monologues, while he

21

made his rounds, to engage the rabbi, the calligrapher for the wedding document, and the tailor to make the girl a new dress for the ceremony. For those three weeks it took to ready them both for the marriage, he did not touch her. *Perhaps,* he reasoned to himself, despising his own hypocrisy, *even virginity can renew itself. God is good,* he prayed.

Too late, on their wedding night, he became aware that Sosia was not the victim of men; that the act of love was as natural to her as eating. She was not unwilling; she was not frightened. She was dismaying in her appetites. He realised that it was the seep of flickering memories from her skin that cluttered up the air around her. The shock of the first revelation did not leave him. Once he had imagined her body curved around another man's, he could no longer look on her without that vision writhing in front of his eyes.

At first, it sickened him; sometimes, when he acknowledged that he did not love her, it raised in him a kind of excitement he felt to be unhealthy. He knew of booksellers in Venice who could supply woodcuts of the kind of scenes he imagined; he knew that noblemen among his patients exchanged these pictures. So far he had fallen from grace, from dignity: he was now bonded in honour by a primitive act to a woman whose soul was as anonymous to him as one of the participants depicted in those obscene prints. He could not meet his own eyes in the mirror; he shuddered at the speculations of the neighbours. He knew that in Venice they were always omniscient.

He stopped looking at Sosia. It was in looking at her that the trouble had started. He no longer cared to know whether she was beautiful or vile of face. Doctor and wife now exchanged information with their eyes averted, for Sosia, it seemed, had no more desire to reach out to him, except in the basest, physical way. When he asked her to read aloud to him, to spare his tired eyes, she seemed to turn the purest poetry into cold and dizzying licentiousness, without changing a word or the monotone inflection of her voice.

It was a mystery to him how she did this. Perhaps it was the contradictions: despite what seemed the deliberate iciness of her voice, she could not disguise the pleasure she found in the words. When Sosia was reading, it was an act of her whole body. She held the book in four cupped fingers, one hand like a tray of sweetmeats, poring over it. Her body squirmed like a child's, too excited to contain the knowledge it was ingesting. Rabino disliked watching this. *Sosia loves to read,* he thought, *but I hate the way she loves it:*

22

He no longer followed her to the pantry, and rarely joined her in their bedroom. These days he clung to the side of the narrow divan in the *soggiorno* rather than join her in the darkness. The conjugal bed, with Sosia in it, had become in his exhausted mind a kind of terrifying mollusc with a slimy, greedy mouth at the centre. In outline, in the moonlight, Sosia's body under the coverlet looked to have a hundred grasping limbs. She slept restlessly, churning her feet and grunting like an animal. He would look down on her when he arrived home at midnight, and lift the sheet as if to join her. But at the last moment abhorrence overcame him and he stole away, wiping his hands on his tunic.

Rabino longed to talk it over with his friend, the surgeon Smuel Ben Shimshon, but Smuel could not be expected to understand, and his sympathy would be painful. *He* shared a tropical joy with his own young wife. Rabino knew – from Smuel's eagerness to return home after even the most pleasurable evening's discussions, from his rueful tiredness some mornings – the nature and extent of his friend's physical and sentimental happiness with his Benvenuta. Once he had asked Smuel, 'What's that beautiful smell?' Smuel had blushed and stammered out a confession. His wife liked to put sprigs of lavender in their bed; at night they released their oils.

Rabino imagined Benvenuta strewing the fresh herbs over the linen, smiling in happy anticipation of sharing their delectable scent with her husband. He had no idea what Sosia thought about when he was away from home, what she looked forward to, if anything.

He did not know how she passed her days, whether she had friends. There were other Serbs in the town; fewer Jews, as all of them, except physicians like himself, had been exiled seven decades before. Was she lonely? he wondered. Was she perhaps homesick? Did she seek out her own kind?

Perhaps she longed for a child, he thought, but he could no longer bring himself to do what was necessary to fulfil such a desire. Anyway, his professional eye had long since detected some slight malformation in the bone structure of her hips, which explained her loping walk. It would be difficult for her to bear a child to term.

Rabino stayed away from home more often; volunteering for night vigils over dying patients, relieving other surgeons like Smuel and sending them gratefully home to their wives and families. He would go to the dread island of Santa Maria di Nazaret, the *lazzaretto* for those infected with the plague and the depository for all contaminated goods. He was there so often that the monks gave him his own cell with a clean, hard pallet. But he had to go home, sometimes. During the day he snatched some hours' sleep while Sosia went to the market. His signal to rise hurriedly from the bed would be the sound of her key in the latch. He would pass her on the stairs with a polite greeting that she ignored or to which she replied, mockingly, 'Tired, are you, Mister Doctor?'

Over their mid-day meal he remained as silent as she did. The food was unappetising and he did not comment upon it. He did not even wish to draw attention to it by adding condiments or peeling the burnt crusts from sippets in the meat porridge. He knew that it was not mere incompetence that resulted in sustenance as revolting as the messes Sosia placed in front of him.

It was hatred, quietly and passively executed.

Chapter Three

He just lies like a log in a ditch.
He knows so little about her
that he might never have had her.
This idiot of mine sees nothing,
hears nothing,
knows less,
whether he's coming, or has ever come . . .

Rabino assumed that Sosia hated him for his neglect. In this he was completely in error. Regarding her husband, his absence was the only thing that gave Sosia pleasure. She had loathed reading Petrarch aloud to him, hated watching the softening of his eyes and the way he looked to her to satisfy the tender needs the poet created in him. She had soon made sure that he stopped asking. She had other fish to fry. Unsupervised, Sosia took to stealing pleasure where she could find it. She had become an expert at procuring it and detecting those who also knew where to look.

On the Venetian ferryboats Sosia stood close to other women, close enough to gauge the percentage of sweat mixed with their civet perfumes, to know whether they menstruated or had copulated that morning or afternoon. To those smelling of the latter events she would give a crooked, complicitous smile that made them look to their baskets of cherries, the knotting of their shawls or the ribands of their children, in blushing confusion.

The street-whores turned away from her, defiantly. They did not want to be complicit with such as Sosia Simeon, even if they did not know she was a Jewess. Her foreignness chafed with them, her unwholesomeness was so pervasive as to be contaminating. She seemed capable of stealing their own slender strand of innocence by polluting the sweetly shabby memories in their heads.

Although she would automatically always say, if asked, that she hated Venice, the city suited Sosia Simeon and her purposes. She might live like a character in a book there, rather than as a mere person constrained by circumstances. When she was not reading aloud to Rabino, Sosia loved books. She loved the choice of universes they offered, far from the restricted life of a Jewish doctor's wife in Venice. In reading a book, Sosia could be male or female, potent or passive. The more she thought about it, the more Sosia considered herself free to try those other kinds of lives, sampled from intrigues of the Old Testament or picturesque, amoral tales of the Orient. The values that she prized were those of the fabled East: cunning, superbly executed malice and secrecy.

Venice was, it seemed, built for all these things. From her Crusades, the city brought back more than physical plunder: she stole ideas of beauty too, but made them subtly her own. Her architects had taken the traceries and arcaded courtyards of the East and turned them outwards, so that the modesty of inner sanctums became delicate but flagrant display in Venice. What was impenetrable in Aleppo was permeable in Venice. Anyone might walk the unnumbered streets and peer through shapely holes in the stone to see Sosia and her kind at their honest and dishonest pleasures. And she would be aware that she was watched, and find the sensation conducive to further enjoyment.

If Sosia feared the stone lions' heads fixed in certain Venetian walls, their mouths gaping open for anonymous denunciations, she did not show it. She loped briskly past them, on the way to her assignations.

Rabino was correct in one theory about his wife. Sosia was not born the way she lived now.

Her parents, on his brief meeting with them, had seemed decent and kind. So something, Rabino reasoned, must have happened to the girl. The one thing he always remembered, guessing that it must be relevant, was that her mother had not looked at Sosia when she said goodbye.

Rabino could not know that Sosia's mother had not met her daughter's eyes since the day her family fled their home in the mountains of Dalmatia.

On that pewter-grey December morning heavy footfalls in the forest had filled up all their senses with terror, finally growing into the tall silhouettes of men gaunt as nails against the pale gold of the field.

Sosia would not talk to Rabino of what had happened next; about the garrotting of her grandfather and the beating of her grandmother, the pulpy noise as the wrinkled faces collapsed; how ineffective had proved the cunning with which her parents had hidden the children in a wooden crate in the dung-heap. The soldiers were wise to farmers' tricks. They were farmers themselves when they did not have better things to do.

They had prodded the box with pitchforks, none too careful with them. The children, screaming and bloody, were tumbled out into the dung, where they sat blinking and passionately sucking their thumbs. The soldiers sent the baby flying with a sharp butt of the fork to a heap of hay where it lay ominously silent. Nor were the younger children of interest. But they hoisted Sosia, the eldest, by the neck of her dress and held her kicking and scrambling above the dung-heap while they looked up her skirt. She squealed and twisted.

'She's ripe,' said one.

'You reckon?'

'Well, I'm ripe.'

'You go ahead then. What's stopping you? The Venetians don't tax it yet, do they?'

'The Venetians wouldn't touch a scrawny piece like this. They'd throw this one back. They wouldn't touch her, dirty little Serb.'

'Not even going to be pretty,' observed his companion.

'Not even going to be anything,' laughed another, with menace, brandishing his pig-slaughtering knife.

The consensus was that it would be more enjoyable to torture her than copulate with her.

The only man with a semblance of uniform ostentatiously turned his back while three men approached her, spread her flailing limbs like a windmill against the colourless sky. A fourth wiped his stiletto blade across the sweat of his forehead to moisten it. Sosia's heartbeat gulped to every noise: she could not hear their words any more. Deep throbs blockaded all her senses, as if each beat excavated and threw a heaped load of snow from an endless drift. Her scream was thin; she was choking on bile in her throat.

They slashed through her dress and carved a large, shallow S in her back, having ascertained her name from the other children. They laughed and shouted as she whimpered, writhing on the post.

After the soldiers had melted back into the forest, Sosia's parents emerged from their hiding place in the barn. Sosia's father tipped her off the pitchfork, into the mud. She rushed to her mother, pulled at her arms, tried to make them encircle her, but in vain. No one would look at Sosia, and when she made to climb on to her mother's lap, she was pushed away.

With the simple fervency of childhood, she decided to die as quickly as possible. She refused food and water. They were not offered again.

Somehow it didn't happen. The wound swiftly sealed, without infection. Physically, Sosia thrived. But the bereavement of her mother's gaze damaged her in ways that ran beneath the skin.

She assumed a new persona.

She did not cry, she who had been known since infancy for the readiness of her tears and the softness of her sensibilities. She did not refer to what had happened. What she had made of the words the men had used to her was a mystery. She did not mention them, or the soldiers. But their cruel glances began to cross her own face and their coarse phrases started to take part in her own sentences. Those sentences became opaque, and as brief as possible. Her glare was poisonous, her hand quick with slaps and pinches for the other children. Suddenly Sosia, like a basilisk, was someone to be feared.

Within hours of the soldiers' departure the family had fled. Sosia's father closed up his school and posted a regretful notice on the door. They travelled down from the mountains. Sosia leapt into the cart at the last minute. No one welcomed her, but nor was she denied a place.

They came warily into the walled port of Zara, looking for a passage to Venice, where, they were told by the workers on the docks, all those with skills were made welcome: so rich was the city that she needed endless supplies of foreign labour to support her luxurious existence. In the shade of Zara's fortress wall, inscribed with reliefs of the winged Venetian lion, the father negotiated a passage with a Greek captain, who neglected to mention the fact that Jews were excluded from the island city.

In Mestre, the land approach to Venice, they slipped off the boat, grey as a family of rats in the dawn light. A great truculence of porters, swarming round the arriving merchants, cast them such contemptuous glances that they fled the crowded docks immediately.

Sosia's father hid them in a Christian church while he went to look for work. No other refuge could be found from the iced wind screaming in from the lagoon. That night the younger children screamed in their sleep. The dismembered saints painted on the church walls seeped into their imaginations and took possession of their empty bellies in the dark. The looming figures soon seemed to resemble the soldiers who had come to their village.

Inevitably, given the nocturnal shrieks of the children and the stink of urine in the darkest corners, they were discovered. A priest, arriving at midnight to exorcise the church of suspected ghouls, found the family stretched in uneasy sleep behind the altar.

They were taken into custody. Rabino Simeon, the Jewish doctor, was called in by the *Provveditori della salute della Terra* to examine them for plague, lice and venereal disease. Except for Sosia, the children were found to be diseased with one proscribed illness or another, gifts of the fetid vessel that had brought them. The family was to be put on the next ship. Rabino could not know that the memories they had left in Dalmatia were worse than the church, worse than a Venetian prison or *lazzaretto*. They did not resist, however. The faces of the parents wore the immutable acceptance of those who face a slow death, without even the means to foreshorten what would be an entirely miserable life.

When he had examined Sosia, Rabino found more flesh than on the other children. The large letter S on her back had healed astonishingly well, though he could see that its infliction was recent. She would answer no questions about it, merely looking at the ground as he traced the slender scab with a gentle finger. Turning her around to listen to her breathing, he found small breasts and definite hips, though with an odd curvature to them. There was a slight murmur in her heart, but if she were kept well fed then this would not harm her. *A miracle*, he thought. *This little girl has a chance to survive.*

She spoke only once, to ask, 'You are Venetian, yes?' When he nodded, she gazed at him appraisingly. Discomfited, he turned to examine her siblings.

As an afterthought, he offered to take the eldest girl as his housekeeper and assistant, even to pay her parents something towards their journey back. They pressed the cold coins back into his fist with their own spider-like hands. They would not accept money for Sosia.

Very soon, he began to understand why. The girl was vicious. She drove the maid from the house, bleeding and weeping. The tradesmen were terrified of her. She ate as if about to die, though the hips and breasts did not develop any further. And then there were those looks she gave him, enough to madden any man.

In just three months she had driven him to the act he now regretted above all others.

It was during the passage on the boat that Sosia had first discovered the commercial uses of her body. A sailor had shown her how she might earn money with her mouth and fingers. Another sailor was found, less cautious than the first.

The only question she asked them was, 'Are you Venetian?' and the only men she refused were those not born in the city.

Starved of her mother's caresses, she began to enjoy the sailors' eager hands upon her; was quick to learn what gave pleasure and what earned the most. By the time she arrived in Venice she was able to read men's needs expertly as a shepherd might scan the clouds. The doctor Rabino Simeon was no mystery. He did not attract her as the sailors had, but she felt no repugnance in performing that same act with him. She assumed that it would be required at some point, in recompense for his rescue of her.

The work of a housekeeper did not suit her. Expecting at every moment to pay for her salvation in a different way, she did not feel grateful for the haven Rabino offered. At the house in San Trovaso she splashed her anger against the floors, smeared the windows with gritty rags, slapped rugs over the windowsills, beating them like delinquent boys. When she became Rabino's mistress, and then his wife, her freedoms increased. Her housekeeping became ever more desultory; Rabino often foraged for himself in the kitchen now. During the few, but interminable evenings when her husband was at home in the early days of their marriage, he taught her to read Latin and to perfect her Italian.

Nervously Rabino complimented her, telling her he was astonished at the absorbency of her mind. Words seemed to lodge in Sosia's memory with no effort on her part, grafting themselves in clusters rather than singly. The longer the word, the more quickly she learned it. Rabino did not know that she refined her vocabulary even further on her own, pretending, with him, to be slower than she was. When he was not at home, she ranged the studio restlessly, looking for unread texts, particularly any he thought unsuitable for her. Now that she could speak Italian, she quickly learned Venetian as well, and this meant that she could go outside, and, wrapped in the shadow of her cloak, find entertainment and revenue in the streets. Even with her yellow badge, Sosia was able to find physical relief and her own unusual kinds of emotional enjoyment among the Venetians.

She sold herself at variable prices, becoming expert at gauging what the market would stand and what she could afford to give away because she would have willingly paid for it herself. She refused, despite the dangers, to affiliate herself to any one madam or pimp, but sought to supplement her pocket money from random eye-contacts in the crowd. Her business was usually transacted in silence, in alleyways, disused buildings or the luxurious studios of the rich or noble. The only question she asked was 'You are a Venetian, yes?'

She spent her earnings on ephemera; a ripe peach out of season, a pair of jewelled shoes she would never wear, silk chemises she wore once, with someone, and then used to clean the phials in Rabino's small apothecary studio. Then she burned them. She bought books, trading them away for new ones as soon as she had read them. She bought a row of pink pearls from a pawnshop. She knew they carried a tragedy of their own from the way they recoiled in her hand as she examined them. But this innocent pathos of the pearls was their power. When she wore them, customers were drawn to her. The pearls looked like a row of small, hard nipples, never yet touched.

Sosia was not a proper Venetian courtesan, protected and spoiled. She was not educated as they were, in the arts of poetry and luxury. She knew of such women and saw them in the street, sometimes. The Veronese scribe Felice Feliciano had explained their courses to Sosia: they would engage with a steady clientele of five or six noble lovers, each of whom might grind his grain with her on his appointed night of the week. The days of the society courtesan were hers to sell or repose in as she wished. Felice Feliciano would always say that there was something erotically attractive to these young noblemen in the idea of sharing one whore between them, and perhaps also a competitive edge to be honed in the bedchamber. From this, the courtesan could only profit, financially and physically.

Sosia had no such aspirations. She preferred brief encounters, as many as possible. She liked the variety. To attract it, she presented herself variously. She could change the expression of her face so that it seemed to alter its lineaments. Some days she went out as a beautiful woman and attracted the kind of men who loved only faces. Other times she went out as an ugly woman, and attracted the true sensualists.

And so, in the first twelve years of her marriage, she had made her preferred kind of acquaintance with merchants and senators, barrow-pullers and shopkeepers, and finally the scholar-nobleman Domenico Zorzi and the mad scribe Felice Feliciano. While she insisted on variety, she did not object to repeating the same from time to time and so some men became regular appointments, the regularity of the encounters always decided by Sosia herself. She took different pleasures from each of them, and kept a diary, recording each man in one of three columns: *Golden Book, Bourgeois* and *Gutter*.

Merchants and shopkeepers kept her well dressed and fed with luxuries. The barrow-pullers were humorous and often surprisingly refined in the arts of love. Domenico, she took for power and for his library, Felice for the glamour of procuring something universally desired. And because there was something about Felice Feliciano that even she, Sosia Simeon, could not resist, perhaps she less than anyone else in Venice.

Chapter Four

No one sees what's written on the spine
of his own autobiography.

By the time he was nine, the only thing that Bruno could really remember about his father were the pads of his fingertips. Signor Uguccione had been a musician in the private orchestra of the Doge, playing every kind of wind instrument, a quiet man, eloquent only in musical notes. Bruno and his sister Gentilia grew up to the love-songs of the flute leaking from under the door of their parents' bedroom every night.

In those times, even more than now, Venetians were truly amphibious, moving without fear and indifferently over water and land. Indeed in those vigorous days of early empire, land was changed into sea and shore into land at will with bridges, irrigations and reclamations. The Venetians treated the sea with a familiarity bordering on disdain, receiving respect in return, as with any slave and mistress. The sea surrounded the city, pounding like the unquiet breast of a bird. Only occasionally it reached out the claw of a wave and pulled one or two Venetians into its jade-green depths.

As it did with Bruno's mother and father, caught in a sudden vicious storm on the Day of the Dead, as they went in their little *sandolo* to the island of San Pietro in Volta to pay their respects to three generations of Bruno's paternal ancestors buried there.

The bodies of Bruno's parents were washed up, side by side, on the shore of the Lido with the next tide, the petals of the flowers intended for the grave speckling the shallow water around them like funereal confetti.

An aunt and uncle from Pesaro arrived in Venice to decide the fate of the two children.

The uncle planned to take the children home to Pesaro. But he soon realised that, Venetians, they would not thrive away from the lagoon. When he explained his wishes to them, they stared uncomprehendingly, as if they did not believe in a place outside Venice. Their very language was contaminated, as he saw it, with the sea. In conversation, their every image was watery; their little hands swam in fluid gestures. Their Italian accent was poor; he could barely understand their strong Venetian dialect. At the funeral of their parents, they clung together, like two fish caught on the same hook.

The uncle wrote home to his own father (in a letter Bruno found on his desk and skimmed guiltily) that his nephew was to be enrolled in the boarding school of the Abate Guarino. Gentilia was to be taken in as a novice at Sant' Angelo di Contorta, which appeared to be the best-known convent in Venice.

Sant' Angelo was conspicuous for all the wrong reasons, but the well-meaning uncle from Pesaro knew nothing of them. There had been no time for investigations during his hurried days sorting the affairs of his inconveniently unworldly sister and brother-in-law. Venice appalled him: the leached light, the skittering reflections, the choking damp, the Byzantine ways of the people. *The city herself is a courtesan, cloying, corrupt, confusing,* he wrote to his father. *The quicker we act, the sooner we may leave the pernicious place. I am drowning here, I cannot bear it.*

The aunt and uncle kissed the tops of the children's heads and both cheeks as they delivered them to the convent and school respectively. Bruno asked only one favour: that Gentilia might be taken first and that he might accompany her there, and say goodbye to her in her new home.

Neither child cried or asked questions on the journey.

'Shock,' the uncle mused aloud standing unsteadily at the prow of the boat with his upright little nephew. 'Mercifully. Time enough for grief later.'

As the boat docked at the island of Sant' Angelo di Contorta, the uncle asked his wife, 'Am I doing the right thing?' His thickset little niece clung moistly to his hand and he found the sensation unpleasant.

'Better with the nuns,' the uncle mumbled and his wife nodded. 'She won't find a husband in Venice. She's as ugly as a punch in the eye, that one. The boy got all the looks.' Bruno looked at Gentilia, hoping that she had not heard. She seemed unconscious of the words, lost in impenetrable thoughts. Luckily the abbess at Sant' Angelo di Contorta had agreed to take her in immediately. It did not occur to either uncle or nephew to wonder why.

A young boatman with patrician features thrust a plinth across the jetty to the boat and the family filed ashore. Bruno and Gentilia marched side by side to a cloister where a blonde nun greeted them with a meagre display of warmth.

Kneeling to examine the child's face, she had snorted and risen abruptly. 'She'll be a good girl, I fancy,' she said. She slapped Gentilia lightly on the rump and pointed to a gated entrance.

It was said that more scholars came out of the Guarino school than armed men from the Trojan horse. But Bruno hated the place, in which it was a wonder he retained any education at all.

Mayhem reigned in the classroom. While the teacher bravely read aloud from Aesop or Cicero, the boys fought duels, made paper boats, beat each other with their slates, stabbed each other's fingers with their slate pencils, deployed their rear ends out of the windows, doodled in their precious palimpsests, produced dishevelled blinking parrots from their pockets.

Somehow, despite the distractions, Bruno prospered in his studies. His command of Latin was faultless; his ancient Greek had soon surpassed his master's. He had an instinct for perfection; a misspelled word on the page seized his attention like a sharp stink in his nostrils. Only his handwriting marked him down as an imperfect student. It grew out of proportion to him. His passion for swiftness ruined his ability to write beautifully. Tall ascenders and descenders leapt tangentially from tiny rounds in his script. Gradually, with his teeth gritted, Bruno forced his handwriting into an uneasy harmony, but he would always regret that his calligraphy lacked grace.

As he grew from child to adolescent, his personal appearance, in contrast to his writing, was entirely pleasing, though he was unaware of it himself. He never noticed older women turning to look at him in the streets; never caught the warm eyes of girls his own age.

He visited Gentilia every week on the island of Sant' Angelo. Even as they grew too old for fairytales and games, they spent hours devising stories in which they took the important roles. Bruno, the official scribe, recorded the stories on second-hand manuscript paper, inscribing *Volume Two, Part three*, in his rapid script. Gentilia always ended up marrying her brother, with a voluminous output of babies.

'But you are going to be a nun,' Bruno would object.'You are to be married to God.'

'God loves all babies,' said Gentilia, stubbornly. She blew out through tight lips and hopped heavily from one foot to the other.

'But you may not have them, if you are a nun.'

'I will make such beautiful and so many babies that God will be proud of them and love them better than all the rest,' she replied, implacable, sucking a hank of hair and knitting her brows.

Gentilia added, 'And if God says no, then I shall become a witch or a courtesan.'

Bruno worried. His fellow schoolboys made sure he could not close his ears to all the rumours about Sant' Angelo di Contorta. He asked his sister: 'Has anyone tried to touch you? Have you seen things that trouble you?'

To such queries, Gentilia turned a blank face, and took up a dry lock of hair to chew.

At fifteen, Bruno had passed all his examinations with distinction and was sent by his uncle to be educated at the University at Padova. He proved a brilliant student. He also made brilliant friends, including the incomparable, eccentric scribe Felice Feliciano, who had bustled up to him in the street one day and grasped his hand, saying:'Yes, it's true you are the most beautiful boy in this university.'

Bruno had blushed and replied – for everyone knew Felice – 'But my handwriting is inexcusable.'

'I forgive you,' Felice had replied.'Your face excuses you. We shall be friends. *Intimate* friends.'

From the beauteous Felice, whose tawny colouring and perfect features were one of the wonders of Padova, this was a potent compliment. Bruno blushed and turned away modestly. When he looked up, Felice was still nodding and smiling with delight.

The two of them spent all their free time together, making expeditions into the forests to practise their archery. Bruno excelled at the sport, though he was sad to come home with long poles of sapling strung with tiny songbirds.

When Bruno's studies kept him in his rooms, it was Felice who visited Gentilia on the island of Sant' Angelo, taking letters and gifts from her brother. When he could, Bruno went too. Gentilia appeared to be neither happy nor unhappy. She was clearly well cared for; she had gained a significant amount of flesh. The lace edge of her chemise was clean; her hair was combed to a dull shine, the parting straight and translucent as the spine of a feather.

But he had lost the ability to read her eyes, which disturbed him.

'Are you content here?' he asked, where no asking would have been necessary before.

Gentilia merely squeezed his hand, which was invariably in hers, and showed him her needlework, humming under her breath.

After two years Bruno returned to Venice to take up his position with Johann and Wendelin von Speyer's printing works. He worked hard, lived frugally, socialised only with scribes and other editors, and, when he could, made the boat trip to Sant' Angelo di Contorta to see Gentilia. It was a small life, a life ascetic in the antique sense, intensely focused on the written word, the written word of the past.

He lived in relative penury in two rooms above a silk-dyers in Dorsoduro. Slugs made slimy trails across his wooden floor by day and night. He had learned to reach out with an experimental finger before placing his feet on the floor when he woke in the morning, lest he experience the moist squelch he dreaded between his toes.

He was grateful for the separate entrance to his rooms. Unlike most tenants, he did not have to pass the gamut of the neighbours' curiosities to enter his private quarters. A small stair led up directly from the street to the space that was his alone.

Not quite alone. He had two pet sparrows. He had acquired them after first hearing of the famous sparrow poems of Catullus, a mysterious Roman poet whose work could be read only by the privileged scholars who had access to a handful of manuscripts in circulation. But the fascinating poems were becoming known by word of mouth. Bruno was able to memorise the sparrow poem in a few minutes when he heard it from a scribe in a tavern. By coincidence the same day, at the Rialto market, he spied the two thin little birds at a twittering stall. They were huddled together, palpitating in unison like two chambers of a single, feathery heart. He had carried them home in his pocket.

The sparrows had flourished under Bruno's affectionate hand. In May of that year they presented him with five tiny eggs, ash-blue in colour and spotted with brown. He took it as a good omen.

It was 1468, an eager spring was cluttering the cracks in the paving stones with tiny daisies, Bruno was eighteen years old, and Venice was alive with possibilities for a young man of his very talents.

Chapter Five

But what a woman says to her desirous lover
should be written on the wind and the running water.

Every year Venice married the sea. Each June, in the ceremony of the *Sposalizio*, the Doge sailed into the lagoon and dropped a golden ring into its acquiescent depths.

In exchange the sea brought to Venice a dowry: a merchant empire. She brought Barbary wax and rock alum from Constantinople, furs, amber, pitch and hemp from Russia, horses and wheat from Crimea; ironmongery and bowstrings from Bruges, spun cotton from Damascus, molasses and preserved fruits from Messina, cochineal from Coron, wormwood borax, camphor, gum arabic, seed pearls and elephants' teeth from Alexandria and Aleppo, glistening currants from Patras. Never was a bride so luxuriously dowered. The match seemed sure to prosper.

For many years the sea admitted none but Venetians to the rich trade route to the Indies, batting away the advances of her rival, Genoa.

Venice or no one said the sea proudly, *even if God himself were to come a-wooing.* (Thus, as always, in the early days of mutual discovery and passion!)

From the outside the marriage looked healthy and successful, profitable even. Nobody realised that things were going to the bad.

For lately the sea had been making long eyes at others, yielding to the lisping blandishments of the Spanish and Portuguese merchants and even to the guttural grunts of the English and the Dutch. The Turk of course had reclaimed Constantinople by force in 1453 and was nibbling at the knees, in none too affectionate a manner, of the rest of the Venetian empire. Albania, the Aegean Archipelago and Cyprus were slowly succumbing to the Ottoman.

Of course, the sea's infidelity was not entirely unjustified.

Like any pampered spouse, Venice had also been neglecting her partner, the sea. The city's merchant-nobles had become so enervated with comfort that they could barely lift themselves from their velutinous gondolas to enter a workaday galley. They were rarely to be seen at trade on the Rialto Bridge, leaving it to the enterprising middle classes. They sent their money, not their sons, on long ocean voyages; so had their ardour for the sea cooled. Nor had Venice been a faithful partner to her spouse. In marrying the water, Venice had not ever quite cast out from her breast desire for conquest of the land. All through the fourteenth and fifteenth centuries there had been teasing enmities and violent seductions. Ferrara, Pisa, remnants of the old kingdom of Naples fell under Venice's wandering eye, though not her thumb. Venice had not yet been taken in adultery, but it lurked in her heart.

The long-married pair, Venice and the sea, still operated like any old couple. Each kept an absent-minded or lazy eye upon the other. To some extent, little infidelities were used to fuel jealousy, which remained the only way they might still rouse the dirty spark of their former passion for each other. They fussed and quarrelled; they lost respect and occasionally surprised each other. They brought each other trophies.

They brought together Sosia Simeon and Bruno Uguccione who met on the water, as must happen half the great meetings of mind, body or spirit in Venice. That it happened in a storm of ice was perhaps the sea's and city's gentle warning as to how this meeting might turn out.

Chill dawn on the seventh day of March 1468, a *traghetto* crossing from San Tomà to Sant'Angelo: a meeting of two pairs of eyes, one yellow-green, the other calf-brown, glowing in pale faces like bleached seedcases on slender stems. In those days the Venetians dressed in black, craftsmen and merchant alike, all the year round. Only senators like Nicolò Malipiero affected red robes. The encasement in black had the curious effect of rendering each face more vivid. With the clothes a virtual uniform, the individuality of each person's features was shockingly evident.

Sosia smiled at Bruno with her eyes – the yellow pulsing out of the green – to engage his attention.

Bruno, his *bareta* pulled low over his hair, looked like any other Venetian, if immeasurably more attractive.

Nice boy, thought Sosia, *nice eyelashes, nice mouth.*

She liked the way his eyelids were delicately shaded with mauve. His lips looked like the detail of an exquisite painting. His black robe was closed at the front and fastened at the throat with a dribble of pale ribbon. A white chemise showed above the collar, visibly abrading the slight stubble of his chin. She checked the ridges under his cloak that informed her that he wore hose and a silk *zipon*, a close-fitting waist-length jacket. His sleeves hung down like bells. He had draped a long scarf over his shoulders.

Yes, thought Sosia, *the pretty young man is a borghese, a bourgeois*. At home, she saw in her mind, he would have three other suits, a fuine, a squirrel back, miniver and thin silk for summer. She sniffed: *He's not so poor as to smell of the streets but he cannot afford musk and civet to protect himself from their stench.* She imagined that he would have a sister or two in a convent and perhaps one married upwards to a minor nobleman.

Sosia was also dressed in black. It was the safest way to go about the town for someone who wanted to attract attention only at times suitable to herself. Underneath, she wore a luxurious dress of which her husband Rabino knew nothing: a high waist and low neckline. Her sleeves were elaborate: laced segments of brocade, between the gaps of which little puffs of her chemise emerged like sighs of breath on a cold day. She wore her hair coiled at the back and a thick curled fringe at the front. Unless she was engaged in her particular kind of commerce, she kept her eyes downcast.

The second time, she smiled with her mouth. Bruno blushed. He had not dared to suppose that her first smile was for him; now her stare was unmistakable.

Sosia thought, *Ah, a virgin, how lovely. Doesn't even know how to bring me on.*

She had felt drawn to Bruno on first sight, an unfamiliar sensation to her. The very discomfort of such a strange feeling kept her interest aroused. From his face, she could see that he was kind. From his movements, she could see he was both quick and gentle. Yes, she would take him, she resolved, seeing the way through to the inevitable sad resolution, even as she contemplated the pleasures of beginning such a *storia*.

She smiled again, and now she spoke, and Bruno saw the yellow badge that she had pinned on the underside of her sleeve. It startled him, but it was already too late. She had moved closer to him.

She said, in a clattering foreign accent, the consonants slanting away from the vowels and then slapping down on them, 'There are snowflakes in your hands, *Signor*.'

It was true. The *traghetto* shuffled across the canal through a heavy fall of snow. All the Venetians standing motionless in the black boat were dusted with snow like statues. Bruno's hands, lacking gloves, were curved like little alabaster bowls against his thighs. The snow had gathered between his mottled fingers where it did not melt.

He met her eyes. A smile was drawn out of him, an idiot's grin spilling out of his mouth, *like a skater spinning off the ice*, he thought. He said nothing; nothing came to him, and he looked down in embarrassment. *Why should a woman like that address me? Like that, a foreigner, a Jewess, some kind of courtesan, probably, but so beautiful. Such golden skin, such a fascinating slant to her eyes.*

When he looked up again, she had disappeared. He had not yet, in any case, thought of what to say to her. He felt a scalding sense of loss at her departure, a hot confection of regret and embarrassment at his own social incompetence and a small element of relief. He knew without doubt that the unknown Jewess represented the kind of shameful excitement for which Venice was famous, and which he, so far, had managed to avoid.

He inspected his hands for the snowflakes she described. But after this brief encounter with the strangely fragrant woman, they, too, had melted away, as if they could not withstand the heat of her close-by body.

Sosia had slipped in front of him and flattened herself in a doorway as Bruno passed, abstracted, studying his hands.

Hidden in the crowds, she followed him to his work, all the way into the

Fondaco dei Tedeschi near the wooden bridge at Rialto. She knew that the large squat building served as a guild for the German community in Venice and as accommodation for the visiting Teutonic merchants. Rabino was known to them, and respected by them, frequently called there to attend Germans suffering from the rigours of the perilous journey over the Alps.

The young man did not look like a Northerner and nor was he dressed in their style; so he must work for them, as many did. Perhaps he was a *sensale*, she wondered, one of those trained to monitor the German traders and extract their taxes, keeping a nice percentage for themselves. But this dreamy young man did not have the look of a coin-counter, and nor did he seem prosperous enough to hold the lucrative post of *sensale*.

She trailed him through the first open courtyard, now a-grunt and a-jabber with tall Swiss and German merchants at negotiation while their neat servants waited patiently in the arcades. It was easy to see which of them had been in Venice for a long period: those men used their hands when they spoke. The newcomers kept their arms stiffly aligned to their bodies. The water gates were open. Men were carrying in boxes that jangled with pewter and iron utensils. When the canal stirred a smell of beer and sausages poured forth from the kitchens like a sigh of well-being. Sosia walked to the well in the centre of the quiet second courtyard and spun slowly around, looking upwards.

The design of the place was sternly theatrical, like a court of judgement. She imagined an audience of men crammed into the serried arches above her. The young men would not resist certain hand gestures and smiles. The older men would look at her with the eyes of weary connoisseurs in whom life is rekindled at the thought of a new taste. There would be those who would look with sharp slits of eyes, like the arrow slots of a castle, on whom she would have no effect.

Bruno had disappeared up one of the four staircases. So she stretched back against the well, craning her neck for a glimpse of him among the columns. Her hands, behind her back, felt the face of the well's winged lion; it was worn to silk by the sturdy legs of a thousand Germans who had leaned against it.

She caught sight of Bruno's smooth cheek flitting between two arches. She glided to the mouth of the nearest staircase, ascending quickly, with her eyes downcast. A man appeared in front of her. He looked at her curiously, but she did not give him time to develop his speculations, walking swiftly to the next floor. She saw no one there except her quarry, whose black robe swirled around a corner out of sight.

Following ten paces behind, she let him pass through an open door. Then she approached the entrance herself, hovering in its shadow. Through it she saw a group of men bent over a metallic apparatus the size of a wheelbarrow, a boy carrying away quires stamped with black lettering, two other men hunched over fine metal rectangles, another stirring a cauldron of swirling black. Someone slapped a blanket over a metal plate with a sound like a large fish being landed.

Above the door she observed a sign carved on cherry wood. JOHANN AND WENDELIN DA SPIRA, she read, and the name was familiar to her.

A fume of hot minerals jolted her from these thoughts and reminded her of the young man whom she had followed here.

So this is what he does, she thought, *the nice young man.*

Chapter Six

That man seems to me to be a God,
No, more than a God,
who can sit opposite you,
and can at the same time look at you and hear your
sweet laughter; but miserable, I
suffer all my senses to be ripped from me.
For when I look at you, Lesbia, even for a moment,
I can no longer speak.
For my tongue has snapped in my mouth,
For a sudden frail fire scuttles under my skin
For my ears roar
For my eyes have fallen into the night.

'Mister Doctor,' said Sosia over the grey polenta she had drizzled meagrely with gravy, 'You should have some papers with your name and address on them. Wealthy clients find this kind of detail comforting. You could profit from more rich clients. They get more expensive diseases for which the treatment is longer.'

Rabino, who had watched two children die of plague that night, raised fragile eyes across the table at her. Why did she look blurred to him these days? He wondered when he had found that repulsive smell attractive. He could not make out what she was saying in that fuzzy voice. Why did everything he ate taste so metallic? She was his wife, but she did not even feel like family. She might well call him 'Mister Doctor', never using the name 'Rabino'. When he touched the skin of his patients, there was more intimacy.

'I never heard of such a thing, my dear, but if you think it's important.' He felt the need to be respectful with her, to compensate for the absence of the proper feelings.

She said: 'I'll organise it. With Venetian on one side, and Latin on the other.'

'Very well. I – I must go now. The mother of those two children was nursing a bubo in her sleeve. She tried to hide it from me, because she wanted my entire attention for her babies.'

'Christians?' asked Sosia, wrinkling her nose.

'Human beings, Sosia, suffering.'

'Can they pay?'

Rabino lied: 'Yes, they've already given me the money for the apothecary.'

'Then give it to me. I'll use it for your papers.'

There was no money. Rabino had planned to pay the apothecary himself. Or to trade some of his own herbs for the *prezioso liquore*, the *triaca*, in which the Venetians had so much unfounded confidence. He would go to the Struzzo on the Merceria, or the Carro in the Frezzaria or the Fenice in San Luca, and all the others, if necessary, to see what business he could do for the young mother.

He envisioned a long, cold walk, faces uplifted cynically to him, at the Fircone, the Siren, the Lily, the Apple or the Sun. The Venetian apothecaries loved to name themselves poetically, as if to add a wreathing of spells to the incantatory nature of their fragrant trade. And if they would not help him, there were smaller places that might do so in exchange for an hour of his time with their own patients or some written advice for a sceptical noble client. Rabino Simeon's name was worth something in Venice, in spite of his race, or perhaps because of it. *In extremis* many noble Venetians had more faith in the quick, silent Jewish doctors than in their own fashionable chattering physicians.

Sosia was still holding out her hand across the table. Rabino leaned back imperceptibly in case she actually touched him.

'Another day, my dear. I have other medical expenses this week.'

He hurried away, forgetting his threadbare hat on the table. The wind would burn the thin skin of his scalp today. She did not remind him to take it.

'You are pathetic,' said Sosia, to the hat. She cleared the table. There were many glasses. Last night, Rabino had been able to gather a quorum of ten men to worship. There was as yet no synagogue in Venice herself, and those on the mainland were too far distant for a busy doctor to attend. So the articles of their faith were enshrined in a room in the doctor's house, and all those Jewish men of business who visited the city on the fifteen-day passes, knew to come to Rabino Simeon's home in San Trovaso if they had need to drink of the comfort of their faith, or to feel his gentle hands upon the damaged limbs and flesh that pained them.

Sosia was supposed to keep their records in order in quires of paper Rabino bought cheaply from the *cartolai* when he could. Among these rough sheaves she sometimes hid her own ledger, a more elegant document altogether, bound in oxblood leather and containing the finest watermarked paper from Bologna. It had been a gift from Domenico Zorzi, who thought Sosia was interested in poetry, and that she might pen some lines herself. He could never have dreamt the use to which she would put it.

That morning she opened it and found the column labelled *borghese*. In it, she drew two lines, with a space in between, in preparation for a new entry.

Sosia cleared the table, washed inside her mouth, her face and between her legs, and set off for the *Fondaco dei Tedeschi*.

It was yet so early that the sun had not yet sponged the cloudy albumen of dawn from the outlines of the town, and not a single boat cleaved the melted pearl of the canal.

By the time she arrived at the opposite *riva* the sun was rising squarely above the blackened silhouette of the *fondaco's* slender frill of roof ornament. In a large room in that building, she knew, was the boy with the mauve-lidded eyes and the silky eyelashes. His skin bore the unmistakable fragility of one who rose early: he was sure to be at work already.

She raised her arm to shade her eyes. The jut of Sosia's breast drew forth an automatic chorus among the passing boatmen. Some grunted rhythmically as if already in congress with her; others cried out their wares verbally or with eloquent motions of their hips. A few nodded and smiled with encouraging familiarity. Some threw languid glances that seemed positively post-coital, as if performing the act of love with her was a foregone conclusion. One articulated his appreciation in grimaces of pain: how could she deprive him of herself for a moment? Another man, gross-bellied and tall, merely opened his mouth to its widest extent, to show how greedily he would consume her – in one bite!

47

She was not angry. She knew the provocation she presented: a woman, standing shamelessly alone at dawn, must be a harlot, worn soft and sweet by the night's grinding of grain, pungent with the sweat and semen of a dozen customers.

It might have been so another time, reflected Sosia, *but not today*.

When she found Bruno she wanted to be the kind of woman *he* wanted. So she arranged her features into the expression she deemed most suitable: sweet docility surprised by unexpected longing. With this touching struggle inscribed on her face, she walked over the bridge to the *Fondaco dei Tedeschi*.

It was Bruno himself who greeted her as she walked into the *stamperia*. He had been at his desk since the early hours, deep in a manuscript. At the sight of her on the threshold he started up.

'You? I mean, *Signorina*, may I help you?'

'Yes.' She did not contradict him. Time enough later, if it were necessary at all, to let him know that she was married.

She walked towards him, harshly outlined in an envelope of light. Behind her, through the windows, the Grand Canal glittered like an animal's eye. The shadows of the room seemed to Bruno to be leached with the yellowness of a sudden dawn. The tables and chairs, the printing machine itself, shimmered in radiant dusty haloes. Sosia stopped abruptly in a pool of light, interrupting its good intentions with her dark silhouette. Her body seemed to be gulping up the brightness of the day. Bruno twisted his head to try to discern the expression of her features, but he could not.

Her voice, foreign, cool and low, rasped softly from this churning hourglass of blackness. 'You are a printer, yes? I am Sosia Simeon. I need some small sheets. With a name and directions printed on.'

Sosia? thought Bruno, *Sosia, meaning double-image? No Italian mother would give a child that name. Of course she's not from Italy*. He wondered if Sosia herself knew the sinister meaning of her name in Italian. She spoke the language fluently, it seemed, so she must. *Why had she not changed it to something more acceptable?*

Sosia stepped closer to him. She emerged, still wreathed in golden motes, from her cocoon of light.

'Can you help me then?'

'But of course,' said Bruno, bowing. *Of course I can. It's not my kind of*

48

work, but I know how it's done, and there's no one else here to be of service to the lady at the moment. This request is entirely reasonable, the idea is good even though it is a new one, and her presence here is a mere coincidence of fate, as happens in any town, as happens so often in Venice, he told himself, squirming at the facility of the internal lies. He did not address the question of why she should be there at seven in the morning, when any respectable woman would be indoors.

It had started from there. Bruno persuaded Wendelin that they might accommodate her needs, as an experiment in a possible new market, though the press itself was enormously oversized for the tiny sheets she wanted.

For all their minuteness, the sheets required substantial deliberation. There were many consultations early in the dawn hours, when Bruno, she had ascertained, was often alone in the office. A proof was to be made first, and then rearranged to suit the *Signorina's* very creative ideas. She was most intriguingly concerned about the mixture of majuscule and minuscule characters and the choice of paper. Bruno had never met a man, let alone a woman, sensitive to such nuances before. Even his colleagues showed less interest in their typeface. It was necessary for her to stand very close to Bruno while he adjusted the letterforms himself with hands made suddenly clumsy by her presence. It was close enough for him to smell her.

He noticed, in the course of their deliberations, how quickly Sosia did everything: how swiftly she moved, spoke and thought.

'You are Venetian, yes?' she had asked early on and then changed the subject without a break in the flow of her words.

She was like himself, who, since his schooldays, had always sped through everything, leaving his dearest schoolfriend, Morto, stumbling behind. Felice was always urging him, 'Slow down, Bruno. Savour. Slow-ly.' He could not bear it. Venice herself was too slow for him, some days. She always seemed to be dragging at him, as if pulling at his ankles when he hurried through the city. It was impossible to run; she would trip him up. He watched the bird tracks fading slowly in the mud with an impatience no one else could understand. This confluence of their rhythm made him feel closer to Sosia. There were so few people who shared his compulsive fleetness.

But regarding Sosia, Bruno hung back, afraid. His imagination fought his good manners; there were questions he longed to ask which had no place in a

49

purely commercial relationship. Only after ten days did Bruno dare to enquire in oblique terms about her relationship with the doctor Rabino Simeon whose printed sheet he was preparing. Bruno knew of the doctor, of course, and his great reputation for skill and kindness, though he had never met him and knew nothing of his family circumstances.

'Does your father prefer . . . ?' he stammered.

'My husband,' said Sosia shortly. 'Though of course he's much older than me.'

She considered him, reading the tragedy unfurling in Bruno's eyes with the precision of a soothsayer perusing entrails. *Ah*, she thought, seeing the hot pain written there, *it's gone far, further even than I had hoped. He is nice, this boy. Help him, I will.*

She said: 'I hardly know what he prefers; I hardly know the man, really. It was – is – a marriage of . . .' she lowered her eyes, as if in pain and then appeared to recover herself bravely. She shrugged defiantly. 'I would far rather have your judgement and advice on such an important thing as this paper. After all, you are a sensitive man who understands the printed word and its effect on people. My husband only consorts with sick and dying people and he uses his hands.' She shuddered delicately.

Those hands he lays on you, thought Bruno, scarcely able to support the obscenity of the thought. This time he could not wait for her to leave. It was too much. When she was gone he slid to the floor and laid his cheek on the cool marble there. A vein throbbed uncontrollably in his forehead. A hot skewer seemed to be pushing through his bowels. When he closed his eyes he saw yellow haloes and green lights pulsing; they were still there when he opened them. He lay there for many minutes, until the thud of feet on the stairs announced the arrival of his colleagues.

But the images he had manufactured in those minutes, of Sosia in the arms of her old Jewish doctor, would not be shaken loose from his mind.

Again and again, the sheets were set and revised. Just before the resolution of each infinitesimal variation, just as they reached the end of each blind alley, Sosia would change direction. It was not just the work in hand that altered in style and mood; every day Sosia herself was different. Sometimes she came drooping with a kind of pathetic submission. In these encounters, Bruno felt that she was about to fall into the arms he was too frightened to hold out to her; it was as if she felt his unexpressed desire for her as a cruel oppression on her fragile shoulders. Other times she came in flames: demanding, arrogant, exciting. She drummed her fingers on the table and spoke quickly, from the corner of her mouth. Once, drawing the edge of a fine vellum violently across the table, she left a long red gash on his wrist. He was sure that it was deliberate, and he treasured the weal, stroking it for days until it puckered up.

One morning, while snatching samples from racks of paper, she appeared to trip on the hem of her cloak and strike her head a glancing blow against the wooden shelving. She staggered, seemed dazed and about to fall. Bruno, at her side, opened his arms to catch her. Somehow she collapsed with her mouth pressed on his, and that mouth slack so that the tongue fell out upon his lips. She might have been unconscious, for all the movement in that tongue, and Bruno, breathing into her open mouth, felt its wet heat invade him. His hands fluttered around her back, her hair, not knowing where to rest, where to support her. It seemed that he took her entire weight, slight as it was, upon his lips.

So they stood still like this, mouth to mouth, for long moments until Sosia slowly slid to her knees, sliding her lips down his chin, throat and breast, till they came to rest at his groin. Her nose stabbed his pubic bone. He whispered *dear God!* for surely she would rouse in a moment and feel for herself the effect of her intimate proximity upon him.

Quickly, he knelt down too, taking her shoulders in his hands and holding her, just a little way from him, so that he could see her face. Her head hung like a heavy grape on its stalk. With one hand, he tilted her face up to him. He could hear the tread of feet on the lower stairs. Any moment, the door would open and the apprentices would arrive thudding and groaning for their morning's work.

'Sosia! *Signora* Simeon!' he whispered, desperately. She murmured under her breath, in her own language, something incomprehensible. Her eyes remained closed; the lashes rested trembling on her cheek. With one finger, Bruno stroked her face. At this first contact with her skin, he shivered and hunched up his shoulders like a child.

'Wake up!' he urged her. 'They're coming.'

His eyes darted from her face to the door.

But Sosia was recovered now, looking into his eyes with her own yellowish ones.

'Where do you live, Bruno Uguccione?' she asked throatily. It was the first time she had spoken his name. 'It is alone, I think?'

Chapter Seven

But the fact that you don't lie lonely by night's
proclaimed by your bed, reeking out loud of
Eastern unguents and garlanded with flowers,
not to mention the pillow and mattress dented evenly
both your side and the other one and the
creaks and trembles of the poor old bedframe
as it perambulates the room.

While their country cousins practised their wedding nights in copses and hedges, the Venetians – as always, forsaking Nature or improving on her – took to their gondolas, each a tree cut, carved, painted, cushioned, curtained, perfected. Rich lovers could be distinguished by their slender boats, gracefully rocking both ways at once. Those too poor to buy an hour of passion afloat pursued their pedestrian loves in slithering corners on moonless nights.

Or invited them home, and opened their hearts.

Bruno knew that Sosia would hurt him, but he opened the door to her anyway. A single knock, and there she was, with one hand on her hip, looking over his shoulder to appraise the size and comfort of his accommodations. Her cloak was dusted with snow that she shook off briskly. Flakes of it spattered on his face, the coldness sharp as needles.

Until he opened the door, he had almost felt safe, with his feelings for her contained in the stone walls of his rooms, battened together and sealed in with layers of paint to enclose him. But willingly he went to the door at the sound of her sharp rap, and willingly he let her into his life. He knew that from this moment on his life would be lived as an art form, an exhilarating nightmare like a ride on a seabird's back through the dead hours of the night. He would be as alive as he could be without being nearly dead. He would at last know for himself what it was the poets wrote of.

Bruno had rehearsed this scene in his mind for hours. He imagined her falling into his arms on arriving at the door, trembling at her own audacity. He imagined soothing her hair, kissing the top of each of her fingers, then laying her hands together as if in prayer, and playing to her a melody from his father's flute in the candlelight, watching her eyes dissolve with tenderness as his mother's had done in response to the same melody. He had lain sleepless for hours planning just how to kiss her eyes: he had finally decided upon three soft slow kisses for each lid. He would lay her down on the pallet, kneel beside her at a reverent distance, gazing on her in a calm, loving way to inspire confidence. He would lie beside her, and cover them both with a blanket to warm their trembling limbs. Gradually he would steal a hand around her, and then another, laying his palms flat against her sides without rifling with vulgar haste among her clothing. Then he would talk to her, mingling the words of the poets with his own specially composed declarations. In each of these visions, Sosia lay sweet and passive in his arms, while he, subtly and gradually, convinced her of the purity of his passion, to which she would finally and blushingly submit, barely able to raise her eyes to his as he lowered his lips to her mouth.

It was not like that.

On the day she came to him, she pushed past him into the room and walked directly to the carefully groomed straw pallet on the floor. She looked down on it with a smile, and turned back to him, reaching out an arm. She took his head in the palm of her right hand, ran her tongue down the groove between his nose and his lips, while reaching with her left hand inside his stockings. Her hand was cold and somewhat moist as if it had been boiled and then plunged in brackish water.

'Nice,' she said, closing her fingers around him. 'Bed, now, Mister Editor.'

She drew him down to the pallet.

Sosia was used to all kinds of beds, from greasy rugs on cellar floors to the bed of the nobleman Nicolò Malipiero, which was notable for the great luxury of two mattresses covered in crimson satin, one on top of the other. That bed was seven feet long and six feet wide, and its canopy of green brocade lay upon eight veils of such sensitive gauzy fabric that it billowed with their every breath. The valance was in cloth of silver, figured with velvet and lined in changeable taffeta with a deep silk fringe. It was caught up with long gold hoops and buttons of bullion. The headpiece was also of crimson satin, and sprouted six ample plumes, each containing two dozen ostrich feathers of varying hues, garnished with a festoon of spangles. This masterpiece reposed on a dais with panelled head and footboards, painted images, gilding and carving. The counterpane, in the summer, was of tangerine coloured silk, quilted, and lined with sarcenet of a hue just a shadow darker than itself. For the winter there was a velvet and silk coverlet lined with three kinds of fur.

Other men had other beds. Sosia had become a cataloguer of the prevailing styles – the discreet *Lit à Alcôve*, the *Lit en Baldaquin* with its canopy against the wall, the *Lit en Baignoire*, with its integral bath and small linen chest. She particularly liked the *Lit Bâtard* with all the accessories and grandiosities of a grand bed, but everything executed on a smaller scale. The owner of that bed, a dwarfish merchant from the Castello quarter, had looked a man of normal dimensions inside it. Indeed, he was nothing less than a man, she remembered. She had once pleasured a Golden-Book Cornaro in a *Lit en Dôme*, looking up at the gilded stars studding the canopy, and had tumbled, dishevelled from an encounter with a Dandolo on a *Lit à Deux Dossiers*, a kind of sofa without a back.

Sosia, pulling Bruno on top of her, noted the smell of cheap tallow soap sighing from his tired sheets.

She looked up at him, noting the smoothness of his cheeks and the curls and the clarity of his eyes and the fullness of his lips.

But Sosia also thought, in that first moment with Bruno, of straw beds rumpled and sour as old nests, curtained beds stately as galleons, dark creaking beds like prison hulks moored at wharves. She thought of a kitchen floor near Rialto, among the egg baskets, and remembered the meat ants marching in and out of the addled eggs. That reminded her of a hectic dawn in a gondola, the rising sun orange as a pigeon's eye, and the gondolier's skin salty in her mouth.

She turned to face Bruno, her eyes filmed with memories.

Bruno was also thinking about eggs.

On his straw pallet, the thin covering was soon untucked. The bald straws pierced their skins. Sosia was Bruno's first full experience of physical love. He had never concentrated on anything quite so hard in all his life, but even so there was something he could never quite forget amid the mingling of their hair and fingers, toes and elbows, the sheets driven into coils and ridges, the imprints of her teeth on his shoulders and the emptying of the desire inside him, inside her.

The image of an egg was always in Bruno's mind. Felice had told him once that in Albania, when a child was born, visitors to the new mother and infant bring a white egg, with which they rub the face of the new arrival, saying 'Pashi bar, Pashi bar', 'May it be always white!' They meant this: that the child's growing face should never have cause to blush for its actions.

As Sosia slid around him, breathed against his teeth, and rubbed her face against his, the white Albanian egg hung in Bruno's mind, glowing faintly in the red-black of his squeezed-shut eyelids.

He was only half-awake when Sosia prepared to leave, rising naked from the pallet with no self-consciousness, as if he were not there. His first thought was of his old enemies, the slugs. He feared more than anything that one of them might slime Sosia's naked foot and make her feel disgusted. When he heard her walk to the window, he covertly scanned the floor for their silver trails. Finding none, he quickly closed his eyes. She looked down at him briefly, seemed satisfied with his comatose state. He knew instinctively that it would be wrong to reach a hand out to her; that this first encounter should end, as it began, without words. He also knew, though not why, that this would not be the last time Sosia came to his bed. So he feigned sleep, watching her dress through lowered lids. He restrained himself from exclaiming when he saw the 'S' carved into her back.

But he had not fooled her. She paused, finally, with her hand on the door handle, and asked him in a neutral tone of voice: 'Do you see Felice Feliciano today?'

He shook his head. He knew it would cause damage to ask why she wished

56

to know, or how she knew Felice, so he gave a brave impression of caring not at all. But he did not wish Sosia to leave with another man's name on her lips, the echo of that man left hanging in the air, so he said: 'Shall you feel safe, walking home alone? Shall I accompany you?'

She laughed: 'There's nothing more dangerous than me in Venice!'

As the door slammed, he whispered to the thrumming wood: 'No, no, no.'

He sniffed the scent of her saliva on his arm, where she had fastened her teeth in a bruising kiss some time in the course of their lovemaking. He lay back, treasuring each moment of memory, of her long dark eyes closing in on his, her golden skin lambent in the shadows of the afternoon. She had shown him such passion he was sure that she had meant love by it.

And so Bruno was transformed into a dishonest man. Sosia made him a person of the shadows, a person afraid to be seen. A person who could no longer find contentment, anywhere, for all his pleasures were concentrated in her, and had thereby become compromised and complicated. He accepted Sosia's apparent valuation of him, and marked himself down to a remnant of his former worth.

He became solitary, for now he lacked confidence to offer his company to friends and colleagues. His altered state, sometimes wretched, sometimes euphoric, was obvious to all. The translucent paleness of his complexion had taken on the desperate sheen of the gallows. Many were the solicitous enquiries, the gentle offers of a shoulder to cry on. Blushing, he waved them away and changed the subject. But he could not bring himself to confide in anyone, not even his oldest friend Morto, and most particularly not the fastidious Felice Feliciano.

Now that he nursed an unclean secret, Bruno suffered a sense of being cast out of his old quotidian world, of losing acquaintanceship, of even fleeting intimacies, as with the bird-seed merchant, slipping away. Exhausted with thoughts of Sosia, he no longer found smiles for them.

Conversely he found that he had a softening of heart stealing over him. He was absurdly vulnerable. Now that he no longer transacted love on a small, gentle scale, he had lost the impermeability that had once stopped him breaking down in tears at the sight of a grieving young widow or a lame beggar. He noticed the profound sadness of ageing waiters and the empty eyes of widowed grandmothers gazing down from fourth-floor garrets. His eyes were drawn to the blackness of unlit windows, profound as the eyeholes of a skull.

He felt everything more distinctly in his worn-thin heart, so painfully that at times he wished she had never walked into the *stamperia*, even though before Sosia he had been but half-alive, fed only on books, shyly eager to know what real love did and was.

By candlelight he usually saw Sosia, in a dark place. Candlelight rendered her features crude as a primitive carving. She looked hard, not soft in the haze of the flame, like a Goddess of Vengeance, implacable. He could not say any more whether she was beautiful or not. He searched the blackness where her eyes should have been.

She never stayed long. Sometimes it seemed to him that Sosia used his house like the street, making her way through it, not looking back. Now that they were lovers she only occasionally came to the *stamperia*. These were precious moments to him; he hungered all day and all night for the sight of her. It seemed to indicate a reciprocal feeling in her, when she came to his workplace, even when there was no possibility of physical gratification. And better still, she still showed an interest in his work sometimes. She understood Latin, and the new manuscripts, in which he lost himself daily, seemed to please her. She herself carried a book of her own around with her everywhere. When he tried to show an interest in its contents – perhaps she was a poet? – she rounded on him, 'Hardly!', so he guessed it was some kind of diary.

When they were alone Bruno touched her everywhere he could – on her bodice, at the waist of her dress, on her workbag, on her stockings. She asked questions, had him scrabbling at the lower shelves for early proofs to show her. Once, at her feet, he noticed one of her shoelaces undone, and humbly retied them. She did not acknowledge it; she had not been looking at him, but glancing impatiently about the room.

He showed her a poem that moved him, from Catullus, of course. He had written out one of the poems he had memorised, on the back of a discarded proof.

> *I hate and I love. Perhaps you'll ask why?*
> *I don't know. But I feel it happening, and it's crucifying me.*

Sosia met his eyes mockingly over the manuscript.

'This is what you call "love"?' she said. 'It doesn't seem much good to me.'

She took another look and smiled, 'But the lettering is very nice.'

Bruno woke at night, sick with guilt. He was cut through with the thought that he might have a choice. But he needed her. He did not need his love of himself. He would let Sosia have him; he would be the creature she wanted. He had given up his place amongst the righteous.

Bruno conducted so many imaginary conversations with Sosia that at times her name came to his lips involuntarily. If a flicker of dust scraped his eyeball, if he dropped something (which he frequently did; despite the former grace of his movements Bruno was as clumsy as a drunk since he began to love her), then he would gasp 'Sosia!' as an imprecation, as an invocation.

She sent messages. She told him to wait for her. She did not come. He dared not go to the dark house in San Trovaso where she lay by night in bed with her husband and by day mixed the doctor's potions and washed his linen. *His intimate linen*, Bruno thought sometimes, and a queasy pain nudged his stomach.

Bruno daydreamed guiltily of Rabino being done away with, carried off by diseases contracted from his patients, or poisoned like . . . a husband. Sosia was amused at the idea.

'Ah yes, every corner of the house shall stink of him,' she laughed.

For the first time in his life Bruno found himself looking at other men, monitoring their attractiveness, not in an aesthetic sense, but in terms of whether they would appeal to Sosia. Not that he could second-guess her taste. Many times she had shocked him by pausing in the street to bestow a slow stare on a fat gondolier or an ageing merchant. Foreigners, she ignored.

'She does this to taunt me,' he consoled himself thinly, 'she does not really want those men.'

He added, 'She does not need them. She loves me.'

He waited for her on the stairs of his studio when he knew that she should come. Outside the door, on the crumbling staircase, he was already ten paces closer to her. He invented a game to control his patience, lacing a finger through each of the spaces between his splayed toes, one at a time. He started full of hope: by the time he had finished the lacing of his toes she would be there, he told himself; or by the time he finished the next lacing.

When she came in the door, always tormenting minutes later than she had promised, he used the sound of the slamming to mask his own creeping footsteps back into the studio. So when she strolled in he was bent over his work, as if he were fully occupied and had not noticed at all the lateness of the hour.

He could not deceive her. She would walk to him and run her finger over the last line of his text to see if she could smudge the wet ink. She held up a dry finger, which she then put into his mouth. When he rose, she slapped the dust of the staircase from his rump, none too gently, while he hung his crimson head.

His happiness was at her disposal.

Once she left her diary by the bed when she left. When Bruno found it he struggled with himself, desiring and fearing with equal intensity to read what she had written about their love affair. In the end, he found it in himself not to open the book, hoping to earn a reward for his abstinence. When Sosia came to reclaim it she looked at him sharply, 'Did you read it?' When she saw that he maintained his serenity, she herself answered: 'No, you did not. You are a rare one.'

Bruno often closed his eyes with Sosia, whether because he could savour their lovemaking more that way or because it spared him from seeing the inappropriate expression on her face.

He wanted to say to her: 'I love and trust you. You are indispensable to my happiness, and my sadness. When anything happens to me, I want you to know that moment.'

She would say: 'Take your clothes off. Do this. Touch me there.'

Sosia's lies and her rare, cruel truths were so compelling as to have their own moral world. There were certain truths etched in stone for her, between her and Bruno, like the tablet of the Ten Commandments:

I do not have to tell you that I love you.

You may not ask me where I have been.

If you displease me, even for a second, I will leave you in that second.

If your expression changes to something that I dislike then
this is also a fair reason for leaving you.

Bruno had his own litanies. He told himself: *Truly it's better to love someone like her. It's too easy to love the soft slack women that Morto lays himself on. It's too easy to love someone beautiful and affectionate. I have chosen a love that asks more of me.*

But the love never came true with her.

Sosia shrugged off any questions. He knew nothing of her past. She would not tell him how she had acquired the S carved into her back. He knew nothing of her earlier loves. There must have been some, for there was nothing she did not know about the satisfaction of physical desires and how to arouse them. Sometimes Bruno felt she was working him grimly through some erotic manual of positions and contortions less loving than improbable. He worried less and less about Rabino Simeon – he sometimes even felt sorry for his original rival – than about the legions of unknown, mysterious lovers who had been with Sosia and taught her all these compelling things she knew.

What Sosia had lavished on others, he could not bear to ask, did not know if the reason that there was so little tenderness for him was that it had been spent irretrievably elsewhere – or had she still saved it inside her and was he not sufficiently desired by her to release it? He felt he had failed to be attractive enough to inspire her passion.

She was not curious about his past; she had shown no interest in his family, had cut him off when he tried to tell her of his own innocent early loves, a friend of his mother's with lagoon-silver eyes and blonde hair, of an older woman who had caught his imagination for an entire winter merely by opening the shutters in her chemise one memorable dawn as the schoolboys tramped through the street beneath her house. Only Bruno had looked up at that moment, seen the shadow of a nipple through the crumpled linen, seen the other breast bunched up under her elbow and suddenly swinging loose.

He was wiser now, years older in the weeks since Sosia had first come to his room. Spring was creeping into early summer. He had meanwhile lived whole seasons of passion and disappointment.

He could say to Sosia: 'Before I knew you, I thought love was a delicious mystery. Now it's not a mystery. I know so many things about love, but I find there are many of them which I did not wish to know.'

'Shall I go then?' asked Sosia, rising, with seeming indifference.

At this, panic rose inside him, sharp as garlic.

'No, no, no, my sweetheart,' he gasped, pulling at the hem of her dress. 'Please don't leave me.'

'Mmm,' said Sosia, looking out of the window.

Below her in the street, the men strolled.

PART TWO

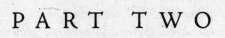

Prologue

Sparrow, darling of my darling,
with whom she plays, keeps at her breast,
to whom she always hands when he begs, her fingertip
arousing him to tiny little pecks.
When it is my darling's desire to play this way,
I wonder if it is for the solace of her own pain,
I believe so: that the hurt that burns her might be soothed.
Let me now play with you myself, and find, as she does,
a way to ease this soul-ache.

December 63 BC

Lucius, Lucius,

So many questions! (And how much brotherly censure packed into each one.) I see you're not finding it easy to be sorry for me.

Nor are my friends quite racked with sympathy. Once they stopped whistling and rapping their chests like monkeys, they all teased me, a chorus of nauseating monotony, like the ear-scuff of a single dog barking, 'So you've got Clòdia Metelli to your bed? A mundane Transpadane like you? You want her to stay there, too? You're dreaming.'

They told me. 'This is the best bit, for her.'

They mean that it's part of her legend that for Clodia the ending of a relationship is its summit. All Rome knows that the art of dismissal is her special talent. So she cuts all her men to measure. I should know too: she's discarded me and called me back to her so many times now, each parting barbed with a piquant new twist of cruelty.

At least I've had four months, so far, of dismissals and recalls. I'm lucky, you might even say. She's rinded me diligently as a scribe working over a papyrus; she's unrolled my whole history between those nipping fingers. With other men, I've heard, she's been in such a hurry that the amatory episode was but perfunctorily consummated and the lover never once recalled to her bed, or even remembered, except for the way in which he served her, a sharp physical memory entirely detached from the man's face.

It seems that I have misconceived my muse, Lucius.

I know now that Clodia, unlike the pleasure-stained Sappho, hates love, hates everything lovely with a flint-eating, savage coldness. She hates so much that beneath the rose oil and civet she stinks of hate, foreign and metallic. She has the shades of Orcus inside her, which eat up anything beautiful.

The purest distillation of happiness is what I long to taste when I make love to her, but it's as if I merely suck on the cool stopped-up bottle in which the sacred juice is sealed. The bruising repertoire she puts me through, while gratifying my every inch, is painfully inappropriate to the delicacy and sweetness of my feelings.

I know. I *know*. The fashionable thing would be to let it pass, to enjoy what I can and then let her go. But I'm incapable of playing a cool hand with her. *Because* she's the way she is, not in spite of it.

At the beginning, I loved her blindly. Now I have opened my eyes to her nature, I still love her blindly.

Clodia has many ... gifts, shall we say, which are the stock-in-trade of a prostitute. She's the most fascinating package of purity bundled in lechery, the pure inner frigidity of a courtesan gift-wrapped in the fake outer frigidity of an aristocrat. She scintillates with allure and danger like the sun on the water. I cannot keep my eyes off her.

And as you know, Lucius, I would never have wanted a leftover woman, whom no one else wanted. So I was always destined to be with someone like her.

My very jealousy enriches her worth in my eyes. She even seems taller, the more she hurts me. I dread to lose her, even when I hate her. And such hatred, such dependence has somehow become aphrodisiacal. No matter what Clodia does, it still excites me, shakes that bottle of undiluted love so it effervesces. As she well knows, her servant will always find me waiting at the door. I bathe four times a day so that I'm always ready to follow him straight to her house to face whatever humiliation awaits me. I lie lightly in my unmarried bed all night, hoping for the familiar discreet tap.

She would say, and did this very morning, drawling on the words with a mocking smile, 'It's your problem, the way you love me.'

You can imagine, Lucius, that the truth of this remark does not make it any more palatable, and nor does its frequent repetition on her biteable lips.

Indeed the first time she said it was the moment I began to think about making a wax model of her, and now I find its image floats comfortingly into my mind each time she hurts me. Without it to soothe me, I assure you, I should grow as mad and wild as the Spring Equinox.

Early on she said to me, 'You're greedy for pain.'

I shook my head mutely.

'Without it, you couldn't write a couplet,' she laughed. 'You feed off me. So don't whine that I'm eating your heart alive.'

'What about my happy poems? The Thousand Kisses? The Counting Poem?' I countered as a distraction, though I knew she was right.

'It's clear they're written in retrospect.'

I panicked at this, for she was as yet in my arms, and, as far as I knew – idiot that I was – exclusively so at that time. 'Are you warning me about something?'

She raised herself on her elbow and looked down on me, amused. I noticed the fold of a wrinkle in her neck and stared at it as if fascinated. She was not embarrassed; she nudged her flank under mine and brought my hand around to grasp her downy haunch.

'My whole life should have been a warning to you,' she said, starting to move, slowly and deliberately. 'Were you too stupid to see this when it started?'

I continued to gaze maliciously at her wrinkle, a fold in that skin which, Lucius, I must tell you, remains as finger-friendly as a Saetaban napkin from Spain.

Finally she stilled her motions and asked, 'Why are you staring at me like that?'

I replied: 'I'm taking the measurement of your features for a wax doll.'

She laughed, uneasily this time.

I said, 'So give me a curl! I need something from your body, a toenail clipping will do.'

'Go fuck yourself,' she said, baring her teeth. So I waited till she'd left the room to bathe and then sidled round to her dressing table where I raked a swatch of loose hairs from her comb. I noticed that the roots were tipped with white, which made me feel vaguely triumphant. I raised her perfume bottle, shaped like the glass ghost of a bird, to my lips and gulped some bitter drops from its beak.

I've written a poem to commemorate the bothersome little beast, her self-important sparrow, damn its black-splotched breast. She seems to love the bird, insofar as she can love anything. What Clodia loved, I would love too, with all the talent I possessed: out came my charming tribute, fluttering with delicate syllables. I thought she would reward me for it, but she threw down the tablet after the merest glance.

'Do you like it?' I asked, eyes downcast.

'Don't expect *me* to love you more poetically because you fancy yourself a poet,' she drawled. 'And don't think I don't understand the double-entendre, either.'

(You see how quick she is, brother. She saw immediately that my poem referred also to the little bird that flutters between my own legs at the thought of her.)

'Are you not a little pleased that I write about you?' I pleaded. She shrugged, as if to say she's no virgin to the role of muse.

Clodia! You ask what it is about her that could make up for her coldness. Many men have tried to work it out. Now it's my turn. I would say that Clodia's incomparable lustre is merely the reflected gloss shined up by the lust of many men. Each sees her as a woman wanted, at one time or another, by anyone who was anyone. She refracts desire, rather than welcoming it into herself, like, and not just in this way, a dusty lantern, which seems to shed light but in fact just spreads ghastly confusion in the darkness.

I know all women have fantasies; that they can conjure a new lover in their minds any minute, sometimes when the old one is still on top of them. Fantasies are one thing, memories are another. Clodia does not need to imagine what it's like to be mated by any of the highborn and many of the lowborn men in Rome. She has only to consult the archives of her skin to remember their endowments and their finesse or stamina. When I lay down with Clodia I was in no way alone with her. A blind bat in a cave colony might suppose himself alone in just the way I was.

This thought makes me shudder, as it must make anyone shudder, but me more than anyone because I fear that the other men have made their way from our lovemaking into my poetry. These men have grown one in my mind, a colossus called 'not Catullus'. At moments when I should be forgetting everything I'm pricked and snagged by reminders of them: my nails and hair and teeth catch on jewels she was awarded by those other lovers. She never takes them off. Even naked, she's hatefully scabrous with ridges and crusts of gold and ruby.

Clodia does indeed write a little herself, witty little party-pieces, and I begrudge her every word about love. I cannot be sure it's about me.

69

For Clodia, the love that comes from me, Catullus, is no more bothersome than a fly.

But my poems about her are another matter. The trouble is that they are unforgettable. (Unlike those of Caelius.) My songs have served to burnish her reputation: Clodia's more famous than she was before, because of them.

It was not long before my friends were passing copies around. Somehow my poems have leaked out of our circle and on to the streets where lovers no doubt quote my songs to one another. Roman memories are absorbent of sweetly flowing words.

And of course anyone may turn a second-hand phrase to his advantage if he likes the sound of it. So I don't know whether to rage or smile about it, but now salesmen of all kinds cry their wares with snatches of my poems. The Syrian sausage seller and the Egyptian nut merchant have come to know them by heart, and they are scrawled on the walls of the Baths. My name is not yet attached to them. I am anonymously famous, not what I planned at all.

So when I went to the man who makes the wax models and began to describe her, he straight away quoted two lines of the sparrow poem to me, with his eyebrows raised.

Chapter One

If you keep your tongue locked in a closed mouth
you throw away all gifts of love . . .

A certain invention by Johann Gutenberg had raised a sharp alarm among the members of the Venetian *collegio*. Printed books from Mainz were flowing into the city, overtaking the production of the native scribes. There were even rumours that the Germans planned to set up their presses in Venice herself. An intemperate faction called for the proscription of printing in *La Serenissima* and the preservation of the old scribal culture.

Domenico Zorzi, book collector and scholar, begged to differ. On 18 March 1468, the nobleman addressed his peers on the subject of Johann Gutenberg:

'Some of you mutter darkly at his name, whisper that he is Lucifer's henchman. What kind of talk is that? Peace! Instead, let us contemplate with our famous Venetian rationality this astonishing invention that has come not to blight our history, but to marry the past to the present.

'It seems that this Gutenberg was born some seventy years ago, a junior nobleman of Mainz, not a commoner, note, my Lords. His first act of genius was the mass-manufacture of mirrors, something that should ever endear him and his imagination to the Venetians! I am informed that the idea of letters cast in metal probably came to him while pouring melted lead or tin over a glass plate.

'Some time around 1450 this Gutenberg invented movable type. I see you wrinkling your brows, but I tell you that this is not a difficult concept. It's merely a process that makes it possible to print pages of continuous text made from metal letters slotted together in wooden forms. I would have liked to demonstrate the simple tools – but of course they are as yet still barred from Venice.

'This diagram shows the simplicity of the process: here are the parts separately and together. So simple is it that I cannot imagine why it was not invented before! Like Our Lord's ingenuity with the loaves and fishes, this miraculous device enables writers to feed the minds of the multitudes, individually but all at once and at a price by which any respectable man can enhance his library.

'I ask you, my Lords, with the Turks and Genovese clamouring impudently at our doorstep, if we can still indulge ourselves? Turn our backs on such advance in the world of machines? Stand like storks in the water, putting our heads under our wings, so as not to see how the world outside Venice races ahead?

'Moreover, can you see the beauty of these sample printed pages? Of course, they are *German* in style. But how much more beautiful would they be if the letters were fashioned by *Venetian* artisans! In the right hands, printing could be like oil painting, my Lords, like the art of Giovanni Bellini, a fine new thing come to adorn our city.

'And not just adorn it: printing will enrich our minds, too. Some people sneer that we Venetians have no intellect in the purest sense; that no philosophy will ever flow from us; no deeper thinking will ever flourish here. The city is a paradise for the senses, outsiders observe enviously, and eats up our ideas the way the water penetrates the paintwork and makes it fall in flakes.

'I quote from a letter I have received this month from the famous scribe Felice Feliciano, who loves our city but sees it from the affectionate distance of Verona. He writes:

There must be a repository somewhere at the end of the lagoon where all the pieces of Venice that have floated away are kept. I see it as a hollow, airy Venice, reconstructed from these fragments, a coloured shell of the city, a kind of book of the city, the city expressed in two dimensions, more beautiful than it is in three.

This is the true soul of Venice, this bubble-city in my dreams. She's like a transparent floating book, where the pages are concepts visible in colour. Not a thing of the mind, but a piece of beauty dedicated to the senses alone.

'Now, my Lords, I ask you, is this what you want? For Venice herself to propagate the slander that we have no minds, that we lack substance, that we are nothing more than a bubble? A transparent egg as hollow and light as a letter of the alphabet? An empty-headed courtesan of a city?

'Compliments on our beauty have rotted our intellects with vanity. It's time to prove to the world that Venice has soul and wit to match her peerless face. Now, my Lords, I close. Let us hear what the rest of you think of this new invention of printing and whether we should welcome it into our city, or close our minds against it. What shall it be? Shall we listen to the priests and the pessimists who cry down every new thing? Or shall we open our gates to innovation? Over the Alps, there are men waiting to turn us into a city that prints books, and prospers on it.'

And so, within months of Domenico's speech, over the Alps came Johann and Wendelin Heynrici from Speyer, with an instinct for success and with letter moulds in their pockets.

They carried with them letters of introduction written in Italian by Padre Pio, a Roman cleric seconded to the very powerful bishopric of Speyer. Padre Pio, amiably corrupt, would under normal circumstances write such letters for anyone, for an almost negligible fee, but in the case of the two brothers he had done so out of purest friendship. Something about them, at the very first interview in his commodious office, had attracted not just his acute commercial instinct but also his affection. The elder brother was nearly thirty, the younger just five years less. Yet both had the tender patina of the schoolboy about them. As yet, no disillusion, no disappointment had shaved that sweet and eager optimism from their faces and their fair hair was fluffy as chicken down.

Padre Pio was vastly interested in printing; among his tasks was the propagation of volumes in the bishop's library. He'd been to Mainz to acquaint himself with the process of movable type, and envisioned nothing but success rolling out of the printing press. He was also one of those surprisingly numerous liberal clerics who saw no danger in the revival of the ancient Latin and Greek texts.

'They're merely picturesque allegories for God's true values,' he always said. 'Not blasphemous. Anything so enjoyable must surely be a gift from Our Lord. As are grapes and whipped cream.'

Padre Pio himself had never been to Venice, but he knew what it had to offer an enterprising and energetic pair of Germans with something beautiful and practical to sell.

On the day they left, he accompanied them to the boat that was to take them down the Rhine to Basel. He embraced them firmly on the quayside, urging them, 'Go straight to the Locanda Sturion, remember, don't let them take you anywhere else, and then to the *fondaco*. And then, to the Piazza! The canals! The courtesans! Ah, Venezia! I wish that I were five years younger! You must write to tell me about it. Everything!'

He waved until their boat disappeared around a bend of the river. The last sound of home the brothers heard was his voice floating over the churning waters: 'The Sturion! Look out for the sign: a silver fish on a red flag.'

Turning on his heel, Padre Pio thought to himself, 'I wonder if they'll be back?'

As they landed, shivering, at Mestre, that cool dawn in the late spring of 1468, the brothers from Speyer stood among boxes and trunks being unloaded on the quay. Had they but known it, a good omen was betokened by these boxes. In them lay the first shipment of Cardinal Bessarion's gift of his entire library of manuscripts, destined to make Venice a more bookish city. A thousand new volumes, mostly in Greek . . . for the moment they were carried off to the Doges' Palace until the library was ready for them.

The brothers stumbled ashore, dragging their trunks and satchels. Wendelin carried the lion's share. Johann was by far the inferior in height and strength; he had been from childhood slighter and weaker in his person. Wendelin enjoyed all the physical robustness of the family. But Johann's presence was more intense. He absorbed the attention of those around them, moving people almost to unease by his investigative gaze.

In their halting Italian, acquired from archaic tracts and with the help of Padre Pio, the brothers commissioned a porter to carry their bags, heavy with matrixes and iron letters, to a boat. And what a boat! The only transport turned out to be a serpent of black wood, rearing up out of the water at them, slim at the hips and slenderer still at prow and stern, with a beak of silver gnashing in the pale light of dawn. The brothers sat side by side on a velvet banquette, while the porter crouched on a painted bench. They watched a fairytale of a city form in gauzy silhouette in front of them. If they had not read about it in books, they would have thought it was an invention, a fantasy brought on by the extreme rigours of their journey. Tall towers rose against the sunrise; the city seemed like an open book, its pages fanned up, floating on a tray of beaten gold leaf. White palaces, fretted like lace, levitated over the misty water. Others were encrusted with mosaics and painted in tints of lapis lazuli.

The brothers were silent, afraid to infect each other with their fears by uttering them aloud. Wendelin and Johann clung to the sides of the boat, enthralled, half wishing themselves back in the velvet hills of Speyer, reproaching themselves for their stupidity and arrogance. Who were they to approach this fabled city, and to think that they might bring something new to her?

The sun rose. The city materialised from its ghostly outlines. A warm breeze tweaked their hair at their scalps, making them quiver. As they approached the shore, smells assaulted them: buttery pastry, sour olives, garlic and lilies. They heard singing, the cries of the street-carriers and, surprisingly, birdsong, infusing the salty air with delicate excitement. Everywhere they saw other foreigners – Turks, Greeks, Egyptians – and heard the clatter of barbarous tongues. Their gondolier poled up the Grand Canal, past *palazzi*, churches and warehouses of a grace seemingly at odds with their vast scale and utilitarian purpose. The brothers sat up straighter on their banquette, trying not to feel intimidated, thinking of the wonderful new invention in their leather bags.

We have something to offer, even this miracle city, thought Wendelin, tapping the buckles of his trunk.

'What's that handsome house?' he asked their gondolier, passing a *palazzo* of unusually upright comportment and slender lines. Wendelin noted with satisfaction that its plot was exactly the length of a gondola.

'You don't want to go there, sir,' growled the porter. 'That's Ca' Dario. It's haunted to hell and back.'

'So you believe in ghosts in this town then?' Wendelin smiled indulgently. It was somehow pleasing to know there was a weakness, a whimsicality here.

'He who does not believe in ghosts will be destroyed by them,' came the lugubrious reply.

At Rialto, they disembarked with their porter who led them immediately through narrow streets to the inn of his cousin's wife.

'Beds soft enough for the seraphim to die on,' he told them over his shoulder, as if this were a recommendation, 'Food to satisfy a friar.' The establishment into which he ushered them looked respectable enough for neither angel nor clergyman. An unkempt woman, a baby clamped to her breast, offered them a scant welcome. The room they were shown reeked sharply of sweat and was so dark that the landlady had to light a candle to locate the bed for them. In its halo, Wendelin saw the giant shadow of a flea leap in silhouette from the mattress.

After some altercation with the porter, they persuaded him to take them to the Locanda Sturion where their rooms were already commissioned, in advance, by letter. Red-faced with the effort of thwarting the Venetian, and with dragging their heavy bags through the myriad alleys, the brothers felt their hearts beating like flapping sails. Venice had put them to the test already, embroiling them in her Byzantine corruptions. This time, at least, they had won. The porter shot them tenebrous looks from beneath his slender eyebrows, but he now took them, by a miraculously foreshortened route, back to Rialto and their rightful accommodations. As they reached the peak of the wooden bridge Wendelin caught sight of the little silver fish on a red background, just as Padre Pio had promised, and breathed a tremulous sigh of relief.

The immaculate aspect of the Locanda Sturion seemed to confirm the wisdom of Padre Pio, and reinforced their confidence in all the advice he had dispensed. At first, the beauty of the landlady and the luxury of the rooms, hung with blue and green velvet, silenced them. They caught sight of their own pale faces in mould-tainted mirrors, which trapped the reflection of the water below, and seemed to be melting inside their frames. As soon as the landlady glided from their room, with the most restrained and alluring of smiles, the brothers fell into their beds, which were mercifully and surprisingly free of vermin, and exchanged exclamations of surprise and pleasure for a few minutes. Having settled the question that their landlady was absolutely not a courtesan, they fell asleep and remained unconscious for twenty hours.

When they awoke it was with a sense of security, a happy memory of the information imparted by their landlady when she had handed them their key, that just a hundred yards away across the Rialto Bridge lay the *Fondaco dei Tedeschi*, the German guild hall, where they knew they would find comradeship and efficiency, competent information and logical ways forward. In less than an hour they were walking through the Rialto market, marvelling at the sunray clock of San Giacometo. As they passed, it squalled the hour of eight in the voice of a cock. It was reliable to the minute, Wendelin ascertained with an expert look at the sky.

A passer-by stopped to talk to the brothers. A Venetian, he was curious about the strangers, and to hear what they thought of his city.

He preened and smiled as Wendelin stammered out a halting list of fervent praises.

'And even your clocks are beautiful and work perfectly well,' Wendelin concluded breathlessly.

The stranger informed him, smiling, that the internal workings were of course of Sienese manufacture, for it was well known that Venetians could not make clocks which ran to time.

Wendelin, noting that a quarter hour had passed in this pleasant but profitless discussion, already suspected that Venetians retained no wish to mark their hours in disciplined units.

However it was impossible to dampen his spirits on this unclouded morning. It even seemed to him a good omen, this successful integration of a foreign machine at the very core of the city, an outsider heartbeat throbbing healthily at Rialto.

By the end of that morning the brothers had negotiated the use of two bright rooms within the *fondaco*, and hired two bilingual apprentices. They had made the acquaintance of five German merchants. One of the three Venetian nobleman who supervised the *fondaco* had welcomed them with a graceful courtesy that mitigated his condescension. Even that seemed well and good to the brothers: everyone must know his place and they had not yet shown the town what they were made of.

The brothers von Speyer had already learned from their new expatriate friends, that the polished Italians, and most particularly the effete Venetians, regarded Germans as boorish and deficient in creativity, good only for making useful objects and fine mechanisms like scale balances which did not fail (another skill singularly lacking in all Venice). Even the famous German painters were admired only by a small group of connoisseurs in Venice.

So Johann and Wendelin decided, after earnest debate, to re-christen themselves 'da Spira' to render themselves more acceptable and less foreign to their adopted city. No one took any notice. The Venetians, hearing their voices, still turned their heads away from them in the street, lest the famous metallic stink of 'German-ness' invade their nostrils.

They grafted themselves, like the twin shoots of an audacious vine, upon the society offered by Venice, quietly forcing themselves, with a becoming modesty, into the company of Venetians, whenever possible. They attended local *festas*, church benefits, processions; any event where women might decently be met. It was unspoken between them, but they were looking for wives, Venetian wives, to make more intimate their bond with the city with which Wendelin, at least, had been secretly and tenderly in love since that very first day.

Within a few months of their arrival Johann von Speyer married Paola di Messina, the daughter of a painter. Pale and cool of eye, she was somewhat past first youth. Already widowed once, she brought to the new household two silent, swarthy sons by her former husband. She accepted Johann's hurried courtship without requiring any trappings of romance whatsoever. This was as well, as he retained little time or energy to devote to the process. Johann laboured and worried to excess. Wendelin hoped that marriage would modulate his brother's appetite for work, which even to him seemed intemperate at times.

Wendelin lost his heart, in his charmingly stiff way, to a beautiful, impulsive young girl of the Rialto, the daughter of a bookseller. With her white-gold curls, warm apricot complexion and her slanted dark brown eyes, she was confusingly familiar and unfamiliar to him in her lineaments and colouring.

Wendelin had supposed all Italian girls dark, in the same way that German women tended almost universally to fairness. He was astonished at the prevalence of blondes in Venice. Johann, informed by his new wife, explained that Venetian women dyed their hair with noxious substances. Furtively sniffing her

78

hair and gazing at her downy parting, Wendelin immediately dismissed any suspicions about the naturalness of his bride's supple curls. With that matter settled, he relinquished all other trepidations at the notion of marrying a Venetian.

'We shall indeed commit matrimony?' he had asked her, when it was already obvious to all that no other course was possible to them. When he handed her the ring, he descended laboriously to one bended knee. Awkward as a puppy, he held out his short arms and inclined his large head to one side. The girl, already madly in love with his slightly crossed pale blue eyes, and firmly decided upon the number of their sons, had fallen into his arms, laughing.

'I shall be married to an angel?' Wendelin asked, amazed. 'You even like me?'

'Very much. This much,' she smiled, kissing both his eyes. The next day he appeared at work, his hair rumpled at the back, a sure sign of erotic dreaming. His Venetian employees smiled to themselves, and thumped each other on the shoulder.

Chapter Two

Who's seen beings so beatified?
Or so sweet-omened in their love?

My ma was got with me when she'd no more years than I have now – five short of an old crone of twenty, five more than a child of ten. She told me it was on a horse. I think that was to throw me off the sniff of her tale, for how often does one meet with a horse in this town?

It served her well, the horse. All I could do, for I was then but small, was ask her about the horse – I loved those beasts with all my heart.

'Tell me of the horse!' I would cry. I wanted to know every small thing about it. Had it in fact four legs each as tall as a man and did it run fast as a boat flies on waves at high tide? Was it white like foam, or grey like an old barrel? Did it make a noise like a long wet sneeze in March?

For years, in fact, I asked of nothing but the horse. Only when I first lay with my own man did I think to ask my ma for the rest of that tale of how she was got with me. It turned out that she was in the country, in a trap pulled by a horse, when my pa had got to love her just there and then. The rear end of the horse, which was in fact a white one, moved so sweet and smooth that his thoughts, which were then wet with wine, turned to acts of love and he could do nought but grind grain with my ma in the trap with the horse all loose in her reins and half in the road and half on the grass all the way from one town to the next.

So then there was me. I was born on the land, where they kept a farm, though both of them were from this town. But by the time I had five years my pa had moved us all back to this town. He'd made our land water-sick by too many irrigations, 'That madman tries to make Venice on *terraferma*,' I heard one farm-wife hiss to another.

And so it seemed – for soon he could not live one day more with no sea smells in his nose and no sea light at play on the walls. He gave up his great water-stained farm, and all the horses (there was a small one for me), cows and wheat and vines and peacocks, even, that screeched in the yard, and came back to the old wet house in Venice where he'd been born.

He had then to put up with the whisperings of those who said he'd failed on the land. Though all knew in their hearts that to be gone from this town, if you were born here, is like to a living death, and that one day you must own it is so, and make your choice: to live like a worm on the dirt of dry land – for a rich, fat worm is still a worm – or to come home to the clean, good sea and live like a fish, but a fish with a soul.

So then I would wake in a room with sea light at play on the walls, and I grew, first two feet above the rim of the sea, then three, then four.

My father bought a shop, a small concern, which he planned to grow bigger. He worked and drank and worked and drank. He came home with the stench of wine on his mouth and I did not want him to kiss me. He did. I made a sourpuss purse with my lips and would wait till he'd gone before I would breathe again. Then I went out to the canal, spread my arms, and turned around and around and around, until the stink of his kiss was unravelled and blown away.

My father's shop was a *cartolaio*, which sold books and the ingredients for books. His clients could contract the making and binding of handwritten books or bring an old book in for decoration with new boards on the outside or letters painted in gold and tempera at the tops of pages inside. In his small dark shop at Rialto the smell of ink nudged the smell of fish out of my nose when I went in there. (Of course, I was not allowed to touch the books he sold, just to smell them when he held them out to me.) I always begged him: 'Hold the page to the light,' so I could see the watermark – a bird, a gauntlet, a unicorn, perhaps! I loved these more than the words on the page, though I'd learned to read those too, with ease, more fluent even than my pa himself.

My pa tried to make a big noise in the town with smooth paper made of rags and oils, finer than the skins of goats but at half the cost and with a sweet dusty scent to it. He bought from mills on *terraferma* and set up to sell it in the town at profit.

The great objects of his ambition were those outsiders who'd come here not long back who said they could use it to make books. These were not those books that scribes make, one each year, each word carved as if from wood. No! These were quick books! Eight score books born at the same time like a brood of flies and each one whole and good, and each word in it whole and good too. My father was on fire with a dream that these quick books would make us rich.

They came from the North, these men who made the quick books. They brought with them small sharp tools that were special for books. Each one of those tools made a piece of a word. Each word made a piece of a page, and so it went.

One day my pa took me to see the men from the North at work on the quick books. They made them in the *fondaco* of the Germans by the Rialto Bridge. I was to wait below while pa went up to see if I might be allowed to come in to watch them at work.

So I sat on the steps of the bridge and looked up at the house and in the glass of the third floor, just then, I saw a face which I knew though I did not.

Straight away I felt that kind of shiver that starts in your neck and forks out through your body searching for a way out of you. There was a melting in my privities and a taste in my mouth like a citrus liquor and the light went strange, as if the sun had been taken with a fever and smeared its white eye.

I did not wait for my pa. I ran up the stairs in the heart of the *fondaco*. I knew just which way to go, though I did not. My pa looked shocked to see me there. He stood next to the man with the face, who smiled and smiled, but he was curd-pale with shock just as I was. He was fair as a chicken and wore his clothes stiffly, like a new pine coffin. I lifted my right hand up to ask leave to wait while I caught breath. They let me pant till I could speak.

My pa said: 'I would like you to meet my . . .' but I stopped him with my hand on his. I said, fast as if the words could be set free from my mouth, 'No, no! You see, we are to be together.' While I said this I held my palm up in front of the man's face, like a flag that says 'Love Me'.

'Yes,' said the man from the North, and I heard snow and spires and pine trees in his voice. I saw he had perhaps few years more than me and this seemed just right. Then he too held up the palm of his right hand, like a fish tendering its fin, like a flag that says 'Yes'.

My pa looked from him to me and me to him and grew quite old in two jumps of a flea. It was as if the horse and acts of love were gone from him now for good, as it was my turn.

Then my pa's face split in a white-tooth grin like the foam wake of a boat. I knew at once why he looked so pleased. For in this town of trade we sell all the things we love, and my pa saw that he might now sell his own child, me. My price was this: the man from the North might have me if he would buy all the rag stuff – which is called paper – to print his books from my pa now, and never mind the price, if he was to have acts of love with me, as I could see he wished to with all his heart.

And so did I, with him.

In the time it took my pa to bring one boatload of paper to the house of the men from the North I was betrothed to the man whose face I knew and did not.

Wendelin von Speyer wrote to Padre Pio:

I've not forgotten that you asked us to tell you all about Venice. So here are my impressions. As yet, I write in German, but indeed my Italian has improved beyond measure, and for a reason you might easily guess if you could see my face . . . but back to Venice!

How to compare it with Speyer? Speyer is a good little nun. Venice is a beautiful pirate. Before we came here we were told they were a lewd race, but to my mind the Venetians are not so full of the fleshly vices as a love of things. I believe they would sell their souls for spices, dyes, aromatics and salt from Egypt, furs and slaves from Tartary, soft wools and worked metals from our own northern lands. I never saw a town with such a lust for stuffs of all kinds! And even if Venice does not want those things, she still likes to handle them a little as they pass through. It's a law that every sack of cinnamon, every twist of pepper, every bar of gold, which comes through Venice, even if merely on the way from Corfu to Flanders, must be traded at Rialto, to the profit of the town.

She (so you must call her, for Venice is more feminine than any place, if not always exactly a lady) has become a repository of precious and edible goods. And things of forms so exotic that one can only guess at their origin and purpose. Every day I see vegetables I cannot name and fabrics I could not dream. Even humble pumpkins are spiral-cut in airy slices, just for the joy of it. When I take the air with my bride-to-be — (Yes! I cannot resist inserting this information in the middle of my account of Venice: I am to be married!) — we often go to market, so she can teach me more about the town.

Rialto is our university, she declares. In this case, she says, I am the student and she the teacher. She giggles then, whispering shyly, 'But in other things, you will be the teacher.' She barely utters the words before she blushes and covers up her huge eyes with her tiny hands. I too find myself scarlet, but wave upon wave of pleasure crashes inside my whole body.

With so much of the exotic laid out for them on stalls every day, the Venetians seem to think themselves characters from some oriental tale, wily as Sinbad, mystical as giaours . . . yet in them all this orientalism takes the form of a mysterious languidness. They need more sleep than a cat, and it's beyond them to come less than one hour late to any appointment, yawning and plaintive. It is no shame to them to send a boy to say they are simply too tired to come at all.

It fits when Lussièta explained to me this day that the Venetians are worn out — sodden — with a communal dreaming of the Orient, which has flowed (with no effort on their part, of course) into their imaginations, both from travellers' tales and even more so, I think, from the flavours and perfumes of the spices in the market, which travel up their noses and embed foreign pleasures in their very brains.

We stood on the docks this morning, watching the trade galleys take flight to the horizon. My bride explained in great detail (she's so wise in the workings of this town) how the Venetians, never stirring from their opulent gondolas, instead send their money on voyages. A round trip to Alexandria repays the investors one thousand per cent dividends. Even better, they are trading practical things, like iron and timber, for picturesque luxuries. I have a vision of the hopes and fortunes of half Venice floating on the sea, or trotting on the back of a camel twenty days east of Byzantium. (So the boat-builders are not always sleeping, then! This is good to know.)

When you asked me to describe the town I think you meant how it looks. Venetian houses are not like other houses. They are like boats, always ready to make a journey to Aleppo or Damascus! You do not enter a Venetian house, you embark upon it. And once you are inside — the sunlight reflects the waves on to the walls until you feel as if you've gone underwater to some strange new city below the waves.

This is of course all most outlandish. But Johann and I find that we are well suited here. You were absolutely correct in your advice, Padre: the Venetians have built a fine fondaco at Rialto for her respected German businessmen. Indeed all 'Tedeschi' merchants must stay and live there — I suppose, to ensure they do no smuggling or private enterprise untaxed by the town. It's here we have set up our business.

Like German trade with Venice, the fondaco building has grown like a wild plant that flourishes so the plan is not particularly symmetrical. However, it is pleasing. The courtyard to the south, where we have our rooms, boasts seven splendid arches in each of its arcades.

The fondaco *has its own kitchens and cooks. There's a spacious dining room on the first floor. There are good wells with fresh water. The wine-store is open all night for our use. An excellent house master, appointed last year for his whole life (if he likes the work — there's no keeping a Venetian in servitude), keeps the whole running smoothly, dispensing fresh sheets for the visiting merchants, keeping an eye on the porters, the boatmen, the weighers, the stampers and packers. He reports to a committee of three Venetian nobles, the* visdomini. *It's all run rather like a college or a friary, well ordered and peaceful. Each merchant has his own* sensale, *a kind of Venetian broker, to advise what tax he must pay on each transaction. And of course* Signor Sensale *must have his little packet too.*

It's locked up every night against the robbers and madmen, of which, I regret to say, there appear to be many in this beautiful town, though probably not as many as they told us recently, when they increased the charges for guarding us.

We ourselves no longer live under the fondaco's *roof. We've finally persuaded the Venetians that we are not traders; that we are here to stay. We shall be citizens now, by grace of our marriages, of which I shall tell you more. We have rented two small houses behind a square known as San Pantalon.*

We are both so happy with the women we have found. Imagine this: we might dandle Venetian babies on our laps next year! On the bad side, my father-in-law-to-be makes his demands upon us — he supplies us with good paper but drinks his own business dry and looks to me to help him. Johann is more lucky in this respect: his prospective father-in-law is a portrait painter of great renown. But Johann's Paola is of a colder disposition than my Lussièta, and I am glad with the choice I have made, if you can call it a choice.

I am learning not to be hurt by the Venetians. Ach, so strange! Sometimes I think I have made a friend here; the next time I see him his eyes are opaque and he barely acknowledges me in the street, as if I've caused him some deep offence.

I believe now that the Venetians are like the water they live upon: they're extremely sensual in their manners, always dragging their hands with slow pleasure over all their smooth stones and banister-rails. They change mood according to tides of success and happiness, according to light and darkness. The town affects them so much: how can it not? To live in such a strangely poetic place, full of windows and water and reflections!

I confess that I myself am not immune to the sensuality of the place. I feel the love of Venice in me in parts where I should not feel love for a city. But I fear that I grow boring in my enthusiasm for my new home. I shall now desist. Please convey my news to my parents when you see them in church on Sunday. Next week, when there is more time, I shall write to them. Lussièta is calling me. My little sweetmeat! She embodies this quality that I can only describe as 'towardness', which makes all living things, I included, incline towards her in the expectation of pleasure, which she unfailingly delivers. As for me, she warms my heart like hot beer! Sometimes, when I catch sight of her, I just raise my hands like the old saints at prayer and I say to myself, in my new tongue, 'Ecco qua! Un miracolo!'

You will say that I live as yet in the idolatrous season of the newly-betrothed, but I feel certain that this balmy time will last for ever.

All this I have now, because you helped us to come to Venice. I never stop in my heart thanking you for sending us here, Padre Pio, never.

On 18 September 1469 the *Collegio* of Venice conferred upon Johann von Speyer the exclusive right to print the letters of Cicero and the *Natural History* of Pliny 'in the most beautiful form of lettering'. Fines and confiscations protected this right if any other entrepreneur should commence a rival printing works.

Johann could not fully understand it, but the German merchants crowding round him at the *fondaco* to look at the elaborate document, thumped his shoulders and shook his hand. They read aloud the signatures of the *Consiliari*: Angelus Gradenigo, Bertuccius Contareno, Franciscus Dandolo, Jacobus Maureceno, Angelus Venerio: there were no more noble names to be seen in Venice.

A tiny man, bandy-legged as a turnspit-dog, tried to push through the crowd to the front. The Germans calmly joined ranks with their arms and elbows, keeping him to the back. There was a sound of whimpering and scurrying and suddenly his pocked face and one scarlet ear appeared between two German waists for a moment. The other half of his head was hidden in the hood of his cloak.

'Who's he?' asked Wendelin with distaste, 'I mean what's he?'

'A spy from the priests at Murano,' hissed a merchant. 'They hate the thought of this monopoly. Unless it's the Bible, and in Latin, they hate the whole idea of printing.'

To dream about your future love, they say you should remove the yolk from a hard-boiled egg and put salt in its place. Eat this for supper, just before going to bed. To know the trade of your future husband, crack the white of an egg into a glass of water. The shapes formed in the liquid will tell all.

I'd no need for such things. I knew my man and what he did, before I knew I was ready for a husband.

I saw him every day after that first one. He came to sign for me, to meet my ma, to sign some more, to try the ring. (He kneeled to give it to me!) He could even then speak the tongue of this country quite well, but not fast. When he speaks a small part wrong it charms my soul to see how it grieves him. His worst mistake was – and it is still – to tuck the word of action deep in the far end of the sentence so I must hold my breath for a long time to see where his thoughts are going.

When he was not there, I starved for him. For hours I would look at my ring and feed on the light of its small blue stone. Once I saw him in the street, he did not see me for I was on the first floor and looked down on him. He walked slow as trust past my house, his head stiff and sad. I saw he did not do well without me, and I did but poorly without him, and I wished our day yet more close.

A maiden should not think of how it is to share a bed with the man she shall wed. Yet in my mind I held that image: the great globe of the earth slowly rolling with our bed, and us in it, perched on top, like a wind vane.

And the other image I kept always in my mind was that of his face, that face I knew yet I knew not. I never thought to marry an outsider! Yet that face of his seemed the very opposite of strange to me. Sometimes it reminded me of a kinsman I'd loved when I was a child, who had died, or gone away and at last come back. Sometimes it called to mind my first-born doll: it was so smooth and pink and round in its lines, and so perfect that I longed to lay myself down beside it and gaze into the eyes till sleep came.

When it lacked but one day to the one when we were to be wed, I did not see him at all. But as I lay in bed that night, his kiss came to me in the dark, on its own.

The nobleman Domenico Zorzi, to whom the events at the *fondaco* were reported in less than an hour, called for ink and paper. He scribbled a brief, gracious note to the German brothers, congratulating them on their monopoly and asking to be included in the subscription for their first edition.

'It cannot hurt', he said aloud, 'to be kind to these Germans.' Domenico knew that the von Speyers had seduced the *Collegio* with the beauty of their typeface. He had himself fallen under the spell of their samples, the lettering impeccably even yet lusciously full in contour, like a slice of a slim black eel that has recently swallowed an egg.

By the end of that day, Wendelin and Johann were in receipt of fifteen such missives scrawled in aristocratic hands. At Wendelin's wedding, on the Saturday of that week, liveried servants from three noble families arrived bearing nuptial sweetmeats on platters embossed with the crests from the Golden Book. And there was a gift of wine, too, from Ca' Dario, the haunted *palazzo* Wendelin had admired on the day he arrived. Giovanni Dario, who spoke more languages than any other man in Venice, had put his name forward as a subscriber for the new quick books. But when Lussièta heard of its provenance she insisted the Dario wine should be tipped into the canal.

'No one shall be poisoned by ghost wine at our wedding!' she insisted. Wendelin dared not remonstrate: she looked too beautiful to be argued with at that moment.

Embarrassed by the attentions of the noblemen, Johann was distracted throughout the day. Wendelin stammered through the service, his eyes fixed on his new wife, as if she was the Holy Star. There was no wedding journey, for the bridegroom was needed at the *fondaco*. Johann was not entirely well; something caught persistently in his throat and he was unable to keep down food. His energies depleted, he could not spare his brother. After two days secluded with

Lussièta in their new apartments, Wendelin returned to work, flushed with the exhaustion of his conjugal felicities.

And so the brothers von Speyer, dimly aware of what was riding on their shoulders, set to work on their business, began traditions, teaching the Venetians what it was to manufacture learning at a thumping pace instead of a slow-breathing one.

Chapter Three

The bonds of marriage bind all creatures.
See the bulls spreading their broad flanks over their wives,
the bleating ewes crowd into the shade with the rams,
the lake rings with the hoarse love-song of the swan.
The Goddess of love forbids the melodious birds
to close their beaks.
The nightingale chants in the poplar tree
so that you would think she was uttering in music
the very emotion of love . . .

It's too quick to be wed. The words are gone before you can taste them in your mouth. The ear of your soul limps along behind: 'Wa—it' it bleats, 'Wait! I do not know where to fit this news inside my heart; I shall burst.'

So, yes, we were wed in San Giacometo at the tenth hour of the day. It was small as well as quick, our wedding. From my side came my ma and pa; from my man's, just Johann and his new wife Paola, who must be my friend (though how I'm to succeed in this friendship is beyond me as Paola lacquers her face with something so no expression reaches her lips). And the scribe, Felice Feliciano, who dressed so fine as to seem a bride himself.

Acqua alta had paid its devotions before us. In the swooning damp of the half-drowned church, Johann coughed all through our rite. I did not like this at all, for with each cough of his kin, a new groove was carved on my man's smooth pink brow. Paola seemed not to notice, never offered him a hand or even a handkerchief.

I looked behind me, through the open mouth of the church. Outside the grape-black pigeons throbbed 'I do – I do – I do' and the colourful scents of various articles of spicery rose up from the market stalls like wedding banners in the flaunting sun.

You do not say much, when you say the most in the world. You just listen to some words, which are about God and chairs and tables and houses, and you say just 'Yes, I do,' and 'Yes, I will,' some few times and your name and his, and then it is done, and you are sealed by law for life.

Then you stand mute and stunned at *una festa* while all congratulate you, but you hear their *auguri* as if they were speaking down a tunnel in the earth, and presently (and mercifully) you retire to a room where you mix all your flesh with all his.

I thank God for this.

I have but a plain tongue in my mouth, but I tell you our love is a thing to make stars bloom by the light of day. It is love on stilts, and it does reach for heaven . . . indeed though each new act of love's the same in its conclusion, it's yet as variable in the splendour of its execution as the quotidian dawn.

We cannot be unmixed now. Even as he goes about his work, and I go about the business of being a wife, we've only to close our eyes a moment to feel ourselves back in our bed, and the whole day folds up like a box, bringing us together from the diverse parts of the town.

My man's quick books are no small thing to make. It's the hardest thing I know to get work from the men of this town, so much they love to doze and dream. Most things float here to us; we need not raise a finger, let alone a hand. As with the anemones that flower beneath the sea, our nourishment swishes in!

And so it seems the work of God for my man to find the hands he needs: it's just as though he must fashion a whole new world here in Venice, a little German world that clicks and ticks on time like a foreign clock.

92

The new art of mechanical printing was hungry for human hands.

Wendelin and Johann went out on the streets of Venice, into the salons, the workshops, the bookshops, the studios, looking for the right kind of hands to help them.

In some ways, the new business of printing was little different from the old one of creating manuscripts: first the ideas and then the substance. So Wendelin and Johann made it known throughout the town that they sought editors. Knowing the vanity of scholars, the brothers insisted that they wanted only editors capable of selecting the most refined manuscripts, correcting their accumulated scribal errors, and writing the most alluring introductions and flourishing dedications to flatter the hoped-for noble patrons.

From the resulting flood of applicants, they selected Gerolamo Squarzafico, the bibulous classicist, and the scholar Giorgio Merula.

The next to be hired was Bruno Uguccione, a decent young man of Dorsoduro, who was to assist the senior editors. The scribe Felice Feliciano, who had insisted that the von Speyers meet his protégé, put his name forward. Bruno brought his old friend Morto, now a jeweller, with him to his interview. He guessed correctly that the German brothers might find uses for Morto's clever fingers, but more importantly he cherished the hope of working alongside a familiar face in this foreign enterprise.

It was evening when Bruno and Morto came to the *stamperia*. The summer's day had persisted in coolness when the heat should have burnt off the dew. So the sulphurous smell of the night had not been shaken out of the weave of the town's streets. Even at midday the leaves had lain shadowless on the stones where they had fallen limply as tears hours before. The town's dogs thought twice about lifting their legs: it was too much effort. The sun had remained just a drop of molten glass in the sky, awaiting the attention of a master glass blower. The Venetian carpenters fitting out the *stamperia* with shelves and tables were gripped by desire for sleep. They yawned, stretched themselves extravagantly without inhibition, as if still in bed.

Everyone stopped and looked up as the two young men entered the subdued room; ten pairs of eyes followed them to the desks of the two German masters who stood whispering in urgent colloquy, Johann making many small, tight gestures towards a proof in Wendelin's hand.

Wendelin and Johann, both wiping their perspiring brows with a simultaneous and identical gesture, looked benevolently on the two young men, one with the delectable lineaments of a schoolboy, the other gangling and deathly pale, his nose an unpleasant wedge that blocked out the light. Bruno's letters from his teachers were enough of an introduction. Moreover, he possessed the kind of face that it would be most pleasant to work alongside. A prepared contract was placed in his hands.

Morto, who lacked academic references, was set to engraving a tiny slab of copper.

'Ummph,' said Wendelin, leaning over Morto's shoulder to see the perfect sparrow he had engraved. 'You're hired.'

When I married my man, my women friends told me that I would have a great job of mending to do, not just the normal things – for example to teach him the difference between a mother's breast and a wife's, but also to instruct him in all the words of love I would like to hear, and how to button up his rear end to stop crude sounds and worse smells, and many more things besides . . . but this one, my man, was not even Venetian, and they said he was therefore almost a case beyond hope.

The women told me that men like the love of their wives only at the start. It's a sore thing, for they're like spoilt boys who take just one bite of the peach and leave the rest to rot, or open a bottle of cordial for the white sigh of the bottle and one lone swig, and then go wandering off to look for beer. Worse, there are those that even grow to hate their wives, and do them harm.

'Wed her, bed her, put her in the ground,' chanted one of the women, and we all stared at her.

She said, full of her own defence, 'My husband sings that when he's in his cups.'

Well, it's not like that with my man and me. Nothing could rot the delight we find in one another. The first time we lay together was not so lovely as the last time.

When we have fallen apart, panting, I love to sleep with my man in this house of ours. It's a gaunt, auntish little house and we live its every inch. I set flowers in all places, lamps and enough glass from Murano for a tiny cathedral, my man says.

In each window and every place where light falls, I put glass of red and blue and violet and green . . . perhaps that's why my man and I sleep so sweetly, for we are enfolded in colours, like the sparrows of Bengal who, it is said, ornament their nests with living fireflies.

When we wake, we pull the frail threads of shared dreams from the lids of our eyes. He lays his big head against my breast and I feel my breasts crushed beneath the weight.

Sometimes, when we lie like this, I feel a great desire to be a part of not just his present life but also his past. I want to know everything that he remembers. I ask him to make me see his own town of Speyer. He starts to tell of the proud priests and merchants and the fine houses, how it's bigger even than Heidelberg and can be seen from exceedingly far off.

I break in then.

'But where is your water?'

'Our water?' he answers, dimly, to obey my need but he struggles to do so.

'Yes, your water to live by.'

'Oh,' he says, understanding at last, and he puffs himself up. 'Well, of course we have the Rhine,' he says proudly, as if that meant something to me.

I look on him adoringly, proud that he knows so much that I do not.

He takes this in, but wishes me to know about the Rhine without his telling me, for he also wants me to be great of brain and soul, as he believes I am (just because I penetrate the mysteries of the market and the dialect, and know the morrow's weather from one glint on the sea. Such things that are natural as kissing to me.)

So he says, 'You know, the great river, the one which brought me here . . .' and he goes on to tell it for me, painting pictures with his voice. And he describes the mountains he came over, the great lakes of the Alps and the deep woods of Germany. All men of the North, he tells me, love their forests with a fervour. 'A wood is a cathedral,' he says, 'but more beautiful and refreshing to the spirit.'

I find that thought ticklesome and simple. We of this town love nature only when the hand of man has improved it. Was the Grand Canal still grand before we built our *palazzi* along its edge? I think not.

My man tells me that the *palazzi* of his town are shut-up dark places, full of gloom. They've great wood doors with iron studs and drawbridges. The folk of Speyer may not make a great show of their wealth lest a great army comes marching across the plains to take it. Instead they build watch-towers – six and seventy of them!

The main street is five and thirty paces wide and the buildings on either side are fair of form and painted with stories and scenes, some of battles to save the city from those enemies who covet her, and would put her citizens to slavery.

We are much safer in Venice, where our enemies must float over the sea to us (which they're not used to, and they are clumsy as pigs on their boats) and should they be so foolish as to dare it, we could easily see them from the horizon and put them to flight. The Genoese pirates got as far as Chioggia once, but we soon saw them off.

My man is intrigued that I know so much of history and practicality. I am amazed that the girls of his town do not, and many cannot even read. All my friends can read. My sister-in-law can read. Even the harlots of this town are educated, I tell him, to change the subject hurriedly (for he's forever nudging me to call on Johann's wife Paola, and I hate to do that. She's cold as winter with me, and does not wish an intimacy. This is poor behaviour on her part for she and I have much to do to help our husbands, and it would be better if we could do it together).

The harlots of Venice prove a good distraction from the subject of Paola, and I explain many things to him that make his eyes open wide as a lake.

So many conversations we have like this.

My women friends, when they see me yawning at the well, laugh that I have not slept much. 'It's not what you think,' I tell them (though it is that, too). 'We talked until the fourth hour this morning.' They shake their heads in disbelief and ask 'What do you talk about, all those hours?'

I say, 'This is what happens when you marry a man who is not of your race. The discovery is never over.'

'What about the nuances?' they carp, 'the tiny things, the little words?'

What of them? If some love has transpired in the steam of translation, I tell them, how very much more has got through!

They laugh at me, and say I'll tire of my big bear soon enough. They sneer at my happiness.

Happiness such as mine, however, laughs at sneers. And yawns with a smile.

Chapter Four

Gates, unfold your wings!

As Morto and Bruno left the *fondaco*, Johann von Speyer had already turned away, frowning.

A month was not long, and there must be work awaiting these two when they came back to him; work that would earn its keep.

In that month, the brothers von Speyer knew that they must find their raw materials: manuscripts to turn to print and the paper on which to print it.

Wendelin and Johann gently persuaded Lussièta's father that his *cartolaio* could not supply all their needs. Deferentially, seriously, they went about the town. There were bonds to be drawn, hands to be shaken, brown eyes gazed into, directly and unfalteringly, by blue and grey ones. And before that there were honeyed words to be spoken, modest glances to be cast at the ground, for the greatest of *cartolai* were rich and pompous and had to be flattered.

Nor did the oiling of the wheels stop there. The brothers knew they must secure the interest of patricians, particularly Domenico Zorzi, who read everything and knew everyone, and who manipulated his way with consummate grace around the Senate, obtaining favours and custom for those he patronised. They could not take his early support for granted.

To make their ink Johann and Wendelin scoured the painters' studios for smoke-black, boiled linseed oil, turpentine, Greek pitch, marcassite, cinnabar, vermilion, rosin, hard and liquid varnishes, nutgalls, vitriols and shellacs. They bought wine from the wine merchants to dissolve the gall, and wooden batons from the *falegnami* for stirring their black mixtures. They recruited a well-paid ink-mixer; his recipes were crucial to their vision of printed pages, on which the letters would fly in front of the eyes as if cast simply by wishes upon the air.

For the styling and casting of the type they hired engravers and metal-workers like Morto with the lightness of touch and artistry to sculpt jewels of letters in reverse on the end of hardened steel punches.

They found a master jeweller to work as *compositore*, with the task of plac-ing the tiny letters in sequence, ready to stamp on the paper. He was a skilled craftsman, but, just to be sure, they also hired a corrector to shadow his work. They trained operators, *torculatori*, to run the press. For inkers they hired stu-dents and unsuccessful teachers.

For the people to ornament their printed pages by hand, Wendelin and Johann recruited artisans from the *scriptorie* of the monasteries, and nuns, who, with their delicate fingers, were quicker and cheaper than some of their male counterparts and certainly more tractable than some arrogant scribes, who did not yet know that their big day was nearly over, and sneered at the printers as a weak and short-lived pestilence.

Wendelin asked Felice and Bruno about Sant' Angelo di Contorta: 'This is where your sister lives, no, Bruno? Do the nuns there undertake rubrications?' While Felice giggled, Bruno had blushed and lowered his eyes: 'No, they're slightly more skilled with the needle, I believe, sir.'

'Ach, a pity,' sighed Wendelin.

Felice smirked, his face alight with mischief. Wendelin would have liked to ask more, but could see that the turn of the conversation was distressing to Bruno. He addressed himself quickly to more pressing matters.

The brothers personally took on the training of the illuminators and scribes in their new work of decorating *printed* pages. They had also to ensure sufficient stocks of gold leaf, azure and saffron for the voluminous labour ahead.

Once the three hundred books were printed, each sheaf of folios might meet a different fate. Some would be destined for noble libraries. Such clients would want full colour illumination; lesser clients might also order the books in advance for the pleasure of savouring the wait, but they could afford just the decoration of some red hand lettering. It would be prudent also to allow for a few to be handstamped with pictures whittled on wood blocks.

They lined up binders to take over when the sheets had been printed and decorated. In their workshops the tall folios would be bound in boards of wood covered with tooled or stamped calf, fastened with thongs of leather or bronze clasps. Lettering and patterns would be gilded directly on to the leather with heated rods or into the impressions after the leather had been tooled.

The much-handled sheets would finally come full circle. For the new printed books would be marketed by the same *cartolai* that had sold Wendelin the original manuscripts and then the paper on which to print. But the booksellers had to be briefed on how to speak enthusiastically and knowledgeably of the new invention to their own clients, how to demonstrate the beautiful regularity and clarity of the von Speyers' typeface.

By August, everything was in place and the real work was about to begin. Wendelin and Johann, it seemed, confronted and surmounted all the problems that face a printer of books, problems unknown to makers of manuscripts. They had even become used to the limping shadow of the little spy from Murano who trailed them in all their various enterprises.

At that moment Johann von Speyer fell ill under the strain of the administrative toils and the heat of the Venetian summer, to which neither brother had been able to accustom himself. Wendelin watched anxiously as Johann's cheeks hollowed day by day. The bark of his cough filled the *stamperia*. Every thud of each machine and the cadence of every conversation were now punctuated by the rasp of Johann's punished lungs.

Wendelin wanted to put an arm around Johann's bony shoulder, but gestures of physical affection came awkwardly to the brothers.

'Don't worry about me. What about this ink mixture, then?' gasped Johann, clutching the desk, a grey sweat pearling his forehead. Wendelin could smell the sickness on him, and grieved for it. His brother, always small, seemed to be diminishing in substance every day. Each morning he seemed to use up less of the leather on the chair at his desk, till he looked like a large-headed child who insists on sitting at his father's place.

Wendelin knew that Johann's wife Paola had called in the local doctors and wise women, who applied all their unpleasant concoctions to her husband's chest and head. Now, according to his own wife, Paola should be calling in a

Jewish physician. Listening to Johann's laboured breathing, he hoped it was not too late.

Does she not see that he's mortally ill? Does she not care?

My sister-in-law Paola shows no feeling at all for poor Jo. Instead she drives him on, interferes with his business and asks him impudent questions about the accounts in front of his family! How can a woman be so shallow and so thick-skinned all at once? I only wish my man's press ran as fast and sharp as her tongue.

There are better ways to help a husband.

I lie in bed at night and tell my man stories I've heard about the town. He loves to hear them, and in this way he learns more about us, which is good for his work. He can lose himself in my tales and for a while forgets his problems at work and the sound of Jo's cough.

However, his taste in stories is not exactly mine. He likes accounts of things that can be explained by practical means or human nature. When I tell ghost tales, then he shifts in the bed and fidgets and wishes that I would stop, not because he's frightened but because he's German.

Of course the world's mouth gapes open at Rialto and this is where I go to hear my stories, while I poke my fingers among the melons and lift the eggs up to the light.

There's a tale from Rialto this day of a man and wife, chicken farmers of Sant' Erasmo. The wife was of large breasts and those breasts were the man's joy and delight. And the wife was just as proud in their regard. Her breasts, she said, held her man to her like glue.

One day the wife took it in her head that she would hatch a chick in between those breasts. A mother hen had died in the night and left one small egg in the nest. The wife saw the egg, lonely as a single white teardrop, and grieved for the hen who was a favoured one of hers. She reached out and took the egg and put it in between the fold of her two breasts. I think that for a moment it must have been cold with the death of its mother, but how quick it must have cleaved to the heat of her breasts – and how soon it must have taken to itself their pink tint. In my mind's eye I see it there, a peep of pale shell against her skin . . . but I run off my course. The tale had a sad end.

For her man did not like the egg in that place. They say that late at night when they lay a-bed the wife would not let him have his acts of love for fear that if she took out the egg it would die of cold and if she left it there while they coupled it would be crushed.

So the man was left unsatisfied and could but look at her breasts where he thought his own head and lips should be. I can just see his look, sour as a pickled herring – how would my man be if I chose an egg for my breast, not his hand or his lips?

As I said, it had a bad end, the tale, for the man in the end could not bear it. He took an axe as if to split the egg, and the wife, even with the glint of the steel in her eyes, shrieked that she would not take out the egg. And he cursed her and said that if she loved the egg more than him then she was no wife. And she sobbed that the egg was in need, for its mother was dead. And he yelled that he was in need of acts of love and a wife who would not give them might as well be dead.

The screams of both of them were heard by all nearby and then a dread noise – the smack of the axe that cleaved first the egg and then her whole heart in two.

My man grew pale, asking 'Is this true?' and I gave him comfort sweet as grated sandal-root, so he forgot not just the question but the tale.

I did not tell this part to my man – that when I heard this tale I was moved to try my own breasts with an egg and I stole to the box to take one. But my breasts are not so large or so slack that they can hold an egg. The one I chose – a large brown one – slipped to the ground and smashed on my toes.

As I cleaned up the mess of yolk and shell, I wondered if my sister-in-law could hold an egg between those gaunt breasts of hers.

The answer is, of course, that she would not think to try. Just as she will not call in a Jew to tend to Jo, though he begins to fail. There's one called Rabino Simeon who saved my pa from the drop-plague last year. He lives at San Trovaso, and he always comes, not only to the rich but also to anyone who needs him. I'm sure he would help Johann.

Paola's one who cleaves to the old school of thought and hates his race: I've heard her say so.

'Don't print their tracts, there's no market for them,' she said once to my man and his brother, and I blushed for her that she'd no shame in ordering our menfolk about.

She stinks of pride – granite-breasted, the sourest-natured woman I ever met. Paola has a horse's face and horsebreath too. I smell rotting greens when she leans over to me.

No, she won't call the Jew to save Johann. She sets more store on dry doctrinal things and the clink of coins than on the love of her husband, even though she risks his life in doing so.

I tell my man that Paola must call the Jew.

My man looks full of doubt, and I tell him that the Jews are the best doctors. The Venetian quacks are just butlers with big bags and fine long tongues for flattering the noble ladies.

'I suppose that Paola forbids it?' I ask, with scorn in my voice. He shakes his head: he always defends her.

'Do you fear the Jews?' I ask him. 'Perhaps you know them not? Do you think them dirty? Perhaps there are none in Speyer?'

He tells me this is not at all the case; that Speyer has many Jews. They are treated well, have the respect of the town. They live in their own quarter, where they conduct their kind of mass in their own church and even a special bath, called a *Mikwe*, where they wash before they pray.

'So no,' he tells me, 'they are not strange to me, nor dirty; they're the cleanest race.'

'So let us call this Simeon, then. I hear he's a wonder.'

Still he resists, and suddenly I realise what it is. I think he knows that Johann has taken the damp on his lungs, the kind that does not heal, and a good doctor will tell him this truth he cannot bear.

Paola shows no sign that she understands her peril. How can she be so cold? If I lost my man or his love, I would have no more wish to live. As the year turns round I love him more by each season, more and better, and with a fiercer passion.

Bruno and Morto, and all the other newly recruited workers, looked up anxiously as Johann von Speyer passed them, coughing like a wet cat. He appeared gradually less and less at the *fondaco*, leaving Wendelin to manage alone. One day they heard that Johann von Speyer had taken to his bed. He was not seen at the printing works after that.

Wendelin doubled his efforts with the Venetian dialect. He was determined to learn it fluently; he wanted no barrier between himself and the men at the *stamperia*. It was his task to transmit the detailed knowledge that at present belonged only to Johann, and to a lesser extent to himself. Now that Johann was no longer visible to the men, he needed all the more to ally himself with them. He knew he must learn to speak with his hands, like the Venetians. The arms hanging neatly at his sides while he talked marked him as an outsider.

But his wife fervently wished him to become accomplished in her language, so she suggested that he ask Bruno Uguccione, that nice young man, to come to their home after supper some evenings and coach his *capo* in Venetian dialect. There were stories about the town that Bruno had become involved with an unsuitable woman and it seemed a kindly thing to take him off the streets and have him pass his evenings in a loving household.

Of course Wendelin's wife meant kindly. She had no conception of the convulsions of jealousy she would rouse in the young editor, every time she ruffled her husband's blond hair, or slid her cheek alongside his, the better to kiss his nose.

Wendelin worked harder. He could not sleep. While Johann dwindled under his damp sheets, stiller and more silent each day, Wendelin felt too much alive, oversensitive to every physical sensation. It seemed to him, in the early hours, that the very birds were nagging the sky to dawn more quickly, that as he paced through his courtyard garden, the plants were squeezing out dew that urgently needed to be transpired into the sky. His ears were tickled by a maddeningly subtle noise, which, he realised, was the slight cracking of the carapaces of rosebuds on the verge of a flourish of petals.

He could not bring himself to call the Jewish doctor. Paola had dismissed the suggestion, and he could not go against her. Each morning he visited his brother's bedside, held the waxy hand in his, and talked of business matters. Johann's eyes flickered in the dim light, but Wendelin could not be sure if his brother had heard anything at all. He took comfort in the thought that he'd told everything. Johann hated not to know what was going on at the *stamperia*.

At night, in bed, Wendelin clutched his wife, listening to her breathing, gasping with fear if one breath came a little slower than its predecessors. One morning, hurrying to work as the sun rose briskly at the far end of the Grand Canal, he shook his fist at it and said, 'Wait, wait for me, wait for Johann. Please! Wait.'

But three weeks later, in the offices of the *Collegio* a clerk scrawled across the document which had guaranteed the printing monopoly to Johann von Speyer: *Nullius est vigoris, quia obiit magister et auctor:* 'Of no significance, because the said master and petitioner is dead.'

Chapter Five

Through many seas and many nations
I come, dear brother, to take this pitiful leave of you,
to make last gestures at your grave,
to utter pointless words over your silent ashes . . .
Now and for ever, brother, hail and farewell.

Wendelin took his brother's body back to Speyer.

He could not bury Johann in the shallow ground of the floating town. Death became the city; her very beauty was morbid, but Wendelin felt that Venice was not *substantial* enough to keep his brother's body safely. He had horrifying visions of the thin corpse rising up in the mud, the arms still crossed over its breast. He saw himself encounter it, floating down a canal, as he walked over a bridge. Within a day of his death, Wendelin had resolved that Johann must be buried in good firm German soil.

When rumours of Wendelin's decision reached the *stamperia*, two theories vied for grim precedence: that he'd gone mad and that he would never return. In anticipation, the men mourned the printing works – its fascinations, hoped-for profits and the pleasant hierarchies that had begun to take the shape of a family – but no one complained. Wendelin's transparent grief for his brother was impossible to criticise.

His wife, to whom Wendelin confided his visions, lay in bed beside him, inscribing pictures of his fears on the black palette of her closed eyelids, so that she might feel them too. 'Yes,' she agreed, when filled with these shared terrors, 'we should take note of them, but should we let them lead us to danger for our own selves?'

Gently, she reminded him how long the journey would take, and the body, as yet still fresh, would soon become less so. He countered with the coldness of the season. Already there was snow and on the mainland tramps were freezing to death in doorways. They were found in the mornings by the street sweepers, who closed their eyes and dragged them to the nearest church.

'To carry a body all the way over the Alps, though!' keened his wife. 'How can you think such a thing? There's no cart that can take those roads in the high snow.'

'We shall think of something.'

'Can we not send Johann with a good courier? His soul has gone before him.'

'No, this is something I must do for my brother.'

When she saw that he was obdurate (a thing always signalled by his return to German syntax even within the Venetian dialect), Wendelin's wife insisted that she would come too. She would not be separated from him, she declared. At first he thought this a mere gesture of loyalty, but her very quietness in its reiteration made him realise that she was in earnest. He tried to dissuade her, then found himself disarmed at the thought of her beloved company, at least until the Alps, when he was sure that the hardships of the journey would force her to turn back. There was also the possibility, given the enthusiasm and frequency of their lovemaking, that she might at any moment find herself with child, in which case he would never put the baby at risk in such a venture.

It was a week later that they set off. Johann's body, kept in a side-chapel of San Bartolomeo, was set as ice.

'You see,' Wendelin told his wife, 'we have preserved him.'

She wailed: 'It is so now, but we must be afraid of every ray of the sun!'

Paola made no objection to the plan, merely opened her pale eyes wide and nodded. It was she who made sure that Johann's body was washed in vinegar and anointed with musk, then laid with aloes and other spices in a lead coffin, encased in cypress.

The weather was in sympathy with their plans. In the Brenta canal, along which the horses pulled their boat against the current towards Padova, the water was grey as stones, with no reflections. The first wagon taking them west towards Brescia jerked through a sere, dead landscape.

As they rose up into the hills the colour drained from the land as well. Pale, seemingly translucent spires, like ghostly nibs, jabbed the sky. The sumpter horse that bore Johann's impossibly small coffin plodded on, his eyes demurely on the ground. On the other side, to balance the coffin's weight, the horse carried a sack of Venetian tooled bookbindings and packets of ink mixture for Padre Pio in Speyer.

The other packhorses followed at a discreet distance. Wendelin, watching the sumpter and its burden, found that the monotony of the journey imprinted a litany in his mind. He could not refrain from chanting to himself, to the rhythm of his own horse: *My brother and the things he died for, my brother and the things he died for.*

Lussièta rode beside him, as close as she could, holding his hand.

Why did I come? How could I not? How could I send my man on such a sad trip all on his own?

In the end, I saw why he had to do it. Johann's corpse must go north. He never bonded his blood or soul to Venice, not as my man has done. He could not learn the dialect of our town. His wife was chilly to him: Paola is not a Venetian herself and was already a widow when he married her. Sicilians are strange: small in body, huge with temper. They can brood for a decade. Paola is like that. I know she does not like me. In her sly way, so none should criticise her, she sneaps at me, without seeming to do so, every little word stabbing my ears.

'A nice piece of fabric,' she will say of my dress, all the while prim as a nun at a christening. In other words: my gown itself is badly made and ill fitting. She, of course, is always stainless and elegant.

I could never think of Paola and Johann joined in acts of love: easier to conjure them bent over the account books of the household. Their marriage was of the earthenware kind. Still, it must have happened, for there was a daughter and lately a son, to add to the two boys she bore before with her Sicilian man. Johann's children, young as they are, have taken after Paola in their characters and we do not often see them in our house. I feel that Paola merely borrowed him from Speyer, never took possession of him, as I did with my man.

So yes, Johann's remains had to go home. I just did not see why my man was obliged to take them.

I hated the whole idea. My secret fear was this: if my man went back to Speyer, after this great sadness had befallen him in Venice, he might never come back here. I thought that if I went with him, to remind him hourly of the joys of our town, that he would never forget her necessary beauty, and would not stay long away from it.

I also saw my task was to keep up his pride in himself. He was lost without Johann, deathly afraid that without his brother the business would falter and fail. If he was alone all those days on the road, I just knew the black picture he would paint for himself. Though I nourish no great affection for printing works, which keep him from me all the day, I've never wished him to desist from this employment. Indeed I had some ideas for him, to help him more in the town, and I thought this long journey would give me time to air them all.

So good were my intentions, but this trip was never fated to be happy, was it? All the sweetness that I'd planned to flow into his ear was soon stopped up in my mouth. Far from mellifluous, I fear my voice more often bore the stale timbre of a scold or a nag. The more sordid were my discomforts on this journey the more ugly were my complaints.

We sat, endless, endless, behind the flanks of the horse, which sometimes contracted to squeeze out lumps of manure. In spite of this, the rump of the horse made me think of how I was made. I licked my lips and looked to my man to discover if his thoughts drifted likewise and I hoped that he might ask to stop a while so we might retire to a bush. For a moment I was cheered at this prospect but it came to nothing. With Johann's body stretched in its box behind us and the tops of these great trees drawing my man's eyes up to God like infernal tweezers he did not think of the tale I once told him of my ma and pa and the horse. He wanted of me just to hold my hand and stroke my hair.

Va bene, I sighed silently.

Sometimes I could not stand the shake and jerk of my mount any more and I told them to let me down to walk a space. Then the land came up to slap my feet till they were sore and I had to ask to be helped up again.

Tall grey birds, more like ghosts of birds, stood still on the ponds we passed, their beaks pointed up as if in reproach. Perhaps it was the process of Johann's coffin that made them do that. Certainly all the folk we passed along our way would cross themselves at the sight of the box, and sometimes they would spit to forfend his ghost.

Some people love to travel; even some Venetians are known to take to the road with relish. I cannot comprehend why. Most seasoned travellers are insufferable folk, full of themselves and tales as unlikely as their complexions. My man and I were appalled at the vulgar people, the pompous priests, the know-all merchants, we passed on our journey: how they grated on our nerves, drove us deeper into our satisfaction with one another!

I was frightened of those inns where the men eyed me, for my man had explained that there were those who sold their wives' favours to strangers by night to pay for the passage on. In those inns my man, for he's great in size, pulled me on top of him and I slept on his belly, with his arms around me, and I felt safe then.

I preferred the nights we slept in fowl-houses – for yes, we did that too. I liked to fall asleep to the soft noises of the roosting birds. Their sleepy shufflings sounded a little like the cluck and gurgle of water in a back canal in our town.

'Doesn't it sound like home?' I asked my man craftily. 'Is it not a delicious noise?'

But he did not answer, and I could see that, even though we were but little advanced on our journey, the word 'home' had two possibilities in it for him now, and the one uppermost in his mind was Speyer.

The roads became steeper. Crossing Valtellina, they moved up to the pass of Aprica. Fellow-travellers, smirking over their beer in the inns, told them that they must regard these cold and steep roads as a mere rehearsal for the torture of the high Alps. Wendelin, remembering his journey to Italy, knew that this was true, and was at pains to point it out to his wife.

'Whatever cold you feel here, whatever wind, whatever tiredness, you must, if you are to come over the Alps with me, double and triple it. And there are highwaymen and worse . . .'

His wife replied serenely: 'They will not trouble us when they see the coffin. It would be bad luck indeed to raid a funeral party.'

She set her lips in a narrow line and smiled. 'Take me higher.'

Wendelin felt the warmth of relief flood his skin. He really did not know what he would do without her arms around him every night and her sweet breath against his neck while he slept.

Every night, when they laid Johann's coffin in whatever stable or anteroom the innkeeper unwillingly provided, Wendelin would spend some time alone with his brother and in kind words for the gentle horse who bore the burden all day.

He spoke aloud to Johann's box, bidding his brother a soft and peaceful night, before joining his wife in the nest of blankets she had already warmed for him.

But there were other nights when he sat down in the straw with one hand on the coffin, and talked to Johann of his fears for the *stamperia* and all its staff.

'How am I to continue, Johann?' he pleaded. 'I have not the will and anger in me, as you had. I have told the clerk to pay the men as normal while we are away. But with our present funds, as you know, the money cannot last beyond the spring. What am I to do?'

I was seasick; I grew clumsy. I felt dizzy all the time, as if I had drunk something strong. It was too quiet. I fancied I could hear the birds breathe.

I did not like the hilltop houses, with their black roofs folded over them like the hunched wings of a cormorant.

'Where's the water?' I mourned silently, 'Where is it?'

My man heard me, anyway, and pointed when he could to streams and falls.

It was the wrong kind of water.

Up there the water was everywhere tortured by the land, carded over sharp rocks in shallow rivers, crashing down mountains as if taking its own life because it couldn't stand the burden of height any more.

'Poor water,' I kept murmuring under my breath.

Meanwhile the wind, like a beast that sought advantage, found a way under my cloak and gnawed at my legs.

The horse that bore the box with Johann inside walked slower and slower, holding all of us back. We lingered on the road, until we heard the old horse's breath behind us, and then we moved on, slowly, never looking behind.

This journey gave me a new respect for my man. To think he and Johann made this dreadful trip alone, knowing nothing of our town, just in faith that they would find it good. Now he made it in reverse, I saw he thought of that himself. In coming to our town, he had lost his brother, had started a big concern that may bleed him dry of all his savings before it succeeds.

'Was it worth it?' I asked him, once.

'For one kiss of your lips, it was worth it,' he smiled, even though out of breath from the climb. (Leading my horse, he often stumbles but before he saves his knees or his wrists, which are black with bloody grazes, he looks up to me, to make sure my mount is steady and that I am in no peril.)

At that moment a wedge of geese flew south over our heads. My eyes followed them longingly, and my man's followed mine, regretfully.

When they approached the foothills of the Alps, Wendelin asked his wife yet again if she would return home to Venice.

In the mountain passes the party would be forced to abandon their carts of provisions. There was no road for wheeled vehicles through the Alps: a combination of packhorse, foot and, when the need arose, boats across lakes, were as yet the only ways to cross the mountains. They would be heading for Basel to join the Rhine, and take one of the canal boats up towards Speyer.

But before then the roads would rise up so that the tops of hills would be lost in the mist. The temperature would drop to half of what they endured now, and by night black ice would creep over the pathways.

When Emperor Henry IV had crossed the Alps nearly five hundred years before, his entire court was placed on bullock skins, like magic carpets, and drawn by ropes up the passes. But there were no such luxuries for ordinary travellers of these times. If they were lucky they might be offered the use of the Castilian Threshing Machine, a tree loosely harnessed to an ox, so that as it proceeded it rolled its bush of leaves around, clearing the snow to make a path for the horses.

There was peril of avalanches, so that each hour their servants had to discharge their muskets into the air, to bring down any loose snow. A false step in any direction and the powdered snow would dissolve, plunging the traveller into a narrow unmarked grave two hundred feet below.

Herds of shaggy cattle, which terrified Lussièta, roamed the passes. There were tales of dragons around the Luzern Alps, and the ghost of Pontius Pilate in the lake.

At this, her eyes widened, but she held tight to Wendelin's hand and declared that she would not leave him.

At first it was just unpleasant.

There were even good times, when I myself could see the beauty of the place. The trees were crusted with gold like burnt cream pudding. I liked to watch the birds swirl off in funnels of beating wings as we passed. I loved the quick change of mood in those short days: one dip in the road, at three after noon, and we were all of a sudden in regretful evening light. I watched for the moment each day but it always took me by surprise.

For many miles we travelled behind a cart laden with trees, as if we were great lords and ladies who went abroad only with their own private garden to accompany them, lest the view be for one moment not lovely enough for their spoilt eyes.

Sometimes we rode above the clouds. I saw the white vapour boiling below us and we were so high up I felt that God might at any moment look down on us, who trespassed so in his realm of gold – for gold it was. The light was gold and the hills seemed to have a great cloth of gold shrugged over them. I confess I wished this God would say to us, when he poked through the clouds, 'Go home to Venice now. Leave Johann here in my care.'

God never showed his face though, and soon enough we would go down right into the cloud where we walked like blind men, our horses tied to one another and each step a terror to us.

The cold was not too terrible as yet. We wrapped parchment round our chests to keep out the worst of it. There was nothing to be done to keep our feet warm. At night a kind landlady would sometimes put them in bowls of cold water, and then she would add cups of hot until we could feel them again.

I hated the high mountains. When I looked at them I felt sick and many times I varnished the side of my horse with the contents of my belly. And it was a cruel place for beasts that must be deformed to live there. All the cows, for example, had legs considerably shorter on one side in order to keep their grip and stay standing on those steep slopes. It was not natural, the land like an old courtesan, lying on her side, with everything sliding off her at an angle. I hated the grim cleavages and scars of the ravines.

I began to see why mountain people set so much store by God. Of course we Venetians believe in another world, but it's as delectable as this one, and in the same style. I explained to my man that on still days we see our whole world reflected on the water, and that glittering vision is probably our conception of Heaven.

I did not feel any closer to God in the mountains.

I told my man what I was thinking and, to pass the time I suppose, he argued with me about it. Kindly and gently, of course.

'No, no – it's the greatness of God, incarnate,' he insisted. 'And it's a kind of Calvary on Earth. When we struggle up here, we bring our souls as well as our bodies a little closer to Heaven.'

'It does not look like something God made. It looks as if some monstrous dogs dug huge holes with their paws and threw up the clods of earth.'

Of course the Alps are most direfully haunted to hell and back. At night, in the inns, the travellers whispered stories to us. If my man left the table, they lowered their voices and leant over to me, to give me more and more dreadful details.

Worse still, it's well known even in Venice that the Alps are bristling with dragons, all kinds that fly or slither or merely stink. There were, we heard, many sightings of these beasts by respected travellers, and each sighting served to confirm the truth of it, as in respect of their appearance the Alpine dragons are always the same; they have the head of a red hairy cat, with whiskers, sparking eyes, scaly legs, a tongue like a snake's and a tail which is spread in two forks. They prance up on their back legs like a mantis, or take to the sky, always with the front claws raised in front of them.

The road became harder, higher still. Through St Gottard the wind blew round them, and the track that marked the tiny progress of a whole day was pitifully visible from the next station. The travellers were obliged to stuff the mules' bells with wool for fear of dislodging avalanches. The sumpter horse that bore Johann's coffin was disturbed by the stark lack of soothing bell music. It went a little mad, and performed three somersaults. It was only stopped from a fourth and certainly fatal one, for it ranged near a crevasse, by the presence of mind and brute strength of the muleteer who caught it by the tail and brought it to its knees, where it brayed and foamed.

The coffin remained sealed, but for many hours afterwards all in the party continued in silence, their minds' eyes fixed on images of poor Johann's remains inside, surely splintered and broken.

Wendelin's wife strained her neck, constantly watching out for the cat-headed dragons. All she saw was strange northern sparrows, their head-feathers drained of colour.

'Poor little beasts,' she said.

Her own body, formerly blessed with the elasticity of a young rabbit, grew bowed and cramped with cold. Even when she dismounted, she walked like an old woman.

Everything was denatured in the mountains. The ground was lighter than the sky; the lakes were solid, the complexions of the travellers glowed like those of saints, and even the horses, now shod with protective spikes, looked like dragons.

They stopped at towns that were cut off for months at a time, which showed fearful evidence of in-breeding, worse than what Lussièta knew of the small islands of the Venetian lagoon. At one place, all the shopkeepers sported the same hairy goitres on their necks. At other villages only the cretinous section of the population was to be found lolling by firesides in otherwise deserted houses: those with their wits intact were out working in the small pockets of tillable land or guarding the sheep.

They took a boat across the lake of Luzern, ploughing the still water that held tight to mirrored mountains wigged in blue-white. Johann's coffin was placed upright on the deck, as if he could see through its lead and wood the beauty of the landscape. At the far end of the lake it was again laced to a horse and continued its journey horizontally.

The further north they went, the more arrogant became the innkeepers. When they arrived at the nightly inn, the landlord no longer deigned to come to the door to meet them. At their knock or call, he would put his head cautiously out of the window, like a tortoise from its shell. He listened in silence to their requests for shelter. If he did not refuse them, they might enter. If they asked for the stable, he merely pointed to it.

As for the rooms, they were always told that the best were reserved for the noblemen, whom he pretended to be his regular clients. There was but one common room to change their clothes, wash, dry their wet cloaks, and that was also the room reserved for eating.

The innkeeper would never prepare food until the whole night's company was assembled. Wendelin and his wife sat wrapped in one another's arms, their stomachs barking up the fumes of starvation, sharp and sour. At vast prices, morsels of unkempt food were served late at night.

Not surprisingly, some inns had suffered the rage of their guests too often, and the landlords ordered all knives to be taken from travellers on their arrival. Others boasted sheets that were washed but once every six months, no matter how many had slept on them. Some offered beds that were nothing but high cupboards, reached by tottering ladders. Inside were ticks filled with greasy feathers, never replaced and never beaten to scare away the vermin, whose nightly welcome was eager and diligent.

The more north we went, the more Northern my man became. I did not like it. He started to walk stiffly again, as if trying to copy the fat burghers here who wear their hose pulled up high over the barrels of their guts. In Venice he had learned to walk as one should, easily, as if swimming through light air. I did not like him to forget how to do that.

I spilled a tankard of beer on him, and myself as well, in Freiburg. He turned German again, or at least to ice. He could not look at me.

'Are you mad?' he asked quietly. I could see in his face he was embarrassed to have a wife such as me. A German wife would never have done such a thing.

'No, just stupid,' I said, full of my own defence. I could not turn away fast enough from his closed face. Venice has been good for him, I thought. It's reshaped him softer and sweeter. If he'd stayed here in Germany, he would have become entirely rigid in his ways.

The landlady took pity and hustled me away to her kitchen to clean my beer-sodden skirts. She used me very kindly, plying me with pickled salmon and conserves. 'You are such a little sweeting,' she said in German (words I understood, as my man used them also when he flowed with love for me). She would not desist from cupping my numb cheeks in her great rasping hands. Then she ran her fingers, tarantula-like, over my breasts and my hips, all the time sucking in her breath, as if to say: 'How can anything so tiny really be grown and married?'

Soon my man appeared in the kitchen, shamefaced and sad, to take me away. The landlady made a sorrowful noise at this, and gestured passionately to my man.

'What is she saying?' I asked.

'She says, and I suppose it's the truth, that you are so delectable she could just eat you up. Also that they never saw a little Venetian lady here before.'

This splintered the ice that had grown between him and me since I spilled the beer, and I ran to him. He was full of sorry-ness and tender as a mother. So I comforted him in turn and all was well with us again.

Every night we ate more than I could have thought possible. It was our only protection against the cold.

The food lay on my gut as if it had died there. It was the 'wild' season, they say, by which they mean it's the time to kill and eat all things that run fast with blood dark enough for rich gravy. So we chewed on deer and wild pig and wild goose, all doused in cream or floating in it. Cream soup with mushrooms, cream sauce with cabbage, cream custard, cream pie with rhubarb. I begged for some fish, and a stinking thing, awash with yellow cream, was brought to me. Lake fish and river fish are different from sea fish, I told them, and thrust the creamy dish away, like a spoiled child, which pained my man.

He looked as if he might be wrathful. A strange affray went on inside him – anger fighting against sadness, and sadness winning. He went out to the stable where they let us rest Johann's coffin and stayed there a while. I guessed he was talking to his brother about the business.

Some nights I hardly cared. My guts grew most mutinous on that diet. I was stricken with the cramp colic and I rolled up in a ball on the bed. When he came back to the room, I lay with my back to him. He always forgave me my whining, and stroked me until I slept. If I woke up in the night, feeling better, then we made what I call 'mountain love', that is, the superstitious kind which keeps out your fears.

But when we got to Freiburg, I said, 'Enough.'

We were staying at an inn called *Zum Roten Bären*, the Red Bears, so we could be close to the parish church which was said to be the most beautiful in Christendom. Its spire was picked out like a veil, and that was pleasing, but otherwise I could not see what was lovely in its flat red stones and the horrible gargoyles who leered at me down every gutter.

We'd taken a diversion there, because Johann had always wanted to see it. My man wished to light a candle for him in the Münster so that at least his soul might rest more easy in Heaven, with one more dream achieved on Earth.

I knew we lacked but a few miles till we could be in Speyer, and that I would now not meet his ma and pa. I knew it was not kind of me, but I could not go on. By that time, I'd run out of patience with the mountains and the roads and the high skies and all that cream.

Of course there was a graver reason than that. I was deeply afraid of going all the way to Speyer with him, more afraid than I had been even of the cat-headed dragons and the ghost of Pontius Pilate.

The journey had opened up a little glimpse of a chasm between me and my man, made us see the invisible glacier that runs between his German-ness and my Venetian nature. He found the mountains beautiful; I found them repulsive. He'd showed me his stiff and closed side for the first time. I'd let him see my childish tantrums. Something was spoilt between us, who had hitherto only shown the best of ourselves to each other.

Now I could not come to Speyer, present our flawed love to his parents, show my flawed self to his town. All those clear-eyed Germans would see right through me. They would say to my man, 'Stay here! Why go back? Johann has died; you cannot run a business by yourself in that strange town. Stay here, and there will be work for you without worries. Your wife must do as she's bid.'

And I had one last secret fear. I worried lest I should get with child in Speyer. Sometimes it surprised me that I'd not fallen yet, and I expected it at any minute. If I should conceive in Speyer, how much stronger would be the demands of that town upon him! For then our baby would be more than half German. My man can count. He would work it out. He would start thinking on it. And what a catastrophe, what an ill-starred thing that would be.

Chapter Six

Do the milk-white
girls detain you?

Wendelin argued with his wife, wasting precious days trying to change her mind.

'My parents will adore you,' he told her. 'I want you to see Speyer. Now that you are married to me, it's partly your home town, too.'

At this, she had stuffed her hand inside her mouth and turned away, her eyes full of tears.

Wendelin tried to tempt her with tales of Kraichgau streaky bacon. He tried to make her laugh with menus of '*Schnippelbohnensalat*', and '*Rahmpfifferlingen*', which he told her were 'fairy' mushrooms in cream sauce. At the word 'cream', she made a childish face.

Something had broken in her in the trip over the Alps. She had become more dependent on Wendelin and at the same time more distant from him. She interposed herself between him and everything he wished to see or do, demanding attention, and yet she was remote with him.

She is not well, she's worn out, Wendelin told himself. *This is the only way I can account for her behaviour.*

A happier thought struck him: *Perhaps she is with child. Things are not quite right between us and she wants to wait till a beautiful moment to tell me. This is how women do such things. This is how she would do it.*

Whatever was happening inside the impenetrable lead coffin, Wendelin felt increasingly anxious to inter his brother. When he saw that his wife would not be induced to join him, he made reluctant plans to sail up to Speyer without her.

It was two more days before he arrived in the outskirts of his town, catching his breath at the sight of the familiar walls looming over the edge of the Rhine plain, and the turrets of the Dom spiked above it. With the help of his servant, he loaded the coffin on to a smaller boat. In it, they took a fork into Speyer's own town river, arriving at the port on a cold morning. Pausing on the Sonnenbrücke, he listened to the panting of the Speyerbach flowing below him, and looked over the rooftops of the twisting lanes of Hasenpfuhl, remembering the hare hunts there in his boyhood, but it seemed like someone else's young days he remembered, not his own, as if he'd once long ago read a story about two young boys growing up in Speyer, as if Venice had claimed not just his present life but his memories, too.

Feeling like a ghost, he felt almost surprised to know his way from the port to the busy wood market, next to the fish market. How mean and poor seemed the display of grey fish compared to the vivid drama of Rialto! He sniffed, remembering which of the sharp stinks was that of a barrel of salted fish from Cologne, which was a freshly caught sturgeon. Or perhaps not so fresh, he thought, wrinkling his nose. How restrained were the cries of the fishmongers; how pallid and lumpen their wives, he thought, shivering. Even the pretty young girls selling apples seemed as mild as milk pudding in colouring and character.

Hiring two men and a cart, he took the narrow streets to Little Heavens Alley and the family home. Both parents came to the door to greet him, stepped quickly out to the street to gaze at Johann's coffin. His father thumped the wood once. His mother whispered consecutive prayers expressionlessly.

Padre Pio appeared, waddling up the road at a surprising speed, his round cheeks slick with tears. When he reached Wendelin, he took him in his arms, and cried heartily on his breast, 'My son, my poor son.'

Wendelin, rocked in the priest's embrace, whispered hoarsely, 'I never thought we would come back like this.' He pulled away and gestured to the coffin, and to his own gaunt frame, pared away by the hardships of the journey. His parents, hearing their son speak Italian for the first time, exchanged frightened glances.

'Where's your lovely wife, my friend?' asked Padre Pio, continuing in Italian, for he'd observed the parents' discomfort.

'She's not well, she could not come all the way,' mumbled Wendelin, scarlet-faced.

'Not well, *in a good way*, I hope, my son?' Padre Pio leaned forward, gesturing at his own round belly.

'It may be that, I hope . . . but we must think now of my poor brother.' Wendelin's voice broke on the last syllable, and Padre Pio enfolded him in his arms again, and let him heave and gulp for a moment or two. Wendelin's parents turned away in embarrassment.

The undertaker, already sitting with his hands folded in the parlour, was summoned out and discreetly took charge of the cart. As he handed his brother's remains to the man, Wendelin felt a moment of rebellion. Why should a stranger take over these intimate duties that until now had been his own? He'd become used to the presence of the coffin; it had taken on a familiar personality, quite separate to that of his brother. He realised that in a strange way he would actually miss it.

But his parents were so convulsed by its presence that he could not reasonably leave it any longer in their sight. He saluted the undertaker with perfect civility, bid an affectionate farewell to Padre Pio, put arms around each of his flinching parents, and drew them inside. He realised that neither of them had asked of his wife, and by this he knew that they wished he might not leave them again nor return to Venice. In the quiet ways of the family, though, he also knew that this would never be discussed, and that they would at some point allow him to depart without fuss, as they had done the first time.

I made him leave me in Freiburg where baby canals ran through the streets to carry water for fires and for the beasts. They are called the '*Bächle*' which means 'little brooks', and I soon saw the Freiburghers took the same bad delight in them that we of our town take in our canals when they wrong-foot the foreigners who come here. So often I saw a man of the South or further North, black with wet up one leg to his thigh where he'd mischanced upon a *Bächle* or walked backwards into it while gazing up at the spire of the Münster.

So my man went on to Speyer without me, and I stayed on at the Red Bears. He told me he would be back in a fortnight, and left me one manservant, who straightaway disappeared to the fleshpots of the town. I did not care. I spent my days sitting by the arched windows of the dining room that gave on to the street. I watched the Freiburg folk outside.

These Germans look so rich, I thought, *with their thick clothes and their thick buildings*. But I wanted to scream, 'You are poor, you are poor! Rat-poor in the things that matter, for all your cream and butter. For how do you amuse yourselves? What do you do for fun and laughter?'

But I liked their wardrobes painted with birds and flowers, and I liked the width of the German ladies. I imagined their shape under their clothes – their bellies must be oval as plums with the cleave of the haunch starting high up at the back and the front all taut and soft and rounded. Walking behind two of them, you could see just a thin hourglass of light chipped between their bodies. I wondered if I, little as I was, could slip between them and not be noticed.

It was late autumn so there were still gourds in dream shapes in the windows, in oranges and green. With all the sights to amuse me, I thought I would do fine without my man, but I was wrong.

Within an hour I'd started to miss him and to regret my stubborn nature. I begged a piece of paper from the landlord and I made a big square. I divided it into many little squares. And then more. Enough for one tiny square for each hour my man would be away. As each hour passed I coloured in a square with a little kindle of charcoal. When the time seemed to pass too slow, I would go out, so that when I came back from my excursion – to the Münster or the icy river or the mossy park – I might blacken two or three of the little squares at one time. So tiny were the increments of my relief that I thought I might go mad.

The day after Johann's funeral, Wendelin made his way through Markt and Krämergasse, crowded with stalls selling cereals, wood and vegetables. Everything was scented with the earth, he noticed, wrinkling his nose and pulling his cloak more tightly around him. He realised that he was missing the tang of salt in the air. He remembered fondly the lush perfume of the Merceria in Venice where the scent-merchants burned pastilles of Egyptian incense twenty-four hours a day to attract custom.

A canal ran through the centre of Speyer's main street. Wendelin looked at the water, his eye seeking the sparkle to which it had become accustomed. But the city canal ran dully, not mirroring the ashen sky, but shadowed by it, and in a dead straight line from the city gate to the Old Mint, as if, he thought, it lacked the wit or curiosity to weave even a little from side to side in its course.

He laughed at himself, thinking, *This is not my thought: this is something Lussièta would say. I wish she was here to contradict me.*

He looked hopefully at blonde girls in the street. There was no one who resembled his incomparable wife: none with her slant almond eyes or that rich bloom to her skin. There was no one as *complicated* as Lussièta. The young girls were simple as dolls in their mien, stiff, pretty little dolls indeed. They lacked the vivid plasticity of his wife. The older people he passed all looked the same; square, handsome, tall and fair, prosperous, relentlessly decent, well upholstered in firm flesh against the cold.

Yet in Venice he had remembered Speyer as cosmopolitan, sophisticated, with Jews and foreign merchants enlivening the city.

Speyer is changing, he thought to himself. *Or is it me? Perhaps the damp of Venice has eroded my sense of myself.* He counted in his mind the good things about Speyer, the crispness of the sheets, the fresh dryness of the air, the joy of understanding everything said around him, the bite of the beer, the proximity of his parents and the affectionate Padre Pio. But at night in his narrow childhood bed, unable to sleep, his thoughts and desires turned constantly to Lussièta.

In the street, Wendelin picked up a retinue of curious acquaintances from former times. Every time he stopped at a stall, merchants clustered around him, asking about Venice.

'Is it true that there are gold tiles in the Markusplatz?' they asked him. 'Do the women show their breasts in the streets?'

Others clamoured to know if those streets were truly made of water. Or were they just like Speyer's own town canals, exaggerated, Italian-style, in the telling?

Wendelin laughed but he did not answer them, for he did not like the way the questions were put. He resented the cynicism of his fellow-townsmen, and their lack of imagination. *It's not my role to be ambassador of Venice*, he told himself. *Let them go there for themselves – they'll never believe what I tell them, anyway.*

He continued on to the cathedral, walking fast enough to leave his questions behind.

He had always boasted to his wife that Speyer's Dom was one of the most important in Christendom. He'd told her of its immense size, its political importance. She had asked him, impatiently, 'Yes, but how beautiful is it?'

He had described it for her proudly, 'A church built by Emperors and chosen for their final resting place. It's like a . . . like a great full-breasted ship, like a galley at sail that you can see above all the rooftops.'

Looking at it now, its immense straight body and its stumpy little towers, he could no longer answer her question with unequivocal loyalty. Yes, it might still be said to resemble a great ship. But it was rooted immovably in the ground. Its triangles and cones seemed the pieces of a primitive toy building set, put together by a child who lacked fantasy.

He shook his head, as if to dislodge these inconstant thoughts, and stepped inside the cathedral.

He found it, as ever, full of light – clean, scouring unmysterious light – with everything made clear; the very opposite of the shadowy Venetian churches. The cathedral had expressed to him, as a young man, everything great about his faith. *Ordnung und Klarheit*, order and clarity, it had personified both, on a grand scale. Now, he was forced to confess to himself, it was unsatisfactory to his senses. Its colours were cold and wintry. Its interior failed to raise on his skin the goose-pimples of sacred mystery, as always happened at San Bartolomeo in Venice.

He proceeded, as he had planned to do, to the *Taufkapelle* on the right of the nave, where he wanted to light a candle for Johann. The capitals of its four squat columns were carved with acanthus leaves. He could not help but compare them with those he had left behind in Venice where the art simply flowed from the hands of the artisans so that their leaves twined around columns as if still growing. Here in Speyer the stone acanthus stood stiffly upright, as if dying on the point of a pin.

Wendelin lit the candle for Johann in one of the crypt altars and prayed, briefly, in German, stumbling over the words. Among the many images of his brother which floated through his mind were two of Johann at the *stamperia*: one, the moment of hiring young Bruno Uguccione; the other of the day he had brought back to the *fondaco* the precious monopoly document.

He was filled with exhaustion at the thought of the *stamperia* and the problems that awaited him. His funereal duties to Johann himself were now completely discharged; he was emptied of that responsibility. It was time to shoulder the ones Johann had left for him to complete. This pivotal moment, between one great task and the next, also offered him an escape, he realised, rocking on his knees on the cold stone floor.

I could stay here, Wendelin thought, *I don't need to go back*. But the empty space inside him suddenly flooded with desire for his wife's voice, her arms around him, and her eyes.

Then he rose and strode back to Little Heavens Alley.

'I must leave now,' he told his parents. 'My wife is waiting for me. And my business. My and Johann's business, which I shall carry on in his name.'

They nodded, politely. They did not accompany him to the river-dock, but waved from the window of the house. By the time he reached the river, he had thoughts of nothing but Lussièta in his mind.

When he asked her what he might bring her as a souvenir of the riches of his town, his wife had requested only a portrait of himself as a child. This, extracted from his mother, was now wrapped in sheep's wool at the top of his trunk. It had been handed over with some difficulty (he could read her thoughts – his wife would have him by her all the time now, it was she, his mother, who needed the mementos). He had glanced briefly at the sketched likeness, hoping to revive his memory of his childhood self, which now seemed so fugitive. But the drawing was badly done, wall-faced and unalive – *unless*, thought Wendelin, *this is how I really was before I went to Venice?*

Chapter Seven

*Sirmione, sweet little eye of all islands
and peninsulas that Neptune lifts out
of the liquid waters and vast seas,
how happy the heart that beholds you!*

At last he came back to me. He slept in my arms one night at the Red
Bears and then we set out again, this time, blessedly, southwards. I
was light of spirit for he'd shown me in an instant that he forgave my
selfishness and my coward's heart and that he had not guessed my
motives for staying behind. The first thing he did was lay his hand on
my belly and look at me full of hopeful query. When I shook my
head, he took me to his breast straight away, and said, 'Well, we
begin again now.'

Afterwards he rose from the bed and went to his leather box. He
brought me the picture of his young self, which I kissed. I hoped
he'd understand from this that I can love his Speyer self as much as
his Venetian self, provided, of course, that he keeps the Speyer self
by my side in Venice.

Of our journey home I shall not trouble you with an account for
it was filled with the same discomforts, all intensified by the onset
of truly cold weather. You must imagine for yourself the waterfalls
weeping ice tears through black rocks, the lakes with their tattered
fishnets of mist, the bite of the snow on my cheeks, the old ladies
in scarves strapped to the tops of carts like corpses . . .

Imagine the horrors of all before, doubled, but yet sweetened by the thought that we were on our way back to Venice.

Coming *down* mountains was worse than going up, if anything, as the way was more uneasy. It seemed to me that I but held my breath until we came down from the Alps again, to the Lake of Como. I did not start to feel myself until the mountains began to flatten, like the whipped white of an egg left in the sun to subside. It was only when we were within scent of the sea again, with the houses and churches in rabbles of colour, that I felt free from the dragons, ghosts, frostbite and fear of the mountains. And not till I was home in the plains above Venice that I could let my shoulders fall from their stiff hunch.

And yet there was one good time along our way. When we passed Lake Garda, though I longed and yearned for home, my man persuaded me that we should go to Sirmione, where the Roman poet Catullus lived fifteen centuries ago. Even at that time, you see, my man had conceived his notion of printing the poems of Catullus, those poems that would soon cause our lives to change for ever. A certain manuscript had come to Venice, and all the scholars were talking of it.

There were the ruins of an ancient Roman villa at Sirmione. Felice Feliciano and his friend, the artist Mantegna, had been there before. One evening at a tavern they'd filled my man's sweet head with pictures of it. Those two had arrived by boat and picnicked in the shade of the ruins, fancying themselves the new ghosts of the young Catullus come to life inside their drunken bodies, no doubt. It was those two, of course, who were loudest and most persistent in pressing my man to print that dangerous book, even though he'd not yet laid eyes on it himself.

Even so, I was not curious to see this Sirmione, for every moment I thought I could catch the tang of Venice air blown westward on the wind. Yet my man insisted, saying that the place was lovely and I should see it once in my life.

In the end, though it cost us two more days, I am grateful that he put me under duress.

If I one day committed some dark crime, and was made to leave our town, there is one other place in the world where I could live, and that is Sirmione.

Everyone should go there.

It sleeps on the lake like a dream, in a veil of white light, a little headland nosing long and slender into the centre of the water. This light makes the near shores look transparent, like a sketch in pencil, and it rubs out the far shores, so the place looks like heaven, floating on the clouds, seen above and in reflection on the water.

We walked through arches that framed the lake like a theatre, and the bird choirs lifted our hearts with their sweet music and refreshed our souls. Sirmione was beautiful not only for its flowers, but also for the shade of its orange and lemon trees. Water streamed from springs, fruit still hung heavy from the boughs of trees like lamps holding the sun in their kernels. We found many traces of antiquity: the marble columns were dimpled with inscriptions.

Sparrows fluttered everywhere, their brown heads as glossy as chestnuts. I reminded myself, when I saw them, to tell young Bruno Uguccione about them, and also about the northern sparrows that had frightened me with their strange pale heads. These were proper Venetian sparrows – the males with black-blotted breastplates and serious skullcaps, their downy dim mates hovering at tender distances, their brown gowns muted as if left in the attic many years past.

There was not much left of the great Roman house, but we could see that it was vast. My man wandered around, picking up stones, looking through his fingers and squeezed-up eyes at the crumpled walls. I guessed that in his mind he was building it all up to splendour again, with its waving flags, its mosaics, its fluted columns and the happy young Catullus lounging in a portico writing his love poems and gallivanting with his mistress.

Sitting on a cool rock in the shade, I watched my man from a distance.

He was not alone in his sightseeing, it seemed, for I saw a young man flitting in and out of the trees too. He was strangely dressed in a tunic that was nothing to do with Venetian fashions. But I'd seen all kinds of costumes on our travels and nothing surprised me now.

Even from a distance I could see the young man was not well. He staggered, and his whole slight frame was racked with a most terrible cough, which reminded me sadly of Johann. I hoped my man could not hear him.

Every few seconds the young man stopped to loose what pressed on his breast and he grew weaker by the moment. Finally, he leaned against a tree and collapsed, sliding down the trunk to the ground where he lay in a mess of thin elbows and knees. I rose to fly to his side and assist him, but then an older man, also strangely dressed, appeared as if from nowhere. He seemed to be calling out. When he saw the young man he fell to his knees and gathered him in his arms. I could see from the way the young man's head lolled back that he'd fallen in a deep faint. The older man, who must have been his father, held him tight against his breast and I saw his shoulder shaking with tears.

I was so absorbed in the piteous sight of the young man that I did not notice the roach that crawled up to join me, not until its tiny antlers tickled my hand. My scream echoed around the natural theatre of the site, but the roach stayed on my hand. In a moment my man was with me. Weeping with fear, I held up my hand, on which the roach seemed glued, for even when I shook it, the wretched beast stayed there. My man brushed it gently aside.

'Kill it! Kill it!' I shrieked at him.

In an instant he snatched up a heavy rock and dashed it down upon the roach. I still sobbed, feeling the imprint of the beetle on my hand. I calmed myself only when he lifted the stone to show me the shattered carapace of my tormentor, cut in two halves by the sharpness of the blow.

'All gone, darling, you're safe now,' my man said, rocking me in his arms, his eyes on the horizon over my head, which he kissed and kissed.

I too looked up and was ready to tell him all about the sad sight to which I'd just been witness, but the older man and the young one had vanished. I thought then that in the heat of the sun I had perhaps become drowsy and dreamt them.

So I did not tell my man what I'd seen. He's not fond of ghosts, real ones or dreamed ones: since our parting in Freiburg I'd tried not to mention them too often. Also, I felt sorry for him. I'd interrupted his reverie most brutally, and we had come all this way to help him think about Catullus.

'Go, darling, go and look at the rest of the place,' I said. 'I'm perfectly well now. I can see that the thing is dead.'

'Are you sure?'

'Yes, yes, go!'

He left me, finally, with a long kiss on the lips, and many looks behind him. I waved at him each time and blew kisses, until he was quite out of sight.

It was then that I saw something glint in the cavity left by the rock with which he'd killed the roach. I leant down and put my fingers where the shining was. I touched something soft and cool, like a candle in a larder.

I knelt down and dug gently around the object, thinking it some little souvenir I could give to my man to remind him of this place that gave him so much pleasure.

With a little digging, I loosened it and pulled it out of the earth. I turned it around in my hands, blowing the grains of dirt off it and dislodging clumps with my little finger.

Then I dropped it on the ground with a cry.

For I had seen what it was: the wax figure of a woman with nails in her back, one each for her kidneys, her liver, her spleen and her heart, with dark hair wrapped around them to form a number 5 or the letter S. A witch figure! A bad love charm! And I had touched her with my own naked fingers. I wiped them backwards and forwards against my dress.

My man had heard my second cry and was hurrying towards me again. My instinct, sharp as a squirt of civet, warned me that he should not see the figure: it would trouble him and spoil Sirmione for him. I did not know what to do; all my thoughts were scrabbling in my head as his dear outline gained substance running towards me. In the last minute as he approached my side, I leant down and scooped the woman up into my sleeve, just to hide her. I planned to drop her again as soon as he was not looking.

'Is it another roach?' he asked breathlessly. 'Where is it?'

'Y-y-y-es, but it ran away. It's gone. I'm sorry I frightened you.'

'You're sure it's gone?' He foraged around the grass nearby with his hand, looking for it. Then he turned to me, 'I don't mean to frighten you, darling, but shall I look in your clothes?'

'No!' I said vehemently, with such force that he took a step backwards. 'Let's just leave now. I'm tired from all these beasts.'

We walked slowly back to where we'd left the horses, hand in hand, stopping sometimes to kiss.

Truly, I meant to drop her on the ground somewhere when he was not looking. But it was not to be: inside my sleeve one of the nails on the figure had hooked itself to the fabric. She hung there, like a fly in a spider's web, and no matter how I shook her, surreptitiously, she would not drop out of my dress. The wax had lost its fatty coldness and became warm against my skin. I stopped shaking my sleeve.

She means to come to Venice, I thought. *Or whoever made her wants her to come to Venice with me. I have been chosen to carry her. Who am I to stop him? Whoever made her: his will has become mine now.*

As we left the grounds of the old house, my man put his arm around me, and turned me to face the sunstrewn ruins one last time.

'Is it not lovely?' he asked. 'Is it not sad that it has fallen back into the past?'

I could see then what he was thinking: by printing the poems Catullus wrote, he could make Sirmione come alive again. I did not say anything, because I did not agree.

It was beautiful enough for me, just as a ruin. I do not see why we need to bring the past back into the present.

Why not let it stay there, where it was happy?

PART THREE

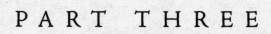

Prologue

For there is no crime more extreme to perpetrate.
Not even if he were to lower his head and swallow himself.

October 62 BC

Greetings, brother!

What tidings from the East? I hope these last months have not erased my name from the tablet of your memory?

I hear nothing from you, just stale news via our father. Have you a wound in your writing-hand, soldier? In your profession, silence is frightening for those who love you. Write.

My news? Nothing of war or gain. I'm writing all the time now; that is, when I'm not scintillating with the drink. I spend my sober hours with the other young poets of the Alexandrine school, in which excess, delicacy and, naturally, the courses of Venus are celebrated. Our coterie likes everything small and perfectly formed (we abhor an epic). My Phalaecean hendecasyllable is a thing of polished beauty and my limping iambics positively gambol! Even Caelius has something tumescing his normally flaccid verse these days.

We are interested in the concept of synaesthesia put forward by the Greeks: how, in writing, combinations of two or more senses give a disproportionate amount of pleasure. Also, why the sound of certain consonants harnessed to certain vowels can move a man to tears, even when he has no idea of the language.

So, for example, I've coined a new word for 'kiss'. Old 'osculum' sounds to me like what snails do. It has all the sensual panache of sucking a pip from an orange. I've borrowed from our Celtic dialect in Verona and come up with 'basium' on which the mouth can linger at least. And instead of mere kisses, I write 'kissifications' – the kind that leaves you wishing for another mouth, so pillaged is the one you own.

It's a rare day when a poem stays trapped inside me.

I have plenty of hours – sometimes days – when Clodia doesn't require my services. I don't wait around moping. I burn up the time between our encounters. I do everything. I go everywhere that's fashionable. I wave away the hand that pours water to dilute the wine. I know the hazy pleasures of wandering drunkenly through midnight Rome, my arms linked in those of two poet-brothers. I bypass all those earnest transactions in doorways of exclusive clubs, for I, Catullus, am always waved in indulgently. I drink and gamble with my slaves and on the Kalends my animal mask was more grotesque than anyone's. This year I was a small deer with enormous horns and a nose of ember-red. Clodia was a hyena.

Her brother Publius Clodius wore women's clothes, of course. There are rumours it's not only at the Kalends that he does this. I avoid his company, for he puts the glad eye on me when he sees me. He'll reach out a hand too, if I pass too close, and it's horrible to feel, soft as a baby's sneeze. He makes me uncomfortable in ways I cannot name. It's not just the excess of fondling he lavishes on his sister, even or perhaps especially in my presence, or the wall-eyed thugs who lurk in knots on the stairs when he's with her. It's a sense of something limitless in his corruption. There's nothing Clodius would not do. He would bring down the edifice of this city if he could, temple by temple, brothel by brothel.

I'll admit it, I myself love to shock.

Not like Clodius. With me, it's just a bit of fun, a savoury jest at someone else's expense. Mostly.

The stink of Aemilius' mouth, I quipped, is worse than the stench of his arse, because the latter at least lacks his long, rotten teeth – which are like the slats that stop manure from falling out of a cart. I've dedicated another poem to Rufus, who smells like hell. I put about, in sonnet form, the story that a rutting goat is lodged under his armpit, frightening away the women. Of Furius, so mean he can't bear to excrete, I wrote that his infrequent stools are dry as beans and smell of rose petals.

Other writers are my best game. I insult the very tissue of their work. *Cacata carta*, I say of the wretched paper smeared with the *Annals* of Volusius, *beshitten paper*; cursed even are the flames to which the tedious words are inevitably consigned.

And when I cannot insult someone I know, I'm ready with some anonymous witticisms, dirty as you like. The prick, as I write it, is a sausage that makes its own gravy.

Our father sends pleading letters from Verona, for my health continues to deteriorate. Sometimes I make the journey home, but Rome is the place to be if your heart's being slowly dismembered in front of you. Not achingly lovely Sirmione or the gentle fields by the lake.

Rome gives me plenty of material for metaphor. The mutilations Clodia performs on my feelings are enacted every day in the public places of Rome with less subtle instruments of torture; scourges, barrels of boiling pitch, the rack, whips with spurs, flaming torches held directly against the skin. Every day I pass men stretched out or doubled up on the little horse of the lyre rack. I pass an open door and see a slave being flogged in an atrium (they always make such a punishment as public as possible to discourage insubordination). I see the *carnifices* on their way to torture the criminals in the forum. I've seen the impaled corpses up at the Esquiline Gate. Even radish and mullets, supposedly harmless foodstuffs, are used as painful suppositories for the adulterous, administered in public places where the mobs may see the pain and humiliation of their peers for themselves.

My best weapon remains the verses.

'Good morning, wax tablet,' I say, like a gladiator saluting his lion. Indeed I sport on my tablet like a hardened killer, murdering reputations, cutting down rivals, branding them with the vocabulary of the brothel, scribbling ugly marks on their immortality. My words, my hired beast-boys, go out ball-breaking, just like Clodia herself.

'Aha!' I say, 'Take that!' brandishing my stylus, my little arm that will reach into the future.

As will the little wax doll I have commissioned, of course, my darling *devotio*, soft and silky to the finger and tender as the nape-parting of a little girl's hair.

December 62 BC

Brother of mine,

All Rome is up in arms about their antics now! Clodia and Clodius.

You know of the *Bona Dea*, do you not, Lucius? She's a Roman goddess. Her temple rites are held in May at her dwelling on the Aventine. But more important and more luscious, they say, are those secret ones that take place in December, performed by all the high-born women of Rome and the Vestal Virgins.

We men cannot exactly know what happens among them or the style of the ceremonies they perform together. They are rightfully called 'The Mysteries of the Good Goddess'.

It *is* known that at midnight both the Vestals, the more proper matrons and the pregnant women retire. At this point comes an act thought to be obscene in nature, lubricated by a special wine, which, for the sake of the goodness of the Good Goddess is called *lac*, or milk, and is carried to the house in a honey pot.

The women return from their night's exertions radiant and serene, as if after a protracted orgasm.

It's these very rites that Clodia and Clodius have violated.

I bribed a young Vestal to tell me about it. Some of them are surprisingly venal.

This is what I had from her little puckered mouth as we stood in the shadow of the temple.

She started pompously, informing me that this year's ceremonies of the *Bona Dea* took place in the Via Sacra residence of Julius Caesar, he being Supreme Pontiff, in the presence of his wife, Pompeia, and his mother, Aurelia.

'I know, I know!' I said impatiently.

My eyewitness then began to gasp and roll her pretty eyes as a prelude to reliving her important memories.

Annoyed, I stared her down until she calmed. 'Just the facts, if you please,' I told her sternly. 'No hysterics.'

She shrugged and lowered her eyelids. Apparently, the mêlée started just before the ceremony reached its height. (I hoped my Vestal might elaborate on that point, but it seems nothing will make the women break their silence about it.) There was a collective intake of breath – my Virgin demonstrated – as the realisation spread among them all that the unimaginable had happened: Clodia Metelli had smuggled her brother Clodius, dressed as a woman, into the sacred rites.

My witness thought it was Aurelia, mother of Caesar, who first detected the faint scribble of beard on the chin under the turban and veil of a dancing girl. But she'd also heard it said that it was a pungent male smell that suddenly maddened the brains of the women near Clodius. She herself had scented it.

'Oof, disgusting!' she shuddered, yet I'll lay money on it Clodius was not the first man she'd sniffed in her life.

I told the Vestal that it would be just like Clodius to be contemptuous of detail: not to bother with hiding his own rank odour with feminine lotions. Or perhaps he suffered a moment of normal human fear – in the presence or eminence of the Good Goddess he might have begun, unusually, to sweat.

She nodded sagely and then spat on the ground.

To myself I kept the thought that Clodius had longed above all to see his sister in her moments of greatest excitement, and that in his jewels, his cosmetics, his slender body exquisitely conscious of the strange garments he wore, he must have felt a rare excitement. I pictured him, his dark curls dripping sweat, his features, so like his sister's, rendered identical with paint.

Gossip whispered that Clodius had swallowed the *alectoria*, a crystalline stone the size of a bean that is to be found in the gizzard of certain magical cock-hens. This stone is said to give its ingestor not just the usual endowments of strength and potency, but also invisibility. It's hard to say if Clodius, never the most spiritual of men, could believe in such a thing, but in all events, if he used the *alectoria*, it did not preserve him from the enraged eyes of the female celebrants of the *Bona Dea*.

The women went mad, with their special kind of violence. I pressed my witness to describe what she meant by this, and with an extra coin in her hand she found the words to paint the picture.

Like adolescent girls caught naked, the women felt the shame and helpless rage of violation. The screaming was of a thousand of sibyls. Some women beat him with their hands. Others tried to cover the implements of their sacred rites from his eyes. A handful reached out to gouge those eyes. They shredded his robes with their bare nails and tore the turban from his head.

To make matters worse, Clodius was discovered to be wearing a girdle of myrtle, a final insult to the Goddess; the plant was forbidden in her temple for she herself was said to have been cruelly beaten with rods of it by her father, Faunus.

Clodius carried a lute, with which he tried to shield his private parts from the tearing fingers of the women. Only that, it was said later, saved his manhood.

'What about Clodia?' I asked. 'Didn't they go for her too?'

But apparently no one touched Clodia. They merely averted their eyes from her. She was beneath their anger or contempt. Pompeia, Caesar's wife, wisely fainted. Rumours whispered that Clodius had tried to seduce her, and may have succeeded. In this desecration of the Good Goddess in her own home, he'd certainly violated her in a public way.

'So how did it end?' I asked. 'How did Clodius survive?'

Eventually Caesar's guards came to save him, bleeding, semi-conscious, but still grinning at his success.

'Too bad we didn't kill him,' said my witness, viciously, before she slipped back into the shadows of the temple.

Lucius, you cannot imagine how bad this is.

Rome is convulsed, shamed in her own eyes. After all, the people are saying, these monsters are bred from the noblest blood of her people. What's worse: they have got away with it. Clodius has bribed his way out of his punishment. No one can prove Clodia's complicity, or dares to try.

When the Vestal had gone, I stood in the garden of the temple, turning bitter thoughts around in my head, then retired to a tavern where I seethed like a cutlet in cheap red wine for hours. I, too, felt a biting wrath against Clodia and her brother. Goading my personal fury was a perverse jealousy that Clodia had excluded *me* from her plans. Our intimacy is strictly rationed. She would not even take me into her confidence about her outrageous, tacky little plot. We might have giggled over it in bed, extracted all its pleasures and then I might have persuaded her against enacting it, perhaps. But no, I remain peripheral to her high and low moments, called in and out of the arena of her life like an attendant at the lion-pit.

I prayed that now, alone, disgraced, hated, she would come to me for comfort.

She did not. The next time I saw her she sneered the compassionate expression off my face. 'Don't think you can save me, you patronising little boy,' she said. But she was stepping out of her robe as she said it and then she lay down in front of me, grinning and breathing faster, as if the memory of her crime aroused her.

My feelings and my temper were worn to a blade. I pulled her hair back from her face, to whisper harshly, 'I love you' into her ear. But she hates me touching her there and slapped my nose stingingly.

It's nearly finished now, my little *devotio*. On my next visit, the craftsman promises it will be ready to take away. He just needs a few more of her hairs to finish it off. I undertook to bring them soon, stroking the little white doll with my fingers. Although she's tiny – just the size of my hand – and simply done in white wax, the figure has caught the spirit and style of the woman exactly. It's so very like her that I became suspicious.

I asked the craftsman, 'Have you done her before?'

He smiled discreetly.

Chapter One

And shall he now,
proud and profuse,
perambulate all men's marriage beds,
like the white dove of Venus, or Adonis?

For her precious little son, beautiful as God on a cloud, Felice Feliciano's mother chose the name that means 'most fortunate'. It sounded just like 'Fenice', or 'Phoenix'.

The first morning Felice was able to crawl, he slithered straight to the cupboard where the silver platters were kept. He reached inside with his small plump arms, selected an elegant little platter with a scalloped pattern on its rim. He squatted over it for a moment, delivering a small, neat stool. When his mother walked into the room, he lifted the platter and presented it to her, smiling as graciously as a courtesan might offer convent-made sweetmeats to a noble client. Perhaps, in his kindness, for he was an observant child, he had also detected and wished to reward the very natural delight of his mother in her son's every bowel movement. But there was no doubt it was the presentation of his own first work, in style, which had chiefly inspired little Felice.

He was an adorable child; *a cherub, a little angel,* cooed the women of the family. He was presented to widows and rich town-ladies of Verona like a truffle. By the age of six he was speaking like a miniature Petrarch. He knew how to please, and loved to do so. Plumes of compliments – of a sumptuous texture and colour not found even in the love-songs of the age –

unrolled from his pretty lips; he lisped 'The noble lady's eyelashes are like the legs of a slender grasshopper or autumn wheat waving in the zephyr.'

At first, everyone thought he would be a writer. But the gift of invention was not in Felice; merely that of decoration. Words were of importance to him only in the moment of their immaculate execution at his lips, or, more importantly, his quill. A story, for him, was better deconstructed down to the last descender of its most perfect alphabetical letter. The little boy who could have been anything decided to become a scribe. He affected the costume of the ancient guilds, carrying his work materials in a case appended to his girdle.

In the world of manuscripts, Felice's opinion soon came to matter. It was known that he endorsed, for example, the long-tailed Q, the curling R, the double serifed M. These things immediately became not just the fashion but the rule.

People quoted his aphorisms about letters: 'A good script is a god that dispenses happiness. An ugly one is not merely incompetent but an act of hostility against beauty, like a pustule on the complexion, like a lovely poem spoken in a brutish accent.'

What a charmer he was! When he held a quill in his hand it was a magician's wand. Only errors of taste offended him. In the spirit of friendship he had appointed himself the muse of the painter Andrea Mantegna, to whom he dedicated a collection of Roman epitaphs, and of Andrea's brother-in-law Giovanni Bellini, whom he counselled in the draperies of angels.

Felice's reputation as a lover went before him. His kisses were said to have the finesse of a heron in flight. His very musk was known to be perfumed as if with sandalwood. However, his heart never seemed to be engaged.

He would look at women long and critically. He was aware of the daily fluctuations in their skin and eyes. He would greet them with a question, 'How lovely are you today?' Their fingers would fly to the blemish he had detected.

Surprisingly, the quality of his female provision was not always of the best. 'Perfect beauty,' he claimed, 'like pure water, is tasteless.' And so women of unusual lineaments or dimensions were explored for their very particular pleasures.

People were sometimes suspicious of him, as they might be suspicious of a man who did not love wine or shellfish or music. He was like a beautifully set table: china translucently expensive, golden candlesticks, flowers, but nothing on the plates that could nourish a red-blooded, tender-hearted person.

However, in the end his charm got them, anyway, the suspicious ones falling hardest of all.

Felice was utterly clean of the dust that clings to some antiquaries, but he was not untainted in other respects. It was faintly whispered by some and obscenely roared by others, in the taverns, that the fragrant Felice loved a boy. In 1467, lascivious, unnatural poems were found, apparently in his unsurpassable script. The provenance of the poems was thought sufficiently credible to have him banned from the town for a period.

And so Felice drifted from Verona to Venice, to embrace the printers, rather than to make enemies of them, as did most scribes, short-sighted as they were, in his opinion. He did not think the printers would rob him of work – they would give it to him. And of course Venice might have been created specifically to serve the pleasures of Felice Feliciano. It was just the place for him, an effeminate town whose fused and febrile spirit could not separate her industry from her arts.

He spent everything he earned in the town, on pottery, silk, jewelled swords. Better than the view from the Campanile for him was the sight of the glass blowers of Murano. Felice stood by with his slate while the men emptied their lungs down a tube into a nugget of molten red glass. Later, he would practise alphabets whose rounds were shaped like the glass blowers' fragile shells of colour packed with air.

When Felice came to Venice he stayed at the Sturion at Rialto. It offered every comfort: clean beds, good food, and a vantage point over the liveliest part of town. The famously lovely Caterina di Colonna, who ran the Sturion, was the real reason for its success. She dressed with care merely to supervise the emptying of the slop bowls. All who caught sight of the red-gold halo of her hair would pause and wait for her to come nearer: it was always worth waiting to see what ingenious confection of silk or gold wire or flowers – never too ostentatious but always a gift to the eyes – she had twisted into her curls, to which clung, at all times of the year, the delicate scent of wisteria.

She ministered to her guests like an apothecary, distributing rooms with canal breath or morning reflections as if administering just the right potion for whatever ailed them. What mostly ailed them was a fierce desire for her own person. Felice knew that when married couples came to the inn the fine dust of the house was disturbed every afternoon by a rhythmic thumping during which the husbands pretended that they were showing Caterina di Colonna the skill born of their ardour for her, and the wives pretended to be the landlady herself. With their eyes shut each spouse achieved loud and wonderful climaxes and fell asleep immediately without opening an eyelid, in order to preserve the perfection of the fantasy.

In the presence of such beauty as Caterina's – indeed, Felice always declared, as a natural response to it – happiness kept breaking out everywhere in Venice, in the form of impromptu festas and routs. Felice loved the parties and often ornamented them with his presence, always making certain to leave so that his absence was noted.

It was at such a party he had met the Jewess Sosia Simeon, whose intriguing features somehow soaked through her mask so he could read her vivid face in a far corner of the room.

It had not been difficult to extract her from the fat nobleman she accompanied. She had walked with him in a pleasing silence to his inn where she had performed, also in silence, and without instruction, a number of acts he had previously commissioned only from boys.

She had looked startled when he asked her to leave.

'You don't want me to sleep the night with you?' she asked. 'For later?'

'No, thank you, my angel,' he replied pleasantly, handing her the chemise she'd discarded two hours before. 'Let's not spoil it, shall we?'

He had lifted a book from the small stack near his bed and commenced to read before she even left the room. In his hand he held the stone letter T he had chipped from an ancient grave near Verona. As he read, he fondled it continually, pushing his fingers into each angle and niche.

Sosia stood silently for a moment with her hand on the door handle. She had not come across such a man before. She was surprised to feel not merely insulted but also a tearful prickling at her eyes and a sad constriction at her breast. She scribbled her name, which he had not once asked, and directions to her house on a piece of parchment she found on a table near the door. He did not look up, kept caressing his stone letter with an expression of satisfaction she had not seen on his face even at the most hectic moments of their intimacy.

It was suddenly clear and devastating to Sosia Simeon that the fascinating Felice Feliciano loved the crevices of the alphabet the way other men loved the crevices of women.

Chapter Two

I snatched, while you played, sweet-as-honey,
a kiss sweeter than sweet ambrosia;
But I paid the thief's price for it;
For I remember that I hung an hour on the cross
stammering, snivelling my apologies . . .
If this is the way you punish a kiss,
I shall never steal one again.

*A*fter you fall in love, Bruno had noticed, you must adjust your sight to all the old things. You may think you have absorbed the love entirely, swallowed it up inside you as the sky inhales the dew, but then you visit again a familiar place where you have not set foot since your heart made that fatal somersault. *Eccoqua* – the old place must be re-addressed. You must sit there quietly and allow your soul to transact a negotiation to admit you as the new creature you are – in love or beloved – or, if you are very fortunate, both.

Bruno smiled bitterly, thinking, *It's possible that the place may not believe you. It may slyly undermine you, start to persuade you, with its own implacable permanence, that nothing's changed at all, that the love you thought in your grasp is mere delusion. In the face of this proof, so tangible and familiar, the love becomes ghostly, scarcely credible even to you.*

That morning he had faced Sosia inside the courtyard of the Ca d'Oro, where he had brought some folios for the nobleman who owned it. In the absence of Wendelin, the editors had taken it on themselves to keep the reputation of the *stamperia* alive with constant diplomatic missions to Golden Book houses where they presented samples of their work and flattered the noble clients as much as they dared. He had surprised Sosia, who was leaving the *palazzo* as he entered it. Now the wind was blowing her lies through the columns out to the water, stippled like beaten pewter in the fitful autumn breeze.

She was agitated. She didn't want to be there. Bruno wanted to detain her but he could not, any more than he could hold in his fingers the glassy morning light slowly crystallising around them.

Within seconds, their conversation had taken its usual dismal turn.

'So, do you sleep with him? Why can't you just tell me?'

'Of course I sleep with him. We have just one bedchamber.'

'No, I mean, as you know, do you share your body with him, as you share it with me?'

'Rabino's rarely at home. If he comes to my bed, I try to lie above the coverlet, so he doesn't touch me even by accident.'

This, too, was an elaborate lie, thought Bruno, but he pursued it anyway.

'So he does not want you?'

Silence.

'Would he suffer to know how I touch you?'

'He sees me as his wife.'

'Are you not his wife?'

'We live separate lives.'

'But you stay together, so he must love you still.'

Sosia chose to take the practical interpretation of this question.

'He's too tired. He looks at me without seeing. I see through him without looking at him. He falls asleep before I finish a simple question about the herbs we need for the apothecary. I think sometimes that he sleeps cunningly so he does not have to face me. It's what I do with him.'

'In the bed you nevertheless share. Sometimes.'

Silence.

'In which you do other things than sleep, sometimes.'

A more dangerous silence.

He could not guess that Sosia deliberately portrayed a greater intimacy with Rabino than was true, for otherwise Bruno might importune her more daringly, more tediously. The truth was that her marriage to Rabino did not disgust Sosia. She could easily live with its small privations; she had contrived it so that it cost her no pleasure. When Felice Feliciano had sent a messenger to the house not a week after their first encounter, Rabino had wearily transmitted the subtle message, pretending not to know what it meant, and when he saw how she bathed and dressed to attend the appointment he had simply cast his eyes down to the floor and turned back to his herbs.

Later, in his apartments, where he had lured her with promises of silent gratification, Bruno asked Sosia about her mother. She spat and turned away.

'Here in Italy, motherhood is sacred. Is it not so in Dalmatia?'

'My mother was a mother.' Sosia dragged out the words with contempt. 'I saw only the degradation. I also saw that she was nothing in that she had us, little rats, sucking and pulling at her all the time. She was nothing more than a feeding bladder, a kind of meal for us to consume. We devoured her. She loved us so she did not even put up a fight.'

'Did you not love her?'

'She became a stranger to me in the war. I did not love her any more. I remember better loving a pomegranate a sailor gave me.'

'What sailor?'

'A sailor.'

Sosia was already walking away.

'Could you not stay till morning one time?' he begged, abandoning his dignity at the last minute.

'You would only fall asleep on me.'

'I would never, never . . . You're not talking about me. You're talking about some hideous creature, some composite man you've invented so you can hate all men.'

'You think I don't know men, Bruno?'

He walked moodily to the cage where his two sparrows sat. Their eggs had not hatched. The stain of rotten meat had watermarked the pretty shells and he'd put them away in a drawer. Perhaps this was his fault. When Sosia stayed away from him, he fed and overfed them until they were unwell with it, their little paunches stiff with seed.

Just once they spent the night together.

Bruno extorted it from her.

He spent the day in preparations, buying precious fruits and dried meats from Rialto, scouring the dust from his room, then stacking his books and papers at rakish angles to mitigate the too-careful effect. Although winter had not yet begun to bite he laid a welcoming fire.

She would not eat the food he had bought at such perilous prices, finding an old milk loaf in the cupboard and scooping out its heart while she strode around the room like a captive lioness, flinging open the windows so all the neighbours might witness her presence.

'I'm choking,' she said. 'It's too hot.'

He'd thought all he had to fear were the embarrassments of chamber pot and water pitcher, morning breath and his own all-too-visible lack of a change of clothes. But despair came from an unexpected quarter. She would not make love to him.

'I don't feel good. I feel you forced me to come here. I don't understand what game you're playing, Bruno, what you're trying to prove.'

Then she kissed him erotically, licking his lips, but when he moved towards her with paddling hands, she snapped: 'Be more sensitive!'

He said: 'But when you kiss me like that my body, this poor primitive con-. struction, thinks this,' he touched her thigh. 'That's what it's used to.'

'You've upset me so much with all your demands that I can't think of you like that now.'

Is it like this with Rabino? he longed and dreaded to ask.

He mourned silently. *She'd rather spend her energy not giving me what I want, than the little it would cost to grant me a speck of happiness. Why is that? It's not even efficient. Because with a few loving words she can release behaviour in me which makes her happy, which gives her pleasure? Perhaps at heart she's stupid, after all?*

'Don't poke me like that,' Sosia said, as they lay on the pallet.

He lay beside her, in the permitted position, every part of him just one inch from her, not touching.

Now she was smiling at him, wanted to examine him in the candlelight.

'I have to leave very early in the morning,' she announced, watching his face. 'There will not be time to make love.'

'You mean when the *mattutino* strikes?' The pre-dawn bell marked his normal hour for waking, for his first thoughts about her each day.

'No, later, the *maragona*.'

These two bells, one an hour before dawn and the other as the sun rose, punctuated all sleepy early-morning fondlings in Venice.

An hour later, thought Bruno. *But we might rouse ourselves at the* mattutino *to make love or even talk for an hour. Even more, for in Wendelin's absence there's no reason to arrive early at the* stamperia. *We merely wait for his return, if truth were known, and act as if we do not fear for our futures at all . . . But no. She does not wish it, I see. She's determined that I never demand this of her another time. Indeed, I've learned my lesson. I would not ask for a night like this again.*

'I can sleep now,' she told him. She kissed him, as she'd never done before, chastely on the cheek. He choked on tears, the imprint of the kiss stinging at the side of his face. She was leaving him, going into unconsciousness, just like leaving him to go back to Rabino. If anything, it was more insulting, more diminishing. It showed how she was able to forget him when he was still at her side, breathing and hurting. She slept heavily, snoring and grunting. Twice, as he stood by the window, looking at the moonlight on the canal, she muttered angry words in her own language. He watched the phosphorescence on the water until his legs numbed.

In the morning, as he lay hunched and sleepless beside her, she woke and nuzzled his neck. He asked fearfully, hopefully, 'Do you want to make love then, Sosia?'

She said, 'No. I felt a bit of a stirring this morning, but on the whole no.'

'So you love me again?'

Silence.

'So what is different?'

'Ten hours, I suppose.'

He recoiled.

Seeing that, she said: 'But I have to go now.'

Throughout the day he would feel a dyspeptic fizzle to every swallow, a kick nursing in his gut, the bile curdling in his stomach.

Kind, decent Wendelin von Speyer would ask him, if he knew, 'Is this the kind of woman you honour with your love?'

His friend Felice would say, 'Come with me to Catalani's. Forget her. What's so special about her? There are women who will give you pleasure in the having, who will enjoy you.'

He didn't want them. He looked at the bed.

The sheets, full of unspent passion, hung haggardly over the side of the pallet.

For some reason, the sight of them reminded him of his sister Gentilia.

Chapter Three

*May you be sacred
by whatever name you please.*

When the doctor Rabino Simeon was summoned to the island of Sant' Angelo, it was usually to deal with a clumsily aborted pregnancy or a clandestine delivery gone hideously wrong. The baby was often dead by the time he arrived, in those cases, and the young mother already sedated by the puissant liquors the nuns brewed for themselves. If the girl was a noble-woman, the nuns would call Rabino to see to her, rather than a gossiping Venetian physician. The middle-class girls were left to fend for themselves, he surmised, as the accents of his patients were always patrician.

He dreaded the calls that took him to the island. One such came to him a mild late autumn night, the boatman of Sant' Angelo rattling at the door in San Trovaso in the early hours. Stumbling from the *divano*, Rabino sighed as he recognised the man's outline downstairs in the moonlight. He shrugged on his robe and gathered certain instruments together. He was out of the house in a few minutes, pausing for a second on the first floor landing to see if Sosia was asleep in the matrimonial bed. She had not been at home when he went to sleep but she was there now, one eye glinting, the other buried in the hair on her pillow.

'Off to do some good, Mister Doctor?' she whispered. He nodded miserably and turned to run down the stairs.

The boatman saluted him cheerfully and guided him down to the comfortable seat inside the gondola. Rabino hunched over his bag, trying not to think of what awaited him at Sant' Angelo.

A nun with a lantern met him at the jetty and hurried him through the cloisters, even at this hour noisy with the whispering of prayers. Rabino, unlike most visitors, knew that the monotonous chanting came not from devout nuns but from caged parrots kept in every corner. The birds had been trained to pray continually; their chorus drowned the noise of other, less pious activities, taking place at all hours behind the wall of the cloister.

'It's too late for the child,' the nun hissed, raising her voice over the mumble of the birds, 'but we cannot lose the mother. She's Golden Book.'

In the cell, Rabino knelt by the luxuriously appointed bed to inspect his patients. Marks on the baby's neck and the whimpering of the young noblewoman betrayed the heinous scene that had preceded his arrival. The girl was drugged and did not know what had happened to her. She was not even aware of his gentle hands on her.

As he lifted her arms, heavy with bracelets, she called out a man's name.

'The father?' he asked the nun.

'Could be. Could be someone else, too. Likes the men, does this one.'

Rabino was saddened but not surprised. He knew, to his cost, how the noble nuns of Sant' Angelo 'escaped' without difficulty, and went abroad about the town with more liberty than their married sisters. They enjoyed debauched picnics on neighbouring islands. He'd overheard his rich patients gossiping: tales of satin sheets spread on crisp grass; pressed mullet eggs, salted and smoked, laid out on the bellies of naked nuns for their companions to lick up. It was all one, it seemed, to the Venetian noblemen to secure some courtesans or some nuns for an afternoon's open-air eroticism. Indeed, for some men the nuns were a more piquant choice. After all, Rabino reflected bitterly, the corrupt nuns of Sant' Angelo did for pleasure what courtesans merely did for money.

'How old is she?' he asked, looking down on the pale childlike face. The older nun looked mutinous, so he added, 'I need to know so I can measure the drugs for an infusion. She seems small, but I want to give her a full dose.'

'Fifteen.'

Fifteen and already more than one lover! A bastard child fathered in lust and then destroyed! *Is there nowhere in Venice,* Rabino thought wearily, *a woman who knew how to love decently? Who valued the gift of love more highly than her jewels and her own pleasures?*

He called for warm water and fresh linen, opening his bag to find a pouch of herbs.

At first he barely noticed the little nun who carried in the steaming pitcher, but she did not leave the room, as they usually did, and the heaviness of her breathing drew his attention to her face.

For a nun of Sant' Angelo it was most unusually ugly. She was staring at him fixedly.

'Is she your friend?' he asked, pointing to the young noblewoman now muttering to herself in her sleep.

The ugly little nun shook her head vehemently. Rabino observed from her features that she was of humble stock. It was unlikely that the aristocratic young sinner would have condescended to befriend such a girl.

'Do you serve her, then? She will survive you know, but I'm afraid that her little baby has perished.'

The nun shook her head again, and put her thumb in her mouth. Rabino thought, *Ah, she's simple, then. That's why they entrust her with these sordid tasks, poor creature.*

But at that moment the lantern-bearing nun returned, and swore loudly to see the ugly girl in the room.

'You've been told not to come here, Gentilia. This part of the convent is for the Golden Book families. Are you satisfied now? Have you seen all the horrors you wanted to see?'

The nun turned to Rabino, 'She's a real ghoul, that one.'

She gave Gentilia a push towards the door. 'Go on out of here. What is it?'

The girl dipped her head and mumbled a few words.

'Yes!' exclaimed the older nun, impatiently, 'yes, he's a Jew. That's what a Jew looks like. You've seen one now. So go.'

The girl shuffled away, her head down.

Rabino packed up his instruments. As usual he refused the coin brusquely proffered to him. He could not accept money for this dirty business.

As he walked through the cloister back to the boat, he felt eyes on his shoulders. Looking behind him he saw the nose and fat-sheened forehead of the ugly nun, pressed against the bars of a tall gate.

He thought to himself, *And she probably thinks me the most ghastly thing she saw tonight.*

Chapter Four

Suns can be extinguished and rekindle:
but for us, when once our little light is extinguished,
there is just sleep for one unending night.
Give me a thousand kisses, and then a hundred,
then another thousand, and then a second hundred . . .

An unremitting torrent of rain, the first of the autumn, slapped against the windows as Domenico Zorzi presented his private manuscript of Catullus to a select gathering of scholarly nobles. The book, cased in jewelled leather, sparkled with Felice Feliciano's illuminations in gold and vermilion. The codex was laid open on a velvet cushion, candles flickering at either side. A Bellini Madonna gazed serenely down on it. Domenico raised his voice above the thrum of water against his tall window.

'It's an old and a new story, my friends, a story that never stops unravelling, like the rain.

'A young man loved a cruel woman, and died of it. No commoner, the flower of his noble family, who died without a son to carry his name into the future. The dedication of his book shows that he fixed all his hopes on the immortality of his poetry. Life and love had failed him: literature would not. In this he trusted.

'Alas for Gaius Valerius Catullus. It was not to be. Short years after his death, his poems fell silent, fled from the tongue of memory. The most notorious poems of ancient times seemed to have gone to the tomb with him after all. The poems and the poet were extinguished for a thousand years, a thousand years in which the art of writing itself fell away.

'Nevertheless, some things do not die of scorn. The poem-book of Catullus in fact continued to germinate quietly in the dark, like a mushroom. There were whispers of Catullus and his songs through the succeeding centuries . . . the especially learned among you will have noted a word in Boethius in the sixth, a couplet or two clearly Catullan but not attributed in Isidore of Seville and Julian of Toledo in the seventh. I personally deduce, from his writings, that Bishop Rather of Verona read the entire work in the tenth century, but this cannot be proved. Then silence.

'Catullus still had a little longer to wait; another four hundred years. Until almost now, my friends.

'A merchant found the first Catullus manuscript of modern times in or around 1300. The man, unusually well educated for his class, pulled the sheaf of paper out from under a corn measure in a storeroom in Verona. He had no idea of the age or value of his find and sold it on cheaply to a paper dealer who also traded in manuscripts. The dealer paid by the weight, no doubt, and probably did not spend too much time pondering over it. If he had bothered to count them, he would have found that his bundle contained one hundred and thirteen poems.

'The paper dealer would have faced a choice: should he rub out the old words and sell the fine old paper again as palimpsest? Or should he take the manuscript to a scholar and see if it would fetch a higher price with the words left on? The chances of Catullus surviving were just so slender in that crucial moment.

'Fortunately, it was exactly the right moment for Catullus. The world was just then starting to lift its head and look to the light again. For those who wanted to read, the last ten centuries could offer little inspiration. The glorious classical past, in contrast, was now gleaming in the scholars' imagination like a diamond in the rock.

'And so the Catullus manuscript found its way into the hands of a scholar who gave it to a scribe to copy, lest something should befall the original. And another scribe. And another; until the first manuscript blossomed into a hundred versions of itself. Petrarch himself was said to have owned a copy. My own is my greatest treasure. Freshly illuminated by Felice Feliciano, I've brought it here to share with you tonight, for this very week I plan to send it to Gerolamo Squarzafico, the editor who works for Wendelin von Speyer, the printer from Germany who has brought his great machinery here and begun to print, by grace of our kind patronage and inspiration.

'Yes, it's true that the monopoly we granted him has lapsed with the death of his brother, and that von Speyer has accompanied his brother's body back to Germany. But his *stamperia* still thrives, or at least survives; the men await his return, which is, I understand, imminent. There's word from Padova that he will be back in the city in two days, storms permitting. I have heard that the weather is already beautiful again at Lake Garda.

'It is my intention that then this very manuscript of Catullus poems will make its way into the hands of the person whom I hope to persuade to give them their new life in modern times.

'One hundred and thirteen poems by an unknown Latin poet. Wendelin von Speyer will take his future in his hands if he accepts the manuscript I shall offer him.

'Catullus will open hearts, deftly as a blade, and they will not be closed again after reading him. Wendelin von Speyer shall need the encouragement of all of us and much help in subtle ways. It will not be an easy decision for him. There are things about these poems . . . Well, I leave it to you to judge, my lords. If Wendelin von Speyer decides to print Catullus, his reward will not necessarily be gratitude from all quarters.

'We must help him deliver the book into print: to give this single precious manuscript of mine three hundred lustrous heirs.

'And if he proves a little unwilling, a little fearful, then we must see to it that it is less frightening to print Catullus than to leave him unprinted. Let him know that responsibility falls like the rain – most times you may take shelter if you choose, but one day you will be caught in it, with nowhere to hide.'

Chapter Five

It's hard to slough off a love that has grown years on you;
It's hard, but you can find a way.
Only you can do it. Only you shall do it.
Whether it is possible or not.

The clouds had parted in front of them all their way back to Venice. By the time Lussièta and Wendelin set foot in Mestre the warm rain had evaporated, leaving the streets shining with puddles dizzy as shaken mirrors. The next day the air in the *stamperia* still hung heavy, saturated with damp. Wendelin wiped the moisture from his forehead and plunged in among his men.

He spoke kindly to them, each in turn, encouraging them with scrupulously appropriate praise. He gave attention to whatever minute operation this man or the other concerned himself with. Gradually the heads bent over the presses and matrixes again, and their fear, like a sharp fume, dispersed, as if through the open windows. After an hour the *stamperia* had settled to its ordinary noises, the thud of paper, the raze of the copper plates, the clicking of letters into forms. The hum of voices rose again.

Wendelin retired to his corner where he sagged into his chair, discreetly rubbing his taut shoulders against its oak back.

Nowhere was Johann's absence more painful than here at the *stamperia*. Wendelin listened to his workmen, and missed the voice of his brother, the family voice, that timbre so like his own, but quicker to rise in irritation or inspiration, and quicker to cool as well. He felt unruly tears nudging the corners of his eyes, panic gnawing his stomach. He'd lost more than his brother, more than his business partner and collaborator. In his brother's voice, he realised now, he had preserved his last memories of their home. He thought, *outside the fondaco, I shall never speak German again. I shall lose my language and become a nothing-creature, neither German nor Venetian.*

Twice, he half-rose from his chair to say, 'I am sorry; I cannot go on without my brother. You are welcome to everything I have – it's but poor recompense for the devotion you have given us.'

Each time he sank down again. He could not do this. The best way to honour his brother, he knew, would be to make sure that Johann von Speyer would be remembered for all time as the man who brought the first printed book to Venice.

And so Wendelin von Speyer resolved to continue, hoping that the *Collegio's* five-year monopoly had given him a head start. Since returning to Venice he'd discovered ten new printing works in varying degrees of readiness.

From that first faltering day, he laboured doggedly, finishing the St Augustine *De civitate Dei*, which Johann had left uncompleted at his death. Wendelin worked without a pause. He kept his men so busy that they had no time to worry about their livelihoods. While the press ran he went out on the streets, sniffing the air, trying to second-guess the currents flowing through the market place. His earnest, wide-eyed face was becoming well known in the area. Everywhere he went, he pressed book-bearing strangers by the hand, looking into their faces, asking them about what they were reading, begging, with the greatest civility, to be informed what they would like to read next. He waylaid respected scribes, questioning them about newly discovered manuscripts. Should he print them? Should he be looking at them? With his head on one side, he asked, 'It is the coming thing, yes? It is what is wanted, yes?'

Then he would shuffle-run back to the *Fondaco dei Tedeschi*, full of plans, muttering to himself, planning where the money would come from to subsidise this next new project.

Only at the end of 1470 would Wendelin pause to count, and be amazed to realise that in eighteen months he had published thirteen books, in editions of three hundred or more. He knew he should examine the ledgers, to see how many of them he'd sold. But the piles of printed sheets around the *stamperia* and the pinched faces of the booksellers told him more than he wished to know.

It sounds hard, but what woman does not long some time to have the man she loves cast down some, so that he may need her, desperately? Be lost without her? Look to her for all things, not just food and sons and acts of love?

When Jo died, my man was sick at heart. It was I who went to the works to tell the men of the journey to Speyer in our own words. It was I who told them to wait for us, to keep their faith in the work. I promised them that I would bring him back. I rushed; I did not leave him more than an hour alone all those dark days.

And so I also left alone Jo's wife Paola. She did not cleave to us in her loss. She discharged the requisite spoonful of tears when we came to her with our plan. After that I did not see her at all, except in glimpses. I saw the darkness under her eyes like ruts in the road as she turned away, pretending not to see me. But I heard things: that after Johann died she still had the maid set the table with his place, and cook the foods he liked best. But it was also said of her that she would do that until a new man came to take his place. Perhaps I fancied these things because I could not bear to think on my good luck compared to hers: I still have my man and she has not, and he and I still make love that scorches the curtains.

Now, moreover, we are sealed together for ever by our long journey which, when I shut my eyes, still comes to my head so I feel dizzy with the roll of horses' hooves and blinded with snow. I've shown my love for him, and my little failure, close to the end, and his ability to forgive it, are just the proof of that. Our love is still great, merely alloyed by the small disappointments which happen in every marriage, and which must be forgiven, out of love, in order to preserve love. Or so I tell myself.

Since we came home, I've found a sack of new ways to bring him comfort. I know I cannot be for him what Jo has been, yet I can be something more.

Each day, I bring new information to help him on his way in our town. Ways he could not find for himself, I mean.

If he has a fault, then it's a tiny one. That carefulness which is the heirloom of his whole race does sometimes cork up his brain. He's not enough imagination to deal with Venice. He's too much in love with logic and so the Venetians elude him, like drops of water falling through his fingers. If he wants to sell a book, he talks of the good words inside and the fine cut of the type; he's puzzled when the Venetians become vague and walk away. To capture a Venetian customer you must tell exotic tales of the hunt for the antelope whose skin is tooled for the cover, and talk not of the book itself but of the dreams that will follow from reading it.

Everything is strange and spectacular to him, but touches him intimately for he lives here, and is no pilgrim or merchant. It's like a play where he may sometimes go up and mingle with the rich-dressed actors on the stage. Sometimes they acknowledge him, sometimes not. That's Venetians for you. I tell him it's not personal.

For I admit we Venetians are not at all times kind with those strangers who come here. Perhaps we fear they take the joy of this town in the greed of their eyes, tear it off piece by piece: if we were to let them do this, Venice would lose her shape and its style, worn down by their desire, and one day we would have but the ghost of a town to live in and the rubble of our memories.

So we have our ways to keep the strangers out, even when they are still here. In the crowded *campi* we slender Venetians walk fast around them and trip up their legs; in the narrow streets we spread our bodies like starfish so they may not pass. With our carts we nip their slow toes. We are quick with the crooks of our arms. We do not smile at them, not once. They must think we have no teeth! Some men of this town will watch with eyes of slate while a foreigner flaps and sweats. He will snarl from the edge of his mouth as fast as he can – the words fall like the pips of a grape, the meaning clear as stones to the poor foreigner, who feels himself a fool. When the Venetian must finally address the poor foreigner in a way he can comprehend, he does so with a sneer, as if to say 'Yes, the whole world, and your shabby race the most, should wait for our town. No one else measures up to her.'

So I warn my man, for example, to keep away from the *traghetto* at Rialto – use any of the other twelve but not that one. The Rialto gondoliers are vicious and will incontinently carry any foreigner straight to a place of worship or a brothel, no matter where he wants to go and whatever the *bagattino* proffered in payment. Though my man can speak some words in our tongue, there's no mistaking him for a Venetian, and I hate to see him embarrassed by these acts.

And I explain to him that if he must do trade with nobles, then he should go to the *Broglio* at the palace of the Doge, beneath its arches. To make an appointment in their office for a set time is not sufficiently serpentine to give pleasure to the lords – they will not be interested in what he offers in a plodding way. No, he must go to the *Broglio* betwixt eleven and twelve of the clock in the morning or five and six of the clock in the evening ... and his conversation must not start or end with the business in hand, but only approach it by long and pleasant paths.

It is I who suggests he takes samples of his work to sit in the public rooms of the Locanda Sturion. There they bask in the beauty of my friend Caterina, and the people who finger them under her lovely gaze will be moved to come and buy copies for themselves. I hope. I know she will help us if she can. She's my greatest friend, although we are so different. Caterina is so serene, so quiet! Compared to her I've a mouth like a beggar's clack-dish.

Fortunately I have not an indigestion of aunts and cousins, like most Venetian families. I make sure the few I have do not trouble him. Very secretly I tell him which of my cousins are good for him to take into his employ and which of them will steal the ink and fornicate with the cook maids at the *fondaco*.

I fear so much he will end like Johann. He comes home ill some nights, hunched over as if he still carries Jo's coffin on his back. He's still not used to such savage and unreasonable heat and cold as this town turns on us as the year rolls around.

Now that I've been north I see how it was for him – *each day* a six-course *meal* of hot and cold. In the North one moment the sun gilds the hairs on your cheek and next comes a cold wind to slap it and sweep you off your toes, then a splat of a quick rain and some time of grey light and then a burst of blue . . .

'I am parched for weather,' he says, as if what we have is not that. I try to see his point but it's hard for me. I think we just have better weather than in the North, and there stirs in me the old fear: Is he homesick for Speyer, does he want to go back there? What did he promise his parents when he was alone with them? We've never talked of it once in all these months since we came home.

The little lines cluster around his eyes like pink pleated silk from crinkling his eyes up against the hot white light. There's no hue to his skin. He burns to red at the lightest touch of the sun and then it makes me laugh to loose his shirt and see the cream-white chest thatched with blond hairs beneath his red face, as if that face were that of some other man entirely. I love both of them, in any case!

But when I see his white chest, it reminds me of the waxen doll from Sirmione, who now lives here in this house. She hung on my sleeve all the way to the next inn, and there I detached her and hid her in my trunk. When we returned to Venice I put her away in the depths of my mending basket, beneath all those shredded hose I shall never make good again but cannot bear to throw away. I've tried to forget about her.

Chapter Six

I have come away incandescent
with your elegance.

Still intoxicated with his own eloquence, Domenico awoke with the dregs of his speech on his lips and an almost post-coital sense of well-being. His first feeling was of exquisite private pleasure, to have the Catullus manuscript to himself again after a long evening during which the noblemen had too eagerly and roughly handled it. The rapture had in every other way been highly satisfactory. He examined the pages scrupulously for damage, was relieved to find it slight, and laid the manuscript reverently on his desk, flicking away an invisible particle of dust.

The words are so light that they float above your eyelids. You might grow blind waiting for them to become solid. So Domenico thought, standing motionless in a finger of the sharp sunshine that had followed the downpour. Tall and slender, his silhouette seemed like a deep crack in the light.

The poems of Catullus had attached themselves to Domenico like adopted children who turn out to be your own bastards. *These poems are already inside me;* he had thought when he read them the first time. *How strange,* he mused, *that on the hardest things we use not knives but words. Against the hardest things we launch armies of words marching left to right across the page. When we want to hurt someone to the core we aim not spears at him but needling little words. The softest, sweetest things, too, we use words to obtain them.*

Domenico thought about Catullus, wondered at the fifteen centuries' reach of the Roman poet's words forward into this glorious Venetian future. Could Domenico's own thoughts reach back to Catullus? he wondered. Was the poet, trapped in some similar sunlit moment in the past, sensitive to these feelings that now held Domenico still as silence?

Domenico marvelled at how little he knew of the writer: only one salient and consuming fact – that they inhabited the same wasteland of desire. For Domenico, in the very rhythms of the Latin poet there lurked a seductive spell. The words fell like limbs thrashing in a bed, sometimes violently, sometimes languorously, and the repetition of the most throbbing phrases had a climactic cadence to it. The whole book was heavy with hard caresses given and received. To a connoisseur of words, like Domenico, who swilled them in his mind like a wine-lover his favourite vintage, the Catullus manuscript was a living thing, more alive even than a woman in his arms.

Domenico picked up the manuscript and sniffed it, nosing each poem individually. *And they are full of delectation (for the eyes, the nose and the mouth speaking it)*, he thought, *full of the fragrant resin of the lasarpiciferius and its odoriferous liquor.*

It smells, he thought, *not unlike Sosia Simeon, this manuscript.*

Did Catullus want to die when he thought of Lesbia, the way I want to die when I think of Sosia?

With characteristic restraint, he suppressed these thoughts in a single sigh and leant over his desk to address a letter to Wendelin's scholar, Gerolamo Squarzafico. Such poems must be published. Gerolamo would make Wendelin see sense in the end.

In the meantime, Domenico had the manuscript to himself again for a brief while. He opened the pages again, petal-skinned from so much use. Domenico could not help himself; he started to read again.

'One last time,' he said aloud.

In the following hours, Domenico waved away his wife and his secretary. He ate a loaf of bread, tearing the pieces off with his teeth, while reading the book. He took the book with him to his bedroom and placed it on his bed as he undressed, leaning over and never taking his eyes from the page. He fell asleep with the manuscript cradled in his arms and the candle flame still pointing at the ceiling. His wife, offended, did not join him. It did not matter. It was not her that he wanted. It had not been, for some time. He had loved her once, he dimly remembered. But soon after the birth of their heir her caressing fingers in the dark had begun to feel like the talons of an owl.

Now this book had disturbed him again. When he had closed the binding, he placed his finger in his navel and pushed until the nail drew blood. This made him realise what was bothering him. He wanted Sosia Simeon. He called for a servant and despatched him to the house at San Trovaso.

Three days later, when he judged the manuscript sufficiently rested from its travails, he greeted Gerolamo Squarzafico and placed the bound papers in his hands, with certain instructions.

'Read it first yourself, so you may better plead its case, then take it straight to him,' he begged Squarzafico. Knowing the editor's reputation, he added, 'Not via the tavern, please. And choose your moment. I don't want to frighten him. Give him time to settle himself back in Venice. Try not to patronise him too much: these Germans can be ridiculously oversensitive. But make it clear that he may not forever take for granted the patronage of the nobles if he does not make it his business to indulge our tastes . . .'

Recoiling from the fumes of stale wine on the editor's breath, Wendelin abruptly turned the sheaf over in his hands, so that the edges of the paper fanned wood-scented air into his face. It was Wendelin's predisposition to mistrust but feel a timid, desirous affinity with enthusiasm. Squarzafico had been somewhat over-eager to press this work upon him, and was standing just a little too close to him as he cast his eyes down the first page.

Wendelin sucked in his breath, scanning the pages. So *this* was the famous Catullus, in his own hands at last. A cold light fell on the page, perforated with the delicate shadows of the frost patterns on the windows of the *stamperia*.

Words of love and lust tripped up his eyes. There was something about a sparrow in the very first poem. Was this not an indecent allegory? That 'sparrow' was surely the poet's virile organ. In a blushing conversation, Wendelin had learned from Bruno that this was also so in the modern Italian idiom. He searched back in his well-archived memory for the disturbing association – *Ah, yes*, sparrows were sacred to Aphrodite, Goddess of erotic love, for they drew her chariot across the skies.

He groaned. Even from the first page, he knew, the Catullus manuscript was the kind of thing that could be used against an honest businessman.

'So why this one, Gerolamo? How can we justificate it? It is filthy like a hound!'

Squarzafico lurched closer, gesticulating with hands not quite synchronised in their movements. Wendelin steered him subtly away from the matrixes. In these moments, less lucid than liquid, Squarzafico was likely to break delicate equipment.

'Surely, Wendelin, you know that the market is ripe and clamouring for such things from antiquity. I thought I would write a little biography to re-introduce Catullus to the world. Something to mitigate the more difficult aspects of the poetry, you know, make them think "other times, other morals", look upon it with indulgence.'

Wendelin looked hard at Squarzafico, who was lapping inside his jowls as if trying to extract a last wine-sodden breadcrumb from between his teeth. Wendelin observed the deep groove from each side of the corner of his mouth, and a long simian curve between his nostrils and condescending upper lip. His hair was surprisingly neat, moulded to his head like a helmet.

'But are you sure it is genuine? The ridicule for printing a fake, we cannot afford it. Our dignity is very important . . .'

'I am sure.' As he stopped talking, Squarzafico's mouth commenced to bulge with his tongue's investigations.

'You worry too much, Wendelin. Trust in me. Domenico Zorzi himself has provided me with a complete dossier on these poems.' Gerolamo made a low sucking noise in his throat.

Aha, thought Wendelin, *he's found that nourishing speck.*

'Show me then.' Wendelin handed him a goose-feather.

Squarzafico dipped the pen, stabbing once or twice ineffectually before achieving the narrow mouth of the inkpot. In jagged strokes he sketched a single word.

'"Veronensis,"' he said aloud, dragging out the syllables. 'The very first manuscript, discovered in Verona in 1300.'

Wendelin nodded; that part of the tale was well known to him already. His shelves were stacked with unique manuscripts rescued by similarly slender chances.

He asked: 'But this is not the original, is it? This copy is no older than I am. Look at the vellum, not yet discoloured, and the ink still bold as night on the page.'

Squarzafico said: 'You do not disappoint me in your eye for detail, Wendelin, so meticulous, like all of your honoured colleagues from the North. No, this is not the original. But it is an immaculate copy! At least a hundred such paragons are known to exist.'

'How can we be sure it is one of the true hundred? So it is identical to them?'

'Again, Wendelin, your immaculate instinct for the difficult impresses me. It is unfortunately true that all those manuscripts do not always agree in every detail of the text. But you are doubtless aware of the very good reasons for that. As usual, some of the scribes mistakenly thought that the original manuscript was inaccurate in parts, and so they wrongly corrected it. Sometimes they made unlucky guesses about missing stanzas and words. Other times, they saw things that made no sense, but copied them anyway. But this manuscript is a legitimate offspring of that very first one, a descendant, copied by Felice Feliciano himself, from a manuscript in the library of Pacifico Massimo, who commissioned it himself, and it is now the property of our distinguished friend the nobleman Domenico Zorzi.'

'Pacifico Massimo, the pornographer?'

'Yes, the very one.'

Wendelin sighed. 'And what if *that* should become known? It's hopeless, hopeless. We shall be blamed. They will say we are all merchants of lust and godlessness. They always say that. It will come to trouble with the Council of Ten. Remember, I am a foreigner here. I cannot put my head above the ramparts without someone throwing stones at it.'

'On the contrary, you will be admired for your courage and your taste, to bring such a delicious thing into print.'

Squarzafico raised an imaginary goblet, and drained it, smacking his lips. 'It will be like nectar for the Venetians,' he said. 'Remember, this is Venice, not

Rome. This book will save your business. In fact, not to print it . . .' His voice trailed away and he looked significantly at the floor.

Wendelin flinched to realise that Squarzafico was aware of the dire state of affairs at the *stamperia*.

'I know not, I know not,' keened Wendelin. The editor had a point, he knew. This book could make money, could solve half the problems of the *stamperia* in one edition. Nor was he deaf to the subtle threat underlying all the editor's flattery: he knew him to be a creature of Zorzi's.

And Squarzafico was right: even from a brief glance he could see that the poetry was unusually beautiful. The editor contrived to hold the manuscript relatively steady under his nose.

Why be a printer if not to print such things as this? he thought. *That's what Johann would have said, or is it?*

His eyes still dragged over delectable images, as Squarzafico wafted its pages in front of him. Wendelin sniffed at the manuscript. Why did they always smell of cypress trees in the autumn? It made them so hard to resist. So many times he'd tried to catch a manuscript out in an unfragrant moment. Yet always the vellum breathed sweetly on him, making a pleasure of his business, which seemed to him, quite possibly, to be a sin.

Squarzafico frowned at these procrastinations, so intent upon suppressing a belch, that he inadvertently broke wind. Both men blushed and Squarzafico fanned the air apologetically with the manuscript.

He said: 'Wendelin, at this point I merely ask you to read it all. It will not take you long. Then you will want to publish it.'

Wendelin shrugged his shoulders. He could not help but feel Squarzafico's disdain. He knew his own editor looked down on him, not just for his Germanness, but because he inhabited the sordid world of business. Squarzafico thought he lived without a soul. Perhaps the publication of Catullus, if Wendelin dared it, would show the twice-sodden bore that he was mistaken.

Wendelin read. His Latin was workmanlike; he paid people to have souls in this language. Italian and the Venetian dialect caused him enough problems.

However, even Wendelin von Speyer could not resist Catullus. After three poems he stopped trying to do so, and merely revelled in the unaccustomed voluptuousness between his thighs. A book had never reached him there before. That night, he turned to his wife, and wished to love her as Catullus wrote of love.

'Little sparrow,' she whispered lovingly as he raised himself above her.

They spent themselves, as always, at the same moment. As his thoughts powdered to a scintillating nothingness, Wendelin thought, 'Little sparrow. *Little sparrow?* Has *she* been reading that manuscript too?'

When he woke in the morning, light as an omelette in his spirits, he was already justifying his decision. He disentangled himself from his sleeping wife, smoothed her hair over the pillow, and prepared himself for work.

His employees were all Venetians, as were his readers. His first books had been Pliny and Cicero, to answer the Italians' new craving for their classical past. It was no passing phase, it seemed, this rebirth of desires for ancient art and writings. After bringing out the obvious candidates, he'd been obliged to dig deeper, to look for more obscure texts. The educated drawing rooms and clubs of Venice, as far as he could see, had always run amok with greed for pleasures: perhaps this Catullus would answer to them, and better and more profitably than anyone had done before.

But he needed more affirmation before taking such a risky step.

Wendelin had handed the manuscript to his young editor, Bruno Uguccione, Squarzafico's capable assistant and substitute on the days when the senior editor could not rouse himself from the Falernian stupor.

'It is possible that we are going to publish this.' Wendelin regarded the young man with great earnestness.

Bruno said: 'I've heard about it, *Sior*. And I know some of the poems already. Do you really think . . . ?'

'Take it home and read it, my son. I would like to know what you think of it, as a young man, and as an editor. Does he write the truth about love, this Catullus? Will the Venetians love him?'

So he came home one chill night with poems in his sleeve. That's how it started.

'Catullus,' he said as if it were a good-witch word. 'Finally, I meet him in person and I should like to introduce him to you. Let us go to bed so I may read them to you.'

He was already puzzling at the latchets of my dress.

Poems in the bed? thought I. *Oh, no. Poems are for the wise ones, who bend over their desks. Or to wrap mackerel in, if they fail to catch the hearts of the public. Not for those of us in love.*

Not fair, I thought. I try not to show the hurt when he works late or the midday meal is missed or when he comes home with nothing left but a faint light behind the eyes.

But it is too much, yes, and more, if he brings work home now and worse still to our bed, where he should be mine and I his, with no book between us.

He saw my face then and smiled. I could not be fierce after that. I tucked my head beneath his arm and walked up the stairs with him.

So the poems were read and did their work on us, which I've no need to describe, as everyone has read and felt them now. Later, as we were at the rest that comes just when love has been done, then he asked me, 'Should I print these poems?'

'How can you not?' I asked. 'He's a god, I think, this Catullus, it would be a sin not to print them.'

'In this town you choose your gods for your high tastes,' he laughed at me, 'not for their high tone or good souls!'

I thought then of the wax-lady from Sirmione, certainly not godly at all! I did not mention her.

'For this', said I, 'shall these poems make you in this town. We shall be rich as Malipieros . . .'

'Or break me. There are risks.'

'I care not,' I said. 'Read me once more the poem of the kiss and the sand.'

'I have no need to read it,' he said. 'I can tell it by heart.'

And so he told it, and so he kissed it, after.

The next morning he took them away, and I was sad, but I knew that it must be so, for the journeys of those songs had only just begun.

Nicolò Malipiero, delectably plump as he was, was starting to bore Sosia. She enjoyed the soft linings of his skin, knowing them to be lineaments of wealth. Inserting a hand into the folds beneath his belly, she closed her eyes. Malipiero had grown this way on oysters, peacock-flesh, wine-essences and cream sauces.

The contents of his belly were pleasing to her, but when he spoke to her, when he held her in his tentative arms, when he kissed her uncertainly, she felt a raw and cheap anger against Nicolò's pampered softness. He'd never needed to grasp for anything with both hands, hard. When she seized his head and forced his lips to hers, she felt indelicate. She blamed him; he made her feel feral. Her body seemed poor and stringy, in comparison to his lushness. She did not hide her irritation, terrifying him with glares and rants of insults. When these did not relieve her, she resorted to pinches and bites. She nipped the thin skin at the top of his ears, which always made him whimper, though he never asked her to desist.

What incensed her more was the pathetic way in which he was always trying to be careful of her, treating her like some kind of wild and dangerous animal that would destroy the world if wrongly provoked.

If only he'd show a bit of backbone, she thought, *I'd be nicer to him. Why doesn't he understand that?*

Sosia thought to herself that she'd never really realised before the sheer emptiness of the space between Malipiero's large, aristocratic ears. She was starting to stare in wonderment at some of the comments made and questions asked, and the endless repetition of things already said, the important names and high connections reiterated so many times with fresh flourishes as if she'd not heard them a hundred times before and as if she cared a *pajanca* for any of them, the first time or the hundredth!

She no longer found it amusing that he was a part of the Malipiero clan, entrusted to control the outbreaks of prostitution and vice in the city for decades. No, Nicolò did not enjoy the double standard, and so she could not. For hypocrisy to be enjoyable, it must be relished *à deux*, and sauced with a little irony, she thought. The way Felice did it.

Sosia suspected that other women, kinder women than herself, had in the end found it very sad and in fact felt sorry for him. Nicolò Malipiero lived in such a perpetual mist of blurred intentions and the maladroit expression of them, that he was always apologising for something or other. His money and privilege could in most cases protect him from his deathly errors of tact and taste. However, sometimes, pitiably, he himself was even aware that he was lacking, and it felt terrible to him, transporting him to a place outside his birthright, a grim wasteland of a place where he wandered alone. But he was usually rescued by a profound inner smugness, a sense of his high place in the world, of being one of the 'top' people; this consoled him. It disgusted Sosia.

Until he had produced the borrowed Catullus manuscript and insisted on reading passages of it aloud before they made love, she'd been thinking of leaving him. But there were ideas in the text, and shivery feelings to be got in the execution of them, which decided her to prolong the *storia di Malipiero* just a little more. He had been lent the manuscript, penned by Felice Feliciano himself, by the humanist nobleman Domenico Zorzi, who was also Felice's patron. For reasons unknown to Nicolò, Sosia knew that the manuscript was now somewhere else, a humbler location altogether.

She had last held it in Bruno's sparse apartment, when she'd arrived to surprise him the night before. Seeing the well-known pages open on his desk, she had suppressed any sign of recognition and had allowed Bruno to read the very same poems to her, as if they were fresh and new.

Her thoughts returned to the matter in hand.

'*I'll have you upstairs and downstairs,*' she quoted, tunnelling through the crimson satin to find Nicolò's nervous organ with her fingers. It was unreliable, tentative as its owner, but she liked the way it nestled between his fat thighs.

As Sosia did this Nicolò Malipiero was wondering if he could divorce his aristocratic wife and marry her. Such a *college* was not unknown – noblemen were occasionally permitted to marry down into the privileged lower class of 'original citizens' and with daughters of doctors, lawyers, spice merchants and glass workers of Murano . . . Sosia tightened her grip. All Nicolò's thoughts were extinguished in a spasm of pain and pleasure.

Outside early snow piled up in pale swathes, like the unbought pages in the *stamperia* von Speyer.

Chapter Seven

When her husband's around,
Lesbia calls me every colour of black.
The old fool thinks it so funny.
Ass.
If she had forgotten me and ignored me,
she would be cool.
Instead she snarls and scratches.
She not only thinks about me,
but, what is worse, she's on fire.
She's hot to whip me, with her tongue.
Watch her fume, watch her speak.

I do not wish that Giovanni Bellini would paint me, great though he is. Great and kind and a friend of my man, who is most proud of that fact.

I've no desire to rest frozen in one spot, with one smile, and one look in my eyes to be so summed up for ever – when I've a sack of thoughts and smiles to share – my face may not hold them all at once; my features are dappled with them, like the sun on the sea. No, and I've no wish to be trapped and mounted up on the wall.

I am strange in this, for most in this town are mad for the face. The nobles think that each painted face on their wall shows how pure's the line of their blue blood. They trace the family nose or lip down the generations and persuade themselves each father's son is fully legitimate.

My man also loves each painted face he sees. He tells me they talk like a book and in his terms he can say no more than that.

Felice Feliciano says it is like that with words. He says that everything you want to know lives in their letters.

Ha! That's where he's wrong. It is wonderful not to know things. It means you can speculate and imagine, look beyond what you can make out with your poor limping senses, and into the world of magic and ghosts and many marvellous things besides.

Felice, of course, sees just what he wants, no more; he lives as he likes, he dares to say anything he pleases, for he's no love in him, and so no fear. He only *likes* things, like letters and words. As if *liking* was enough. It's like saying that *kissing* is enough! He's the kind of man who goes to the Rialto market because it looks like a tragic opera for fish – he loves fish not for the taste but for the way they look.

Felice comes to the house when my man is out, shaking the snowflakes out of his head like a cat. He knows he's safe to do so as I am a married woman and may have guests in my parlour. He makes himself at home, sits too close to me and looks at me too hard. He talks to me of bad women; it excites him to disgust me with his tales.

How can you like a man who has no home? He's satisfied with living in inns, buying somewhere to lie, and someone to lie with, no doubt, with casual work.

Yet, yet, he loves to be around women. When he comes to our home and sits beside me, looks at my brown eyes and my blond hair, I see that I please him. He brings me gifts which are just right: a shawl which sets my hair on fire in the winter light; a filch of lace which falls just so on my wrist.

'You are kind,' I tell him as shortly as I know how. And in return for this simple praise, I get a peddler's pack of twisted thoughts from him.

'But you see, I note it each time I'm kind; I am aggrandised by it. So I'm not kind really, or if so it is an accident which occurs while I'm enriching my self-esteem.'

'But the effect is kind,' I insist.

'Mildly, and only incidentally.'

'Did you never do something just out of love?'

He puts his chin on his right hand and drums the fingers of his left hand on the table, and makes his eyes into slits and knits his brows so he looks like the crude mask of a villain who plots the downfall of a virgin in a play.

Outside the snow falls in bundles and I feel trapped, as if drowning in the pool of waxlight on the table.

Felice seems to be waiting for something, and sure enough soon a light footstep is heard in the *calle*. Felice seems to know exactly how long to stay in order to meet Bruno Uguccione on the doorstep, and when his eyes fall on the face of that young man, it's as if a kitten has crawled on to his stomach and kneads with its tiny paws.

'Always hanging around the house like fox pie,' I muttered to Bruno, once, when Felice left, after more embraces than the finale of a play.

'What do you mean?'

'Never goes away, because nobody wants it.'

Of all who work with my man, I like least this Felice. I cannot believe that Giovanni Bellini names him a friend, and gives him the run of his studio.

Giovanni Bellini also wanted Sosia, but not in the way that men normally did. Certainly, he wanted her naked, but she was bemused to see that he wanted her at a distance of six feet, silent and immobile.

Felice had brought her to the studio.

'I think this is what you need for "Vanity",' he said, pushing her forward. Sosia had stood proudly in the light, awaiting approval with no sign of anxiety that it might be withheld. She stared straight ahead while Bellini took in her height and style, peered at her face from both sides with a gentle hand on her chin. Finally he nodded kindly.

'You pay?' asked Sosia.

The painter nodded. Then she looked around her at the boards alight with colour. She could see why the Venetians called Bellini the *Vivificatore*, 'Bringer-to-life'.

Felice had rightly foreseen little trouble in persuading Sosia to pose for one of five small allegories to be set into a dressing table.

'You would like it?' was all she'd asked. 'You'll come to watch?'

She did not worry unduly about the consequences. The table was a private piece and the proposed panel tiny. There was little chance that Rabino would enter a house of the class that had commissioned it, and, if so, he would not have time to examine the furniture as he hurried through the shadows to the bed of the suffering incumbent. And if he did, and he recognised her, would he dare to challenge her? She laughed drily at the thought of her husband stammering his reproaches.

'Be still, please,' said Bellini.

Sosia stood in front of a rich velvet curtain. She was naked, goosefleshed with cold despite the small brazier the artist had kindly placed at her feet. Her hair hung down her back. She cradled a paper model of a large mirror fashioned of silver foil, light enough to hold for hours. Whoever approached her saw their own distorted face in that mirror, captured in her arms. In real life she stood alone, but in the painting Giovanni had given her three fat little sprites for company. One *putto* was childlike and the other was greying prematurely. Both bore lewd horns on their heads. A third *putto* in a grey robe was about to march past, beating a ridiculously small drum.

Felice said: 'I guess you've put Sosia on a pedestal to keep the men away from her, for once. You know she earns her living doing what you're painting her as a dreadful warning against?'

A ripple of amusement ran through the painter's disciples, the *Belliniani*, all hard at work on their own boards, trying to learn how the master made skin tender as a veil and the whites of saints' eyes warm and liquid as the inside of a softly boiled egg. The laughter spread to the actors who stood about in attitudes; they had come to learn from Bellini's heartbreaking *pietàs* how to tell the truth of feeling with eye and gesture. Bellini himself smiled slightly.

Without moving her body, Sosia spat at Felice.

'Gentle, gentle, Sosia,' urged Bellini mildly. 'Look more confident, more serene in your scorn. Aristocratic. Amused, and a little surprised at the folly of men.'

Bellini stroked another tiny smear of paint over Sosia's skin, another coat of happiness for the eyes of future beholders. The *Belliniani* craned their necks.

Felice shrugged. He left, passing Bruno who was just arriving. The two men embraced affectionately in the doorway. Felice traced the tense lines around Bruno's mouth with a delicate finger, and smoothed out his eyebrows. Bruno laughed, but the misery was still inscribed on his face.

Bellini nodded pleasantly for Bruno was a frequent visitor to the studio. He continued with his work, humming sweetly under his breath.

Bruno did not like the painting. He thought that it showed Sosia's evil, and none of her allure. It showed her elongated haunches and small, fragile shoulders. It showed the private parts of her, which no one but he should see. Giovanni, Bruno reflected, was not painting Sosia's features; he was painting the malice under her skin.

The woman in the painting, like Sosia, was not exactly beautiful, but no man could look at anything else while she was in front of him. Her legs and torso were elongated so that the belly was central to everything. It swelled in a curve that could hold the beginnings of a child. Yet the allegory seemed to warn that the man whose face was trapped in her mirror merely believed, in his vanity, to have begotten a baby upon her.

How coolly he sees her, thought Bruno. *Giovanni knows her better than I do. I could not recreate her like this. It shows how little I know her. If I were to paint a picture of her it would be as a monstrous creature – a huge, engulfing pair of lips, nipples and vulva very close by them. Her left eye, the one not crushed in the pillow, all tangled with her hair like a yellow marble in a tiny nest. And I would paint the inside of her mouth, the pink fork of her sex, the sweat on her lip. I would paint . . .*

Sosia showed no sign that she took pleasure in his presence. Bruno gazed at her. She was looking out of the window, hoping that her intense scrutiny of the street outside might bring Felice back to the studio.

Chapter Eight

My life, my Lesbia,
you say that this love of ours will
stay unstained by fighting, for ever.
Dear Gods,
let her promise be true!
Let her be true to what she swears.
Could we live the rest of our lives
in this holy state of peace?

When we were home some months we passed a little spring *festa* in the street and I threw myself into my man's arms, to make him dance with me. I thought we could dance out some of our sadness and trample it on the ground. The snow had melted and so could all our griefs, I declared, smiling up at my man with all my might.

But he stood still. He told me that he could not dance and I stared at him as if I'd seen a ghost.

'But just listen to the music and move,' I told him. 'It's like love. You already know how to do it.'

Bless him, the dear man blushed.

'I have no sense of rhythm, my darling. Also it seems indelicate to touch you like this, out here in front of everyone.'

'But it's a sin *not* to dance,' I told him. He raised quizzing eyes at me and so I told him the tale of an English priest called Robert who gave a mass in the year 1012 on Christmas Day. The folk of his town were gay with festive spirit and began to dance in the churchyard outside his church. He begged them to stop, but the more he begged the harder they danced. In the end this Robert said: 'If you cannot cease dancing, then may you dance without ceasing.' And so it was. Those folk kept dancing for one whole year and felt neither heat nor cold nor the call of sleep. The ground beneath them wore away till they were dancing in a pit. A brother of one girl took her by the arm to make her stop: the arm came off in his hand and she never stopped dancing or missed a single step. In the end a bishop was called and he gave the dancers absolution. Then they stopped. Some died straight away. The rest slept for three days and then woke refreshed and more happy than they had ever been . . .

'Very well, very well,' laughed my man. 'I am conquered by this story. We shall dance.'

And he began to move like a toy with rust in its joints. I could not stop laughing, and he stopped, full of shame and red as a nobleman's robe.

So it was then that I hired a dancing teacher for him. Soon the music got into his blood and jerked his limbs the way it wished. Now he can dance six of our dances. He says this is enough. He does not pretend to be a Venetian, he says.

He's so tired. Quick books are good and they are easy on the body so the problem with them is one of the spirit. In the old days each book was made to order by the scribe. Just one order, just one scribe, just one book.

But when my man prints he's two score men to pay. For reasons I don't quite fathom – he says it is more economic – he prints eight score books and who knows who will buy them? It is a temptation like those in the Holy Bible. Because he has the men, and he has the paper, and he has the speed to make quick books, he's tempted every day to print more. And so the quick books mount up in slow-dwindling piles.

Then there's another problem with the nobles. Like Nicolò Malipiero and Domenico Zorzi. And Alvise Capello. They come to the *stamperia* with big smiles and they order one tall stack of books each time. 'I shall send a servant and a barrow,' they say and swirl off in their red robes. But do they pay? Not always. They think it is enough to give their noble custom and be seen in my man's place of work. It is not. It is in no way just, but we cannot touch the nobles.

And they make their power felt in subtle ways that hurt more than the plain rude lack of payment. They let my man know he should print what they want, or many are the ways that his quick books might come to grief: lack of paper, for they control it; lack of custom, for we depend on them; lack of help in all the rough matters that must be smoothed out, not just in his business but even in the livelihoods of our two families.

My man likes even less the ones from our own class who come in to trade. They think that books in their rooms are like pearls on their wives' throats, a sign of wealth that will help them rise to the top. They buy books they never plan to read. Sure, it is coins on the table, ringing like a bell for us when they come to buy, and they prefer to use gold itself, not promise-notes of it, for they like the shine of it. But my man is sad that they do not read these books into which so much care has been put. They may as well buy false busts of the ancients from Rome, these men, and leave him alone. For they leave him feeling dirty for his trade.

When he comes home I do not pry curiously into his work, for it would make him re-live his problems to tell them. I hope he may find refreshment in my ignorance of his business. Also, if I do not know all, it means I'm always on his side of the question, for I know of no other. No, I don't intermeddle in that side of his life. When he comes home I kneel to loose his shoe-latchets by the waxlight and I kiss his toes.

Of course I am loyal to my man but I do have something secret to tell. It is this. I love *talk* not books. I love to hear a voice. Words on the page? To me they are like the smell of a rose but no rose in sight. You look round for the rose and you miss it.

Literature, I think. So? He wears himself thin for this? People who've a real live love do not have time for love poems. They do not! They make love on a continual basis, and the book lies closed beneath the bed, lies in wait for the sad times when love is not there. What wife would rather have a book in her arms at night than her man? It is his eyes I crave, not little black scratches on dry paper.

A poet is not a lover! Once he's named 'a poet' he might as well be called a businessman. He produces words, because words are expected, to order.

The poets are fools. Lovers do not want them.

They are not interested in a beautifully turned phrase or a long lovely word. They are only interested in the one they love. He is air and light to them. They live on him, feast on him, read his face. They want nothing more. They need nothing more.

However, I am torn, for I would make an exception for this Catullus.

For two reasons.

The first is that he alone among the poets I've seen can tell the truth about love and make it come alive. I remember his effect on me when my man read the poems aloud in our bed. So I think he can help those who do not know how to love, those poor folk who thrash in the dark of some clumsy passion and know not how to express it.

The second is that perhaps he can save us. I believe that if he's printed, Catullus will sell. Not for the reasons of high poetry or art, but because he will make scandal, which will make noise, which will bring sales. The Zorzis and the Malipieros would spend on that book the way they spend on their courtesans: in sackfuls of ducats.

With sales the *stamperia* can survive and my man can stay in Venice. Without Catullus, I am not so sure.

Domenico and Sosia usually met in his library. He was a man of ritualistic pleasures and had early prescribed the style of their encounters.

Sosia was to arrive by the servants' entrance, using her own key and then take an inner passage direct to the luxurious book-lined room. (A library such as Domenico's, she knew, was extraordinarily valuable. It would cost less to line the walls with sable.)

She was to wear the pink pearls and a simple dress that could be removed with a minimum of struggle. Underneath she was to wear nothing, except a silk chemise he had given her. It must be freshly laundered before each encounter.

When she arrived, Domenico was always reading at his desk. Although acutely aware of her presence (indeed from an hour beforehand the thrill of anticipation kept him aquiver), he made no sign of having seen her and continued to turn pages, usually two, before he looked up at her.

Sosia watched him patiently. She liked the way Domenico read, savouring each word like a sweetmeat. Bruno came to any book as if he were opening a little child's fist, afraid of hurting it, which annoyed her. Felice, she always remembered with a visible flush of pleasure, turned pages like a bird pluming its feathers.

Gratified by the smile on her face when he looked up, Domenico would rise from his chair and walk quickly to Sosia. He removed her clothes slowly, folding each garment with the precision of a housekeeper and laying each separately on a shelf.

When she was naked, he would lift her in his arms and carry her to an oversized chair decked with velvet cushions. He would arrange her on his knees so that she lay back with her arms and legs apart, her stomach slanted up to him. She was to lie limply, as if unconscious. He would sit like that, in the exact pose of a Bellini *pietà*, for half an hour. Sosia closed her eyes and slackened her body, like a dead Christ. Domenico lowered his eyes on her like Mary. Sometimes the tips of his fingers twitched but he observed the same physical immobility as Sosia.

Then, with the subtlest of movements, he allowed one hand to move and it began to trace slow circles on her lower belly. Sosia was not permitted to move or even to moan. Domenico's fingers rose individually, walking over her thighs like delicate spiders. First one, then another finger left her skin, until he caressed her just with the tip of his second finger, always moving in tiny circles.

Eventually, even Domenico could not stand it any more, and he stood up to carry her to the desk. He was displeased to note that she always roused herself from her trance then, to what books were placed there. Sometimes she would take one and place it under her hips. Always, he could not help but notice, one penned by Felice Feliciano.

She always left quickly, without endearment or salutation, reaching for her ducat in silence. Domenico liked to think this was her acknowledgement of his station and the important demands on his time. But there were times when he found her haste indecorous. It was almost as though she felt she had somewhere better to go.

In Giovanni Bellini's studio, on the divan bed, Felice Feliciano painted an 'S' on Sosia's left buttock. Unlike the crude scar on her back, at which he wrinkled his nose in distaste, Felice's 'S' was beautifully crafted. The left descender was slender and vulnerable. The right was plump and sleek. He flicked in the delicate serifs. Still, she slept on, curled on her side, her hands pressed together. *If she were sitting up like that, it would be a confessional position*, he thought. He liked that. He had no use for religion himself, but it was an attractive thing in a young woman. Even Sosia, he thought, was cursed with a bit of unconscious goodness, detectable only when she let down her guard.

Felice said: 'S for Sosia.' He admired his slim hand with the squirrel-fur paintbrush elegantly crooked between the second and third fingers. He observed the tableau that they made, he and Sosia, in the tall studio mirror: his own immaculate profile, the gloss of his hair, the athlete's swoop of his shoulders, and, behind him, Sosia's naked body, yellow-pink in the candlelight except where his green ink had marked her.

He recited from his own calligraphic manuals: 'To form the letter S make two circles, one above the other, and practise drawing them so that you make them one tenth thicker above and below. And draw the lower extremity further out than the upper and make it thicker, and it will look well.'

Felice had spent years of his life scraping moss off tombstones in the ruins around Verona. With his measuring tools, he'd recorded every spatial relationship between serif and descender. On each page of his famous alphabet book was a single letter in shades of sepia, encased in a pale tracery of geometry, like scaffolding, by which Felice had proved conclusively the mathematical purity of each Roman letter and established the incontrovertible formula to recreate it in modern times.

In the swells of the 'S', upper and lower, he now painted two 'O's.

Sosia's buttocks looked well, adorned with many practice circles in green ink, like the eyes of so many serpents. Still she slept, her breath rasping occasionally.

She does nothing gently, even sleeping, thought Felice. He frowned. *What were women good for, if not for delicacy?* For more robust pleasures, there were men.

Felice continued: 'To write in green, first seek in the months of March and April the blooms of the Iris and pound the three pendant leaves well and draw off the juice. Add alum. Soak a strip of linen in this liquid and leave to dry. When you wish to draw off the green colour, take a cockleshell, together with some lye and the frothy white of an egg, and press the said cloth well until the green colour comes out. Then write with it, and it will look well.'

Sosia's circles looked well, drying to tiny flakes on her skin. Now she stirred and arched, expanding and puckering the green lettering. Her eyes were still shut and her tongue lay loose on her upper lip. Then she rolled to her stomach, opened her eyes and looked over her back to her painted buttocks. She laughed; *too many teeth for perfect beauty,* thought Felice. She reached out to Felice, trying to kiss his hand, but he batted her away with his brush.

For he'd seen that in stretching she had broken his circles.

The mirror witnessed a transformation in his features; the pleasantness with which he'd previously regarded Sosia had disappeared.

'Sosia,' said Felice, 'the letters are broken.' His tone was bantering, but cold. 'The devil Tutivillus will be calling on me. You've made a *casino* of my script! He tapped the striated colour with his quill, not gently. 'That vowel is flattened; that consonant is sucked off.'

Sosia, feeling her nakedness and the sting of his quill, looked up at him with an expression none of her other lovers had ever seen. She could not bear to feel Felice's displeasure. She tried to coddle his good humour with a joke. She could reach him that way, sometimes, if she concentrated on her breathing. Otherwise, she found that she was always swallowing the air in her throat when she was with him, gasping like a landed fish.

'Felice, I think it's a fine thing. Now I can see with my arse. With all these eyes, I can see who is *coming* behind me, in case I have, in the heat of the moment, forgotten. Bruno says that he wishes he could be the sky, with all those star-eyes to gaze at me. He should see this.'

She giggled and reached out to stroke Felice's ear.

He batted her hand away, saying, 'Plato wished to be the sky, some years before Bruno, in order to look on a woman he loved.'

Sosia scowled. 'That's what editors do, isn't it? Steal from the past. Because they cannot create anything themselves.'

'You shouldn't be so hard on Bruno. You see, now that we spend all our time in these manuscripts of the ancients, our perceptions have become unclear. We do not know when we create, or when we pay tribute or when we baldly imitate. Because of this, every perfect epigram seems stolen from the past, though it may be fresh as the morning. And conversely words that seem still hot from the foundry of the brain are often those merely translated from a fleeting memory that conveniently forgets to attach the correct attribution. I've come to the conclusion that every word we read sticks to our mind like specks of oat in a pot, whether we like it or not.'

Sosia opened her mouth to reply, but Felice held up his hand for silence.

It always astonished Felice that one might talk to Sosia as one talked to oneself or to male friends – her vocabulary was extraordinary. It was easy to forget that she was a foreigner. The edges of her accent merely sharpened her words. If Sosia had been a man, and a Venetian, how far she might have gone! But she was a woman and a foreigner, and, he reminded himself, moreover a person who hurt others as effortlessly as most people breathe. This meant, in the inevitable course of things, that when she lost her ability to attract, she would lose her power, and someone would be waiting, ready to take revenge. It was merely a matter of time. But until that happened, she was worth arguing with. It stretched his imagination.

He yawned and rose, draping a curtain around his shoulders. He sat with his back to Sosia, his eyes meandering around the studio, studying Bellini's work. Over his shoulder he said, 'Sosia, you must get up and go home, or to Bruno, or wherever you're going next.'

Sosia turned on her side and raised her head on her elbow. She looked up at Felice's shoulders. 'How about you – tell me how it feels for you to fuck the woman your dear friend loves?'

Felice turned to her. His smile did not falter. 'It feels regrettable. The path to pleasure is ever disagreeably bestrewn with small moments of ugliness.'

'A little, tiny feeling.' She pinched her forefinger and thumb together to show how small. 'But I thought that men hate to lie to each other; it makes them feel dishonoured and cheap. Lying to a woman is nothing; a slight necessity. But to deceive a male friend, well, there you are breaking the taboos of your kind. So in fact I imagine you really might suffer for what this would do to Bruno, if he knew.'

'Very deft, Sosia.'

'What do *you* feel for Bruno, then?'

'Why should I tell you? Do you care? Or are you merely curious, or filling up the time before I become capable of giving you physical pleasure again?'

'Will that be long?'

Everyone has a different heaven. For Sosia, it was desire in Felice's eyes.

'So what do you feel for Rabino?' Felice asked, ignoring her question. 'If anything? Not too much detail, please.'

He rose and began to stroll around the room.

So he's ready for me to leave, thought Sosia. *How can I make him allow me to stay?*

'I hate him. I hate his smile. It's weak. I hate what he accepts in me. I hate his little boy's thighs. Shall I go on?'

'No, enough. That's a fairly conventional wife's list.'

She did not look at his face; she watched his legs. Every time they shifted she hoped it was the discomfort entailed by desire for her. She'd always thought she preferred larger men, but she didn't know the truth of her desires until she was inside Felice's arms that joined his shoulders in just the right place, on his breast, which pillowed her head at just the right angle. Once this had been made clear to her, other men now seemed put together in the wrong way.

He did not see her face tighten to a grimace. He did not see how her eyes followed him around the room.

Bellini's studio was sultry. His latest Madonna glittered wetly on its easel. It would not dry for days in this humidity. Felice stood in front of it, naked, stroking his chin, leaning closer to inspect the detail.

'I love this painting,' he said simply. 'It's better than a real woman.'

Sosia asked if he would come to the tavern near the Dogana and drink red wine with her among the vines and stars.

'Why?' he asked.

PART FOUR

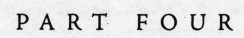

Prologue

For nothing, I called you my friend, for nothing.
No, you have pillaged and broken me . . .
You have poisoned my life!
Now I moan because
you have beslavered my lover's sweet lips
with the filth of your kisses.
You will not escape your fate.
The future will know you, as you are.

December 59 BC

Dear Brother,

Everything is gone between me and Clodia except base sexual passion. Yesterday, when I learned she'd taken up with my old friend Caelius, I made a certain vow to Cybele. I'll not be tamely butchered, me, or destitute of vigour when it comes to taking revenge. Nor shall I do Clodia the honour of renouncing her. No – I shall curse her with my love poems now; they will be the most brutal love poems in the world.

Come to me, you bitch, they'll sneer; *I'll take what you've got anyway.*

Caelius has moved into one of Clodius' luxurious apartments up on the Clivus Victoriae. At first we all wondered how Caelius could cover the rent – then we realised that Clodius is probably keeping him close and convenient for trysts with his sister. Maybe Clodius gives a rent discount for threesomes. Do I shock you, brother? It's only what all Rome is whispering about that smatterer of poemlets, that perambulator in the soul-shallows, that scum-fluff on the surface of all things, that floating bubble, that bantam-strutting disease of friendship, Caelius. Gods, I deserve to be cuckolded by better than *that*!

I've been faithful as a dog until now, but in the shock of this twin-headed betrayal, I've tried the solace of other women; men, too, as it happens. I've lacquered my eyes with wine, so painting my conquests more desirable than they were. I went as far as embracing them. Their lips tasted sweeter for the wine I'd drunk. But when the moment came I could never perform. In the end I have therefore desisted from casual gallantries. I don't want a reputation for impotence in this town. Someone might write a poem about me! And Clodia, who despite everything still summons me to her rumpled divan, would laugh about me with Caelius.

Back to work now. Glyconics, asclepiadeans and priapeans, and above all hendecasyllables for my mistress, who so richly deserves them.

September 58 BC

You tease me about the indigestion of personal pronouns in my letters. Yet is it not the work of a poet to be self-obsessed?

But brother, why do you yourself not write more often? It's months since I heard from you and there are rumours of a fever razing the legions in Asia. It would be a kindness to let us know that all is well with you, and if you cannot find time to write to your wastrelly poet of a brother, at least send word to our father, who fears to be orphaned of a fine son.

Or two.

Death is on my mind.

My chest . . . if I should die before you, Lucius, I would like you to have my blue faience inkpot and my chalcedony seal ring. I would not mind at all if you were to place a little bronze chest, representing mine, at your nearest shrine. I have coughed blood this morning, and though I balled up my napkin to hide the red watermarks the sight of them is imprinted on my memory.

Death is on my mind, for other reasons.

Clodia is a widow! Her husband, briefly returned to Rome from his provincial duties, was suddenly struck down by an eviscerating illness no one could name. Emptied of every drop of fluid in his body, he shrivelled to a corpse in an hour.

You can imagine what is being said in malice. Caelius struts about the Forum, not meeting anyone's eyes, but accepting craven compliments for his risible talent.

I blocked my ears and hastened up the Palatine to pour what loving comfort I could force on her. I found her dry-eyed, composed, and vigorously directing the packing for imminent decampment to her holiday retreat at Baiae.

'You're not still going?' I gasped. A vision invaded my brain: of the widowed Clodia merrily husking her tender green boys in her bean-pod pleasure-boat. I *heard* the creak of wood, the groans, and the squack and skitter of starstruck waters in that melon-cut bay.

'Why not? You're still coming?' She smiled lusciously, as if she shared the image I'd conjured.

Of course I was.

If only I could say that I was her only attendant in that idyllic place.

At Baiae at the end of this summer, she'd gathered an unkindness of young men — how else am I to term it? — and she walked us through her gardens, like dogs, in the cool of each meteor-strewn evening, the sparrow circling her at a more intimate proximity than any one of us was allowed. Even Caelius, I was pleased to see.

The strangest fate befell that sparrow, and this is a secret you must not share, Lucius, never mind that the fame of that bird has spread to Asia on the wings of my poems.

At a certain point one such evening Clodia noticed that the sparrow had ceased to swoop about her, and she snapped her fingers, ordering her young men to scamper around and find her pet. The dying sun still dangled like heavy lemon in the branches of sky and the flit of birds was everywhere. It seemed an easy way to win her favour that night, to find her sparrow.

I admit that like all the others I dropped my dignity (yes, Lucius, you may well add 'what's left of it') behind a bush and threw myself into the search like a child at a serious game with worthwhile prizes. Some of the men whistled up at leafy branches; others scanned the sky. But I knew the spoilt sparrow better than that. He was a plump creature of low altitudes, so I began straight away to crawl on my belly among the caper-berry bushes. I was presently rewarded with a familiar throaty chirp, from just a few yards away and only slightly muffled by the foliage. I knelt by a melodious bush and parted the leaves like the drapes of a window.

Expecting to see the little bird, my shock was then as when a sudden sensation of falling sends you plummeting in your dreams. For what I beheld was another pair of brown human eyes, those of my rival Caelius. For months I'd avoided meeting them, but now they were just a foot away, and fastened on mine.

He too registered surprise and pain – for we loved one another once – but his eyes soon fluttered downwards and I saw what had drawn them. There was Clodia's sparrow, our mutual quarry, and the beast himself was also sportively engaged in the business of hunting. A green mantis, its arms raised in the usual prayer, was laying its eggs on a leaf. The sparrow was scooping them up in his beak as fast as the mantis could deposit them. While we looked on, the bird's beak nipped closer and closer to the insect's tail and finally grasped it. The mantis shuddered, tried to pull away, but the sparrow was greedily drinking its sap while it yet lived.

We owed this horror, I recalled, to Clodia, who fed the beast with bloody delicacies from her table. I'd seen that sparrow supping on cream and gargling undiluted wine while he mashed strips of roasted boar in his beak.

Caelius, for he's a poet too, after all, moaned softly. Suddenly his disembodied hand shot through the leaves, seized the sparrow and snapped its neck. It dangled in his hand, the head on one side, its left eye open and the right eye closed. It looked quite roguish, as if prepared to tease its mistress with one last game.

Caelius and I stared at one another, each face framed by its wreath of leaves.

Eventually I nodded at him, as if to say *well done*!

'What shall I do?' he whispered.

I answered briskly: 'Best close the matter. Crueller for her to keep wondering what's happened to the thing. Don't worry. I won't give you away.'

Together, our faces tight with simulated grief, we went to present the dead bird to its mistress, who was just a few yards away, fanning herself on a rock. As we walked towards her the sun suddenly dropped into the sea as if someone had snipped its stalk. Clodia's servant held up a lantern, enveloping his mistress in a churning veil of grey moths.

When she saw us she immediately grew pink and somewhat out of breath, as if aroused by the sight of the two of us together. She barely glanced at the bird.

'Take it to my room,' she said, and Caelius moved off in a trance, whereupon the bile rose up in my belly and, so help me Gods, I longed to denounce him. I pictured just how she would mourn the bird and how he would console her.

'No, both of you,' she said.

Chapter One

Was it for this . . . that you ruined the world?

Unfortunately for Wendelin von Speyer, someone else had come over the Alps with typefaces in his trunk: the Frenchman Nicolas Jenson.

'We keep our heads down,' Wendelin said, when asked by Felice about the new arrival. 'We do good work. The other printers, they cannot touch us. We are Germans! The fathers of printing!'

But then Jenson printed his first book, a Cicero, *Epistolae ad Brutum* and Venice went mad, not for the well-known words, but for the extraordinary letters which spelled them.

Wendelin wrote to Padre Pio in September of 1470.

My dearest Padre Pio,
It goes badly for us. The wretched Frenchman has arrived here. I have seen his typefaces with my own eyes; I cut tears upon them. They whisper that this man learned his trade as a cutter of coin dies, that he was sent by the French king to spy on the printers in Mainz and that there he befriended Gutenberg himself! The rumour persistently attaches itself to him that he actually learned his

trade from the master of its invention. In my nightmares I see that he will be the subject of a cult.

He took no hostages . . . began to set himself up, insultingly nearby in San Salvador! — even before I had buried my dear brother, assuming that our precious monopoly was forfeit at Johann's death — and I fear the spineless Collegio looks to uphold this robbery from us.

This is typical of Venice. No one gives us Germans credit for our investment: they see something good has been done and they run away with it like a child with his sister's toy. We 'von Speyers', as they persistently call us (never once using our Venetian name 'da Spira', and this is by way of a taunt, of course) — have made the town a handsome gift of our innovation, trained her young men in new and valuable skills. We did this in good faith, thinking ourselves protected. But Venice is a fat baby accustomed to be dandled and coddled by all, a little princess, who expects everyone to adore her and bring her presents. So at the last minute, the Venetians have opened for everyone the field we alone prepared.

Thus, instead of an organised guild, as in Germany, with everyone knowing his place, there's a complete free-for-all, in other words the usual disorganised, catastrophic Italian anarchy.

So now here is Jenson the Frenchman with his letters and his sly ways, running rings around the Venetians, who are easily dazzled by a little bit of beauty.

How can I describe my feelings to you? It's like watching a thousand gold coins you earned the hardest way now sinking into the Venetian slime. I know you meant to be helpful when you reminded me how the great Gutenberg spent the price of forty houses before he printed a single book. That he slaughtered 375 calves to make his first Bible — veal-chops must have been cheap in Mainz that year! But you see I am a mere man, a mere family man, a mere businessman, not a God like Gutenberg. Not a visionary. I cannot stand by to watch the money trickle in slowly or not at all. One in every ten printing businesses here has already failed. Only Jenson prospers. I hear rumours that the printers Sweynheim and Pannartz in Rome are on the verge of bankruptcy. The action of the Venetian Collegio may well do the same to me.

Then, to insult me further, in one of Jenson's first books — Decor Puellarum — he has made what he apparently claims as a mistake but which I know to be his dishonest claim for immortality. He has dated his book M. CCCC LXI, ten years earlier than the actual date it came out. He has thus tried to steal from my poor brother Johann the title of being the first printer in Venice. Jenson would rather suffer the brief shame of an error in his edition in order to steal the regard of eternity. He thinks distantly and coldly, like a mechanical apparatus. This is the kind of man I have unwillingly taken on as rival.

You will ask me, no doubt, what other books he chooses to publish. In this he's not a visionary. Jenson plays safe, repeating editions done already by us or the other north Italian printers so in this last year he has put out Cicero's Tusculans, Pliny's Naturalis Historia and Aulus Gellius. His most important first edition is only a Macrobius, Scriptores rei rusticae, including Cato, Varro, Columella and Palladius. But he's wooing the college of physicians with medical texts now, and has also done a Gloria Mulierum of religious tracts for married women, to keep the Church happy.

Here in Italy, as you know, noble blood is everything. So one always hopes one's book will enter the library of one of the great collections, the Sforza of Milan, the Medici of Florence, the Este of Ferrara, Federigo da Montefeltro of Urbino or the princes of Rome. Now I hear that the Jenson volumes are pushing ours out of these few high places. He has allied himself to all our regular customers, including the Priulis and the Agostinis, and I believe he has even persuaded them to invest in his business! The Agostinis, a big banking family here, are getting Jenson endless supplies of the best paper. He's rolling in their money. And because of that, he can get the best illuminators — even Gerolamo (you know, the one who's always painting monkeys in his margins).

He has dedicated an edition already to Felice's friend and our own patron Domenico Zorzi . . . and through Domenico I fear that Felice's beautiful ideas are now being cut into Jenson's forms. It was told me by my wife that Jenson and Felice have been seen drinking together and a toast was made, to Gutenberg, by the two of them, with Jenson telling Felice: 'Gutenberg himself was a scribe, in the first place.' You can imagine the effect of this on our divine Felice, who absorbs flattery like a coarse cloth drinks milk.

Domenico worries me, too, by the way. If only he can stop dabbling disgustingly with a well-known Jewish whore about the town! The rumours are pointing at him again and he must be careful. It is the Venetian instinct to hate foreigners.

Lussièta says that the Germans (apart from myself!) have failed to win the affections of the Venetians. We are tolerated only because our fondaco yields them one million ducats a year. The old prejudices against our race are coming out, I *fear.* Everyone in Venice enjoys attributing boorishness to us and exquisiteness to the French: they are predisposed to love Jenson's work more than ours.

Now if I, Wendelin von Speyer the German, were to be more extravagant in the type designs, the illustrations, my presswork or the quality of my paper, there would be mutterings of pride and decadence. I would be condemned as sensational or vulgar. But whatever Jenson does is immediately the rage. He has a way of making everything a delicacy.

Trained in making coins, he did his casting himself. Himself! Neither Johann nor I could ever have done that. We always needed craftsmen for this part of the work. Jenson's is perfection, or at least some magical combination of tiny humanities which makes it more beautiful than imperfect. It seems to me that he loves, more than the letter itself, the white space, that airy egg, that appears inside the letter, through its open parts. His letters seem to have a little halo inside them. Among ourselves, we have started to call Jenson's Roman 'White Letter'.

His serifs, weightless but strong, contribute a delectable effect of squareness to the rounded capitals. The lower case is of plump proportions, his ascenders and descenders unusually long. His 'e' has a slanted central line. The stroke of Jenson's 'd' is slightly prolonged; his 'q' has a shorter, thicker tail than ours . . . the refinements, as you see, are minute, but the horrifying thing is that each one is for the better! He dots his 'i's slightly to the right, where ours are dotted just above, and yet somehow his seem juster! How can this be?

Jenson's typeface is so beautiful that it takes all the attention for itself, so that people rave not of the content of his books but of the glamour of his letters.

And in this they — I mean the book-buying classes in Venice — miss the point. Printing is better than scribal manuscripts because even the neatest human hand interferes with the text. It brings in another personality, interposed between the writer and the reader. Johann and I above all tried to return to the classical model, to create a typeface free of the illegible exuberance of the scribes, particularly the Italians, who are far too flamboyant. Even though I count the great Felice Feliciano among my friends, I still think even his work lacks discipline, which may reflect the disturbances of his private life — I understand he conducts an improper relationship with a married Dalmatian woman of this town — and perhaps has a corrupting effect on his work. I go about recommending marriage to everyone, of course, but Felice is not the kind who can love one woman.

(Look at me, distracted by gossip! Like a Venetian!)

Though we all talk of him, Jenson himself is still anonymous. It seems he is a pale grey shadow of a man with scarcely any personality to speak of. It's practically an invisible enemy who is haunting me. He's something like connective tissue between organs, a thing that does not exist in its own right. He never writes his own introductions, preferring an editor to do so. I would have to admit that his colophons are more modest than ours: he's too self-confident to boast of the contents of his books.

And what a businessman! He always knows just how many copies to print. He never needs to reprint, his editions are bigger than our own, and yet he's never left with stock filling up his magazzino with wasted profit . . .

I have always been a little too tender-hearted for my customers. I'm sentimental about them precisely because they buy our work, which seems like love to me. Some of them just cannot afford to pay the whole sum at once. So I allow them three instalments. Jenson, on the other hand, never gives credit; he has no heart. And can you guess what effect this has upon the Venetians? Yes! They actually borrow money to buy Jenson's books!

Perhaps the joy I find in my wife costs me something in the stamperia. Guilt (at rising a little late sometimes, at rushing home to her at night) is what I feel when I see the grossness of our own ink furring and choking up our forms. When it dries it is dingy, smearing and unpleasant to the eye. We cannot afford to boil the linseed oil as long as Jenson does, and when we heat the varnish in the blacking we burn and rubify it so that it loses its brisk and vivid complexion. If we try to stint on the expensive blacking then the ink becomes insufferably pale.

I must tell you that Jenson uses a black ink of a glossiness that I have not even once in three years been able to achieve: it's like velvet, intense and passionate. And this luxurious pitch he stamps on to paper of tints and textures of the greatest elegance, in a uniformity of register that makes me want to weep. There are no blotches, ever! Well, of course, probably there are, but he is too vain to let any such pages be seen outside his stamperia. I imagine him late at night, scrutinising each folio, tearing up any with the slightest imperfection, all while I drowse in Lussièta's arms, work long forgotten.

And now Jenson is spoken of as the man who prints as Felice writes, as Bellini paints! I am not a vainglorious man, God knows, but this hurts me for that was the role I coveted for myself.

I digress. Jenson is also attracting stellar editors, such as the Latinist

Ognibene da Lonigo, that sycophant of the Gonzagas at Mantova — this for prestige, and for the popular vote — that cranker-out of christening poems Antonio Cornazzano. It hurts me to see how my own men are tempted by his blandishments. Merula, I no longer trust for he just sways like a pendulum back and forth between myself and Jenson. Another ambidexter is Gerolamo Squarzafico, who helped with my Italian Bible last year and edited the Latin works of Boccaccio for me — he has gone over to the other side too!

Only young Bruno Uguccione stays faithful to me, but I hear talk that he is wretchedly in love with some cruel older woman who rejects him and uses him badly. Bruno himself has lost the shine on his work: he does what he must, and is always accurate, but I know that he only wants to talk about Catullus, and you can imagine that this is the last subject on which I at present wish to dwell.

All this would not matter if it were not for the state of the market. It is over-crowded with books. It wants novelties.

And guess! Jenson is doing small prayer books, which he contrives to charge more expensively than those of the normal size! I hate those small prayer books! (God forgive me.) They are a typical Jenson stroke of genius. His paper, more delicate than ours, can be folded into smaller sections without making a great book that gapes open like a cave. Almost anyone can carry one easily in their sleeve, or hold it comfortably in the hand while learning passages by heart. There's something about this miniaturisation that is irresistibly refined. Of course the Venetians love it, and they walk about the town holding his little prayer books in their hands, like small beloved pets, advertising Jenson's work for him.

I'm doing what I can to keep my head above the water. I have gone into part-nership with Johann di Colonia, who has lately married my dear brother's excellent widow Paola, and Johann of Manthen. They have enlisted in service eminent scholars and correctors.

I do not know what more we can do, apart from grow fishtails and become Venetians . . . sometimes I have the illusion of doing just that. I begin to feel at home in my own sestiere, looking with distrust on the faces from Cannaregio or Santa Croce. Then I remind myself with a smile that they are all Venetians and it is I who is the foreigner.

I have something else to tell you.

As you suspected would happen, there's already trouble about the Catullus. There's suddenly a mad priest on Murano who's hot for my blood. Somehow *it's become known that I'm thinking of printing him, and this cleric's using Catullus as an example, to show why the new art of printing is only for the Devil, that we print only obscenity and pagan literature. I see more difficulty coming from this direction. I can hardly defend the book. It tears at my own loins, if you must know the truth. I thank you for the honesty of your letter in which you admitted that the sampling of poems I sent you last month has the same effect upon you. But it is literature, and it is life, and I do not wish to shelter the public from it just to save my own skin.*

So despite all, I'm still thinking of publishing him.

Your brave son

Wendelin

Some might say I spend too much on foodstuffs when we are far from rich and the business suffers sadly since Jenson set up his press. I disagree! Food is more than something to put in your mouth. Done right, it also warms the soul. So I buy all the good things I can find.

When I go to market, the fine foods tempt my outstretched hand and deride my purse that is not so full as my desire to please my man. I look at each autumn peach, each apricot, and imagine if it will please him. I put in my basket only figs so fresh the milk yet drips from their prods.

Even though I have other things on my mind there these days.

I try to talk to the wives of Rialto. Just in a casual way, of course. I don't let on a thing.

'What news of the Frenchman? The one who's started with the quick books?' I ask, as if it meant not a bean to me, as if my heart did not thrust at my ribs when I spoke. I do not wish them to know how I tremble for my man, for if I did then the fear would soon catch on, the way plague does.

When the plague first comes, like any bad thing, we Venetians snub it; we give it no truth. If we hold out against it, we feel with all our hearts that it might go away whence it came, with the pilgrims, no doubt, dirty as they are.

But once we give it truth and own that the disease has come once more amongst us, well then the plague swells and fills the town with death, quick as a spring tide.

So it is with bad news. This is why I will not have it said out loud in any place that my man's quick books are not the best. Not once.

Therefore last week I asked for news of Jenson in a light voice as I might ask the fish man if the smelts are by chance fresh on this day. The news I heard was this: on one side that he's a most beautiful man, tall and dark of eye with long silky moustachios; on the other side that he's small and fair as a doll with golden curls and a ring in his ear.

I see, I mutter to myself, *no one has seen him yet.*

But the Frenchman's errand boy has been to Rialto this day, and that little rapscallion told tales of great new lettering lovely as jewels. The folk gathered round to listen and the boy, who must have got his job with his silver tongue, had them eat from his hand and soon there were a score or so gathered round. He told them that his master has caught the hearts of the nobles, and at this the rabble all swoon with pleasure, second-hand pleasure, snobs that they are.

The boy boasted of the pains his master takes to make each single letter and each page, how he toils for all things to be perfect.

At this, I breathed a deep sigh of relief.

For it cannot last, not if Jenson is too slow with new things. You see, we of this town must have some new thing each day, be it good or bad, just so long as it is new. So Jenson has invented one new typeface. It has taken him years. It will take him years to do another one.

For an instance, today Jenson is completely forgotten by all those who gasped at the boy's tales yesterday. The talk is all of one red hen from San Erasmo Island.

This hen, the owner swears, was her best layer for two years. Then, last year, it turned itself into a cock! First it changed from cluck to crow, and then it grew a crest and strutted round the yard as if it were the king. The real cock was old and did not give a fight. But the next year, which is this one, a brave new cock took over the yard. Straight away the hen's crest moulted off, and this year it has made as many eggs as ever. The owner, a fat old island girl, brought her to market, sitting on her clutch. You could still see the stubs of the old crest poke out through the plumes on the top of its head. The crowds round that hen were bigger than the one round Jenson's boy the day before.

When I saw this my heart slowed to a quick tap. *All will be well*, I told myself. *My man will win; he has a new thing each day.*

I added: *And my man has this Catullus, the most new thing that there can be, for he is old and new at once and he knows, though he does not know, the heart of all of us.*

We still do not know if we shall print it, but I think we shall. I think we shall.

On the way home from market, I saw a most bizarre thing: my sister-in-law Paola in close colloquy with a red-haired man, one not of this town. So deep in talk was she that she saw me not, though I brushed past her handsome silken skirt, the gift, no doubt, of her new husband, Johann di Colonia.

Aha! I said to myself, *That Paola disposes of her husbands so fast she must line up the next one while still honeymooning with the last.*

I turned up my nose and marched past without showing her that I'd caught her out in her intrigues.

At dinner last night, I told my man with satisfaction: 'The word at Rialto is all about the red hen from San Erasmo. They have already stopped talking about Jenson.'

I did not mention Paola and her red-haired man. I could not think of a decent way to put it, which would not distress him. Best to talk of the decline in wonder about Jenson, and forget her.

The relief on his face was reward enough for all my spying and prowling in the stinking streets of the market. I'm determined, too, that there's more to be found out, and more to be done about Jenson, and that I am the one to do it.

Chapter Two

*. . . and she reared his infancy
on the perfumed juices of flowers.*

Felice asked: 'Why have you conceived no children, Sosia?'

'I don't know. I take no precautions against it. I just don't seem to need to.'

'You know about these things?'

'Well, if I was to follow the advice in Rabino's books! – I've looked in there. It's all most amusing . . .'

Felice raised an eyebrow encouragingly. Sosia continued.

'Avicenna, one of his favourites, says that we should avoid simultaneous spendings – and that afterwards I should jump violently seven times backwards to dislodge the seed. I'm also supposed to insert a pessary made of colocyth, mandrake, sulphur, iron dross and cabbage seed mixed with oil. There's another one, Albert the Great, a Dominican, from two hundred years ago, who says that women should spit three times into the mouth of a frog, or eat bees, so as not to become pregnant.'

Felice was laughing; Sosia kept talking.

'Then there's Arnold of Villanova. He says that women who don't want to conceive should drink water in which the blacksmith's forceps have been cooled. Where I come from, the Serbian women dip their fingers into the first bathwater of a baby. The number of fingers dipped is to indicate the number of years of barrenness they want. Rabino has other things – goats' bladders and some herbs. He gives them to poor women who cannot survive any more brats or cannot feed the ones they have.'

'This does not explain why you're barren, though? I wonder why it has not happened. You make love like a printing machine, relentlessly stamping yourself on men, like a press! A faultlessly efficient contraption. It's ironic that you cannot seem to utter a page of your own.'

Sosia gave up. 'It would be – if I gave a bite of my nipple for irony or babies. But I don't.'

She was dressed now and stood at the door, slipping her ledger into her sleeve.

'Any new entries?' asked Felice. 'Why am I not in there?'

Sosia blushed.

I could not be seen to ask about his private doings, so I had my friend make enquiries for me. Caterina di Colonna, who reigns at the Sturion, hears everything with her morning deliveries. The news that is fresh at Rialto by nine of the morning is already stale at her inn, where it was brought in with the milk at dawn.

Jenson is not so perfect after all! He has lived here two years and already there are four bastard children born to whores and nuns of this town.

So this Jenson has no fond wife at home, to listen to his worries. He simply buys a whore for her kind of company, and leaves her. He promises, apparently, to provide for any babies in his will, when he dies. He must think this sees off any demands of the heart, and at least it stops the nuns from drowning the little ones.

It made me fume that he had been so fecund here when my man and I had yet to make a child. News of Jenson's babes made more hasty my desire for my own. An heir for the *stamperia*! A loved and legal son! With passion, and with flesh-and-blood, we would defeat the Frenchman. Jenson, who works for abstractions, lives life obscurely as if behind a pane of clouded glass, would not be able compete against that!

I like to think I know when and how we made our son.

I have found *some* good in those heaped scripts my man brings home to ponder as to whether he should print them or not. When he's at the *stamperia* I sit in his study and read. The ones I like best are the marriage manuals that tell how to do all things properly in the bedroom. My man need not know it, but I read all these books, more carefully than he does.

I'm no great lover of books – for I think real life lies in the heart, the home, and the town squares – but in *these* texts I have faith. The books about how to give birth to the right baby and no other.

I did all the things to make the child male. What my man wished now Jo had gone was an heir for the *stamperia*, a little boy to take around the town and show him off. Something Jenson would never do with his bastards.

The act of love took place, as laid down in the texts, one day at dawn in a cooler month. I took pains that we wore nightcaps to keep the heat in: the books teach that seeds and juice must be kept hot and fresh on their trip to the parts where they join. My man lay on top for this is the best stance for the making of sons and I made sure that we gazed deep in each other's eyes all through the act. This brought the scales of our souls in the right tilt.

In the texts, I read sad tales of begettings gone wrong. Some men cannot wait until dawn when the food of the night meal has made its way to the home of the seed. Just one hour before dawn, a spark of too-quick lust will make a girl. Worse still, it can take place that a boy is born who should have been a girl, walks and talks like one, and wants to love his own kind. It's a risk.

The rich of the town go to the bad, weaken and die out, for they do not bide how it must be done! They dine luxuriously, drink wine, then go to bed for slow acts of love just when the seed is at the most weak. They have daughters. The poor, on the other hand, grow sons by the treeful for they come home, eat a good simple meal and are asleep so fast they do not blink. In the dawn, when rest has been had, they turn to their wives full of vigour and strong ripe seed and get sons on them, of course.

I bless this time that most of our kind, and the wives too, are taught to read. Those who row or who sell fish or love do not read, of course, but those of us who have a house, a life, a man – we do. I think that means one third of the town could buy my man's books and I wish with all my heart that they would do so, for how else shall we two feed and raise the son I read all those books to get?

Bruno's sparrows did not breed.

But he could not bring himself to throw away their unhatched eggs. Instead he blew their rotted meat from tiny holes, and their shells became the start of a collection. Now he hunted eggs with a passion. Eggs and feathers of the lagoon birds; the white and grey plumes of the herring gulls, the dark cap feathers of the black-headed gull, the swarthy, greasy tail-feathers of the cormorant. When he could, he went to *terraferma* and haunted the rivers for kingfishers.

While he was away, Sosia spent more time with Felice. She was infuriated to learn that Felice called on Gentilia at Sant 'Angelo. Apart from anything else, such wasted time might have been spent with Sosia herself.

'I didn't know you'd even met her.'

'Many times. Bruno takes me to see her. Sometimes I even go on my own.'

Sosia's face was suffused with dark colour. 'To see *her*? She's not a person. She lives through others, not for herself. Not that she'll ever find a man of her own. I heard she's ugly as a badger.'

She awaited endorsement of this comment, but Felice did not give it. Sosia blanched. Was Gentilia, after all, beautiful? She had not noticed Felice dismissing the concept of Gentilia's beauty with a flicking finger. Fixed upon his face, she'd missed his gesture.

Felice mused, 'Perhaps that's why Bruno looks haunted. Gentilia's living on him, like a growth of vine on a tree, parasitically. He always looks ten years older after he's been to her. He's grateful for her love, I think, but he doesn't look well on it.'

'I think in his heart he must hate her! She wants him too hard, and he feels the pressure.'

'You mean she wants him in a wrongful way?' asked Felice, his brows arching with surprise. Sosia noted with pleasure that she had all his attention now.

He mused, 'Now I think about it, she always was a libidinous little girl. How old was she when I first met her? Twelve? No, littler, littler,' he insisted, patting the air down beside him.

'Even then, she would touch herself, a little too often, in places where it is not done. Bruno never wanted to admit it, but even as a child she made difficulties for him.'

'It's just as I said, then, about her? I knew I was right.'

'The family all thought that inconvenience would be bred out of her. They assumed the convent would bestow purity on her. Bruno's relatives had no idea of what Sant' Angelo di Contorta is about.'

'Some can never have purity,' said Sosia, significantly. 'There are things against it . . .'

Felice passed smoothly over the possibility of her confiding in him.

'You may be right about Gentilia. Take away the downcast eyes, the circumspect words, the seamless form underneath the grey dress, and what have you got: another ravening woman with her stinks and desires oozing at the same time. And babies dropping out of her.' Felice looked at Sosia mockingly.

She smiled. It was good to hear Felice insult Gentilia. It established the bond between herself and the scribe: two canny conspirators against undesirable men and women.

He swiftly fractured her fantasy. 'Wendelin's wife though, now she's different. Even though she's huge with child, she's an utter peach, a little apricot. Perfect, almost as Bruno's perfect. And she hates me, which I love. She crackles with it.'

'I hate you too,' offered Sosia, forcing her mouth into a grin.

It was possible to live modestly and piously on Sant' Angelo di Contorta. The wild girls kept together; those few who wished to follow a genuine calling were ostracised or ignored. Sant' Angelo was a place of pleasure and the pleasure-expert nuns knew that such a thing should not be forced. Any procuring that was done was usually with at least the passive consent of the nun or the foundling girl concerned.

At the age of seventeen, Gentilia Uguccione herself was still, unwillingly, pure, unable to understand her exclusion from the happy wanton life of the convent. As a result, she had become excessively withdrawn. She was so reserved it was impossible to say whether she was pretty. She was not, but she had found a way to preserve the ambiguity of the question. She always turned her head away in conversation with strangers. There was something so sincere about her self-deprecation that it did not even attract the men who came whistling through the nunnery looking for virgins or at least girls who could put up a creditable performance of being inexperienced. Gentilia dressed younger than she was. She framed her dormouse cheeks with ringlets coaxed round her fat fingers. She had cultivated a bow to her lips like that of a little noble girl she'd once seen in a portrait.

All her features were like Bruno's, but each had grown porcine as if she straddled the orders of the animal kingdom between her brother and a pig. Her nostrils, for example, on close inspection recalled Bruno's, but her nose was embedded so deeply in her fatty cheeks as to make it resemble a tiny snout. Her chin curved sweetly like Bruno's, but it was unfortunately one of several. She had Bruno's shapely mouth, but a slight retraction of the gums exposed more of her teeth than could be considered attractive. The silky wave of Bruno's hair was bristly in Gentilia's.

Gentilia liked to linger among the praying parrots in the main courtyard, bent over her lace, picturesquely, as she saw it. She pretended not to hear the masculine voices or to see the shadows of their acts of debauchery falling on the convent walls in the evening light. She sat pleating her thread and tying her knots, spinning cobwebs of white that spread over her legs, which were straight and shapeless as the columns of an old church.

Gentilia was as singular in her handiwork as she was in her virtue. Sant' Angelo was not known for its domestic arts. The convent's output of lace barely supplied the robes and linen of its own priests or the altar cloths of its church. Gentilia's work was often seized from her hands when finished and paraded before the visitors, as if this little display of maidenly application might prove the virtue of the disgraced convent, or perhaps, more practically, to stimulate the jaded palates of the men who came there: those who sought the stimulus of a sense of violation were pleasurably agitated at the sight of the snowy lace, though not at the vision of the stolid little lace-maker.

Gentilia was safe from the depredations of such men. Added to her shyness was the fatty sheen of the middle class on her skin. Any Venetian could read her ancestry in Gentilia's freckled cheekbones and the broad camber of her hips: she had come from robust stock, and not the small effete blood-pool of nobility, known for its feverish sensuality and nonchalant disregard for morality. A noble girl gone to the bad was what the lechers coveted above all.

And yet Gentilia could still disturb a male visitor to the convent.

When she left the room, he would catch a glimpse of her legs – a long glimpse, too long to be accidental – which descended without a hint of taper into her stout shoes. The calves were surprisingly hairy and hideously marked with mosquito bites that had been violently scratched until they blistered. The islands were always haunted by mosquitoes, the visitor would remember, but he could not evade another thought: the well-known Venetian dictum that those whose blood was voluptuously charged attracted the most mosquitoes. A plethora of mosquito bites was the surest indication of multitudinous desires.

Summer has come again. The sun scolds my man's ear-tips till they glow red. On days and nights that are too hot to breathe we go out to sea. Since I fell with child, I feel this need, for the sake of my blood, which must have salt air, and my nose, which must be cleaned by it, and most of all for the sake of my eyes, which must rest on it. Now that I am growing a creature inside me, I need some relief from our town's lace of stone and humps of arch and snarls of stone beasts. While they do please the eyes with joy, so at the same time they tire them out – in a good way, of course, as an act of love with a sack of twists and turns does wear a soul out, even though it is with too much good.

So we go out on the water in a boat. Sometimes we take to the canals and at high tides the water lifts the boat so high that we must lie flattened on our backs as we pass beneath the bridges. We paddle the underbelly of the bridge with our hands to help the boat through, and sometimes the cool stone grazes the plump egg of my upturned belly.

Most times we go to the islands, where live the monks and nuns, those strange folk who choose to be closed up with God. Or not closed up, as the case may be, for there are many who go to the bad and are worse than all. It's here, in this sea, they say, that float the babes, those done to death by the nuns at night, as if God snores and prefers to know nought, like the men who begot those poor babes, some on whores, some on nuns.

And when the babes end up like this, you tell me if it's better to have a nun or a whore as your ma?

I did not my own self ever see one yet but I do hear a lot of tales from those who know a man who did, and so on. But there come to the market the same tales more and more, and I start to think there's some truth in them. They say that these little ones are born on the sea and are in fact in part, because of this, fish. That they have small gills in their necks and small fins on their backs. Some have tails. They float as if they fly, with wings like white-and-pink birds; they have blue eyes not brown, for they're babes of the sea. Sometimes a fisherman will bring a new merbaby to Rialto and the whole town is hushed with horror before we start again with nervous gabbling. But mostly the fishermen leave them where they find them, and do not mention it. We do not want to be reminded of them or their fate.

Bruno's sister Gentilia is a nun at Sant' Angelo, yet she is pure, I'm told. I have not met her. Bruno seems embarrassed about her, though he loves her. (Poor Bruno, he has become so thin! When he comes to our home I try to feed him up, put plates of delicious food in front of him. 'Take the wrinkles out of that belly!' I say, and he blushes. From this, I know that woman of his has no humour to her, or at least none where he's concerned, and indeed he has become most direfully earnest these days.) Even though we are like family to him, Bruno does not ask us to meet his sister and she remains in seclusion, given up to God, and shall never know the joys of love or motherhood. Poor girl. I also heard that she's not handsome, so she can have known only half an existence in Venice, where beauty is everything.

How different life can be!

I carry my own babe like a good joke inside me.

I am never sick; I eat what I wish, just twice as much as before. All the time I am full of joy, for I know he shall be a boy. I know that my man shall soon feel that he once more has male kin; that Johann has come back to him in a tiny form. I know he will be a good baby, just as I know that, if he grows up, he will be a good man.

While I still carry him inside me, I have taken myself to the market to buy us a particular cat. I came home with one who was grey, with stripes and a pink nose, green eyes, and small sag in his paunch. Most important, on his forehead was the 'M' mark all tabbies have, to show they were chosen by Mary to soothe the baby Jesus in his crib. The fishwife who sold him told me that he'd served her well with all young ones.

Now it is too late to think it, I have finally become a little afraid to give birth to a son of a man from the North. I am a small Venetian woman with plump hips but my bones are so delicate, like a bird's. He's a huge tall man with great long bones. What if I should come to bed of a monstrous great babe who would split me down the middle?

Another fear has haunted me all along: I am not ready to be my matron-self. I'm not ready to lose my own self in order to be someone's mother. I fear that in the moment of birth my soul shall go into my baby and I shall be no more.

Chapter Three

Hey girl!
You, without a nice nose,
without a pretty foot
or long fingers,
or a dry mouth
or a pleasing tongue . . .
Does the province tell you that you are beautiful?
Does it compare you with my Lesbia?
Times must be bad and blind.

A plague of baby corpses had haunted the foreshores of Venice for many years. It was not at all unusual for the fishermen to dredge up a few extinct little beings along with their catch, particularly in the waters around Sant' Angelo di Contorta.

A few months after she encountered Rabino Simeon, Gentilia Uguccione had been called to the convent's mortuary. A lone nun, unnaturally blonde and thin as a street cat, awaited her impatiently.

'I hear you can sew,' the nun said abruptly.

'Yes, a little.'

'Can you sew one of these?' The nun held up a tiny winding sheet, ragged at its edges. 'It's for one of those,' she added, pointing to a dead baby, pebbly eyes ice blue, laid out on one of the slabs.

'I – I – think so,' stammered Gentilia.

'Good,' said the nun. 'I hope you're fast. We need a lot of them.'

And so Gentilia became the shroud-stitcher of Sant' Angelo di Contorta. Her long days became industrious. The blonde nun had been right: the corpses were many.

The blonde nun, who never identified herself, gradually became less abrupt with her. After six weeks, she seemed to realise that Gentilia's discretion could be relied upon, or perhaps she had simply heard the truth: Gentilia had no friends to gossip with.

The corpses were so many that at times the blonde nun also took up her needle, swearing as she pricked herself. To pass the tedious hours, she told Gentilia the story of each baby, and if she did not know it, she made it up.

Some, she knew, had died naturally. There were others who had, according to the popular imagination, been murdered by witches, who consumed little souls merely by placing their hands upon them. After a minute under a witch's finger, a healthy baby would commence to perish from a wasting disease. 'Witch-eaten,' lamented the mothers, watching their little ones slip away. They sometimes brought them to the convent to be blessed, though such babies could never be saved.

Gentilia could not hear enough of these stories. She plied the blonde nun with questions in relentless pursuit of inconsequential details until her inform-ant grew bored and stopped the interrogation.

Gentilia continued her researches elsewhere, demanding answers of Felice and Bruno when they came to see her. They tried to laugh at her dark ques-tions, but she would not be shrugged off. In the end, Felice undertook to instruct her in what she wished to know, to spare Bruno the difficulty of it.

Such strange things Gentilia asked! Felice was astonished at the slant and direction of her curiosity. From somewhere she'd acquired smatterings of witch-craft and worse. The crude and simple facts of life interested her not at all; she wanted to know only about unnatural practices.

He did not scruple to indulge her, finding amusement for himself in the lurid tales he told her. Sometimes he repeated whispers from the taverns; other times he used his own invention.

Thanks to Felice, Gentilia now knew that some witches would exert their horrid powers by measuring the swaddling with their forearms and the palms of their hands.

'Ah yes, Gentilia,' he sighed, 'any witch who wants to devour a child, simply makes certain signs over it, saying "God bless this little *bocconcino*," *this little mouthful*, and there's *that* child consigned to a slow death to feed an evil old woman and her cat.'

Remembering Felice's description, Gentilia shivered pleasurably, and hunched over her sewing.

In the event it was not so disagreeable.

My belly was no bigger than any Venetian belly. The midwife was kind and good and the babe slipped out of me in just a few hours that I had rather forget. There was never any danger, though the midwife had, as usual, prepared the syringe of holy water to baptise him in my womb if it looked that he might die before he made his way outside me. She'd stopped at San Giacometo on her way to our house to have it blessed and when she arrived she put it down beside my head as if it might comfort me in my travails. It did not! It made me fight! I kept looking at it, and saying to myself: No! She will not need to use it! The babe shall be born, and I shall live and we shall have no need of that holy water.

For I knew that if I died in childbirth then I would become one of the *fade*, the beautiful women in white who haunt young girls, promising them beauty like their own.

The midwife sent my man away. He did not wish to leave me, but the birthing room is said to be unwholesome and no place for men. I missed him all through the bad hours. When I have a pain in the gut from too many *vongole* or mussels, only he knows how to hold me to make the pain go away. He rubs my belly with slow round movements until I fall asleep, the way he did when I was poisoned with too much cream in the Alps.

In my travails, I cried out his name again and again.

Such was the pain of our son being born – it seemed that only my man's arms around me and his breath on my neck could take it away. And that gentle, sacred look in his eye, such as he always has, when he beholds me. I saw it soon enough when I handed him our son. Then he did not know where to look – at this new priceless treasure or at me.

When I myself first gazed on our son, it was with a pang of fear. I checked swift and quiet to see if he were witch-eaten or jaundiced, or if he bore a mark of the Devil. No, he was perfect in every detail. Just an artisan's small copy in flesh of my man – the same chicken-fluff hair and blue eyes and the same shapely buds of privities all rendered in miniature. He had my little nose, perhaps, and most certainly my lips, for from them came not cries but tiny laughs.

In spite of that, we called him Giovanni, after his solemn uncle. At least I call him Giovanni. My man calls him 'Little Johann'. We gave him both names at his baptism. Many of this town believe that the power to see ghosts belongs only to those children whose godfathers have stumbled over their creed at the font and so I practised Bruno till he was perfect in every word and he said the words without a fault.

In making a babe, I did not lose myself, as I had feared. Now I have my grown-up matron-self, and she rejoices in the baby, and I have my lover-self, who rejoices in my man, who loves me not less but more for I have brought him the gift of a son. And then there's my quiet spirit-self, who knows that there are hurtful things that are not of this world, and respects them, and will keep her new family safe from them, at all costs.

He's a proper child of Venice, our son.

By day he laughs and prattles. But by night, when he cannot sleep he cries fit to wake the dead. Neither the taste of my milk, nor my little finger in his mouth, nor my lips on his hair, nor the rock of my arms can still him. My man cannot quiet him, not with his strange sweet baby songs from the North (which he does not sing very tunefully, but with great tenderness) or the way he has in which he makes a crib of his two huge hands and holds the babe up to God, like an offering. That serves sometimes, and the crib is full of laughs and then, soon after, sweet little snores. But it does not help when our son wakes in the dark of the night, full of fear, as if he has heard in his dreams that a bad time has come, that the witches are clamouring after his toes and there will be no more milk or love in this world for him. I see that the night terrors of Venice were born in him, as they were in me.

So on those nights, when we hear that hopeless tone to his cries, we pull apart (slowly) and rise from our bed, saying not one word, for we both know what we must do. My man goes straight down the stairs to get our cloaks and his oars (we do not pause to dress, just pull the cloaks on top of our nude backs) and I go to our son, change him to dry wraps, and take him down to the door and out to the boat which by that time has come to wait for us with its red lamp lit and my man's face all white as curd under his hood in the moonlight.

I slip in to the boat with the babe in my arms and I place him in a box at the prow. As soon as he sniffs at the wood and the lamp oil he grows more quiet, his screams turn to sobs and he points his toes up to the stars and stares up at them; his eyes still glisten with old tears. He paddles his feet as if he wants to drive the boat up to the silver sparkles in the sky now.

When we leave the shore my man gives a small push with his free leg, just like a gondolier, but once that's done it seems that the sea is in charge of us. It's as if it's not my man who poles through the waves but the waves their own selves who pass our boat one to the other one.

And so we set off down the dark canals. My man poles well, taught by the *stamperia*'s boatman. I sit at his feet, with one arm hooked round his knee and I stroke it soft, soft, and sometimes turn my nose to push at it like a cat will push his muzz at one who sleeps when it's time that a cat should be fed.

The little silvery boat cleaves its prow through the water, like a slim hand through a vat of squid ink. There's no noise save for the waves and our three breaths: my man's quite hard, for he poles with all his strength, mine soft and the babe's little tearings of sob and sigh.

All lie stretched in quiet sleep in each house. There's not a footstep, not a voice: just the waves at play, lively as young mice. Sometimes we stray out to sea, even as far as the island of Sant'

Angelo di Çontorta, but when I see its silver shape against the sky, I beg my man to turn back. It seems to be tempting evil fate to bring a young babe near that dreadful place.

One night, returning, I glimpsed a sight most strange. In a dark corner, near San Salvador, I saw a woman whispering to a man. *Illicit lovers*, was my first thought, *and old enough to know better*, for I could see that neither of them was in his first youth. They stood with their hands on their hips, at elbow distance, as if to deny any intimacy, but why else should they be there at that time of night?

Then a shaft of light from the moon crossed their two faces and I saw they were those of Paola di Messina and the red-haired man I'd seen before.

So Paola misbehaves herself already, and she not long remarried. For shame.

I opened my mouth to tell my man, but it came to me how such looseness in the wife of his dear brother would pain him, so I closed it into a kiss that I pressed on his knee, soft and ticklish as rabbit down.

When we were home, and the baby safe abed, I made good the promise of that kiss.

'Does Jenson have this?' I asked my man when we were panting afterwards. Then I was sorry, for at the mention of the Frenchman in the midst of all our pleasure, his face turned dim and doleful.

Then he lay with his profile instead of his lips to me. I saw despair in the slope of his nose and only half the glitter of his eye.

My small campaignings to do with Jenson do not yet bear fruit. I have started a rumour that his success is ill-founded, or rather founded on ill-deeds. Before he became a printer he was a maker of coins. So when he claims to be selling books in their hundreds, in fact he is quietly smelting the coins with which to pay for new materials. And everyone knows that the materials for printing and for making coins are exactly the same: even I can recite the list of metals that go to make the dies for both type and money. They are identical.

Nothing succeeds like success in Venice. I have hinted that Jenson finds us too gullible in this direction. Nothing enrages the Venetians more than to be thought less wily than a Caliph from Constantinople. And thus, at Rialto, am I stirring my hot stew of little whispers against the Frenchman.

Chapter Four

Do you believe that I could abuse my love, my life,
who is dearer to me than both my eyes?
I could not do so.
Nor, if I could do so,
should I love her so desperately.

My man often speaks of a most wondrous sad-eyed *Madonna* at the home of Domenico Zorzi. It's rare for folk such as us to see Bellini's great works. The nobles keep his paintings for their private devotions. But my man once took me to Bellini's studio and I can never forget the faces I saw there. Of course I am newly a mother myself, and his *Madonnas* turn me inside-outwards.

Those *Madonnas* of Bellini's are so . . . how to say it? I see now that those who own them have no need to go to church. They just kneel down in front of his Mary or Christ Child and it is an act of love for God. That is how good they are, and how full of what is holy.

He has this way, you see, with the small parts of the scene. The foot of the Christ Child will rest on a ledge low down. This means those sweet pink toes are in our world and you feel you might put one to your lips and kiss it, or bury your nose in a crease of His fat little leg and smell its babe-smell like mice and eggs and sweet liquor . . .

It is quite a shock that Christ is in your world and you are in His. The space between you and God is small and you can reach so close to the whole tale, the babe's vile death, and you think how, those pink toes will one day hang down bleeding from the strut of a cross. You feel God as you feel your own teeth and the night crust on your eyes. You are part of Him and He is part of you.

Once you are drawn into his art, Bellini makes you feel more things too. You see from Mary what takes place if you are near to God in the flesh. Where her hands touch the Christ Child, the tips of her fingers turn the pale rose tint of dawn. I felt like that, a soft buzzing in my hands, when I first held my tiny son.

Then again, in the dread scenes at the end of His life, you see his Mother kiss the face of His grown corpse. When I look, I know in my bones how I would feel to hold my son or my man that way. Of course, I would howl, but poor Mary's tears are killed in her eyes. She must hold in her own grief for it is the grief of the world she bears, not some little sadness just for her own self. And yet it is personal to me, too, when I behold it.

There are other paintings in Bellini's studios but I like them not at all. Allegories, they are, and full of witchery and evil. I peered at them, and turned my head away as if I had smelled something bad. Such twisted little children, such devilish men emerging from conch-shells, such yellow-skinned hags pretending at beauty!

My man used to go often to Bellini's studio, for Giovanni is the closest thing he has to a friend in this town. But these days the business ties him to his desk with chains of lead and he never leaves it, except to come home to me, or at least the shell of him comes home, for I believe he leaves his soul in the *stamperia*.

Sosia watched Bellini dip his paintbrush into the liquid vermilion. His hand never hovered; he always reached directly for the colour he needed as if picking the most obviously perfect rose from a bush. She stared at his mild face, pointed and pale, drained of vivacity because overburdened with sensibilities, devoid of the egotism that believes in its own personal beauty and therefore projects it disarmingly upon even plain features.

Bellini is not like other men, she thought. *He has a face that would not rasp against a woman's cheek, or stuff itself with sausages when it was time for love, nor gaze out of the window instead of at me. He almost has no face because it is a face merely to look out of; not to look at. From those eyes he collects beauty and passes it on through paint.*

She sniffed. There was a strong smell of vinegar, of white lead and verdigris fermenting together. Bellini always painted white lead over the gesso with which he prepared his boards, to stop any light being absorbed. It was *all* to be refracted.

How would it be to lie with a man like that; entirely unselfish? Not whining about love all the time like Bruno, not scrabbling clumsily at her skin as if to release the incense of love like Malipiero, not cold like Felice – always looking over her shoulder at his own more gorgeous reflection in the mirror. No, Giovanni would hold her as tenderly as a bladder of lapis pigment; he would unroll her like the little gland of paint; he would gently squeeze the sweetness out of her.

Giovanni was gazing at her belly now; measuring the heat of its yellows and pinks. She imagined that superb hand on her stomach; pressing it slightly.

I could love this man, she thought, *I could love him the way I love Felice, but he would be worth it.*

'Please turn your head a little to the right,' said Bellini politely.

'May I look now?' asked Sosia.

Giovanni did not notice the butter, honey and sugar in her normally astringent voice. He said, 'I apologise, Sosia, you've been standing a long time. Let us break for a while, so you may rest. I'm almost finished with you, in fact.'

He carefully turned the easel to face her. Immediately, she stiffened and her lips became rigid. She looked quickly away and reached for her robe. She could not confront this painting without the protection of her clothing.

He had painted her sag-belly and thigh-thick. He had pulled her nose out like a handle and then pushed it a little to one side. He had pursed up her eyes and painted an idiot grin on her mouth. Her breasts were like hard shells glued to a breastplate; even her hair was coarse as hemp.

Bastard! Old fish-head! In disarray, she tried to select the most potent insult for him. *I shall never pose for you again* was what she wanted to say, and was about to tell him, but the words would not come out. They seethed at the top of her throat, acidly. Instead, as always in moments of extreme anger, she resorted to her own language.

'*Krvavu ti majku jebem*, fuck your blood-splattered mother,' she hissed aloud.

Giovanni flushed. Though he did not understand a word, Sosia's feelings were clearly imprinted on her scarlet face and narrowed eyes.

'Did you after all expect me to paint you *like* a Madonna, my dear?' he asked, gently. 'You know this is not a portrait, but an allegory, do you not?'

She shook her head, vehemently, stumbling from the dais. One of the child-models tottered on his pedestal. She turned and lifted a bare leg to kick him.

Giovanni said, 'Do it, if you feel you must. But remember you were a child once and I see from your face that you know what it is to be kicked.'

In that moment she hated him with a pyramid of hatreds, built on a base of rage and disappointment, narrowing to a sharp point of loathing.

Giovanni, she realised, thought he might sanction her anger, as if it were a small tame thing to be managed.

She withdrew her foot. Kicking the *putto* was not the way to hate Bellini. She knew what she must do: make something ugly.

Sosia prickled with malice. She felt a sense of returning from a journey. The hours of posing, during which she'd thought of loving the artist, had been a brief excursion to another world. Now she had come home to her own.

She had already realised something: this was not Bellini's fault. He was merely a conduit, permeable to beauty or allegorical messages to make the world more beautiful. The corruption in this canvas was Felice's gift, Felice who had stood prattling malevolently in front of it day after day while Bellini painted, not because he loved her company but because Bruno might at any point arrive.

When my man leaves for work each dawn I turn this thought in my mind, like a leaf in my hand: *he is mine, he is mine, he is mine.*

I miss him sorely, but I have my duties to keep me occupied. I have my missions to Rialto, where I continue to dispense hints, like drops of lemon juice, about Nicolas Jenson and his history as a coin-maker. I find the rumour has swelled and spread, even in my absence. Others have taken it as their own, and puff it up with their own ideas. Good. I have other things to do.

I tend to our son and our new cat, whom I must tend more than the son for he has in his small head such brains on fire with the wish of things. That fishwife sold me shoddy goods in him. That Madonna mark on his forehead is a fake! He cares nothing for the child; only for himself.

He sulks when I hear his cry and then hand him straight away a prawn or a piece of bread smeared with fish fat. He wants me to know he's finer than that. Sometimes – (I should know this without his telling me, he implies) – he cries out loud for the shine of my glass lamp or the soft fuzz on our son's arm. I myself, being a busy wife, have not time to take note of these special things, so he, the artist of the house, must do it for me: this is his point of view.

When he feels a lack of attention, he draws patterns in the tray where he dirts. He thinks he is the Bellini of cats!

So he maintains, but that cat has come to me with bad ways in his blood. He steals! Not such things as cats should steal, such as cheese or cream, but silk scarves and filches of lace and anything made out of sandalwood, which he will sniff for hours.

It's his habit to sit on a ledge above our door and cause passing folk to fall in love with him. He makes big eyes at them, opens his muzz to mew with no noise or he will stretch out a paw, so they crane their necks up to him. They want to stroke him, to feed him, some would die for him!

One time he stretched out his paws and took a man's hat. Then he jumped with it back in the house where he lay on it, probably for hours, till I found him. When I tried to take it from him he growled like a mountain devil at me, so I gave it up.

'Be ashamed!' I told him, but he looked no such thing.

This desire for things is for him a thing of need, not mischief. I've followed him and watched him hunt. When he sees a line of fine clothes out to dry, then his paws start to twitch. He hunts those clothes as if they were rats. He stalks, comes close, and springs – ten feet, twelve feet, even more for a scarf with cloth-of-gold trim!

When he gets to the high point, he grabs the thing he wants and beds in his nails and then waits for his own weight to drag the garment off the line. Sometimes he drops straight in the canal, but he cares not. He swims with his prize in his teeth to the shore and brings it to me to dry by the fire. He knows I will.

At first I thought these things were gifts for me, but it soon turned out that this was nôt so. The moment they're dry he takes them in his maw again and pulls them off to his own nest near the fire, which is as bright as Byzantium with cloth of gold and silks and so on. There he sits, pleased as God on the last day. When we come to him with our brows crossed, peering at his nest, he stays suave. We mumble some silly thing and back away.

We fear for the law for what could we say if the *Signori di Notte* received complaints, and so came here and found these things?

That our cat stole them?

In days when we were flusher in the pocket, and fuller with pride we might have laughed at this, but our sense of humour has been smutched with worry, like mending in the hands of a too-anxious maid.

Sometimes my man looks from me to the cat, and I can see in his eyes that he thinks there's some *imbroglio* between us, something Venetian, something feminine, something feline, in any case beyond him. Since I left him in Freiburg, he has these doubts of me, for there I showed him a part of myself he could not understand.

The sadness is that he sees my love of things between the lines as something that threatens us – my ghost stories from the market, for example, more often draw his frowns these days, though I see them as no less than our protection.

Bruno, aware of the kindly glances of Wendelin von Speyer, worked on the Catullus manuscript and it scoured him from the inside. To read Catullus was to call up inside himself the questions he came to work to try to evade.

Wendelin tried to cultivate a neutral attitude to Bruno at the *stamperia*, but the affection in his eyes was clear to everyone. Only his son or his wife could make him smile the way Bruno could. And Bruno had been chosen as little Johann's godfather.

Anyone with bad news for the printer would ask Bruno to transmit it, knowing that the blow would be softened by the young man's gentle delivery.

Bruno would come to Wendelin with the men's requests for holidays or an extra *stipendio* to cover medical expenses.

'You think this a worthy request?' Wendelin would ask.

Bruno would nod. He quickly learned to bring only such requests to trouble his *capo*, sifting them in his head before calling on Wendelin's attention.

Their evening lessons at Wendelin's home were a mingled pain and pleasure for Bruno. While his employers' grasp of the language improved steadily, the domestic joy of the household ate away at Bruno's envious soul at the same rate. He watched balefully as Wendelin's wife made clear her passion for her husband. When she looked at him, her eyes never wavered. She gazed at him softly and intensely. If the child meanwhile started to creep in the direction of mischief, she merely used the eyes in the back of her neck possessed by all mothers, remarking, 'Don't be thinking that the curse has dropped off that door handle, sweeting,' as the baby reached a tiny hand for a forbidden drawer behind her back.

Nor was Wendelin any less attentive to his wife. Bruno noted jealously each time he stroked his wife's flitting wrist, or caught her up in a sudden embrace as she passed. When she put on her cloak, Wendelin was always there to ease the golden bushel of her hair out of the collar, and smooth it down for her.

Bruno was grateful for Wendelin's kindness. He could not have said that he loved his employer, for these days Bruno thought of everything through his passion for Sosia. When he'd heard that Wendelin had lost his brother, one of his first thoughts was *has Sosia lost brothers, or sisters?* She had shrugged off his question.

Raindrops fell outside, hard and cold as pebbles. Inside the *stamperia*, the elbows of twenty men worked up and down.

Bruno read Squarzafico's introduction, marking the errors, shaking the crumbs from the soiled manuscript. He'd learned from previous Squarzafico submissions that these crumbs were particularly absorbent to ink. Enormous blots bloomed from them if they caught a drop from his own quill pen.

Valerius Catullus, lyric writer, born in the 163rd Olympiad the year before the birth of Sallustius Crispus, in the dreadful times of Marius and Sulla, on the day Plotinus [sic] first began to teach Latin rhetoric at Rome. He loved Clodia, a girl of high rank, whom he calls Lesbia in his poetry. He was somewhat lascivious, and in his time had few equals, and no superior, in verse and expression. He was particularly elegant in jests, but a man of great gravity on serious matters. He wrote erotic pieces, and a marriage-song to Manlius. He died at Rome in the thirtieth year of his age, with public mourning at his funeral.

Bruno's eyes strayed to vagrant words from the manuscript, from the proof pages upturned on his desk.

You ask me how many kisses of yours, Lesbia, will be enough for me?

and

she's the one who's stolen all of the allure from all of the rest.

There were parts that were less lyrical; descriptions of the impotent older man, for example,

softer than rabbit's fur, or goose down, or the tip of an ear . . .

So Catullus described Thallus, but Bruno turned away from the text, amusing as it was. He only wanted to read the Sosia poems. Silly! Did he say, in his mind, Sosia? Of course he meant the Lesbia poems, the love poems, the hate poems.

A sudden thought struck him and he rifled through the test proof pages. He clapped his hand on his forehead, scarlet with embarrassment. He'd sent for setting a poem in which the name 'Sosia' replaced Lesbia's! He had wasted time and Wendelin's money, and possibly revealed Sosia's name to the sniggering boys who fed the letters into the matrixes. It would only draw their attention more to his error when he asked them to correct it.

He wondered if Wendelin would really publish them or if he had set the editors this work merely to test his own nerve. Until the manuscript was fully set to type, they no more than toyed with it. Bruno knew all the risks they faced if they brought it out in print, and began to trade in it.

He knew the risks as they stood at that moment, that is.

Chapter Five

In the purse of your Catullus
are only cobwebs

Suddenly, Venice was emptied of coins. They bled from the city like drops from a holed bucket. For decades the Venetians had lusted for the picturesque tokens of their wealth. They hungered for poryphry, agate, and serpentine, for the relics of saints, for silver reliquaries to decorate their churches. There was only one way to pay for all these pieces of beauty: money. A pouch of silver for a Moor with a shipload of Asiatic silks. A sack of copper for a powerfully smelling monk with the mummified leg of little Saint Tryphon in his basket. A purse of gold for a hard-eyed marble merchant from Carrara. La Serenissima's few silver and copper mines were exhausted.

How silent was Venice without money! The jingling of coins seemed to vanish into memory.

At Rialto, rumours of counterfeit rose up and multiplied. There were whispers of midnight smeltings on the Fondamenta Nuova and a conspiracy to destroy the stability of the state and trick the honest citizens of their wealth. The few coins in circulation were examined under bright sunlight, sniffed at and bitten on. No one knew exactly what symptom of corruption they were looking, smelling or tasting for, but every coin was an object of suspicion.

A new rumour was distilled from the sweating stalls every day. The infamously subtle Milanese were said to be foisting a fake coinage on Venice. Other sources of the corrupt money were darkly hinted at: the Turk, the Genovese. The level of hysteria among the citizens was raised to an unendurable pitch. With no coins for food, people stopped buying books altogether. Wendelin and his men continued with their work, hoping for better times, or for the crisis to come to a head.

On 22 May 1472, a shopkeeper refused to accept money offered by a customer. Enraged at the implied insult, the customer drew a dagger from his robe and stabbed the shopkeeper to death.

Venice was paralysed by this new horror. The blood of her trade seized up at her heart. Fish were left to rot at Rialto because people dared not open their purses to buy it.

The next day the Council of Ten decreed that all silver coins be withdrawn from circulation. A new issue was struck, the *lira Tron*, named after the incumbent Doge, the ugly but genial merchant-noble Nicolò Tron, who had as much to lose as anyone from this strange coinless state of affairs.

But Venice still waited, unsure. Wendelin had never seen the city so quiet. It was as if she had fainted. In the silence of the formerly busy streets all he could hear now was the piping of caged quails. The Venetians were always inordinately fond of eating these plump-breasted little birds, who that year increased their life span fourfold, safe from potential purchasers until the *lira Tron* had proved itself a viable currency.

Then, against the counterfeiters, Nicolò Tron launched a reign of terror. Convicted forgers, he proclaimed, would be brought between the columns of the *Piazzetta*, to have their hands cut off and one eye gouged out. This punishment was inflicted on two alleged Milanese forgers on 29 May 1472. Soon forty-nine people had been arrested. Appeased with blood and mutilations, the Venetian public gradually calmed itself. The *lira Tron* had triumphed. Coins began to emerge again from silk purses and leather pouches. Foreign merchants heard the news and began to arrive in their ships once more.

But it was too late for the printers.

Since the currency crisis, those rumours Wendelin feared above all others had intensified. Certain whispers had emerged as battle cries now.

Wendelin's wife was also strangely silent, but he knew, from his men, what was being said at Rialto now. The printers had been implicated in the counterfeit scandal. They were too close to the forgers in the tools of their trade. It had suddenly become dangerous to be associated with the working of metals . . . the printer's *punzone* was almost identical to a coiner's die in shape and function. Even the metal used for casting type, the mixture of tin, lead and antimony, was said to resemble what was found in the crucibles of the captured counterfeiters.

None of the men could understand it, Wendelin least of all. How had the Venetian public suddenly become so interested in and so expert in such technical issues? The Venetians had never before shown curiosity about such unpicturesque processes as printing or casting, occupying themselves solely in matters of taste and style in the finished products.

Now everyone knew about the connection between the printers and the coin-makers, and everyone had a finger to point at the makers of books, or words to mutter behind their hands as he passed in the street.

At their home, Wendelin and his wife sat in silence. They had talked the subject dry, it seemed. But when Lussièta tried to refresh their conversation with a new ghost tale from Rialto, of a miraculous bird that could speak in the voice of malevolent souls long dead, Wendelin turned on her, holding up his hand, his voice unusually sharp.

'I suppose you think it is ghosts who are ruining me? You don't think I have enemies enough, talking evil and walking around in human skins, alive?'

Lussièta bowed her head and shot a sharp glance at a drawer in the cabinet where she kept her linen.

Wendelin, as always, suppressed an unreasonable pang of annoyance at the thought of the contents of that drawer. Lussièta folded their linen as logically as a birdwing but never in a straight, square German shape.

The Doge was besieged with badly spelled petitions for the printers to be exiled from Venice. And a new voice had emerged, sterner and more intemperate than any other. It was that of the cleric Fra Filippo de Strata. The counterfeit scandal had been a message directly from heaven, for a priest who hated printers.

Who are the authors of our troubles? he scribbled to the Doge, and anyone else who would read. *It is the drunken barbarians from the North. And why have they moved here, these brutish Germans? It's because excesses of venery agree much better with any constitution in our soft southern atmosphere than among the rough blasts of the northern winter.*

Yet the fleshpots of Venice are not enough for them. They graft themselves upon the town like maggots and set to work exhuming the filth of the past. Not only are they bringing forth the works of the pagans – full of errors – but they're driving the honest, pious, Venetian scribes into the streets where they must corrupt themselves with unholy works and God alone knows what other subsidiary sins.

Fra Filippo was a Dominican. He was an unattractive man – his face always looked as if it had just been plunged in cold water – but his fulminating sermons had made him a fashionable Sunday morning performer for the entertainment-hungry Venetians. Outside of the pulpit he was less beloved. His irascibility, and perhaps also his lingering personal fragrance of dried meats, had rendered him isolated in his own order. So, for a pittance, he and his assistant Ianno had attached themselves to the elderly Benedictine community of San Cipriano di Murano, where he'd been able to terrorise the frail inhabitants into submission.

Fra Filippo hated everything new: not just printing, but the new style of art, the newfangled organ music, the new interest in the literature of the pagan past, and even the new architecture delicately unfurling in Venice. From his roost on Murano, he watched with consternation the rise of Mauro Codussi's new marble building on the nearby island of San Michele in 1469. The Camaldolese, who had commissioned Codussi, were among the first customers of the German printing press, and one of the island's sons, Frater Nicolò da Malhermi, actually worked on an Italian translation of the Bible for von Speyer. Fra Filippo was horrified. Giving the people the Bible in their own language would confuse and deprave them, without priests like himself to filter and purify the interpretation of certain questionable passages.

Even more incriminating, in his eyes, was the printers' preferred choice of texts.

Heathen writers, he fulminated. *Pornographers, corrupters of the flesh. Greek and Latin eroticists foisted on the minds of the all-too-susceptible Venetian populace.*

God had struck down Johann von Speyer, Fra Filippo observed, triumphantly, but it appeared that his brother was hoping to keep the vile business alive.

Fra Filippo made one valid point amongst his ravings: the work of the early printers left them open for criticism. The editors were too busy to slow down and examine their texts minutely for errors. Blatant piracy of existing editions spread the inaccuracies further. Fra Filippo, who delighted in pedantry, was able to point out, in triumph, a multitude of errors that were fatuous, careless or simply ignorant.

He was, it must be admitted, something of an expert. He spent the proceeds of his collection plate freely, buying up the enemy. All books printed in Venice ended up on his desk, where he turned their pages with a pair of pincers, unwilling to touch the sin-soaked paper, spitting in vast trajectories as he came across yet another obscenity, profanity or scribal error. The lewdness and the inaccuracies all came from the same place, he asserted: the Devil's repository.

And yet the number of books in themselves, piled high on his floor, showed Fra Filippo the size of the enemy he faced.

Fra Filippo could *smell* printed books. Even when people kept them hidden up their sleeves, the subtle effluvia of the pages did not escape him, as savoury to his craggy nose as the death rattle of new carrion to the tufted ear of a vulture.

When a handwritten manuscript of Catullus had arrived on his desk Fra Filippo seized it with a cry, his small eyes round with horror. This was an urgent case, for his spies repeatedly told him that the brother of the deceased von Speyer was thinking of publishing the work. Fra Filippo spent the entire morning with it. As he read, little squeaks and groans escaped from him. He sat with his haggard member unaccustomedly smoothed and erect in his lap. He grasped his quill pen like a child its mother's hand in a tempest.

At the end of the morning, he showed the book to his assistant, Ianno.

'This is what we have to do battle against.'

Fra Filippo noted with distaste how the elderly dwarf was as bandy-legged as a three-poled *briccola* and how the light could be seen to shine between his legs in a way that was hardly Christian.

Ianno twitched his ears, above the left one of which he bore a most unusual and repulsive birthmark. The deformity was a limpet-sized clump of pink flesh, crimped and coiled like a walnut, resembling a tiny human brain. When he was excited, as now, it glowed and appeared to wriggle.

Fra Filippo tried not to look at it; it disturbed him, so he looked over Ianno's shoulder as his assistant lisped: 'Your honour, I should like you to know I have savagely scourged myself this morning, because I detected in my soul a desire to touch a printed book in the library and because I have found myself looking inside some of the printed books I bring daily into your study.'

'Quite right, Ianno, but perhaps you have been excessive. The blood on your tunic might seem blasphemous in that it resembles the blessed liquid soul of Our Lord in His difficulties. Now take this Catullus and read it for yourself.'

The next morning, Ianno reappeared, scarred and stained. As he spoke of the book, in a thickened voice, the brain above his ear glowed red as lava.

'It is indeed the work of the Devil.'

'It is the work of a many-handed Satan. And now there's a German demon who can reproduce this filth three hundred times at once. Imagine, Ianno,' his voice rose to an unlikely choirboy treble, 'that each one of those three hundred books might be read by a dozen men, this would mean more than three and a half thousand souls would be dirtied and sent to hell by virtue of this foul Devil's work of printing.'

'No amount of scourging, I fear, can expunge the evil this book has wrought on me, personally,' interposed Ianno, eagerly.

'And think, if this book were left somewhere a *woman* could find it? Think of the agitation of the womb it is designed to stimulate. Think of the lewd behaviour of such women, informed by this book.'

'I am thinking,' whispered Ianno, tightly. His left hand crept up, as it did in moments of stress, to fondle his little brain. Fra Filippo turned his head, feeling nauseated.

He read aloud:

> *Iuventius, if I was allowed to*
> *kiss those honey eyes of yours*
> *As much as I'd like to,*
> *I'd kiss them three hundred thousand times,*
> *And still not have my fill,*
> *Not even if that kissing was planted thicker*
> *Than stiffly curved corn husks in a field.*

Ianno moaned audibly. Fra Filippo brandished the offending page: 'I have occupied myself with some painful researches this morning better to understand these texts.'

Ianno wriggled in front of him. Fra Filippo wondered briefly if his assistant was verminous.

He continued: 'The strange thing is that *performing* oral or anal fornications was *not* immoral to the Romans, but by some strange pagan hypocrisy, submitting to either was thought a lapse.'

Ianno danced on one foot as if the other was scalded.

'I must leave you now, your honour. It is not possible for me to continue to breathe at this minute, without another scourging.'

Fra Filippo did not hear him, lost in his vitriolic ruminations. 'The grotesque fornications of the pagan gods – all kinds of bestiality! – it is all calculated to stimulate evil fantasies in those who are weak . . .'

Ianno squeaked, 'I must go now, really . . .'

'Fornicators, all of them. Their supreme God, Jove, what is he more than a supreme fornicator, rapist, adulterer?'

Ianno made indistinct noises, backing out of the room.

'When you return, we must start writing letters.'

Letters were written. In his scrofulous handwriting, Fra Filippo made a snowstorm of paper against Catullus. His pen, it seemed, was never still. There was not a nobleman in Venice who did not receive a personal missive denouncing the evil new work proposed by Wendelin von Speyer.

'Look to your sons!' thundered Fra Filippo. 'Look to their sheets and the guilty stains you will find there, if this kind of book is allowed to continue in Venice!

'Do you know that the young men go now to the Calle di Catullo near San Marco, and that they indulge in lecherous games there, in the name of the poet who has put these ideas in their minds. There they compete to spend their seed in the canals, and touch each other in an unclean manner. Even on the Sabbath they drink to Lesbia, the wanton heroine of the poems, and they seem to have found a foreign woman of Venice to personify her for them. This "Sosia", this double-woman, is toasted as the new Lesbia.'

'Let me deal with her,' growled Ianno, on listening to the first draft of this letter. 'I know some men . . .'

'Ah no, leave her for a while. She's useful for us, in a way, and in the meantime you can be sure she's spreading the pox among all our enemies.'

And he sent Ianno to the Rialto market, to spread rumours in the best possible way. That is, he had Ianno whisper, importantly, to the most garrulous of shopkeepers, 'Don't worry, there's no cancerous poison in the printers' ink.' At his sermons, he arranged for young men to heckle: 'Fra Filippo,' they catcalled, 'is it true that the printers use baby hair to make their paper?'

Fra Filippo's sermons were enlivened with a vivid repertoire of gesture. To emphasise a word he would draw his whole body back like a bow when slowly stretching an incriminating vowel, contracting his shoulders at the hissing final consonant, as if discharging a firearm. Those who mimicked him played an easy sport, but even those who had their fun with him unconsciously spread his message.

His voice was taken notice of. His campaign dovetailed most conveniently with the currency crisis. In catching the public mood, he raised his own profile and his power. His status was confirmed when the campaign began to show results. The rumours against the printers were transformed into lethal charges.

Three printers were arrested, a Venetian and two Italians from the mainland. To the printing houses came the *Signori di Notte*, with their chains. As yet, the German *fondaco* was left in peace: the Germans brought too much profit to the city. Too many noblemen were involved in German businesses and showed themselves intent on protecting their investments.

Domenico summoned Wendelin to his *palazzo* and soothed him with assurances. He was fascinated by Wendelin's ponderous German-scented vocabulary, and detained him for many minutes, so he could hear as much as he could.

Of course the man had no sense of the artistry in his presswork, being a foreigner and a German. For Wendelin, an alphabetical letter was a letter, not a small poem in its own right. A letter was a letter, and enough of them together made a sentence, and enough sentences together were a book. And a book was ducats in his strongbox. That was all. It would be simple to calm his commercial fears.

'No one takes this crazy priest seriously,' purred Domenico. 'And what does de Strata offer the city? You Germans have brought us wealth and efficacy beyond the powers of our own creation. Continue with your work. I shall tell you when it is time to be frightened, if that time ever comes.'

'What about the rumour that the printers are making the confect coins?'

'I wonder where that came from? So complicated! It cannot persist.'

'What about Jenson?' Wendelin asked. 'When this dies down, he'll still be here.'

Domenico looked displeased at the printer's lack of subtlety. He did not wish to acknowledge how he shared his patronage these days. He liked Wendelin. And he disliked being caught out in his duplicity.

'I imagine Jenson has his protectors. Nor does he take many risks. Think of yourselves. Remember I have your interests at heart.'

Wendelin repeated these words to his men at the *fondaco* and the men returned to work.

Meanwhile at his pulpit Fra Filippo looked down on his texts, his pale face appeared to be made of folded paper. His nose was just a pleat, his mouth a slot. From it issued the names of the men whom he sought to condemn.

Chapter Six

What an appalling and infidel book!
Which you must have sent to your Catullus
in order to finish him off . . .

My children, I come to warn you of a most vigorous uncleanness that has fallen upon us.

To the other afflictions that grip us – concupiscence, plague, the staggers in our cattle and the adoration of demons, I must now append a dread addition: books.

You may laugh at me, saying: 'Why, a book is just another soulless object, like a cabbage. How can a book be dangerous? Mere paper and board with a light coating of ink!'

And I will answer you that a book is more dangerous than Beelzebub himself. Mere paper and board, you say? No! A thousand times no!

You know not what you say about books, for you yourselves are already beguiled and seduced. A printed book is a triple-turned whore, a cheese full of maggots writhing invisibly! You, led astray by the lies of the printers, see it as a nourishing object; you take the tainted thing unto you, so close you fail to see the pestilence inside.

There are some among you who must hang their heads and admit that they have seen the manuscript of a filthy work by the pagan poet, Gaius Valerius Catullus. I know, my poor weak children, that there are copies of his viper-vile pages in Venice.

It is an unholy work, a lewd work, and a work with no merit whatsoever, which has gained a certain reputation by its power to titillate the low tastes of young men. For a hundred years this manuscript has been circulating in Italy, a monstrous apparition corrupting all who touch it. And now a greater danger awaits: I have heard that the barbarous German printers have taken it into their heads to print the book. In order to support their venal ambitions, they would spew out of their dirty little press not just one but three hundred copies at once.

Printing is quiet like a flood, but it wipes out God's work just the same, dragging decency in its wake, leaving the direful landscape of devastation, the wasteland that is sin, behind it, and the bleached wrecks of men grovelling in the mud. It is the front guard of a scurvy process that will completely secularise the book, making it wholly evil.

The book started as all goodness, with one human hand writing the word of God for the chosen to read. The scribes are good and innocent men; copying the pledges of God is their way of fighting the Devil. Scribes wrestle Lucifer word by word, refuting his rank outpourings by multiplying the pure utterances of our Lord. They toil not just with their fingers but their whole bodies! Do they care how their backs hurt, or their kidneys pain them cramped up in their bellies, or how their chests and shoulders knit together? No! They live only for the sweet relief of the moment when they trace their last lines and can offer their work to their Maker.

The printers, in contrast, do not lift their smallest finger to bring forth what they do. They merely shout for good hardworking Venetians to plough their lazy pages with ugly machinery. The egregious indignity of the actual work is beneath these arrogant Germans.

Now, born from the evil seed of these printers, there grow whole walls of scepticism, cynicism and profanity. When the books were all written by hand, perhaps one a year, the Mother Church could exercise her benign influence, and check the dissemination of heretical or subversive works, nip evil in the bud. Now the Devil's works are running out of control. Because of the printers.

You only have to read their own title pages to see how bad it is. Until recently, they rarely inserted a title page into a book, no doubt wishing to hide their shame in anonymity. But now their pride has grown gilded they're making their own page the showiest of the whole book, decorated with engravings and great flourishes of type. And how they fall over themselves to accuse each other and denounce one another! They claim that their rivals are producing texts that are merely tangled and contorted masses of corruptions. They condemn other printers for greed, by failing to undertake important corrections merely to save money. The truth is that no brawn-buttocked German printer will put accuracy or decency above profit. I see the true scholars among you nodding sadly at my words.

What is a printed book anyway? A black-spotted sheaf of beaten rag and rubbish masquerading as a friend! It is a finger-cutting, makeshift thing, full of errors both intended and unintended, and spitefulness, for those who make printed books do so because they have no decent work to do. Those who read them – the same applies.

What an act of arrogance it is to own a printed book! It positively encourages the vices of pride and sloth! When a novice asked the most holy Saint Francis if he might possess a psalter, the saint refused, saying most righteously, 'When you have got a psalter, then you'll want a breviary, and when you have got a breviary, you will sit in a chair as great as a lord, and will say to some brother, 'Friar! Go and fetch me my breviary!'

These printed books are as full of dirtiness as an egg is of meat. It is typical of our Germans that they think now to print the filthiest thing around – Catullus. This Catullus is an obscene bird of the night: let him fly out of Venice. Let us not bring on this town the shame of being the first to print his book. His is not the art of poetry; it is the art of brothelry.

To read Catullus is to drink to excess of a foul wine. It is enfeebling, it brings disgrace on the individual and his kin, and finally it corrupts even the water in the reader's mouth: he can no longer taste anything holy for his palate has been destroyed.

The publication of Catullus would be the opening of a sewer upon a clean stream, a suppurating lesion left without a bandage for the flies to feed on. It would be a bestial act performed in the open air where innocent women and children might be infected. The putrid indecorum of the work is nothing to the pride with which the poet and now – by association – the printer flourishes without shame, what are in truth nothing more than the clinical confessions of a depraved young man.

The reader would be hustled into the most squalid of bedchambers, stripped of his decent coverings and obliged to take part in acts of shame. For believe me, this is the kind of book which intimidates him into lecherous behaviours, even when he would prefer to be innocent.

You may tell me that Catullus is harmless: he writes of love and makes a little mischief with the bodily functions, that he lets us laugh and dissolves a few of the grey miseries of the day.

This is mere camouflage. Do not be deceived.

Saint Chrysostom condemned smutty songs as much more abominable than stench and ordure because we are not uneasy at such licentiousness; we giggle when we should frown, enjoy what we should abhor. So does Catullus too disguise his grime with humour.

To anyone who loves God, Catullus and all his brother poets of the pagan past are an abomination. Lucretius, Ovidius, Tibullus, Propertius, and worst of all Catullus – what are they but lovers and propagators of moral slime!

They wallow in their intemperate vice like swine in mud.

These books are the poisonous distillations of the Devil himself! And I quote from the learned Tertullian. 'Like the Devil, the Publisher set out to make the dose pleasant by throwing in a Cordial Drop to make the Draught go down. He even steals a few delicious ingredients from the Dispensatory of Heaven. When you see sweet words on a page, remember this! Look upon it only as Honey dropping from the Bowels of a Toad, or the Bag of a Spider.'

I come to the conclusion, as I must, that all books which contain material not to be found in the Holy Bible are dangerous, and those which contain material which is in the Holy Bible are unnecessary, for you have your priests to tell these things to you, in the pure ways of the church.

So let us sweep these corrupt and greasy papyruses into the dust and stamp on them.

And with them, let us get rid of the printers, those misbegotten creatures! Consider the sordid channels through which you get their books! They go from barbarous German printer, to corrupt merchant, to dealer, to small shops in dark alleys. You buy them not in the open air, in decent places, but in such bleak holes as you would visit to buy a concoction to murder your mother.

And when you touch them, the filthy black ink leaves stains on your hands.

And I tell you, that you must be vigilant. My sources tell me that in this year of Our Lord 1472 it has already happened that printed texts have exceeded in number those good books written by the hands of scribes.

Look to your hands, my people, look at them. Are they stained with this new evil?

Keep away from the paper shops. Evil lurks in there.

When you leave this church, and you pass on your way to your homes, you may yourself encounter a printer! Even if he does not utter any words in his gravel-strewn tongue, you will know him by his huge clumsy size and his acrid metallic smell. Turn from him! The best thing you can do to serve your God is to spit on him, taking care not to touch him.

You may pass a man in a barrow, selling printers' books. Do not succumb to his blandishments, his lies. The best thing you could do to serve your God is to kick his barrow over. If you want to buy one of his books, then pay him for it in cudgels, and throw it in a canal. The world will be a godlier place with one less printed book in it.

Chapter Seven

You carry home your lies
and the curses that cling to them.

Domenico's assurances did not comfort Wendelin for long. The accusation of complicity with the counterfeiters attached itself to the printers like a tumour that quickly swelled in its malignity.

One Venetian printer after another was taken away for questioning, brutal questioning, in the upper chambers of the Doges' Palace where their screams could not be heard, except in the minds of those who waited for them at home, thin-lipped and weeping.

Seven printers disappeared. Teachers and booksellers who had associated with them were arrested on charges of sodomy, for which the punishment in Venice, unlike in ancient Rome, was burning alive. And sodomy of course was the sexual art preached by the old Roman and Greek writers, as Fra Filippo loved to remind his parishioners, with all the appropriate illustrative gestures.

Between the columns in the *Piazzetta* books and bookmakers were alike consigned to the flames. Sometimes the books themselves were used to make the pyre. Other books were carried away to serve the jakes, to scour candle-sticks, to rub boots. Some were sold by the looters to grocers and soap-sellers or put on ships to foreign nations, for God alone knew what use. Righteous hands rifled illuminated pages and cut out the pictures, or tore off the bindings for their gold clasps.

Then one of the foreign printers was condemned, a Syrian, a man well known at the *fondaco* for he bought his typefaces from the *stamperia* von Speyer. His works were esoteric, no competition for their own, and Wendelin had come to regard the unfortunate victim, Johannes Sicculus, as a friend.

The news came to Wendelin and his men as they stood by the press, at work on another edition of Saint Augustine. His friend Morto came lurching into the *stamperia*, his howls echoing through the arcades of the *fondaco*.

'They have Johannes Sicculus. There's a charge. He's guilty. They've said that he's to be beheaded and burned.'

'*Porca Madonna!*' whispered one of the *compositori*.

Wendelin muttered to himself, 'Why Johannes Sicculus, why not Nicolas Jenson?' Immediately he blushed, deeply ashamed to have wished such an ugly death on anyone. 'Save his soul,' he said quietly. 'Save all our souls.'

He was not heard. As one man, the printers were already surging to the door, running down the stairs, sprinting to San Marco, all the while fighting conflicting passions: horror at the prospect of witnessing the brutal death of their colleague, mixed with a need to see it done in order to believe such a thing could happen.

News of the impending execution had spread throughout the town, travelling in gondola, work barge and shopping basket from quick mouth to sorrowing ear, from whisper to shout. The printers joined throngs heading in the direction of the *Piazzetta*.

San Marco was porous; so many entrances and exits. In happier times Wendelin had thought these many doors just another aspect of the marvellous democracy of Venice. Now it seemed sinister. There was nothing to separate the streams of noblemen from the fishwives in this rush of humanity, and nothing to nobilitate one man's desire to see the death done above another's. All pressed together in the narrow alleys, stinks and fragrances compressed in a solid fume of human scent above the unwashed or coiffed heads.

This is not what I intended at all! Dear God, what have I done?

I dare not utter a word to tell my part in this. I never thought my rumours at Rialto would have such a murderous effect.

It is so unfair. I meant only to put the finger on Jenson. He's the only printer who knows how to make coins. But now all the printers are in trouble, and it seems he alone floats above it all, serenely, protected by his noble clients. He has greased all the right people in the fist and none will stand bad witness to him.

I would give the price of a city not to have started that rumour that has grown so badly mangled.

My man does not know it but I went today to see the death done. Our son, I left to his milk nurse. *'Fai il bravo,'* I said. 'Be good, go to sleep.' The baby wept some, but soon grew still. The milk of the nurse was rich as mine, and more so, I think. There was no room in my heart for any more guilt – it was full of my man's pain and my sorrow at what I have done.

My gossip has in the end condemned not Jenson but poor old Johannes Sicculus, who never printed an interesting book and never hurt a fly. My eyes turn to puddles at the memory of that scene in the *Piazzetta*, crowded as the roots of my hair with my townsmen wide-eyed to see a foreign printer done to death.

First they brought him out in his chains and put him on his feet upon the dais. He stood, all blink and stare, with his eyes on the sea, full of hope, as if a great fish like Jonah's whale might jump out of the water and save him. A small dark man, he is, Johannes Sicculus, no taller than me, but with yellow skin, purplish lips, black eyes, a good nose with tall nostrils. I saw no marks on him, so I think they knew he did not do it. There'd been no lash nor beating of him in the gaol. My man has always said this Sicculus is good and I know in my marrow that he did not make the confect coins he was accused of. No one did, among the printers. It was all of my invention.

The guards were grim in the face – yet one more thing to tell me that the charge was false. The guards love to kill the bad ones: it gives their work some dignity. But when it's a good one they kill, then they hang their eyes in shame for they know that they're no better than the ones who murdered Jesus.

First they lashed Johannes to a corn cage; then they cut off his hands with pincers, the same way poor Saint Agnes lost her breasts. I can still hear the snap of steel and hot piss of blood on the stones. When I looked up (for I could not bear to see it done) I saw that they had snipped his hands at the wrists and sealed the stump with hot coal on sticks.

Over Johannes' screams I heard whispered around me all the things a Venetian will say at the extreme moments:

'Dio cane!'

'Dio boia!'

Then they threaded the severed hands through a chain and hung them round his neck, put him on the block, his rear end to the sea; his head to us, for more of a view. His neck proved a tough scrag, as it did not cut clean away. It was only after three chops that his head snapped off and rolled into the basket. And in a scant second an enterprise of flies had clustered on the meat of his neck.

At that moment I saw my man's face in the crowd, far away from me, with his men around him. I saw what he thought: *This town kills printers*. I ducked my head. I did not want him to see me there.

When the head hit the basket, all of us screamed or cried, '*Gesù*' in one breath as is our tradition at these times, the men more loud than maids. The children there, and they were great in number, did not cry. A child is sometimes more brave than his father. I think this is because they hear in so many tales on the knee, dreadful tales where death comes in awful ways – and so, for them, all is as it should be when death comes. By the time I myself had ten years I'd heard of deaths by wolf and lion, of babes who starved in the woods, or were eaten by witches, and the real death in front of me did not make me retch, as it would my sweet gentle man, so strong in the soul but so weak in the stomach, because he has not absorbed sufficient tales to protect him.

It was a tragical and doleful spectacle, less than terrifying. 'Not a great death,' adjudged all the folk near me, 'nor a poor one either.'

There were no 'not-me-please-don't-do-this-to-me' pleadings and no noble speech to twist our hearts and make us weep. Johannes just looked as though he could not see the truth in it, why fate should fall on him so hard. Even when he held out his hands for the tool which cut them, he had looked as if to say, 'I came to this town in good faith. Surely you will not do this to me?'

But they did.

And it happened because of me.

The smell of burning, sweet and sour, floated over the water all the way to Murano, where Fra Filippo sat, composing his sermons late into the night. He sniffed the air appreciatively, and allowed himself the occasional smile. Stretching his limbs, he decided to take a walk through the cool depths of the church. He paused at the door, finding it open.

Inside he witnessed the unattractive sight of Ianno, naked, standing, with his back to the door, in the pulpit, his arms stretched up. Candles surrounded him, and their pointed light revealed every one of the ribs that punctuated his pale skin. Motionless and colourless, he looked like an anatomical drawing of a corpse.

From behind, Fra Filippo could see the cleft in Ianno's scrawny buttocks and a tuft of hair sprouting between them. The little brain glowed brilliantly on the left side of his head.

Suddenly Ianno relaxed his taut pose. He reached between his legs and pulled out a large birch of tattered branches. With one hand still raised to heaven he commenced to flagellate himself with the other, groaning loudly. Fra Filippo watched as Ianno beat till the blood came, and then pulped the blood against the untorn flesh until his back oozed like a rotting fig torn by birds.

'Guilty! Guilty! Guilty!' chanted Ianno to himself. 'Take this for your pains! And this! There's no one in the whole world as guilty as you!'

Shaking his head, the priest stole away. He would have liked to find another assistant, but he knew that there was no one but Ianno equipped for the most particular tasks required to serve him.

Each day the reek of charred books floated over the rooftops to the *Fondaco dei Tedeschi*. As yet, Wendelin and his men had been spared. Their religious works were taken into consideration and as Christian foreigners they were not to be judged like the Venetians and those from the pagan East who must be exampled. The noblemen's protection stretched thin, but continued to hold. As yet, Wendelin felt he was safe from prosecution, but not from the odium of the public, fanned to fury by the ever more piquant sermons of Fra Filippo de Strata, who, strangely, never mentioned Jenson in his rants.

At the *fondaco*, groups of printers and sympathetic merchants stood around speaking in hushed tones about the priest.

'But the man is a cretin,' was the general consensus.

'A cretin with a dream is the worst kind,' was the reply and everyone looked at the flagstones, unable to meet each other's eyes. Fra Filippo's dream of a printless world was bearing down on them with the steely edge of reality. A printless world would also be a hungry one for those who sold paper vellum, metal clasps and bindings.

Upstairs, the *stamperia* von Speyer continued with its printing of classical and legal texts. In panic, they had produced too many of both. Bruno knew, with sickening sureness, that his *padron* himself thus contributed to the over-production of books, which seemed to be forcing his downfall.

He sat in the office surrounded by unsold quires. The public was afraid to buy books. Fra Filippo's spies were everywhere, monitoring the bookshelves of their parishioners. Women and old men streamed out of church bent on avoiding, for the sake of their life hereafter, the soul-staling, loin-rotting poetry of those pagan *priapi*.

Bruno, once it became known that he had edited such works, was pursued through the streets by women who spat and screamed at him. At Rialto there were market men he had known since childhood who would not serve him, and crossed themselves as he passed.

One Tuesday, two days after Fra Filippo's latest sermon, Bruno walked through the market, his head downcast, where once it had swung happily back and forth, saluting dozens of friendly merchants. Now he could only take comfort from the physicality of the place, like a foreign pilgrim sniffing the air of a new town for something to remind him of home. The air was warm around him, sanguineous and feathery, as though the plump pimpled breasts of the chickens and geese hanging outside the butchers were still breathing in and out. Pigeons were sitting on sliced-open watermelons, as if being born from them. The fruit men were singing their guttural cries, in chorus.

The air outside the wine shops was heavy with the mingled scents of muscatel, Greek and Malmsey wine; outside the olive-sellers it was sharp and fragrant with oil concentrated in the effort of absorbing black vinegar. Bruno was thirsty but he knew better than to enter the wine shop these days and the olive-seller's daughter turned away from him and hid her face in her apron as he walked by: she who used to smile at him and hand him olives on her fingers to taste. Now, when her mother saw him, she hustled the child into the back of the shop with a slap.

He took a ferryboat to Sant' Angelo di Contorta, feeling the need of Gentilia's or at least familial company. He stood on the deck of the boat winding up the Grand Canal and let the town perform her usual seductions upon him. His mind emptied of thoughts as he gazed on the *palazzi*, each with its little mirror of water in front of it in which to admire itself. Swallows scissored through the blue sky hanging gauzily over the canal. The seagulls flew among them, avidly, as if savouring air somehow enriched by the intense blueness of the smaller birds.

Passing the Locanda Sturion, he found himself searching the windows in case Caterina di Colonna appeared, to make the day more lovely. The apparition did not come, and he found himself unreasonably disappointed. He'd never met her, but Felice had many times spoken of her beauty.

At Sant' Angelo di Contorta he hurried through the courtyard. Recognising him, a sordidly pretty little nun blew a kiss over her shoulder, saying, 'I'll fetch her for you, *carissimo*. And what will you do for *me* in return?'

Bruno blushed and looked at the ground until the echoes of her light footsteps had been absorbed into the stones.

He paced the courtyard, aware of eyes upon him, and disturbed by soft giggles and sighs from behind blinds in the rooms above him and annoyed by the chatter of praying parrots.

Presently Gentilia appeared with her lace in her hands. She drew him into an unseen corner to wrap her arms around him. After too long, he pulled her hands from the small of his back, where they were kneading furiously, and held her away from him so he could look down on her. She craned her neck up to kiss his lips, but he flinched away. It was only hours since Sosia's mouth had skimmed his, and he could not bear to think of the mingling of her imprint with that of his little sister.

Gentilia, who had seemed transported into a kind of trance, became herself again. She seemed to realise suddenly the indiscretion of their hidden position and led her brother to a sunny corner of the cloister. She bent her head over her work for a moment, inserted the needle, and then gazed up at her brother, the lace forgotten in her hands.

Bruno told her about his wretched walk through the market that morning. His eyes swept over her as he spoke. *Why did Gentilia wear such unbecoming colours*, he wondered. And why was her skin was so liverishly coloured and textured, so moist and hot, that he could not bear the idea of touching it, much as he loved her? Sosia, *invece*, had fly-alluring red lips and soft skin on her arms, and there was a tempting glitter even to her toenails. Caterina di Colonna, at the Sturion, was said to have a radiance to her skin, as if something were gently aflame inside her. Wendelin's little wife had the complexion of an apricot . . .

While he was distracted by these thoughts Gentilia seized his hand and began pressing his fingers. She tilted her face up to him and said: 'I hear that Venice does not love the printers any more.'

'Not everyone hates us! We've roused the ire of one lunatic priest on Murano by reviving some pagan texts. He tries to rouse the mob against us in all kinds of ways.'

'You say "we". Are you really so much involved, Bruno?'

'Yes, I am. I'm part of this now. And in spite of what everyone says I still think we should publish Catullus, and his friends.'

'Catullus?'

'A Roman poet; he writes of love, and of – of – physical matters.'

'May I see him please? Bring me some poems, Bruno.'

He snapped, 'That I shall not do! It would be most unsuitable for a nun!'

She looked at him curiously. 'You seem more angry than afraid, Bruno? Perhaps you should put a curse on that priest.'

'What are you saying, Gentilia!'

'Go to a witch, and get a spell.'

'Are you not well? Should I call someone, a sister?'

'An eating spell, to eat him away.'

'Gentilia!'

'And while you are at it, to eat away her who is eating you.'

Bruno backed away, his eyes fixed on his sister. She had started to stab at her lace with her needle, chanting 'Eat! Eat! Eat!' with each thrust. Blood seeped up through the fabric. She threw her work down and held her wounded finger up to Bruno, as she'd done when they were children.

'Take away the hurt,' she commanded, in a high childish voice.

A sharp looking nun, blonde and thin, hurried up and put her arm around Gentilia.

'She's been working rather hard,' she said to Bruno, and hustled his sister away.

Chapter Eight

Now do I grieve, now do I repent
what I have done.

We cling together from fear as much as love these days. That priest on Murano would have my man harmed if he could. The word is out that the priest has hired ruffians to menace the printers and booksellers. But these threats are as yet invisible so we may not go to the *Signori* to report them. We know there's not one thing we can do.

My deft little rumours that were meant only to hurt Jenson have been doubled and trebled in the strength of their poison, I know not how. Now there is an added rumour that the ink in books gives cancer to the skin. Of course, not one case can be shown, but the fear flourishes anyway, perhaps the stronger for a lack of evidence, for the canker in the imagination is ever deadlier than a true tumour.

Now whole days go past without my man selling a single book where once he would do the rounds of the booksellers and hear tales of a dozen snapped up here, two score there. On such days he used to come home full of pride.

Last night he came home and asked me if it might not be time to give up the baby's nurse.

'Is he not grown enough now to do without her?' he asked. He was too proud to say to me that the expense of the nurse, and of feeding her, must now be laid aside. I knew how small an amount is concerned, and by this he let me know what dire straits we are in. And he still does not know it's all my fault!

'Of course!' I lied sweetly. 'He refuses her half the time anyway. I shall tell her tomorrow.'

From this day on I look for cheaper cuts at the butchers and I do not any longer buy pieces of glass to decorate the house, nor any good foods if they are to be got only at grimacing prices. I have taken a vow of humbleness.

And these days too I think fewer bad thoughts about the quick books. I am most grievously sorry for what I have done. I would like to help them succeed again. Another idea has come to me, and I have not yet learned to distrust my ideas. I put it to my man.

It is this: that we should publish Catullus, and as soon as possible. I was brave and bold like Paola when I told him so. 'What, now?' he almost raised his voice, so astonished was he with me. 'When we are so deep in trouble?' He lifted quizzing eyes on me.

'Because of that,' I replied. 'It cannot get worse.'

Then he told me something which he'd guarded to himself I do not know how long (it seems we both have secrets!). Despite the rants of the priest on Murano, the nobleman Domenico Zorzi is also pressing him to print Catullus and promises to buy one quarter of the first run. And there's another noble, Nicolò Malipiero, who has also come to his office, on just that one errand, to ask him to make a printing of that book, says he will subscribe for twenty copies, all on fine Bologna paper. What's clear though, also, is a threat beneath all their fine words. Without the need to say so, their smiles also mean: *if you do not give us what we want then we shall find it elsewhere.* Both these men are known whore-mongers, said even to associate with foreign women, so I doubt their motives. At least I think they're little to do with literature and everything to do with lust.

My man and I do not talk of such things, for with the worries about money a small shadow has fallen between us again, and we are not so free and easy with each other as we once were. We both feel smaller than we did before, diminished in the eyes of the world.

I long to purify myself with a confession of my crime, but each time the words come to my lips a pair of hands inside my throat pushes them back down into the well of my guilt.

The book burnings ceased. There were no further executions or disappearances.

After the purge the stricken printing industry limped uncertainly forward, except for Nicolas Jenson who quietly flourished.

Jenson's type was so beautiful that Wendelin could imagine him struggling to find a text sublime enough to print with it. After him, after his Roman and his Gothic Rotunda, there was nothing left to do but copy him.

And publish what Jenson dared not.

Wendelin took his problem to his sister-in-law. If Paola, clear-eyed and cool, could see wisdom in publishing Catullus then he would almost feel he had Johann's blessing too.

He brought her some pages of proofs, the sparrow poems, and the kissing poems. Although he did not bring the worst of the obscenities, he was embarrassed at the intimacy of watching her read the lines. He stood in silence, aware of his knees pressing together, awaiting her verdict.

She scanned the sheets quickly, and turned to him, 'It's not to my taste, but it will sell. Does Lussièta know you've come to me?'

He hung his head.

'I thought not. Best not to tell her. While you're here, there *is* something I'd like to discuss with you.'

But Wendelin was overcome with guilt for every moment spent secretly in her company and excused himself quickly with a grateful press of her hand. He hurried away from her door, hoping that he was not seen. If Lussièta happened to be looking from her window . . . He hoped she was at Rialto. Sometimes he felt faint qualms at the public nature of his wife's life. She insisted on going to Rialto each day. It was, she said, to choose the best of everything, and to garner what she called 'my dollop of news', but Wendelin was dimly aware that there were other, subtler missions, too.

That afternoon he wrote to Padre Pio in Speyer:

My period of deliberation has already been too long. I begin to think that Jenson will steal this idea from me too. If he did that, should I see him in the street, I believe I could not forfend to smite his nose. But do you know, he's never seen abroad. I have never knowingly crossed his path, even in this town, where I must take threefold the time I should just to cross the town, because of meeting people who must be greeted and consoled (Venetians always have something wrong with them) or congratulated and admired (they have always just bought something beautiful) . . . Anyway, I see my entire acquaintance twice over at least once a week but never this Jenson. Not once.

But Padre, I don't believe you wrote to me asking for more of my futile repinings over Jenson . . . You want to know what I'm going to do about Catullus. I confess that it is at this moment, when I veer towards publishing those poems, that I most feel the loss of my brother. Johann's voice would be so welcome in my ears; his caution would be appreciated.

But to tell you the truth, I think I have decided already. Even if Johann told me not to, I would publish this Catullus now.

There it is, my decision. And you are the first to know it, even before my wife.

Chapter Nine

As soon as it dawns
I will run to the booksellers' stalls

The Venetians liked songs; they liked them a little malicious if possible or at least pungent as a black canal on a midsummer afternoon. They liked little dialogues between mothers and precocious daughters destined for the nunnery, or else illicit mistresses pitting their wits against impudent servants or their own dear but dim-witted lord. The Venetians sang so much that the state was obliged to bring laws to forbid singing at certain hours. But even when they desisted from their melodious caterwauling, the townspeople warmed their throats, humming like cats.

Felice told Wendelin: 'Venetians are not miserable enough to produce a great poet of their own. If they feel a poetical emotion, they ask Bellini to *paint* it for them so they can look at it. Catullus does with words what Bellini does in paint. *Ecco* – they will love him.'

Wendelin nodded. This was also his experience of Venetians. Abstract erudition was not for them – they wanted stories, short and piquant as possible, the ghostlier the better, like the ones his wife brought home from the market. He imagined them distended languidly upon their divans, dozing over their books; undertaking imagined voyages and vicarious romances without exertion beyond turning a page.

'You have not risked so much,' insisted Felice. 'Catullus is just what they want right now. In fact, he's overdue. It would be a relief to give him birth.'

Once he had finally decided to publish Catullus – many weeks after he had begun to invest in the manuscript, assigning its introduction to Squarzafico and the editing to Bruno – only then did Wendelin start to feel true fear. For the first time, when he saw his own staff at work on printing the book, did it seem real to him and even then, when he looked at the first pages, the act of doing so had the surpassingly real quality of a dream. He saw himself from the outside, leaning down to examine the folios. *Look at me*, he wanted to say, *the man who will publish Catullus.*

At the last minute he decided to temper the shock of the new work and to make his investment safer, both at one stroke. He resolved to include in the book the poems of two better-known Romans: Propertius and Tibullus. These two were so famous, so much quoted, so *exposed*, that they were almost respectable, even if their verses were not always so. Why, Giovanni Bellini himself had made neat use of a line from Propertius in the *cartello* under one of his *Pietàs.*

Wendelin quoted aloud to himself: 'When these swelling eyes evoke groans this very work by Giovanni Bellini could shed tears . . .'

In the company of Propertius and Tibullus, Catullus would be safe, Wendelin decided. Just to be sure, he inserted another work too, the innocuous pastorals of Statius.

On the last day of September what Wendelin hoped would be the first three hundred copies of Propertius–Tibullus–Statius–Catullus were printed and piled high in their quires. At midnight, Wendelin and his men ceased their labours and went, as one, down to the waterside, to rest their eyes and compose their thoughts before going home to their wives.

They stood by the Grand Canal, watching the reflections of lamps on the water and listening to the soft breathing of the city. Dark ghosts of gondolas haunted the windows by the water, floating in and out of probability, like dreams. Golden chips of moonlight beckoned from the canal, glittering like the tiny *tessere* of an infinite golden mosaic.

What have we done? the men wondered. Had they made their fortunes or lost their livelihood? Everyone knew that this book, or at least the last and greatest part of it, was different, that it had broken a tradition, that it had startled a foetal idea out of its egg, perhaps before its time.

Wendelin said aloud to Bruno, standing quietly beside him, 'It's just a book, after all.'

But his voice quavered so that his editor gently took his elbow and led him back indoors, where he handed Wendelin his cloak and bid him an affectionate goodnight.

A book may not be unprinted, thought Wendelin, walking home through the dark streets.

So at last the poems came out.

My man came home late, late one night, with the first book in his sleeve.

I had gone to bed but not to sleep, for I knew what great thing he was about. I stretched out there thinking of him at his work, and how he must be feeling.

There's a map in Genoa that shows how Irish geese grow upon trees. The goslings ripen in fruit that resemble apples. Decaying within, the fruit produces a worm, which as it grows, becomes both hairy and feathered. Eventually the creature breaks the skin of the fruit and flies away. That was how I thought of the book: breaking out of the skin of its fruit.

It was the early hours of the morning when I heard his step in our *calle*. His footsteps were light for he did not wish to wake our son, but they were also leavened by the bubbles in his blood at the thought of what he'd just printed.

He came up to our bed where I lay in wait for him. I could see in his face that he'd given that book all he had, as if it were his wife or child. Time was the least of it, but I felt suddenly exhausted at the thought of all those hours that had been used upon it, so much more in deciding to print than in committing the act.

So I felt a piece of meanness for that book in that I knew he loved it in some ways as he loved me. That love I wanted all for myself from him. And he knew that I knew it, so that night he took steps to make me see that the book could be a part of our love, not just something of his own.

When he came into our room, he made a small cough to clear his throat so he might tell me a thing of great worth in a clean voice. He still wore his cloak, and he stood at the foot of the bed, a little theatrical and very conscious of himself.

'This book', he said, 'I have made and the cause of it is you, and my love of you. If I had not known you, I would not know that these poems are true. I would not believe in love like this, think that the poets lie. They seem, the sweet ones, to be all of you or for you, by me, from me. The dark ones are of someone else. I think with fear sometimes that they could be my other fate – the wife who would have been mine, if I did not have you. Your corrupt double.'

'My *sosia*,' I whispered.

We both shook like bells then, and he cried a drop, at so dread a thought. So I held wide my arms and took the book to my bed and my heart. I held it tenderly, that first book, as if it were a babe – and yes, in fact, it was just two hours old when I first met with it.

I rocked it in my arms. It was a big thing, at least seven inches by ten. It gave me its rich smell and then the creamy silk of its pages. It had no binding yet; it was too young, vulnerable as a naked baby sparrow before it grows its feathers.

'Three hundred and seventy-eight pages,' my man said proudly. 'One hundred and eighty-nine folios.'

I raised a page to see which watermarks he'd used – the bull's head with the crown, the scales, the scissors, the castle, the lily, the dragon . . . but my man stayed my hand and said, 'No, just look at the words, this time.'

I saw he needed my comfort for the brave thing he'd done, and I gave what I could. I did not praise the type or the set of the margins. That was not the kind of praise he needed.

So I gave him words of love about his book. I read aloud some lines. I traced my fingers over them. I showed him I was lost in it. I told him it was as wise as the owls of Athens, as sweet as the pears of Calabria, as piquant as the fried frogs of Cremona and as delicate as the broiled quails of Delos.

Then I rose from the bed, and said, 'Let us take the boat now.'

My man looked fully mystified, and I whispered, 'Trust me.'

At this he followed me without one more word to our son's room, where I gently scooped the sleeping babe, and then downstairs to the jetty. All the while I kept the book tucked under my arm.

'Where, my love?' he asked, when the boat was untied and all three of us inside.

'To the lagoon,' I said, 'where the *Sposalizio* is done.'

And so we poled to that same spot where each year the Doge drops a gold ring in the water, to marry Venice to the sea.

Then I rose from my bench and held the book of Catullus above the water and looked back to my man to see if he was in accord with what I proposed to do.

He smiled at me, struck silent with awe.

And so I did as the Doge does. I called on Poseidon, King of the Waves, the Tritons, the Sirens, the Nereids and all the creatures of the briny kingdoms.

'Show the world,' I entreated them, as the Doge does, 'that the ancient times may be married to the present ones.'

Then I set the book softly on the skin of the waves.

I don't know why it did not sink. Perhaps it was buoyed up by our hopes, perhaps being made of beaten wood the book imagined it could float, like a raft.

And so it did, into a path laid down by the moon. We two watched until we could see it no more.

I did not know it would be our fate, that book, that all things would change with it. I thought it just a tender thing, a young thing, made of my man's courage and his love of good words. I thought its printing marked the end of the shadow between us, the one cast by poverty and fear, my way of making up to him for not coming to Speyer, and for starting the rumour which had hurt and killed printers in this town. I thought Catullus would do all that.

How wrong I was, in all things.

PART FIVE

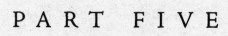

Prologue

So accept this little book, such as it is,
O protecting Virgin.
May it last for eternity and a day.

Lucius, sweet brother-of-mine,

Your accusations fail to wound, being precisely beside the point.

No, I always hoped these poems would raise riot, and that it would last. You know I could never stand to be forgotten, rinsed out of the weave of history, like ink in milk.

And my bid to stay indelible can hardly fail: because of me, everyone may know what it's like to make love to Clodia Metelli, not just the hundreds who actually have.

I *knew* what I was doing. Don't say I was hotheaded. On the contrary, I made a ritual of it.

Those poems were drafted a hundred times on waxed tablets of ivory. I erased as much as I wrote: the flat edge of my stylus was as busy as the pointed one. I melted down successive imperfections without mercy. It was many months before I was satisfied.

Then came the dress rehearsal: for weeks I toiled with almost ungentlemanly carefulness upon second-hand papyrus whose old words had been rubbed out. Finally, when the words had begun to write themselves straight out of my fingers on to the palimpsest, I myself penned the presentation copy for the patron I've chosen, the historian Cornelius Nepos, smoothing down the papyrus with pumice stone till it was silky before anointing it with ink. You never saw anything so elegant. Cornelius would be beside himself – or so I told myself.

I suddenly realised that four years have wheeled around since I started writing these poems: I began them in the late spring and yet again I'm waking in humid sheets and the streets of Rome are stinking of sun-warmed urine in the afternoons. You tell me the sun burns you in Asia Minor, Lucius, but I assure you the stones of Rome are hotter than the ovens of Mesopotamia. My body distils rivulets of sweat, as if each organ separately wept its own tears for snow.

Meanwhile, speaking of sweat, at the bookseller's, anonymous scribes have been grinding out quick, cheap copies of my book, one after another. More than the usual number, for a first-time poet. The bookseller, a low type, but clever in his way, very clever, has great hopes of my work. He knew real pain when he saw it.

'Pain sells,' he told me, spitting on his fingers and running them down the manuscript, which made me feel queasy. But I suppressed my qualms when he added: 'And sells and sells.'

You say nothing of the handsome copy I sent you. Is it not fine? I hope you've done as I asked and made no mention of this book in your letters home. Father must not see it. You know why. Please reassure me on this point, Lucius.

I'm not entirely displeased to draw your attention to the fact that it takes three whole rolls of joined papyrus sheets to contain my book of poems. Even in the cheap copies, the ornamental boss is marked with my initials and each roll is tied closed with those thongs of beautifully stained leather.

('Very expensive,' the bookseller leered at me. 'They'll buy it for the looks of it on their tables anyway.' Forgive me: I know it shows rather vilely in me to be occupied with such low stuff.)

The noblest copy of all was destined for Cornelius Nepos, my patron. I myself supervised the winding of the papyrus and made sure that the leather thongs were polished to the shine of fresh ox-blood. I inspected it one last time in the morning of the day the book was to be delivered. I'd already decided that this would be the moment I cast my destiny upon the waters, in my mind, the hour I was born as a real poet.

I had a slave take it round for me, though old Cornelius is as genial as he's cultured, and I know he would have made me welcome in his tall thin house, built just like him, where he writes his own long, thin books. Like everyone else in Rome, Cornelius has a soft spot for our *pater*, and I know Father respects him.

But at the last minute – don't laugh! – I was struck down by a damnably sudden and most uncharacteristic attack of shyness. I went off with my friends to get drunk, and to them I did not mention the fact that my poems had been born that day, even though thereby I might have prodded the worm of jealousy in at least two of them.

Even while I drank, I was waiting. Eventually I drank so much that I forgot what I was waiting for, but I awoke from my stupor the next day, hungry as rabbit-raddled Celtiberia and blinking painfully at the aristocratically pale sky, still with a ferment of anticipation in my blood.

First, there was silence. Three whole days of it. You, who know me so well, can guess at the torment of those noiseless hours. Then Cornelius scratched me a courteous acknowledgement. It was no more than polite, whereas I'd hoped for either outraged rejection or rabid declarations that his every sense had been ravished by my poetry. I didn't much care which of the two, though I was eager to know which it would be.

Then it came to me, fuddled with the aftertaste of wine, that I was not the only young poet to present his first-born to the eminent historian; Cornelius was not unduly impressed by the honour I had conferred upon him. Probably, he had not even read the work. My pride somersaulted over this obstacle in a second: *So the poor old eunuch cannot deal with them!* I told myself. *Just wait till the public reads my songs!*

271

Silence continued for a few more gnawing days, while copies of my poems next made their way to Roman libraries, to the baths, to the pockets of rich men lolling in the porticoes of houses or on their divans at opulent suppers in private houses. I waited for the talk to start. I decided it would be gradual. A groundswell of praise and opprobrium; gross and bare-faced adulation at the Club; late-night fights in taverns to defend my reputation; in the morning, anonymous praise scrawled on the walls of the bathhouse.

I stayed indoors, modestly reading other poets' works, with an extremely critical eye. (I maintain no poet simply knows how to write a beautiful poem. He only knows one when he sees its image painted on the air, or hears the fluent cleave of its syllables. With a bit of luck, it's his own. If you have to ask why's this stanza short? – then you've lost it. Or why the poet used that particular word. Already it's too late, the poem's expired. Put it in a box with a lily on top.)

A week later, nothing had happened. The sky still clenched its heat, never released a drop of rain. No messengers came to me; no more and no fewer invitations arrived than had done so before my book came out. I almost settled into the belief that I had published my songs harmlessly.

But then, suddenly, I was a sensation!

It all happened at once, ten days after the poems were born: the messengers, the invitations, the graffiti, the claps on the back, the twisted smiles of the other poets . . . so that it seemed in one day I moved from obscurity to fame, or, as one of my friends pointed out, from the bedroom to the arena.

Catullus, Catullus, the public was saying. *What's he like? Lesbia,* they were saying, *Clodia Metelli, rather! Whore of the Gods! Who also peels young men in alleyways and nuzzles stubbly cremators . . .*

I must admit that it was as much for the celebrity of my love as for my celebration of it, that I was the flavour of the moment, on everyone's lips, commoner and blue blood. Why, people who can't even read know *my* poems by heart!

Who could be seen without a copy of my book? The bookseller

was rubbing his hands and opening the Falernian — such a rich sigh bubbling forth from the bottle! — to toast the joy of *his* success.

I smiled, tried to act modestly, as if the poems were mere family heirlooms, nothing to do with me.

But, to be candid, Lucius, I've already begun to worry about the way the book's been received. No one praises my imagery; no one savours my words; no one beats their thigh to the seduction of my metre. They talk about Clodia and her damned sparrow. Will the seedy glamour of Clodia's vices live longer than the songs and eat up my fame as a poet? That thought repeats on me like a rotten anchovy. Outside, at last, it rains in dangling skins of grey, washing my old impatient footprints into foaming drains.

But it's too late to wish I had fallen in love with a better woman. Worse still, it's far too late to cure myself of this hateful love I still feel for her.

Anyway, I have reasons, since last night even, not to give up hope. It seems that Clodia finds my newfound fame somewhat aphrodisiacal.

Chapter One

Then sleep took fright . . .

He just does not see the ghostly perils here in this town, because he does not believe in them. He does not fear the *fade* and *massarioli*, our fays and goblins, who would love to trip him up just for the joy of watching him stumble. Now September is melting into October, the primest month of witches. Each Thursday night they comb their hair to pull out the strands they use for binding spells. In the hours between midnight and cockcrow they unchain gondolas and put to sea for Alexandria.

I try to tell him about the undead spirits of Venice, lest he, with his too-trusting nature, should follow one to his peril, never suspecting that it was a creature of the dark zones with every intent to do him harm. Now that my man has brought this Catullus to life again, like a he-witch who brings back the dead, I fear him a marked man among the spirits as well as among the living.

In the early days of its life, we were frightened that the printing of Catullus would bring the world down about our ears. But the first thing that happened then was . . . nothing. A silence dark as a wolf's throat. We believed each next dawn would bring all the polemics, the praise, the disgust, and the compliments. But from the first there was the silence of the grave and eerie in that way, all the more so for the unnatural heat of this season.

Only three days later was an insult daubed on the door of the *fondaco* – a few foul words wet from the lips of the priest on Murano, that some disciple thought to slap on the wood in paint. For shame, the *visdomini* asked my man to pay for its removal! As if we had not problems enough. A dwarf was seen running from the scene, yet no one took pains to chase or catch him.

Next a rock was thrown through our own window one night, and made a massacre of my pieces of coloured glass. We woke to the crash and lay for one moment throbbing in each other's arms. Then I ran for the babe, who shrieked in his room, and my man went to the glass, which now framed the window like a jagged crown of thorns. When I came back with the babe on my hip, he was unwrapping a piece of paper from the stone. I saw writing on it.

'What does it say?' I asked.

'Some stupid witch-curse,' he said, crumpling it.

'Are you not frightened?' I asked him, anguished.

'Only of the business failing. Or of losing you two,' he replied, touching the baby's trembling lip.

I shook my head impatiently. 'That could never happen, losing me.'

Then, silently, we both remembered I left him in Freiburg, and I recollected how nearly I had destroyed him with the rumour I started at Rialto.

I tried a different line, asking him to remember his five senses, not his single but too-efficient brain. At least I know, to my own pleasure, that his senses have some imagination and may therefore come to know the danger of ghosts.

'But have you never felt the nightmare touch of a cold hand? Or dreaded it, when you heard a scratch at the door in the middle of the night? Did you never hear a phantom breathe on the back of your neck? Were you never insanely afraid at the sight of a wavering light in the darkness? Did you never smell a ghost? A witch-curse is not to be taken lightly, you know that, don't you?'

At all these questions, he just laughed bitterly. 'I agree that in Venice, if you're in a ghost-smelling humour, then there's always a dead rat nearby somewhere, to help you believe in the ghost. If a noise is made, it is by some elastic body. If it has a voice, then it is a beast or a man, with lungs and breath to utter it. If scratching is heard then it is made by some creature with hands or paws.'

I opened my mouth to protest, and he added, 'And as it is with scratchings so it is with dismal yellings and groanings and hidden footsteps and all those noises which are fabled to ghosts.'

His worries are about things he can see, not things he cannot see. The fogdogs at the foot of our rainbows perplex him. The labbering of the living fish at the market makes him uncomfortable. Nicolas Jenson worries him. The cries of our son in the night worry him. This strange long summer makes him ill at ease.

Nothing touches him intensely as ghost fear fingers me.

In the blind dead of a Venetian night, there are plenty of ghosts to fear.

There are so many of them; it is hard to keep them all in mind. I'm always alert to the dangers on his behalf.

When he must go to the bookbinder at the Abazia, for example, I remind my man about the quite-young ghost (in the sense that the living man died not long ago) of the old miser Bartolomeo Zenni.

I warn my man – 'If you see an aged man carrying an enormous sack on his shoulders, if he begs you to help him, do not look him in the eyes. If you do he will turn into a burning skeleton in front of your eyes! And frighten you to death!'

All Venice still remembers how, on the night of 13 May 1437, there was a terrible fire at the Abazia. Bartolomeo Zenni alone refused to help his neighbours to save their children, being too busy dragging his sack of gold and jewels from the scene. Now he's dead himself, and it is his unquiet spirit who implores in vain.

If my man must go to the great ones with the high foreheads at the Scuola di San Marco at Zannipolo, I implore him to take care, for it's in that quarter that the ghost of the traitor Doge Marin

Faliero, his hands tied behind his back, stalks the streets looking for his own head – struck off his body for his crimes. Faliero does not know it is buried between his own legs, poor soul.

Faliero does not wander the streets alone. On his trail is the phantom of the blind Doge Enrico Dandolo, who took Constantinople for us in the fourth crusade. He carries a sword and perforce slashes his hands continually with its sharp blade, this on account of all the innocent blood he spilt in that far land. He chases Faliero to avenge the honour of the city. He never finds him, for neither of them can see: Dandolo has burning brands instead of eyes and Faliero, of course, has no head at all. Were it not so tragic then it would be quite comical, like all ghost stories, wherein lies much of their power.

I hate the thought that my sweet man might meet by chance these violent ghosts, who have few kind feelings for those who still live on this earth and less still for those who are strangers in this town. I fear that if he meets with ghosts my man might be struck with a seizure, or a fever to his brain, for when evil meets good, it's the innocent who suffer the most.

Least of all, I like him to go by Ca' Dario, where a family from Dalmatia owns a house I hate. Though Giovanni Dario's a great lover of books, and buys in good sums from my man, I wish he did not go there. It is the most cursed home in Venice. Giovanni Dario, who conducts a great oriental commerce, and who speaks more foreign tongues than any man in Venice, is planning to rebuild it, I know. Sure it will then be full of eastern traceries and arches – a little piece of Constantinople afloat in our own town! It is at present quite modest in its scale, and plain in its lines, though large in its evil. Now Dario has a daughter he adores and he thinks a great house will make a good showpiece from which to sell her to some Golden Book noble.

But you cannot build strong foundations over a sodden bloodstain; you cannot drive out a bad spirit that way. It only comes back swelled with strength it's gained from the effort of flouting you.

There's nobody who can afford not to believe in magic in Venice. Not even Germans. Their *fondaco* is but a few hundred years old, and does not have a ghost, but if you ask me it's only a matter of time.

Chapter Two

Everything is ungrateful.
In doing good, no good comes to you.

Someone else had been found dead at the old Ca' Dario. Murder or suicide, no one knew and it made little difference: the infallible curse had merely claimed another victim. Again the house was cleared in one more attempt to be rid of the evil spirits that inhabited it. There was yet more talk of a fine new *palazzo* to replace the old one, to expunge its ugly sins with beauty.

The owner's agent sold off the furniture in the Campiello Barbaro, in the shade of a tree. Venetians hurried past, shaking their heads. Who would buy a relic of that tainted place, which, for all its grandeur, ground out corpses like a mill?

Wendelin, walking past the ramshackle stalls, felt his eyes drawn to a graceful cabinet. Lussièta had made sure he knew of the reputation of Ca' Dario, and indeed every haunted alley in Venice. While he sometimes enjoyed her tales, or at least her vivid way of telling them, he did not feel in his own flesh the superstitions of the Venetians. The city failed to frighten him, except in a commercial sense.

'Venice', he would smile at his wife, 'is in a state of story-hunger, that's why she invents ghost stories. It's just a great growling in the intestines for novelty, for visions.'

His wife had shaken her head and told him that Venetians died of these things.

'If they die, it's not of ghosts; they die of too much storytelling and listening and forgetting to be practical. *That* can turn you into a ghost, of sorts.'

His wife had replied with a smile that he did not yet understand the Venetians. They had left it at that, gone hand in hand to look at their son sleeping in his crib, and all thoughts of disagreement were banished from the room at the sight of his soft lips half opened in a smile.

But that day at Ca' Dario, Wendelin found that he had been sufficiently influenced by Venice to be drawn to a beautiful object and to want it for himself. Its purchase might also, he reflected, serve to prove to his wife in a practical way that there was no such thing as a haunted house. An exquisite little piece of Ca' Đario in their own home would cure her childish fears of the *palazzo*, and, he hoped, all such places.

Perhaps it was consolation he sought in the sheer outrageous extravagance of it. At such a grave moment in his economic affairs, it seemed a gesture of blithe and confident faith to invest in something that was worthwhile merely for its beauty.

And he had the funds in hand. That afternoon he had patrolled the local *cartolai*. Not one had sold a copy of Catullus that day. No one enjoyed humiliating Wendelin von Speyer, and various shopkeepers had rushed to settle stale debts, so that his sleeve was knotted round a heavy swag of silver. No matter that there were more practical uses for that money at this moment. He gazed at the grey-green cabinet, running his finger over the ridges of the coins inside his sleeve.

He counted forty-seven drawers, each painted with very pretty and improper scenes of country life. Wendelin drew closer, examining with pleasure the amorous couples entwined in shady groves. Three years ago, he would have turned from it, blushing. Now he regarded the cabinet avidly, noting the four barley-twist legs at the front, the four straight ones at the back, and the dark cracks of age crazing its smooth surface. In the shimmer of the hot day, it seemed to vibrate in front of him, even edge infinitesimally closer.

He opened one drawer to find a hollow sparrow's egg, speckled as a poor child's face. The next drawer held a large black egg, its meat still intact, he judged, from its weight and sour smell. In a third lolled a red egg, hollow and insubstantial as a bubble. A fourth revealed a tiny chicken egg.

A bird lover or an egg collector must have owned this, Wendelin thought, *someone like young Bruno*. The thought of Bruno, of whom he was so very fond, endeared the cabinet to him further.

And a sweet, beckoning idea of how to use it was forming in his head. What a pleasure it would be to bring such a plan into careful execution!

'How much?' he asked the dealer, leaning closer as a noisy wind gusted between them, stirring the soupy air. The man named a sum as ludicrous as Wendelin had imagined.

'It's from Damascus, look at the . . .'

'How much?' The wind tugged at Wendelin's hair, making it stand on end. The dealer showed his teeth.

'This unique and wonderful piece has travelled here over the sea . . .'

Wendelin cut him short as courteously as possible. He was in a hurry to be out of the wind, which had insinuated itself under his collar and was ruffling his stubble uncomfortably. Moreover, there was something tawdry to his mind in arguing over money when the beautiful cabinet stood so close by. How could one put a monetary value on such loveliness and usefulness: it would be like naming a price for his own wife. He unknotted his sleeve and handed the man the three ducats he'd named, trying not to think it represented half a year's rent for a small house. While the Venetian stood open-mouthed, Wendelin explained that two of the apprentices from the *stamperia* would be there to pick it up at three and a half hours after noon the next day, precisely. The dealer smiled mutely and rummaged in his apron for a bill of sale, which Wendelin briskly folded in his sleeve, glad to have documentary proof of his fantastical acquisition.

'From Ca' Dario?' his wife shuddered. 'The Devil lives there.'

'From Damascus, originally. Darling, you know the superstitions in this town about that house are far from reasonable. Men and women die in every *palazzo* in Venice.' Blinded with enthusiasm for his purchase, he did not notice the sad strain on her face as she struggled not to contradict him.

'Please don't bring it here.'

'Ach, now you're being a little silly, my love. It's a beautiful thing. You always say we should live with beautiful things around us. Is that not the Venetian way? Look at all this glass you've collected.'

Wendelin drew his wife to his breast. He was irritated to feel her quivering in his arms. It took the edge off the glamour of his impulse. Was he not permitted a sole picturesque gesture? Such as any Venetian might make, and be praised for it?

'I don't want it here. I beg you.'

'I've paid for it already.' Wendelin handed her the bill of sale. 'Don't cry. You'll see. You'll love it.' He smiled down on her encouragingly.

'I already hate it. It is vile,' she murmured, indistinctly, into his robe. Then she held the paper up to the light, as she always did, to see the watermark. She cried out, 'You see! It's a roach!' throwing the bill on the floor.

Wendelin felt himself unexpectedly roused to sharpness. He pulled away from her and took hold of her shoulders. He spoke more loudly than he needed to, staring into her eyes, shaking her slightly.

'Probably a sacred scarab, not a roach. You're making a big fuss over nothing, my love. You *disappoint* me. This believing in ghosts is a kind of itch in you, which you are scratching out of control, and it is getting infected.'

It was strange and distressing to talk to his wife this way. Yet he could not stop himself. And instead of being frightened by this change in him, it seemed that his wife was moved to equal though softer tenacity. She reached for his sleeve, entreating him in a strangely high-pitched tone, 'Please listen to me.'

A squall of unaccustomed fury rose up in Wendelin. He shook her hand loose from his sleeve.

'This is not reasonable. You're too used to having your own way. You're spoilt, and indulgent of your own wishes. Don't be a little girl. You should grow up, please. Use your mind on wholesome things.'

Wendelin's wife put her rejected hand against her mouth, as if to stopper up a reply. Silence fell between them while they stared at one another.

'Why do you talk to me like this?' she said, eventually, in a voice thickened with tears.

'Like what?'

'Coldly, as if I were a stranger.'

'You are imagining it. Stop this, Lussièta.'

She turned away from him then, and left the room, her shoulders shaking with sobs. He missed her, but he could not bring himself to go after her. He was full of thoughts of the cabinet. In that moment it was more alluring than his headstrong wife: unlike her, it was passive in its beauty, a willing vehicle for his fantasies.

From the moment he'd seen it, he had decided to put the cabinet to work, to serve his love of his wife. He felt that he'd neglected her lately. Worries about work had made him exhausted and monosyllabic in the evenings. He wanted to revive the freshness of their romance. He planned to place a love letter to his wife in a different drawer of the cabinet each day. On all his walks, to and from work, he contrived the details of his surprise for her. Every morning, as he left the house, he would hear upstairs the happy whine and click of drawers pulled open and shut until she found it, the eloquent token of his adoration of her. He would even write in Italian, to prove how much he loved her, never mind the possible errors of nuance or style!

'You are everything to me,' he would write, 'you are the musk and music of my life.'

He would write, 'Never stop loving me, you are grain and grass to me.'

And sometimes he would write out, in his own hand, some lines from Catullus that showed so well how it was to be in love.

For days he planned his love letters; when he had perfected them then the delightful entertainment would start.

He bought it from Ca' Dario on the day the sirocco started.

He should have been at the *stamperia*, of course; instead he was wandering around the town where trouble could find him. The house is falling down with problems, with Jenson, with the priest Fra Filippo, with debts unpaid – and he brings a dreadful costly thing home, paid for with the silver he earned with books!

If he has become so much a Venetian that he must buy luxuries, then why not a ruby from Balashan or a white camel from Kalacha? Or six saltwater pearls from Kain-du? Why this dreadful box?

It's a well known thing that no man or beast nor maid can do a stroke of work when the sirocco comes. No artist paints. The man who sells roast pumpkin and hot pears closes up his stall and goes home to pull the blankets over his ears. The wig sellers in San Marco lower their hairy poles, for the wind will soon tug the curls loose and send shags of hair flying over the square. Even the hungry courtesan gives but sparingly of her favours. And those of us at home are more bitter than yesterday at the sight of our neighbour's dirty stoop.

So I suppose the goat-stinking, plague-ridden *sirocco* blew him to Ca' Dario. But it did not pull the coins out of his sleeve to buy that box! I don't know how he could even go there. I would not want the dust of the street in front of it on the soles of my slippers. He says it's all tales. He says it's just a house. A house cannot hurt you, he says.

But I know Ca' Dario's not just a house. One night when I was a girl I tried to run past it. All the glass was black as it is now since the last man died there and there was not a soul that would go in it, by day or dusk.

Even at ten years old, I knew to run past it. No one had to tell me it was bad. I knew it in the marrow of my bones. The four chimneys worked the sky and each bush of blooms foamed on top of the wall and crawled out with a prod of its branches to take me in. The house craved me.

Then I saw the light in a small window, high above the street. One sole wavering wax flame, held in one thin hand. And I saw another hand that wrote and wrote and wrote. A hand like a claw with no need to dip ink for its own blood poured in a slim black stream down the quill and out upon the page.

I stood and watched for I could not walk away. Finally my mother came looking for me and dragged me home while I kicked and screamed.

I know that was a childhood thing, and years ago now, but I cannot forget it.

Why did he buy it?

This is the first time he has gone against me and now there's a little crack in my world, such as when an eggshell splits with a fissure too small for the eye to see and yet the rottenness still gets in and the life-sap oozes out. Where once I felt safe, I now feel uneasy.

He could read the terror in my face and felt me tremble in his arms, and yet he proceeded with the box in any case. He did not comfort me for my fear, but instead he made cruel comments about me just when I was most in need of soft words . . . His eyes turned the colour of slow ice in the mountains and there was a bitter smell on his breath when he spoke to me so harshly. I cannot forget it! Now my heart throbs as the nose does when someone's struck it hard. And in my belly there's a feeling as if someone has just ripped something in half.

I know it is a trivial and childish thing but when he spoke to me like that my mind went straight to the meal I had made for him that day. I'd cooked two of his most favourite dishes, and brought him a surprise of a peach that should not yet be in season. I thought of the ache in my shoulder from sitting long at my needle to mend a tiny tear in his hose, though my own skirt still has a rent in it – but there was not time to do both. Most particularly I thought of the night, a few weeks back, when he brought home his precious Catullus and I coddled it like a love-child. I wondered that he did not think on these things, and give me some dispensation for them, but all he could do was talk of this wonderful box as if it were a woman and he were newly in love with it.

I realise with a sorry little pain in my heart and lungs that for the first time I do not look forward to the evening when he comes home from work and we may be together from dusk to dawn. I hope he'll work late today and even wish that it was time for one of his trips to the land to talk to the merchants of paper.

This thought brings another, even less welcome.

I fear, in this act of buying the box, that he has begun to be tired of Venice and the sea light on the walls starts to drive him mad. This is the start of his not loving the town, and that means that one day he'll want to leave and go back North, up over the Alps again. And not come back.

You see, after all the trouble and the agony of deciding, Catullus is published and yet nothing has happened. A few noblemen have come in for their single copies and that is all. Domenico Zorzi of course bought two dozen, and speaks airily of more purchases. Nicolò Malipiero is nowhere to be seen. They say he's been taken ill. The *stamperia* is silent with foreboding and hope.

And my man's solution: he goes out and spends money like water! Coins are scarce as white crows, and not just in my purse. Each time I hand one over I stare at its face a long time first, as if it might burst into song. Soon we shall learn to live upon dew like the insects. And he spends three ducats on a vile haunted cabinet!

I fear this box is the start of some bad thing, and I wish with all my heart that he had not bought it.

Wendelin deliberated earnestly as to where the cabinet should go. At first he placed it at the end of their bed, but he saw that his wife gave it wide berth, and that she slapped their son's fingers if he tried to pull at its drawers. He did not want her to hate the cabinet – tried to discourage her from calling it 'that box' – so he moved it to his study on the same floor.

With his hand resting on the cabinet, he would call his wife into his study; ask her to admire the beautiful paintings on the drawers. She stood there, her eyes averted, until he found himself seized once more with anger against her. He spoke a few hard words, watched the tears slide from beneath her lashes. Later, when they ate, she insisted on recounting all she knew about Ca' Dario for the fourth time, in a faltering voice from which all her habitual confidence had been abducted.

Wendelin did not know how to argue with his wife. Her seething quiescence and her intemperate outbursts perplexed him to silence, which he feared she thought cold. If he started to talk about the cabinet, she found an excuse to quit the room, or burst into sobs and incoherent recriminations. German wives were not like this.

He wondered how Johann had dealt with Paola di Messina's cold fire: he remembered that his brother once remarked mildly that the tartness of his wife's tongue could sour the milk. He found it impossible to handle Lussièta's hot eruptions and her noisy tears, and, worst of all, the weary way she interrupted him whenever he tried to explain himself, as if it were a waste of time for him to continue with his speech for she knew how things really lay much better than he did.

He felt as if each harsh word he used scarred their love in some indelible way. Yet, when he saw how she hated the cabinet, he could not help himself: he disliked her for it.

But even Wendelin was obliged to admit the eggs inside the cabinet might not be healthy. They were also in the way of his plans. The night before he started his campaign of love letters, he removed each egg, carefully and slowly, from its drawer. Each was different; each perfect. He laid them in a box, intending to present them to Bruno, then realised that he could not face his wife's recriminations if he did so. Grimly, he walked to the window and emptied the box into the canal from the window. The flotilla of eggs departed immediately, in formation. There was something strange about their movement, but Wendelin could not work out what it was.

Only later that night did he realise what it was: the eggs had floated away *against* the tide.

Fate is barking at me like a rabid dog.

Now the wretched cat has started to ransack my own drawers. He's learned to stand on his back legs and then he worries the handle of each drawer between his paws fast and furious, as if he were trying to light a fire with kindling. Some handles yield to him and he's had much pleasure in sleeping in the open drawers, having first thrown everything inside to the floor. If the drawer contains beautiful things, he simply steals them and takes them to his boudoir, where I must pull them out of his bared teeth if I want them back.

The first time this happened, I came into our kitchen to find a scene of plunder, with five drawers open and the contents scattered. I thought the villain who threw the stone had come back.

I screamed to my man to come down from his study, 'We've been robbed!'

My man examined the scene of the crime with care and slowly. In a few minutes he led me to the cat's corner and showed me the things in there.

'Robbed from the inside,' he said, 'the criminal is one of the family,' and he smiled, but I did not like the way he said it, for all of a sudden it reminded me that it was I who had robbed the printers of their reputations and put their lives at risk, I who should have been looking to their well-being in all things. And I wondered if my man had come to know what I had done and if the cabinet is his conception of a just punishment.

Wendelin prepared the love letters, carefully. He did not want to set up a pattern which he could not maintain, so he drafted the first three score love letters in advance, delighting in the careful sequence of them. He was sure that they would restore his wife's love and trust, which had so mysteriously unravelled in the few weeks since he acquired the cabinet.

Lussièta was eating less than she used to and she was looking less plump than before. He felt great tenderness for his reduced little wife, but when he went to embrace her in the kitchen, she stood silent and still in his arms.

'Is this still about the cabinet?' he asked her.

She nodded.

He pulled apart from her, though she clung to him.

'You are unbelievable. How can you be so stubborn?'

'Please,' she started, but he released her from his arms and gave her a push towards the door.

She moaned.

'You Venetians—!' he started, but she was gone already. He felt a sudden desire to see and touch the beautiful cabinet, which would not flinch from his fingers as she did. He ran upstairs to his study, trying to ignore the sound of sobs coming from their bedroom as he passed.

The air sags between us now, where once it snapped with lust.

He closes down on me. It reminds me of something each time it happens, and I have at last worked out what it is.

In the eighth month of the year when the kind of heat comes that only the poor can bear, then the rich of this town leave their *palazzi* and go to the hills for their cool shades. Those *palazzi*, once full of life, are shut up fast. That's how my man is. It starts with a few windows closing, but soon the sheets are put over everything, the halls cleared out, then at last there's nothing but emptiness in him.

The thing that breaks my heart is that in those moments he's not someone I know. He's the kind of man I know I should flee, and not live with as a wife.

Now I've seen that my man can be like this, I know he can be this way again. This envenoms not just the future but also the past with new fears. I look back on all our acts of love and wonder – were they not for him as they were for me? If they were, then how could he now break the faith between us in this way? Or is it that those years were just the start of a wed life that would become bitter like all the others?

So be it. If I had known it would turn out like this, I would still have loved him with all I had to give.

I know I'm prone to enlarge things, make large of light things. I try to keep this tendency in check.

I say to myself, 'So it is not perfect after all, this love. But why do I weep? Nor is any one day perfect, nor our son, nor our cat, nor one whole thing in the world. I myself am far from perfect. So why should I expect that it would be perfect with my man, all the time, every day?'

I rap my own knuckles on the bedpost, as if that little pain might drive out the bigger one inside.

I look in the glass, to see what pain is doing to me. When I'm sad like this, my mouth feels painted on. The corners are dragged down by the heavy paint. When *he's* ill-pleased with me, as he seems all the time now, his mouth is set in a line and his lips are pulled back inside, safe from my kisses, should I be brave enough to give them.

We still have our acts of love. In the dark I cannot see the line of his mouth. We still talk, though it's hard to get the words out, of daily things – of our son's new tooth, of the cat's latest thievery.

But it's hard to talk. It seems an affront to the real pain we feel to speak of these other things, which matter not at all. I suppose we keep the talk going so neither of us is seen to cut the thin thread: we are both terrified of silence falling between us.

He must have heard my knuckle on the bedhead because he comes into the bedroom, and now he looks wrathfully at me, though for why I cannot guess. I try to smile. Underneath my face, the me who pulls the strings of each feature is sweating over her contraptions, but it's futile. No smile comes.

He stands at the foot of the bed, and looks hard at my face, and says, 'Don't do this to me!'

Chapter Three

That one, whom you see
stepping out in the sordid style of an actress, or a cockroach
grinning like a Gallic beagle . . .

It did not take Sosia long to devise her revenge upon Giovanni Bellini for the insult of his portrait of her. But it took some time for her to effect it. First of all she wanted to ensure that the portrait would never be seen in public and so she ordered Nicolò Malipiero to buy it for his private rooms, where she alone would see it. Giovanni was already working on another one for the nobleman who had commissioned the original piece.

And him of course! she allowed, dismissively, *but what does he matter?*

She made no objection to Bellini finishing the painting just as he wished, even posing one more time at the studio to allow him to perfect the radiance of the light behind her hair. With every appearance of docility, she accepted the coins Bellini counted into her hand. She bade him farewell civilly and bowed to the *Belliniani*, sweating over their copies of the great master's originals. She smiled widely at everyone with the utmost and uncharacteristic decorum. But as she sauntered out, grinning like a dog, Sosia pocketed the key that was resting, as usual, on the ledge of the window next to the door.

She did not to know that Bruno was following her the next evening when she set off. It was not the first time, and he did not invariably do it. But on nights when sleep evaded him he sometimes walked to her house at San Trovaso and watched the door. Often he waited all night, narrowing his eyes at the thought of her indoors with Rabino, in their bed, or worrying that she passed the dark hours elsewhere, with someone else.

More than once Bruno saw Wendelin von Speyer shuffling along the *rio* at strange hours, but thought little of it. For those whose sleep was haunted by business problems or matters of the heart, the streets of Venice were an acknowledged solace. One could not, of course, wander too far from home in the tiny city, and circular perambulations were known to soothe anxious heartbeats. Bruno knew that Wendelin had plenty to preoccupy him, with the sale of books so spasmodic and the executions such a little time past. Only once, when Wendelin seemed to hesitate near Sosia's door, did a flicker of suspicion cross Bruno's mind. *Not Wendelin too!* he'd whispered to himself. Then he thought of Lussièta, and a vision of the many tableaux of perfect love he witnessed in their home put his suspicions to rest.

Bruno sat at the foot of a well, and peered around its edge towards Sosia's house. Three hours after sunset, he saw her slip out of the door.

He followed at a discreet distance, cursing the clumsiness that had overcome him in the last four years, for he often stumbled now where once he'd walked as subtly and gracefully as a cat. He was so occupied in monitoring the quietness of his steps and in not falling over that he did not at once realise where Sosia was going. It was a surprise to him when she stopped at the door of Bellini's studio, fitted a key into the lock. He saw her stand back a moment as the gush of suppressed heat flew out of the open door. Then she let herself in, striking a match on the lintel and holding it to a candle she had brought with her.

His first thought was: *She has a tryst with some lover in there!* But he dismissed it instantly, as too dishonourable, too uncomfortable, even for her. A brief sensation of horror gripped his mind: *Could Sosia have also seduced Bellini himself?* If that was the case though, he reasoned, there was no need to meet in the studio. Bellini's wife was dead; she might have gone to his house, using its discreet entrance.

Bruno's imagination was still fermenting when he saw through the window that Sosia had lit a lantern now. Her slender figure was flitting between the boards and the pedestals, lifting up silk coverings and laying them down again. Sometimes she went back for a second look at a painting, holding the lantern up to examine it closely.

She's looking for something, no, it's less urgent than that, it's as if she's choosing something, thought Bruno.

Finally Sosia stood a long time in front of one board, in silence. Her back was to Bruno. He could see it was a Madonna, Bellini's latest masterpiece, finished but still glistening with wetness. Sosia gazed up at the sad face, her shoulders shaking a little. His own eyes met the Madonna's over Sosia's back. Mary's sweet resignation shot through him, and he crossed himself automatically.

Sosia's weeping, poor darling, she must be thinking of her own mother, thought Bruno. Then a suspicion crossed his mind. *Or she's laughing.*

Then Sosia drew a long, thin blade from her sleeve and raised it to the painting.

Gentilia Uguccione stood at the window, looking out at the water sliding into the courtyard fountain. She shimmered in substantial silhouette through the dusty autumn light. She was motionless. They had been like this for five hours; the brother crouching in the shadow of the room, spilling his pain, his love, his every nuance of guilt and passion, the entire story of Sosia and himself.

Until now, Gentilia had wanted to know everything. Bruno had confided sparingly, throwing her unsatisfactory morsels that merely whetted her appetite for full disclosure.

Today he'd kept nothing back, not even the story that precipitated this confession, of a confused tale of a slashed Madonna in a studio in Venice. This part, no one but herself must ever hear of, apparently, though everyone in Venice seemed to know the character and ill-deeds of this Dalmatian whore who had seduced her brother, this Sosia Simeon. Bruno had forced Gentilia to swear on his life that she would never tell a soul about the painting.

'If it's found out that I saw her and did not stop her . . .' Bruno trembled.

Gentilia shook her head, no, no. She would not divulge that secret. It seemed to her far less important than other details about Sosia, irrelevant to the case, in fact. Why was Bruno so stricken because there was one less painting in Venice? The town was stuffed with them like a watermelon with seeds!

Brushing the Madonna aside, she felt breathless trying to classify and store all she had just heard about Sosia. Sweat trickled down her back. She needed time alone to sift, to divide the pertinent facts from the dross. In the meanwhile, she knew that she must begin the process of separating Bruno from what ailed him, even though she would, in so doing, be forced to add to his pain in the short term. She watched a pigeon alight on a stone trough of water and begin to drink. She felt the coldness of the liquid in his beak, cold as her own words. She did not look at Bruno as she spoke.

'You cannot love her, Bruno. She's thoroughly bad. In fact bad is a feeble word to describe the ways in which she violates everything good people hold sacred.'

Bruno gazed at his sister. He'd never heard her so articulate before. Perhaps he had misjudged her? Perhaps his fears for her sanity were mercifully unjustified? He was only too relieved to believe it so. He answered her just as he would respond to Felice or Wendelin, in a normal voice instead of the simplified language he had been accustomed to use with her since childhood.

'She's not bad, not bad at core, I mean. She's been dispossessed and abused all her life. The abused have only guile or violence to reinstate themselves. She's no worse than anyone cursed with the kind of life she was born with.'

'Cursed? Rabino Simeon has shown her nothing but kindness. She was taken in by a respectable physician who did her the honour of marrying her, who's tolerated her perversions, even those she performs with you. There's no excuse for her. Now that you've told me everything, I can give you only this answer. Before, there was room in my heart in which to excuse her on your behalf, because I love you. Now there is no corner unoccupied with her crimes. I feel it like pain in my side.'

'I feel the pain everywhere, but it's worse without her.'

'Well then, Bruno, does this help? – Think of the millions of men who've never known her and who survive well and happily. Think of the hundreds of men who've had her in exactly the ways you've had her.' Gentilia watched, with satisfaction, as Bruno flinched at this. 'And who now live without her, and are healthier and gladder for it. Think of them. You could be one of them.'

'I cannot endure the thought of being without her.'

'Bruno, you look like a dead man.'

It was true. He reminded her of the men she saw on pallets in the mortuary, awaiting their burials. At the nunnery, Gentilia's duties now included the laying out of adult corpses. She thought of the bodies she had wrapped. Bruno's abject face, his numb-looking lips, recalled those who had left this world. She wrinkled up her nose.

'And you smell strange, like old wine, corrupted in the barrel.'

'I'm drinking too much, it's true. I try to match the oblivion I find with her.'

'Do you want to die, Bruno? That's where she's leading you.'

'If I cannot have her, yes. I must go. She might be waiting at my rooms and she will not wait long!' He groaned softly, 'How can I face her now I've seen what she did to the Madonna?'

'Come back and talk to me again, Bruno. Perhaps letting the words into the air will cleanse you internally. With me, it is safe to talk of such things. With no one else. She's of no immaculate reputation, and yours will be dirtied if the association becomes known.'

'You are good.' But as he said it, Bruno felt unease stirring inside him. Gentilia, he intuited, perversely ashamed at the thought, was not good; she was merely constrained to behave as if she were so. If she were free as Sosia, what would she be like? And her curiosity was morbid. She had asked too many questions; she'd burrowed shamelessly into his intimate memories. She had nagged him for details he had blushed to recount. Now she stiffened his apprehensions, taking his hand and speaking forcefully.

'It's the only thing I know how to be, Bruno. You make me feel that I lack something in that I cannot be the – the love-object – that Sosia is in your life. If only I could,' she whispered, 'then you would not need *her*.'

Bruno shook his hand free and took a step away from her. Gentilia followed him with her eyes. He could hear her breathing, fast and deep, and saw that she was not quite in control of herself. She bore the vague look she'd sometimes worn as a child, when insisting on bizarre rules to her self-invented games. In this trance-like state, he was afraid of what she might say. He kissed her cheek and raised his hand in a brisk valedictory salutation, but she stopped him with an arm flung out to bar his way.

'Don't you understand?' she hissed, 'I'm jealous of her in her *intimacy* with you.'

'I cannot bear to hear this, Gentilia. What have I done to you? Have my confessions made you feel unwell in yourself again? Shall I call *Suor* Nanna for you?'

'It's not you, it's Sosia.'

Bruno moaned, 'No, I cannot bear this. You must stop. Not just saying these things, but thinking them.'

He turned abruptly and strode grimly from the room, leaving Gentilia blank-faced, lost in her contemplations.

Each time he left the island, he vowed that he would not return for more than the normal family visit, once a month, a polite exchange of little news. But every few days Gentilia sent for him, on some transparent pretext or another. He came, sullenly, for he dared not reject her outright: he worried for her.

He also admitted to himself some selfish motives; despite the deranging effect on poor Gentilia, it was a relief to talk about Sosia to someone, anyone. He had run to her instinctively when he saw Sosia destroy the painting. With Gentilia he had no more need to be polite. He might simply give way to his feelings in her presence.

Their conversations became more brutal. Gentilia massaged each of his pains with a prodding finger, sending fiery trails of hurt inside him. On every visit she raised new issues that had enlivened her nights' deranged imaginings.

And perhaps Gentilia was not the only one to be touched with madness. Bruno himself had begun to hallucinate. He saw Sosia in all kinds of places where she simply could not be. Once, on a boat, he could have sworn he saw her leaning from a window in a *palazzo* that belonged to the Malipiero family. He told himself this vision was a mirage, conjured out of the hot air hanging over the canal. Another time, delivering a book to Domenico Zorzi, he felt her presence so strongly in the nobleman's study that it took all his will to prevent him from twitching aside the curtains to see if she was hiding behind them.

Now, whenever she lay in a brief sleep, after love, he sat up beside her staring at her leather diary on the floor. He still resisted the temptation to open it, but he felt unspeakable things soaking through its binding.

Chapter Four

Henceforth let no woman believe any man's vows.

What's more, it was wrong from the start, this strange plot of writing to me. He should not have needed to write to me for I lived in his soul and he lived in mine. The looks that flowed between us were so fluent we scarcely had call to talk. There was no need to scratch it out in ink, as if I was a person separate from him. He had only to smile and I was glad; he had only to sigh and I felt the air departing from my own breast.

So it was wrong of him to write like that, even when the notes seemed so bright with love at the start. I put it down to his love of books and written words. *It has carried him to excess*, I told myself, *so that he forgets there are things so fine they may not be trapped inside a sentence.*

I have been (in secret, of course, – now there are so many secrets between us!) to hear the priest who says books are bad and though he's a wrong-headed man full of hate (and so no true man of God), yet I feel he makes some points which all must yield to him.

He says my man should not print these books of love. Such things should live privately in the breast. Are they not more pure there? More true? Once love is writ, it bears the stain of the man on it, he says, and then purses his mouth like the ejecting end of my cat.

Then I think to myself, *why doesn't the Church – Fra Filippo, for example – turn on the witches?* Do we ever hear him ranting against what is practised in every alley in Venice? Why books, when but a third of us can read? It's obvious. The man cares not to save souls but to win them for his own adulation. If he preached against daily witchcraft, against our little rituals and wise women, he would be ignored. Do you think the public will give up the superstitions that give colour to their lives? No! The public does not languish for lack of books. There are too many books in Venice. And the ordinary people cannot afford to buy them. Why, Fra Filippo might as well tell them to give up dishes of gilded peacock such as the nobles eat. And so the mob's taken to a fine hot hatred of books with relish. It costs them nothing and gives them the pleasure of righteous passion. They're all swelled up with a sense of doing good. Like my man and his love letters.

He acts as if he does me a big honour with them. I'm supposed to be humble and pleased. I am not. I swear there are days when I think he hates me because I do not love his precious box and what comes out of it.

I nearly did not go there – to the box – on the first day. When I woke to find his note on my pillow (which was curt; it just said 'look in the drawer of the cabinet') I should have feigned not to see it. I could have said, if he asked, that the cat had stolen it away, or the wind blew it off. But I was afraid of this new man of mine, who seemed to place more value on that stick of wood than on me.

When I saw the note he had not yet left the house, so I knew he was listening for me from downstairs, and I dared not drag my feet. So I jumped out of bed as quick as I could and walked like a ghost in my chemise to the room where he keeps the box. One of the drawers was a tiny bit open, like an eye that winks, but not very well. I wanted to touch it as little as possible. I saw a flash of cream and I snatched the letter out of the drawer like a cat catching a sparrow.

I left the room straight away. I did not want to read that letter with the cabinet watching me. Yes, it was a nice letter, but nothing could console me for the way of its delivering.

The next one was nice; the one after seemed somewhat less so, and now . . .

This morning, before he left, he drew me out of the bed and kissed me hard on the lips.

As soon as he was gone I went out into the hall, spread my arms, and turned around and around and around, like an octopus dancing in the sea, until the bitterness of his kiss was blown away. I wish I could unravel all my fears this way, as I used to when I was a child.

'You always . . .' he says to me now.

When he starts with this, I am lost. There's no gainsaying those dreadful things he says I do.

'You always make everything worse than it needs to be,' he says. 'Why don't you only put your arms around me and tell me that you love me? It's always I who must make the creeping back to you.'

I'm too frightened to say, 'I am too frightened.' There's no love in his eye, just a cold spark like when a knife blade catches the light.

I feel him take up arms against me. At first he's quiet in his defence. He folds his hands neatly. He tells me: 'You always shrug off what is your fault.' If I'm silent, he seems to feel his enemy – that is me – get stronger. (It's not true of course. I'm weak as a kitten against his rage.) Then he seems to find inside himself a sharp spleen and I fear what he'll say next. It will be without mercy. I leave the room then, if I can, because I see his next weapons are very grievous indeed and it will be hard to repair the damage they cause. He says he hates me leaving the room more than anything.

Now the worst has happened: the pain has spread to our acts of love. He comes to our bed, I think, just to prove he's my man and no one else may have me, like a child with a toy of which he has tired, but for which he'll scream if someone else should try to touch it. He still loves my body each night, but I think it's just to keep up the show and maintain the peace, where once it was the joy of our each day. 'Thank you,' we say afterwards. I to him and him to me, as if we were friends who had done a good turn for one another. Perhaps this is the German way of love and finally it has come out.

He falls back with a yawn writ large on his eyes and mouth. This, I think, is to tell me he wants sleep and I should stay quiet and not press an extra kiss on him or take his hand, lest he thinks I want something more. If I stroke his hair, he does not groan with pleasure, as he used to. He suffers it in silence.

Then he lies still, does not reach for me. He's not asleep, so he can hear me try to eat my tears when they jump up inside of me. He seems to wish to taste my pain, slow and considering, as if it were wine. As if his pride is made more rich because I want him and he wants me not. When he hears me not-weep like this, after a long while, he says soft, as if he dare not speak in a clear voice, 'Did I do some bad thing to hurt you?'

What can I say? Does he really need an answer – or does he mock me? Try to stretch out the pain to make it bigger? I feel shamed, dumb, despoiled, found out. Is it such a bad thing that he does not truly want me? I count the things that bless me from him – he's kind, he loves our son, he works hard, he does not lay a cruel hand on me . . .

I scorn my own self and tell myself that I've the things all wives want. What kind of whore am I that I must have the wild, fresh acts of love, too? I feel shame that I must have them or else be so low in my spirits. I've heard that there's a courtesan in Venice who gives hot and rare service but if not satisfied by a customer, she will pelt eggs at his back when he departs. Am I like that? Have I been spoilt with a superfluity of pleasures in the past?

The tears creep to my lids. I am not a bad wife – even in the spreading of the dreadful rumour about the printers I was acting in good heart – and I wish more than all things to show him love in the way most men appreciate it shown the most, but he bars my way, flat on his back; he folds his arms on his chest as if to ward me off, as if I were a bitch *in calore* that whines to be got with pup. A woman who roams the alleys after red-haired men, like Paola.

How can I give it truth if he says he does not wish to hurt me? If that were so, how could he bear to let me lie like this and think these thoughts – how can he not wish to hold me and roll the tears back from my face?

I think of fierce things. I resolve to go to a witch to get a bond-spell to get his love back. I've heard there's one that can do this, using beans and sage leaves. The witch, they say, takes on students of her crafts. Oh, I hate this! I, who loved, was loved, so well, feel to have fallen from grace, to need a witch, to get just a sign of love from her man.

When I first saw his face in the glass, I did not think it would end like this. I think now that I did not know him at all. When I add these thoughts to the words I must read each day . . .

'I lose all sense of right and wrong when I look at you,' I read. 'Sometimes I want to squeeze the breath right out of you.'

Wendelin lay in bed beside his wife, listening to the little gasps that escaped from her as she tried to hide her tears.

He longed, after making love to her, to roll her into his arms and take her lips to his and comfort her for whatever it was that ailed her. He had hoped that the love letters in the cabinet, which every day he made more detailed in their passion, would reassure her.

If words have any use at all, they must be good for this, he thought. But she seemed so afraid of him. She, whose skin had seemed a part of his, so that when they slept they were one warm beast with tangled limbs, now vibrated in pure misery on the furthest corner of the bed from him. Although she lay no more than ten inches from him, he pined for her as if she had fled to another country, for it seemed to him that she had.

We are in exile from each other, he mourned.

She had shed the animal spirit that had given her such purity and transparency. She had become complicated, hard to read, always tending to some wound that he seemed to have inflicted, looking at him with hooded eyes, her whole body stiff with offence which seemed to have been caused by him.

Perhaps, he thought, *it cannot work after all, this wedding of Venice and Germany. When I see how the printing press fails, it seems that the marriage is doomed. I was proud and foolish to think I could carry this off and keep the love of so extraordinary a woman.*

And yet, even as he explored his misery, he knew that his love for his wife was a thing apart. Even if she no longer loved him, his love for her had an independent existence. It continued to flower; it was a wonder to him that he might generate in his own breast such a poetry of emotion. The condition of loving her had become so absorbing that it had taken his life in hand. Even at the *stamperia* he felt enclosed in the shell of her love, enveloped in the delicate albumen of her tenderness, which comprised all things.

He said aloud, *I did not choose to love her, so I cannot choose not to love her, and if I try to hate her it simply does not happen.*

He had only to touch his ear and she was at his side with some aromatic salve for the earache he did not know he had. She never left the bed without covering him carefully with the sheet. She brought him food to the office, and when he opened the linen packet after she'd gone, the *panino* was always accompanied by a red apple with two careful bites removed to make the shape of a white heart in the red skin. Even these days, though she seemed afraid to touch him in any other way, in the dark she would stroke his hair with a soft hand for hours at a time. He was afraid to acknowledge the tenderness in case he phrased his gratitude wrongly and drove her away.

All he wanted was her love, the way it was before. He told her all these things in his letters, which he tucked into drawers each morning. He could not understand why they seemed to have the opposite effect to the one intended.

After a while, Wendelin noticed that the drawers of the Damascus cabinet were opening more slowly, as if reluctantly, while he waited on the doorstep. His wife used to walk promptly to it, obedient to his wish. Now he waited impatiently while her footsteps dragged as if weighted with leads.

It made no difference that his letters were ever more intense. His wife grew sadder and more sullen. She no longer greeted him at the door, or put her hands into his sleeves when he arrived at the house. The unseasonable heat of this autumn had made her listless, Wendelin thought. The whole town was parching for a drop of cool weather, just as he starved for a return of his wife's affectionate ways. He tried to write it down.

'I want to put my fingers on the tops of your eyelashes,' he wrote. 'I wish to touch your throat with the tip of my tongue while my hands circle around it. I want to see the shine of your eyes again.'

He took her to bed as soon as he could, each night, taking her hand across the plate of grapes and drawing her up from the table into his arms. She hung back. In the bedroom he ached to smooth back her hair from her face, kiss the nape of her neck, her eyes, and the hollow below her ears. She permitted only the simple act of love that for them had been as an evening prayer all their married life. Then she drew away. All night he longed to cradle her in his arms, whispering his love, to make that frightened look leave her eyes, to replace it by glassy joy and grateful tiredness.

He no longer waited on the threshold for her footsteps. She lay sleeping when he left each morning, but he hoped that she would soon awake and go to the cabinet, and find the love letter that he had left there.

I cannot bear to stay in the hot house with that box lurking upstairs like a baleful bear. I go marketing, my eyes darting everywhere for distractions. I find none, only my miseries in echo.

I am shamed in the street. I see wives of men who want them; they're plump and pelting with passion. They fear nothing at all: why should they? They are adored! For them the big issues are: is the fish fresh? Did my ma eat fresh bread with her soup last night? They thump their hands on the counter and want the news, fast!

I go to visit my sister-in-law Paola, to see if she's any more love in her than she used to. I suspect not, in her case, because of the red-haired man, and there is malice in me to see that the new marriage does not take any more than the one to Johann. Paola is my enemy because she did not join me in grafting her man to this town. I still think she killed him by not sending for the Jewish doctor who might have saved him.

You may see bear-fights and pugilists any time you like in Venice but if you want to see low-down dirty combat, look to the women. There's blood under their nails!

She greets me dryly at the door, as if she's little pleased to see me. Her poise is perfect. She gives nothing away. As ever, she's excellently mounted in her outfit. I dress my utmost when I go to see her, but she always bests me. Some little twist of braid, some arrangement around the neck. She's the kind of woman who can stand on one leg even with her eyes shut. (Perhaps because her ankles are thick as a heifer's despite her wispy waist.) She's carroty-pated with a bleached kind of face, nothing lively writ on it. I find no information there, and no way into her confidence.

We talk stiffly of the news of the town, the worst of which is the horror that some madman has destroyed a Madonna of Bellini's. Rialto's ablaze with the story and it's a source of wonder that no one's yet been denounced. Someone must know who did this foul thing.

The subject dwindles. Paola, despite the fact that her father's a painter, feels nothing for art.

Instead, I ask baldly if she's with child again, for at least this answers the question, does she lie with her new husband or is she cold with him – is her marriage to Johann di Colonia just another alliance for commercial reasons?

Then she surprises me. Her face does not take any more colour, and yet I can feel a cold anger poisoning the air in the room, like a dead rat under the floorboards. She turns on me, quivering her whiskers, and says: 'Why, Lussièta, do you play these women's games? You are like a child in the park! Don't you realise what is at stake here?'

I stare at her dumbly. She's taken my breath away with this lambaste. I want to say to her, but somehow I don't, 'Hold your rat-trap of a jaw!'

She continues: 'Gossip and wives' tales are not the way to make the *stamperia* come into profit.'

I open my mouth in horror, for I think she's guessed my secret, that she knows it was I who spread the rumour about the printers and the coins that brought the purge upon us all. I wait for a harder blow to fall on me from her tongue. It's no easier because I know that I deserve it. All this time I have deserved it, and yet I've not been punished directly.

But all she says is this: 'We must act more like men, talk directly and speak plainly of what we want and what will best succeed. This rivalry between the printers is killing all of them. It's a male thing, and must be stopped by women. The men are incapable of helping themselves.'

'You mean Wendelin should give up?' I ask, staring at her.

'No, no, no, no, no,' she whispers impatiently. 'We can be cleverer than that.' Her long sly eyes wrap around me, and I hate her as I've never hated anyone, even Felice Feliciano.

So I do not give her the gratification of asking what she means. I just spin on my heel and say, 'My man is waiting for me. He hates it if I am not home when he gets there.'

'Indeed,' says Paola, gazing at her short, ugly, perfect nails. She does not say 'goodbye'.

Gentilia looked in the mirror more often than a nun should. She feared the straying of a curl, or a smut on her nose, she told herself. She did not wish to draw attention to herself, she thought. But Gentilia rarely corrected her appearance, and with every look she felt more secure.

What did it matter that her ears were placed too high up on her head not to resemble (in conjunction with her rectangular jaw) a sow's? She knew that her large eyes were fine and that her hair was of a fashionable pale gold. Sosia must be dark and swarthy. Her hair would be greasy. She probably had little ears strung with glittering arrows of jet. She probably wore her clothes too tightly and her scant breasts thrust up like spoonfuls of cream.

305

Gentilia would suffer the blind nuns to touch her face, and it was not really suffering. She loved them to read the softness of her skin, linger over her large eyelids. She liked to feel their breath on her, ugly and old as they might be. *Is this how Sosia feels with men?* she thought.

She tried to be graceful and to do so banished the sturdy reality of her body. If she stopped walking, she would consciously place a foot down at an angle to the other, as she had once seen a dancer do in her childhood.

And she could not look on another girl's beauty with detachment. If the other young woman had lovely eyes, Gentilia found herself looking at her own hands, or touching her nose, and weighing their counterbalancing charms against the rival, wondering if Bruno would find them attractive, more alluring than what was hers?

She had asked Felice, once, 'Am I pretty?'

His lip had curled and he seemed ready to reply unkindly. His response however was enigmatic: 'I would rather look at a flower than your face. The beauty of the flower is less dangerous to my peace of mind. There's something about you . . .'

This was, she decided, a compliment and she had glowed with such delight that she distilled a bead of perspiration above her lips.

She thought of Sosia's beauty, which surely stopped somewhere barely beneath that skin Bruno was so sick for. In fact, Gentilia refused to acknowledge what Sosia owned as beauty. It was the lure of corruption, the same thing that made men violate their own daughters, or kill an enemy in a dark alley, taking him from behind in dirty silence.

Sosia had robbed Bruno's heart, and now threw it back when she had, clearly, finished with it. Insult upon cruelty!

Gentilia would make her sorry.

She would tell Bruno this when he arrived the next time.

She would deal him words like blades to excise the memory of Sosia. She would send them as knives into his soft thoughts of her. She would murder the thought of Sosia inside him.

But in her darker moments Gentilia pondered on a troubling fact. A man never came to Sant' Angelo di Contorta without expressing his admiration of her when she was paraded as the very paragon of a demure young nun. Men were often heard to say 'what an unusually shiny purity to her skin', or 'what a saintly expression', or 'this is just the kind of woman every gentleman desires as a wife'. Yes, Gentilia's praises hung on every man's lips, the young ones, the older ones, the smooth and the decrepit. But they looked over her head, with hungry eyes, for Suor Anna or Barbara.

Gentilia had not received one proposal, and not even, she realised, one proposition.

Sometimes I wonder why he still makes love to me, almost on a nightly basis, as if nothing were wrong between us. And then I think of a story I heard long ago. It is an Arab tale of a man who lost a poor, thin, ugly camel. He searched high and low for it and in the end offered an enormous sack of gold for its return. When asked, 'Why do you take so much trouble to get back a beast that is worth less than half the reward?' the man answered, 'Don't you know that the pleasure of finding something you've lost is greater than the value of the thing itself?'

And that makes me think of the wax-woman I found in Sirmione, and who might have lost her. When the cat took to raiding my drawers I pushed the figure to the back of a high one behind some ugly cloths for dusting. I thought that if he ever made his way into that drawer he would sniff the fust of them in disgust and leave it alone.

I was wrong. He found her anyway, and I caught him in the act of fishing her out. I knew then I must find a safer place, and I thought straight away of the least loved and frequented part of our house. It is of course the place where my man put the box from Ca' Dario.

'Of course,' I said bitterly, 'let us put all the evil things together, where I may close the door on them.'

So I took the wax-lady in her swaddle of linen and dropped her in the space between the wall and the back of the box.

The ugly thing seemed to move aside a fraction to accommodate her.

'There!' I said, and turned on my heel.

Chapter Five

Tomorrow let those who have never loved, love;
Let those who have loved, love tomorrow.

She knew it was to do with those parts that men have between their legs.
The ones she saw only when she assisted at the laying out of a corpse. She
herself had laid many such little snouts to one side while other, older nuns
cleaned the softer and even uglier parts underneath, which were also *furred*. She
had turned her head aside and looked at the little heap of nastiness only out of
the corner of her eye, but afterwards she always felt the ghost of its humid
weight on her hands for days.

On the dead, it was an insignificant scrag of gristle. But Gentilia knew
better. She knew that on the living it merely lay in wait, in the coy posture of
innocence, ever ready for the moment in which to show the bestiality of which
it was capable: the kind which brought forth the bobbing baby corpses in the
lagoon and those for whom she sewed the shrouds.

She had already theorised that, in its fornicatory state, the little snout must
sprout many heads, like acorns. Each little head would shrug off its helmet and
grow an eye. Blue-eyed men would sport little blue eyes inside their acorns.
Brown-eyed men would have brown ones. With all those eyes the head of
acorns would look at the woman, the way men in the street looked at women,
but worse.

Meanwhile, Gentilia thought, the hair around those parts would start to stand up stiffly, like a lace ruff. This was to protect the little eyes, like eye-lashes, and to make a courting display, inflated like the prismatic breast-feathers of the amorous pigeons she had watched all her life.

At the sight of the ruff and many small eyes, in Gentilia's vision, the woman would be obliged to disrobe and even her chemise must be removed. She must stand naked in shame before all the eyes that, at the sight of her poor breasts and belly, would open as wide as they could. The snouts would swish backwards and forwards like an angry cat's tail. The poor woman would meanwhile find her thighs swollen apart so that she could no longer close them, try as she might. Her nipples would open up like little flowers, blossoming like the acorns on the male organ. Her blossoms would be pink and red and they too would have little eyes inside them. She must look up at the face of the man to receive her instruction and he, like a father confessor awarding prayers, would choose which style of copulation she merited.

At this point Gentilia's imaginings became vaguer, because in her thoughts it would be Bruno's voice which she heard and his parts in bud before her. It would be Bruno's child planted inside her.

She also knew that she must be very careful not to catch a cold after conceiving the child, because if she sneezed the baby would come bursting out of her nose.

Since Bruno's confession, Gentilia's thoughts had run in painfully tight, angry circles. *Sosia has forced him to commit sacrilege, by consorting with a Jewess. What kind of crime would Bruno be committing with me? I'm a bride of Christ, a nun. He would be making God a cuckold. It is also incest, if God is the Father, then Bruno would be guilty of copulating with his father's wife . . .*

Better think about it a little longer but in the meantime the hour had come to enclose herself in a light cloak of a grey that perfectly matched her eyes, and go to Venice again. She had some business with those lions on the street corners, those stone lions into whose jaws decent citizens might post their written denunciations of those who performed evil acts.

Such stone lions were to be found all over the city, their mouths just wide enough to accept a single sheet of parchment, folded twice. Gentilia always wrote her letters to fit in swiftly and smoothly, as no one wanted to be caught in the act of cramming an accusation through those dread apertures.

Gentilia knew that all anonymous notes, such as hers, were officially burned. But she also knew that the sheer volume and variety of her letters, and the number of months they had been arriving, could not be ignored and that someone, somewhere, was scratching Sosia's name in a ledger on an official desk.

Lately she had begun to think of signing her name to them, a good name, respectable stock and no madness or evil in its past, and of persuading the two old blind nuns with whom she shelled peas on long afternoons to witness her denunciations, which would make them valid currency for the Inquisitors. She need not sully the purity or peace of *Suor* Nanna and *Suor* Elisabetta by explaining the detailed nature of the document they would sign. It would be enough to tell them that she wished to present a proposal for Sant' Angelo to adopt more of the foundlings currently flooding into the city. The old ladies, who loved the feel of a child on their bony knees, would be happy to support the idea of more babies at Sant' Angelo di Contorta and they would fumble their shaky signatures on to her page with a grateful press of their spidery hands.

Far better, the old nuns would sigh, the cries of babies in the night than the disgusting sighs and screams, masculine and feminine, which enlivened the dark air in the cells of the nunnery. The continued hot weather had prolonged the season of late-night visits to the island. The two elderly sisters, like Gentilia, could only but imagine what bestial acts caused their protagonists to ululate in such agonies of joy, drowning out the pious parrots. At least, Gentilia doubted if the old ladies could imagine it in such detail as she did.

She knew the results too. Babies. Hundreds of them. She knew what happened to them, unlike Nanna and Elisabetta. The infants were drowned like kittens. Only respectable babies came to her for their shrouds to be sewn. The others met their fate naked as beasts.

She had seen it herself, several times. There was a place where they went near the inlet of the island. She had watched the shadowy figures dispose of their guilt in the dead of night . . . the babies never seemed to come up again after the quick blow they were given to the head. It was as if the little bodies sank like stones through the water and the soft mud underneath and right back down to the belly of the earth that had not wanted them.

Sometimes I think he just wants one more heir for his quick books. Once he has got me with child and I have brought it forth, then he will act on his threats.

I tried to burn the letters once. But I found he'd used some kind of ink that not just lives, but knows how to dance in the flames. The words were writ in fire then, and I could not help but stare at them. I believe they've burned in my soul. I am branded with his hate.

Now I keep them, for if aught befalls me then sometime my son should know how and why.

When I know my man's to come home there's such a clench in my skin that I can scarce move. When I hear his step, my tongue nips and nips at the roof of my mouth. I gulp like a fish and start to breathe all wrong, in when it should be out, and out when it should be in, so small breaths are at war in my throat and I feel that my life hangs by a frayed thread.

He comes now. I must—

No, it is not him. Just the wind, which stirs the glutinous vapours of the canal, bringing no relief from the heat, merely wrapping its arms around us. Sometimes I wish to hide my son when I hear those steps – *Madonna*, there they are again.

My eyes run straight to the cat's corner to make sure all is in order. For he has lately defied my expectations and climbed into my man's study through an open window. The little wax-woman must have met his fancy for some reason, though she's not made of silk or velvet. Perhaps it is because she's smooth as cold butter. Anyway, he has filched her. When I saw the empty space behind the box I ran straight to his boudoir and dug through the scarves. There she lay, many scarves deep, swathed in peddler's fangles like a gypsy princess.

My heart missed a beat because I fear above all things that my man might find her somewhere in the house and accuse me of witchcraft. I know he thinks me bird-witted because I believe in ghosts, but the wax-woman would be a different thing entirely for she would show that I dabbled in the sorcerers' arts myself. He does not understand the difference of course, though it is plain to me: I love ghost tales but I hate witches.

Even if I were to explain the truth of the wax doll to him, it would show him one more reason not to trust me: that I found her at Sirmione, did not show him at once, hid her from him all this time, and did not leave her in the earth where I found her, as I now wish with all my heart I had.

Rabino, passing Sosia on the stairs, saw a flash of coloured silk under the light cloak she was fastening. He mumbled the usual shamefaced greeting and slid past her. She hummed under her breath, did not acknowledge him.

I'm so lonely here with her, Rabino thought piteously, *yet I must want her to go out. I never stop her. Perhaps it would be kinder of me to try?*

He cleared his throat and looked down beseechingly at his wife's narrow back.

'I – I wish you would not go about the town so much,' he stammered. Sosia stopped for a moment, but did not turn around.

'Does that mean you love me, Mister Doctor? That you want to keep me close in your house? You mean you love me exclusively? You mean—' Sosia broke off to laugh loudly and continued down the stairs, still gusting with laughter.

'I mean I don't want to share my wife . . . with strangers, I suppose. I feel you are being reckless with your – health, and you are not discreet,' he added lamely.

'Indeed?' said Sosia, swivelling round to look at him at the bottom of the stairs. 'I don't ask fidelity of you, Rabino. You're free to find your own pleasure where you want it. Leave me to mine, eh?'

'I don't want to be like you. I'm afraid hurtful things are being done—'

'And if they are? It toughens people up. The softer they are, the more they squeal.'

What did he see in her eyes when she said that?

'No, Sosia, it makes them more vulnerable. Can we at least come to some understanding? You are becoming . . . wilder, it seems to me. I'm afraid for you.'

'Afraid of me perhaps?'

She smiled and turned to leave.

'Where are you going?'

'Do you really want me to tell you?'

Rabino flushed and shook his head, licking his lips nervously.

'Good boy,' she said. 'Perhaps I won't leave after all.'

He recoiled, and would have said *No! That's not what I want at all*, but at that moment the church bell of San Trovaso struck. Sosia appeared to remember something. She jerked and walked rapidly to the door. Rabino felt the cold sweat of relief steaming on his back.

Sosia, on her way to Domenico Zorzi, shook her head in wonderment at Rabino's gaucheness. Surely there was no need to negotiate the terms of their marriage at this late stage?

Then she smiled to herself, recalling that Domenico had promised her a gift that day: her own copy of Catullus.

An hour later, having earned it, she stood with the printed book in her hands. Domenico's thin body was behind her, still caressing her breasts and his lips were on the back of her neck.

'You like it?' he asked. 'Is it not a very fine work?'

'Very fine. Is that Felice Feliciano's hand on the capital letters?'

'Indeed. I commissioned him to ornament the printed pages. Do you know him?'

'Everyone knows Felice,' she said vaguely, pushing her buttocks back against him.

Domenico twitched nervously. There was something in her voice that raised unwelcome thoughts. Domenico, who considered himself the most *classical* of the noblemen of Venice, admitted to himself he was not the most republican. He did not care to share a woman with a scribe, not even if it were the inestimable Felice Feliciano, and the woman a common foreigner too. He tried to

313

concentrate on Sosia's breasts, wrapping both arms around her, enclosing her body and the book in her hand.

'Keep it safe. You know it's very special.'

'Yes, very special. You know that I appreciate it. I love to have my own copy of it.'

'By the way,' said Domenico. 'I should be very happy to look at your own poems sometime.'

Sosia looked bemused. Domenico persisted: 'I know you carry the leather book I gave you for them. There's no need to be shy about showing me your work. Perhaps you have talent.'

Her eyes flew to the ledger lying on the shelf among her carefully discarded clothes.

'I'm not ready,' she said. 'Let's make do with Catullus for the moment.'

Sosia turned to meet his lips, laying her gift carefully behind her as she drew him back to her.

Domenico prepared himself again; Sosia closed her eyes, smiling. He turned her over, reared above her like a mantis and moved slowly inside her for many minutes.

This is good, thought Domenico, *I give her real pleasure.*

This book, smiled Sosia, as her buttocks rose and fell upon it, *is mine in ways he cannot guess.*

Printed on fine Bologna paper by Wendelin, the initial capitals penned in by Felice, edited by Bruno, the book, she felt, belonged more to her than to anyone else in the world.

The nuns warned Bruno about his sister. Certain unsuitable behaviour was hinted at. It had also been noted that Gentilia made more excursions to the town than could be explained easily. It was a matter of surprise to him that she ever left the island. What did she do? She never came to find him. He was agitated at the thought of her wandering around Venice, a dangerous place for an inexperienced young girl and surely perilous for one so unbalanced in her thinking.

The Mother Superior wrote to him, asking him if there were madness or brain fever in the family. Bruno quivered at the thought that his sister's verbal incontinence had already revealed his affair with Sosia or, worse, that Gentilia's own unmentionable feelings towards him had become public knowledge. Until he knew the state of things, he felt he could not be seen at Sant' Angelo.

The one thing he knew was that Gentilia would never tell how Sosia had destroyed the painting: that she had promised him and she would never break her word.

'Please go to her,' he begged Felice. 'Tell me what you think.'

So Felice Feliciano came to visit Gentilia, not for the first time. Bruno liked it when he did so and he had many reasons to wish to please Bruno.

She was making lace at her seat in the courtyard when he arrived, oblivious to the sun scorching the parting of her hair. Felice observed that under Gentilia's fingers, working as they talked, with her eyes downcast, greasy heraldic animals sprang to life, eagles, griffins, crowned lions. She would not answer his questions about her absences from the convent, but made general statements about the weather and her digestion.

Gentilia did not much like Felice; had always felt suspicious of his repeated attendance upon her. He never said much that was of interest to her, just endless judgemental comments on the beauties of other nuns and too many questions about Bruno.

She decided to make use of Felice, just as he used her, for information.

'Tell me about Sosia Simeon,' she demanded, glancing up at him quickly, with a look, which she imagined, blended an innocent curiosity with precocious insight.

'You know about her, then?'

Her reply emerged in jerky phrases. 'A little. She's a courtesan. A Jewess. My brother clings to an unclean attachment to her. I wish he would stop it. It's killing him.'

'Ah Gentilia, you give her too much honour. Sosia is not a proper courtesan. A real courtesan's kept in good style by regular retainers. She's cultivated, writes a little poetry perhaps. Her conversation is exquisite. She offers delicate meat for the body and soul.'

Gentilia's mouth hung open. She leaned closer to Felice.

'A great courtesan's rooms are as beautiful as she is, hung with silks and gold tassels. Nothing that's not lovely is seen around her. There's a famous story about one great Venetian courtesan who was receiving a foreign ambassador. After some satisfactory hours in her company he felt an irresistible need to cleanse his mouth with a thorough spit, and found himself in distress. In the end, he called in his servant and spat in his face.'

'Why did he do that?'

'He explained that in that wonderful place, his servant's face was the basest thing. Everything else was too beautiful. Nothing else was low enough to be defiled by spitting.'

'*O Dio*,' breathed Gentilia. She listened with a childlike avidity, as if to a bedtime story. Felice, noting the expression on her face, continued with added relish.

'True courtesans are *merchants* of beauty, retailers of fantasy as much as their own bodies. Of course there was no reason for that ambassador not to spit on the carpet, as he would anywhere else, but the courtesan had cultivated the appearance of such exquisiteness that he'd been completely transported away from everyday life. The ambassador was pleased, because in her rooms he saw himself as the most elite and refined of lovers; he felt that he'd made the most discriminating choice of a mistress for that night. The courtesan was clever because she sold him not just the use of her skin but exactly the sumptuous illusion he wanted.'

Gentilia interrupted: 'So Sosia, even though she's not rich as a courtesan, is very lovely? She has the ways of a courtesan?'

'No, Sosia is not like this, and nor, I believe, would she choose to be. She has noble lovers – even a Malipiero or two, I believe, but she scorns the beauty aids of the expensive whores. Not for *her* the depilatory lotions, hair pluckers and curlers, perfumed creams. She would not put herself out to attract a man. She just takes the men who come to her as she is.'

'She's lower even than a whore? And she still has a Malipiero?'

'It's hard to explain, but she has something. For example, Sosia, even when she's dressed, walks as if she's naked.'

'As you do?' Gentilia observed.

Felice was taken aback and said nothing. Gentilia continued.

'I cannot understand it. Why would Bruno degrade himself with such as her?' She shook her head violently. 'Is she a witch then, Felice? Does she cast the beans and write *carte di voler bene*?'

Felice wondered, *how does Gentilia know of these things? I have told her something of the witches, but never such details as these.*

'Nothing quite so obvious or tangible, my dear. If I had to explain it I would say it was something to do with the way she smells. If that is magic, then Sosia is magic. She doesn't believe in all the hocus pocus of the wise women and the herbalists. She scorns it. She's more subtle and more intriguing than that.'

He had said too much. Gentilia looked at him with narrowed eyes.

So even Felice Feliciano has been there, Gentilia thought, *to that unclean nest that Sosia keeps for seducing men.*

An idea was coming to her; an excitingly bad idea. She wanted Felice to go away so she could think it out alone. It was a most private plan.

She asked apparently afire with pious fervour: 'Why does this Sosia not go to the *Casa dei Catecumeni* and get herself converted to the true faith? Surely she too can be cleansed of her sin?'

Her question had the desired effect. Felice snorted dismissively and rose to leave.

But before that Gentilia managed to kiss him. Catching him by surprise, she suddenly slid her mouth over his. Even as she pressed herself on him, he kept retracting his lips. Her eyes became long and wide, so close up. He could not make himself move away from her. This kind of kiss was something he had not tried before. He put his head at right angles to hers and tasted her. Her lips were slick and stank of holy oil.

Her blood must be thick like gravy, slow and shapeless, thought Felice. *She could be dangerous.*

He pulled away and hurried to the boat, hoping for a breath of air from the water.

My man brings home not just manuscripts to read but the books of other printers, so he can compare their type with his. These days he has another sad sport: to see which printers have gone to Jenson to buy his letterforms. The house is filling with heavy dark books and sheaves of paper, where once it was light with the glass I used to buy from Murano. I put the books away in drawers without looking at them; by this I try to keep the glass winning over them.

When the cat dug out a drawer this morning, a pile of papers fell on the ground. I picked it up without much pleasure. Usually I put them straight back but for some reason today I began to read what it was about. At first I thought it was a joke but now I fear that it is not.

This manuscript, which is supposed to be some kind of manual for practical use, tells how to choose a wife. Why should he bring home a book like that? He already has a wife! Does he want another? I tell myself this is just another text to consider for the printworks, but I cannot stop myself from turning the pages. I come to passages that make my blood run cold, for they make the choice of a wife seem so venal and unfeeling a thing. The book tells how most of all a man should choose a small wife such as I am.

But for why?

For she takes less space in the bed, I read, so you can save cash and buy a smaller bed! You can save on her clothes; she will not need such yards of stuff. She'll be too tiny to be seen at the window so she scarce needs clothes at all. Then there's the hope, I read, that being small, she might need to climb on a stool to do the chores – and there's a chance she may fall off and be killed, so you'll be rid of her for good.

I shudder when I read this.

And if there is a rope to hand . . . ? I think.

Choose a woman who looks vile, the manuscript says, so she will get sons with none but you. There is no other way to be sure. And how she'll show gratitude to you in the bed, when you've been so kind as not to see how bad she looks.

I rush to the glass. The silver skin of it frowns at me; it sees things I don't understand. I look at my face. Is it vile? I think not. It is much praised. The eyes are large, dark brown, with a tilt up at the edges. Each lash is long and curls. My hair is blonde as it should be, no need to dye it with *acqua solana*. My nose is

318

straight with a soft tip. My mouth is not small but my lips are wine-red. No, I am not vile. Men still turn in the street to look at me.

My man yet looks at me too. It's just I do not now like the way he does it.

He asks me questions which are aslant of the problem, such as 'Do you not like my books? Is it that?'

I shake my head. It's true I do not love the books as he does, but I could have lived with them, if the box had not come along to divide us. But I do not dare say these words out loud as they would make him angry.

'But I love you,' he still says, as if that solves all things.

I look at the floor, as if the boards can tell me more truth than he can.

And I think of the letter I read this morning:

'I can scarcely bear to think about you when we are not together. Such thoughts come to me . . .'

Chapter Six

Since then the poor little lady
has fires devouring the marrow of her bones

'You may not go about any longer, Sosia,' stammered Rabino. 'I have – have heard things which sadden me. I believe also, from the look of your skin, that you're troubled with a dangerous disease, for which the only cure is retirement from the kind of life you've been leading. You've been fortunate to date in escaping it. Some are: I wish we knew why. However, it's come to you in the end.

'I'm leaving on the table some herbs you must boil in pure water. Bathe those parts of yourself you've abused in a tepid infusion. You must do this every day until the sores heal. God will take care of the rest, with time.

'And in the interval, you must not consort with men or you'll spread the disease. Venice has been good to you, Sosia; you should in this way be kind to the Venetians.'

Rabino did not look at her as he said this. He did not add, 'I this morning succumbed to temptation and read your disgusting diary of conquests, and I have put it in the fire.' She would discover its loss soon enough.

He pulled a small leather pouch from his black robe and left it on the edge of the table. His hand shook, and a few crushed leaves spilled out of the bag, releasing a bitter perfume into the warm room. He spoke in a timid concilia-tory voice, but, as he left, he turned the key in the street door, which he had already placed outside, fearing a struggle. He had long suspected that Sosia was capable of violence against himself – lately he'd started to wonder sometimes about the scars and bruises and starved frames of her little siblings. The more evidence he saw of her crimes, the more he feared her.

Sosia had already started screaming as he walked out of the door. As he stumbled along the street, his ears were wounded by terrible noises. She cursed him first in her own language, and then in Venetian.

She shrieked: 'Kind to the Venetians! I'll show you kind to the Venetians! No one has been *kinder* to so *many* Venetians as me!'

Shutters popped open along the street. Rabino burned with shame as he felt the eyes of the neighbours on his back. Sosia continued to make guttural cries, beating on the door, the iron bars of the windows. Then she began to break the plates on the table, clapping them together like cymbals. By that time Rabino was almost out of earshot.

It was then she found the petrified remains of her diary poking out from the embers of the fire.

It took a morning of destruction before the noise of shattered wood and glass softened to a trickle of powder. By then, Sosia had opened the medical cabinet and was throwing together all the herbs Rabino had carefully dried and pounded in the summer past. From the dozens of little bottles she'd made a heap of glinting dust, which, finally, she kicked into a sudden whispering rainbow.

She pried from the wall the birth tray that a grateful Venetian patient had given Rabino on their marriage. All Rabino's fond patients, she knew, whispered at the continued barrenness of their union. On the birth tray, the Triumph of Love was depicted in glowing tempera. Fat Cupid was led in a triumphal chariot. A courtesan rode on the back of a Greek philosopher. The images, showing passion conquering dry intellect in every instance, came from a poem of Petrarch. She threw the tray in the fire and watched the flames cradle, and then devour it.

Her anger was not spent yet. She needed to hurt Rabino more. She eyed the Ark and its silk curtain. The Torah was, as ever, dressed like a princess – the one item of luxury in their home – but she knew that even Rabino's forbearance would not survive an act of violence against the instruments of the faith he supposed that they shared.

'I'll show him what I believe in!' she said aloud. She ran to the kitchen and pulled a slice of curd cheese from a stone bowl. Back in the *soggiorno* she pushed a sliver of it into the hem of the silk covering, squashing it flat. Now his Torah would stink! And he would never guess why! As she laughed, panting, she remembered their wedding certificate, the *ketubbà*.

She went to a cabinet and pulled the heavy vellum document from a drawer. It was about two feet across, almost square but arched slightly at the top, decorated with vignettes of religious scenes. Between two painted columns a scribe had written out in ink and egg-tempera the words with which Rabino had promised to maintain her with all his riches and wealth under the sky, and to hold as security for the future her bride price until all his resources had been exhausted, even the cloak off his back, in life and death, from the holy day of their marriage, for ever. She, the virgin Sosia, blessed among women, had promised him her life, her faith and the performance of all wifely duties.

Sosia stubbed her thumb on the word 'virgin'. She remembered the pallid sheen on Rabino's sweating face as he polluted his faith by signing the document dishonestly. Perhaps this was why their *ketubbà* lay hidden in a drawer and not framed upon the wall, a sanctified piece of the matrimonial scenery, as it would have been in other Jewish households. On their wedding day he had already known that she was no virgin, by his own violation, though he did not know how thoroughly violated she was already. She guessed, as she raised the document, that Rabino could not punish her for its destruction, because it had never been truly holy. She suspected he felt guilty enough to forgive her; certainly he cared for her more than he loved himself. This strange humility in him she found contemptibly weak.

'Who are you to lock me in, Mister Husband?' she sneered aloud.

Well, then, she must destroy their wedding document with the kind of ritual it deserved. She lifted the curtain of the Ark and opened its golden doors. She took from inside the *yad*, the Torah-pointer. The little baton of silver bore at one end a tiny golden hand with its index finger extended. It was forbidden to touch the Torah with impure human skin, so Rabino used the *yad* to point along the dense letters of the scroll as he read aloud the sacred words.

Now Sosia slashed and scored her marriage certificate with the *yad*. She used the golden finger to gouge the eyes of the little figures. Then she raked the *yad* diagonally across the vellum. The words and pictures suffered stripes and weals. Tiny flakes of tempera powdered the table. But the fabric of the *ketubbà* remained intact: it was almost leather. Sosia was unable to spend all her hatred while it remained so smugly intact.

Her fury increased. Tugging at the *ketubbà* her hair fanned out in dark arcs like ripples in brackish water. It seemed to her that if she could destroy the document then she would relieve this anger that burnt her intestines. It came to her instantly, how it could be done. She stopped her slashing and scribbling.

She knew that Rabino kept among his equipment a *maghen kemp*, the small instrument that looked like an ornamental axe-head, used in the circumcision ceremony. The *maghen kemp* was easy to find, wrapped in its ostentatious little pouch of velvet. She had never held it before and was surprised at its weight, which made it seem as if something tugged at her hand, urging her to desist. But still her wrath preserved her from caution.

With her left hand she held the *ketubbà* up to the light of the window and with her right hand she drew the *maghen kemp* slowly down the middle, slicing it in half. The moan of the metal through the vellum stopped her at last. It sounded like an animal dying in a distant room.

She threw the *maghen kemp* on to the floor. How useless, thought Sosia, were these little weapons of mankind! How they worshipped that scrap of flesh between their legs, showing how they feared and exalted it, by cutting it, scourging it. It was indecent. Women, she thought, had no such rituals. Their private parts were private, or as private as they wanted them to be. No woman gloried in hers; every woman kept it modestly to herself, except as a receptacle for the men who desire to fit themselves there and test the length and thrust of their pieces. No lover of hers had ever commented on her parts in themselves. Their grateful commentary was restricted to expressing the nature of the pleasure their own members had enjoyed inside her. How often she'd been invited to admire the length or rosy tint or even the slant of one of them; required to think up poetic phrases in praise of it . . .

Sosia placed the pieces of her wedding certificate on the table. She took a taper to the hearth fire and brought the flame to the remnants. The parchment writhed like driftwood as it burnt, slowly, giving off a smell of roasted meat, exactly, Sosia reflected, what it was. The blaze stained the table black before it died into pale ashes.

In her state of excitement, the itching between her legs had grown intolerable. She went to the kitchen to boil the herbs that Rabino had left for her.

While the water heated, she opened the jar in which Rabino stored their annual rent of eight ducats and slipped the money into her sleeve.

The feel of the coins reminded her of Felice, who never paid her, neither in money nor what she truly desired – compliments. She would go to the Sturion to find him. No matter that she was sweating from her exertions, and Felice hated any human smells upon her.

With a stick of pain in the bowel, she realised that she would not be welcome without an appointment, and that the reason for this must be that she was not the only woman to visit Felice at the Locanda, that some other woman had lain on that bed beneath him, seen his eyes look down on her, felt his body moving intently over her, heard the neat groan he invariably emitted as he spent himself. She saw her rivals, all, no doubt, as blonde as she was dark, their fingers soft as hers were hard.

While she pulled on her cloak and boots she embroidered her painful fantasies. Perhaps even that day, earlier, Felice had been with the beautiful landlady, had unravelled that green silk robe, had cupped those soft, large breasts in his hands, admiring the indentations made by his perfect fingernails. Then he would have slid his hands slowly round to the rear of her flanks and drawn her sex suddenly up to his own. Perhaps at this point, he had rung for the chamber boy, while still moving as yet patiently inside her, and when the boy came, and stood wondering in the doorway, he had beckoned him in, raised his tunic and spilled the little boy's organ out of his hose. Without losing his undulating rhythm, he would use the little pink snout as a handle, pull the boy closer, and suddenly, deftly, withdraw and insert the boy where he had been. The woman, lulled to a happy nervelessness, would smile graciously to acknowledge the substitution and continue to arch and push, smoothly and softly just as before. Only when the boy shuddered to a finish, would Felice draw him away and remount. The boy would sit, drunk with his memories, on the floor, watching Felice and his mistress complete the act.

Then Caterina di Colonna, unlike Sosia, would be permitted to fondle and kiss Felice's downy ears.

Even while she was grieved by this image, it aroused Sosia and she breathed harder. She wanted to run to the Sturion and break in on the scene she had conjured. Felice had never done such a delicious thing with *her*! Then she remembered that it was Wednesday and there was a more pressing call on her time.

'Damn Felice,' she hissed under her breath. '*Jebo bi guju u oko*, he'd fuck the eye of a snake.'

She went to the *armadio* for the wood-axe and crippled the street door lock with a single blow. Pulling on her cloak, she set off through the steaming *calle* for her appointment with Nicolò Malipiero and the boys at the church of San Giobbe, taking care to avoid the wider streets and the shops of those who had reason to be grateful to her husband.

The herbs she left boiling in the grate, forgotten, but she remembered them as she stopped to scratch where she hurt, and wondered idly if the house would catch fire before Rabino came home.

Chapter Seven

Can it make you happy
to remember what you did was right?
That you broke faith with neither man nor God?
If it can, then much happiness lies in store for you,
Catullus, against the graceless pain of this love gone bad.

Wendelin walked to the customs house promontory at dawn. He had not been able to sleep in the study where he lately passed some of his nights. The shadows under his wife's eyes forced him to the conclusion that it was kinder to let her sleep alone, that his bulkiness in the bed disturbed her fragile sleep.

One night he spied on her, arriving home in silence, stealing up to the *soggiorno* where she sat by the fireplace, rocking their son in her arms. In those moments he saw as he used to, her hands busy with gentle touches, her eyes moist with love, her voice thick with it as she sang quietly to their sleeping baby.

For a moment Wendelin was jealous of his own child, but he cleansed his thoughts instantly, guiltily. He watched his wife greedily, observed the glow of the fire warming the parting of her hair, which he had loved to kiss, dwelled on the incline of her wrist which he'd rubbed gently with his own so many times, and on the soft lower lip where he used to rest his own. His longing for her rose up inside him like boiling milk. He took an involuntary step forward and his shadow slid into the room ahead of him. His wife shrank back in terror. Then she gathered up the child in her arms and scuttled out of the door. She brushed him gently with her skirt as she passed. He reached out for the touch, just a touch, of fabric warmed by her skin. The grey linen eluded him and he was left grasping empty air, wondering what had happened to the dresses she used to wear, in vivid hues and soft fabrics. Now she dressed like a nun, as if joy no longer became her.

So he had left her in peace, returned to his study and shut the door, gazed at the beautiful Damascus cabinet for comfort. Later, before it was dawn, he rose from his divan, left the house, walked his usual miles around the town.

At the customs point he stopped, gazing at the waves, which pushed up in soft blocks as if being modelled by unseen hands. In the old days, Lussièta had hated for him to go to the tower of the *Dogana*, because it was said that just below its extremity lay the deepest sea cavern in the lagoon. There lived a terrible creature that, on nights without moon, was visible coiling under the waves. It was known to raise its horse-like head out of the water to swallow seagulls. Its body spiralled rhythmically under the waves while it digested its prey.

This *mostro delle acque nere* had made him laugh, but Lussièta had frowned, and insisted: 'Promise me, you will not go there when the night is black.'

Now she did not care if he came back; perhaps would prefer it if he did not.

Wendelin, acutely aware that he could not swim, rehearsed in his mind the two steps that would take him over the edge of the jetty. A shaft of moonlight fell through the waves, seeming to show him the way, clear as a road. It calmed him, though he knew he would not do it. It gave him a sense of choice, made him feel less helpless. He reflected that even in the dark days after Johann's death he had not thought of self-destruction. But then he'd faced the loss of his brother with the help of his wife. Now there was no one to help him face what seemed to be – what else was it? – the death of his wife's love.

Standing there at the threshold of the world, Wendelin felt that he had become foreign again, dispossessed of Venice. He shivered. The coolness was clammy and intermittent. Pockets of humid warm air floated around him. Clouds hung fat and yellow, as docile as plucked chickens. Soon the heat would well out of the sky again.

Wendelin was suddenly homesick for the crisp bite of a Speyer autumn, for the clean washing hung in orderly procession, observing the proper family hierarchies – not the undignified rabble of nappies and stockings that bestrewed the upper levels of the alleys in Venice. He missed the unindulged babies, the exquisite formality of the shopkeepers in Germany, the unsensuous patter of harpsichord notes in the church, the precise ranks of vines on the hills, the high empty skies of the North, where a rain cloud meant rain and nothing more metaphorical.

Bitterness spilled into him. He had given all that up. For what? For the dishonest lures of a courtesan city.

Like any professional flirt, Wendelin thought, *Venice is utterly insincere. Unless you bring her something that interests her, she's indifferent to you.*

And once you have given her what she wants, she has no further use of you.

And he pictured his wife with feelings discoloured by too much misery. *Perhaps, perhaps I'm too soft on her,* Wendelin reflected. *They say women are of the canine species and prefer a hard hand and hard words – the more she has of both, the more closely a bitch cleaves to her master. Or could it be true all that I was told of the unchastity of Venetian women? Does she crave a man of her own kind?*

He shook his head. That was not the way of his wife's thinking.

Clearly she saw him as a tormentor, with the power and desire to inflict suffering upon her. He knew of nothing he might have done – save the acquisition of the hated cabinet – to cause such fear in her, and he had too much respect for her intelligence to think that a mere piece of carpentry could have robbed her of her senses.

Boats of produce began to appear, scudding in from their various islands to the Grand Canal and Rialto. Friendly boatmen saluted him jovially. Automatically he returned their greetings with polite gestures, making his foreignness immediately apparent. Seeing that he was not one of them, the boatmen turned their backs on him, resumed the conversations that excluded him.

'Have I ever been truly a part of this?' Wendelin asked himself, aloud. A sudden throb of hatred for the city churned his belly. It resembled, in its pain, the hostile humiliation of a disillusioned lover. If his marriage had failed, and his business likewise, perhaps he should return home, and start again.

But a spasm of terror diffused rapidly through his body like a blush, at the thought of being separated from his wife. While they as yet lived together, there was hope that she might come back to him, after all. Their joyous time of love and passion has lasted years: this inexplicable estrangement less than two months. Perhaps the business, too . . . ? With an effort, he distanced his craving thoughts of Speyer. No, he must reconcile himself to this town, find solutions, or at least acceptance, instead of running away from griefs.

I shall bury my feelings with due ceremony, just as the Venetians like it, he said bitterly to himself. *Indeed, this is an excellent town for misery, so long as it is done in style.*

Then he turned to go home, so he might wash the graininess from his eyes before going to work.

The weather had turned. A suffocating veil of fine rain pressed against him. Now, he found with relief, he might shed a few tears and not be ashamed.

He thought I slept still but I wake each time he rises. Though all is broken and now he no longer even wishes to share a bed with me – yet still that string of love that binds his mind to mine pulls me when he stirs.

I heard him wash, soft as a cat, and dress, then tread down the stairs light and quick, though I knew his mind must weigh hard on him. How could it not? He is from the North, yet even there they must have hearts.

I made myself wait till the door clicked shut and his steps went quietly up the path to the street. Then I jumped from my bed and ran down (for I'd kept my clothes on all the night for just this). I padded after him. It was easy to know him, though there were others, miserable as us no doubt, about in the streets then. Here in Venice, when we are wrapped up for the out of doors in this foggy hot-and-cold weather, we learn to know our own kin and friends from just the twist of a shawl or the turn of a hand in a glove.

So I followed his well-known outline, shaving the walls, just one corner behind, all the way to the customs tower that guards the city and looks out on the *bacino*. He walked with the tired tramp of an old horse.

He stood there a long time till the sun rose and the lagoon islands appeared from the mist, floating like trays of soft brown cakes in the sea.

At one point he took a step as if to fling himself into the waves and my heart rose to my throat. He cannot swim! But he did not jump. After a long while he turned, so I hid at the back of a tall stone wall, resting quiet and secret as the water in a well, and he passed me by and did not see me at all. I eeled around the columns, followed him across the herringbone bricks of the *campo*, careful not to slip on the smooth Istrian stone at the edge.

I noticed that he wore too few clothes for the damp of the dawn. Without me to remind him, he does not think of such things. How shiversome he must have felt, out there by the *Dogana*! As he passed me, his eyes downcast, I saw his hair was all clotted with dew and the raindrops, and I could myself feel, with a shiver, the bite of the chill next to his scalp. He used to touch my hair all the time. Now he does not.

When the sun beat down later the hair would stand all stiff and sore with sweat. And then would come those old aches the damp sends through all his joints – how I wished I'd bought from that merchant one of those miraculous woollen girdles from the Monastery of Saint Barsamo in Irak.

Then I saw a skulk of flesh flitting after my man and I felt a squirm of terror in my bowels. From the churn of my bad thoughts about him, my love rose up, and I wanted more than all to protect and save him.

The little figure trailed him until they were both out of sight. I comforted myself that the light was dawning, and that my man's towering shadow swallowed up the little man entirely, and I knew for myself that he knew how to take care of himself, even at another's expense.

Now I have come home with plans for that box of his. Using soap made of ash and boiled water I shall scour it. Till now I did not touch it, just the knobs to pull the drawers and then with as light a touch as I could. I would hate to feel its dust on my skin.

I think now I might have erred there. It has come to me that if I scrub and scour that box then it might lose its bad power. I shall clean the filth from it: the present filth and the past filth. Then maybe all will be good between us again, and I shall start to feel content, which I have not done since he brought that thing home.

In a month it would be Christmas again, though there was as yet no respite in the heat.

Strange smells meandered out of the alleys. The Venetians were already preparing for their Christmas feast of salmon and venison seasoned with hogsheads of honey and kilderkins of mustard. At this time of year the Venetians also devoured herons, bitterns and teal, boars' heads with lemons in their mouths, fresh sturgeon with whelks and roasted porpoise.

With these scents in the air, Wendelin's night-time walks took on the quality of a luxurious nightmare, sensuous and abhorrent at the same time. He was so wearied that his perceptions were equivocal. He accepted every strange sight, every inexplicable vision as yet one more Venetian phenomenon sent to try his tired brain.

The less he slept, the less lifelike and the more unwholesome the town became to him. Lines of washing created strange new beasts in the moonlight. Their shadows danced bizarrely: torsoless legs in their hose, legless torsos in their nightshirts. Treacherous hidden steps lay in wait for him and unfathomable lights cast into shuttered courtyards, reveries brought to sudden despair by the inexplicable advent of a dead end or a canal at the end of a promising passageway, where he could have sworn he had passed unimpeded the night before.

One night he passed a small hooded figure motionless at the corner of a street near Ca' Dario. The face was hidden, as were the hands. Wendelin passed swiftly on. Moments later, there it was again, in front of him, the same hooded figure, and yet he'd walked the intervening hundred yards at a brisk pace, and no one had followed him. He was less frightened than curious, but too polite to scrutinise the creature as he passed it once more. He did not see it again.

He walked until dawn, and then slipped into a tavern at Rialto, which remained open for those such as himself who could not sleep or those who were driven to be early at work. He sat outside, despite the cold, watching the sunrise and waiting for his own apprentices to arrive on their way to the *fondaco*. Their sleepy faces raised fond thoughts in him, and he was in need of such warmth.

Soon a smear of workers, unwashed and slow-footed, appeared. In the dawn light everyone approaching from the east did so in silhouette that rounded into familiarity only as they passed close by. Wendelin found himself making judgements on the gait and garb of strangers – what a scarecrow! lopes like a sad drunkard! – only to find, as the *mattutino* chimed, that the stick figure who approached him was his editor, Bruno Uguccione.

He looked at the young man's face; saw its anguish naked, as yet undisguised by absorption in work. *That woman, whoever she is, is killing my dear young man*, Wendelin thought. *Nothing I love is safe in this town.*

He added, as he reached his hand out to Bruno, and drew him down to the table – *perhaps this is, in the end, what it is to love. Perhaps it always ends like this.*

'Shall we have our lesson here?' Wendelin suggested, thrusting aside his own misery to welcome his editor. He waved at the innkeeper to bring some more of the hot tisane for both of them.

'Why not?' smiled Bruno feebly. There was no chance that Sosia would come to the *stamperia* this morning.

He had noticed that Wendelin was less cheerful than formerly but attributed the downturn of his *capo's* mouth to the problems of the business. In matters of the heart, Bruno, with the arrogance of youth, felt himself the centre of Fate's evil attentions, assuming that the pain in his breast was both more bitter and more poetic than anyone else's.

It was my idea to clean the box when my man was within the house, and to do it myself and not leave it to the maid, so he should see how I tried to serve him, and make the peace between us, to show that I, for my part at least, still wished to keep our love alive.

I filled a pail with water warmed by the fire and carried it, with a pile of fresh scouring cloths, to the study.

I knocked on the door – these days we are so polite with one another! – and he said, 'Enter!' in an abstracted kind of voice. He was at his desk, with another Jenson book, a candle and a magnifying lens on the page.

When he saw me, he started up and a smile flew across his face. Then he looked at the pail in my hand, and the smock I had put on to cover my dress.

'What's all this for?' he asked, knitting his brows.

'I shall clean the box,' I said. It came out all wrong, for what I meant to say, is 'I shall make your cabinet fresh and beautiful for you.' I sounded gruff, and he looked less than pleased, as if I meant some act of war against his precious box.

He said, 'But it's not dirty. Your water may cause damage to the paint. You should leave it alone.'

I hope he did not mean to sound so brusque and cold as he did to me. He was poised on the edge of anger, as if he were at the end of his temper's tether. But his tone made me a little angry, and so I took a step forward and put the pail in front of the box, upright as a toy soldier.

'I ask you not to do this,' he said, and again that tinny ring of choler sharpened his German voice.

'It's the only way,' I said, grimly, and took one cloth, dipped it in the pail, and pulled it, dripping, across the top of the cabinet.

He rose and quickly came towards me. His shadow grew huge in the light of the candle and fell across the stripe of wet that I had made.

So I was looking back at him, trembling, when the roach came out from a crack in the wood. It must have lain there all this time, perhaps from the days at Ca' Dario. Perhaps it had even come all the way from Damascus, hidden in some black groove as the box tossed in the hold of a pilgrim boat, ballast no doubt to make up for those poor pilgrims who had died on their journey.

Certainly I had never seen such a large roach in this town before, or one which had such dark wings and whose antlers were so thick with hairs and whose tail curved over its back.

These were the slow musings of my mind, struck by panic into a slow kind of working, when I turned back to see the roach climb over my fingers and on to my wrist, where it raised its pincers and bit.

It bit most grievously, but I did not even feel the pain, for first came the horror. You know how I hate all things that creep and crawl. I cannot bear even to see them, let alone to be touched by them. And now this vile roach, this citizen of an evil world, had stung me.

I shook my hand to dislodge it and only then began to scream, for it would not let loose from the skin it was pinching. I opened my mouth and the moonlight shot into it.

'Help me! Help!' I shrieked to my man, but he stood still and watched as if this was a play and he had bought a ticket.

'You should not have wet the cabinet,' he said, and turned his back on me. The roach dropped off then and scuttled away under the box.

Chapter Eight

He who wants to catalogue your pleasures
would first need to know how
to count the stars above
And the grains of sands in Africa

When Gentilia became a witch, she found it surprisingly easy to combine her new profession with that of being a nun.

She looked into all sides of the question first, deciding on a mixture of *stregoneria* (simple witchcraft), *fatuccheria* (evil magic) and *herberia* (herbal magic).

She learned the proper adorations of the various demons, how to burn styrax gum, asafoetida and many other substances that give off sweet or foul odours that invade the mind and sway the will.

Most of all she was interested in binding spells, whatever their nature. The first wise woman she consulted taught her the ways of olive branches. Gentilia pretended to be dying of love for a nobleman, and quickly won the romantic sympathy of the older woman.

'We'll get him for you, darling, don't you worry,' simpered the witch, patting Gentilia's hand and thrusting out her hips.

Gentilia's wise woman had nipples that could clearly be seen in outline through her thin aubergine-coloured gown. Her breasts hung slackly between the two great ovals of sweat that spread from under her arms. The elongated nipples were strangely placed, too close to each other, adding to many and various repulsions of her foreignness and therefore the potency of her spells, at least in the eyes of the suggestible Venetians.

Walking through the streets with her, Gentilia was invisible to everyone. All had their eyes fixed on the wise woman, though seeming to look at a point just beyond her. No one wanted to meet the eyes of a known witch; that way madness lay.

Together they went to the market to buy olive branches. In the old woman's dark kitchen they burned the tips of the branches together, tied each one with string, and dipped it in holy water they had scooped from the baptistry at San Giobbe. While they did so they chanted, 'As I bind this wood with this cord, so may the phallus of my lover be bound to me.' Then they took the branches to the garden outside the church and planted them in the ground, chanting, 'As this wood cannot grow green again, so may not the phallus of my lover be inclined to relations with any other woman.'

'Now you go get him,' leered the witch, poking at Gentilia's lower belly with an earth-stained finger.

Gentilia found other women, other teachers. She learned how to skin a bird backwards, sticking two needles in the head and two needles in the tail. She knew to keep its little corpse in a shuttered room and cast spells to conjure the Devil over it, and that he would surely come, as this was the best bait for him.

She learned to pick large sage leaves and write on them, that they might be given to an object of love, who, on eating them, would be possessed with passion.

She received instruction on how to light a candle in front of a tarot card with the Devil on it, how to prepare magical potions to smear on the windowsills and doorways of those to be cursed. She learned how to brush a piece of pork against an unsuspecting Jew, to ensure his downfall.

She learned to anoint lips of would-be lovers with holy oil, warning them to make sure it stayed slick and slippery until the very moment of stealing a kiss from the person they longed to possess. She learned that women who required the undying fidelity of their men must rub their entire bodies with this oil before sexual congress with them. This formula had the added advantage of leaving the woman free and unbound; while her husband might not stray she was able to engage her body and her feelings wherever she wished after this.

Gentilia learned how to revive a man's lust for his wife when he had lost all desire for her. Under the conjugal bed she should place the blade of a plough, and the hoe and shovel used for burying at least one corpse. In other cases she should use the ring in which a young virgin had been married and subsequently died: the affected man must urinate through this ring and would soon find his powers of loving his own wife miraculously restored.

She learned how to package up a *calamita bianca*, a white magnet, in a linen bag with cloves and incense and parchment to bring the bearer good luck in all seasons. She learned how to deliver a *martellata* – a hammering, to the soul of an enemy.

She learned to cast the beans, and how to read them when they fell. She would mark two of the beans, denoting the loved one and the lover, and then throw a clutch of eighteen in front of her. If the two marked beans fell close together then their love was to be trusted. If not, then there was work to be done, probably in the form of binding spells.

She learned that the bed was the most powerful place in any house. A man might be tempted by the maids who performed the duty of making his bed if they put into that bed all manner of small annoyances . . . millet, sorghum, spelt, laurel, apple seeds, roots of flowers from each month of the year, peas, wheat husks, small bones from dead babies, coal, stockings, rocks, wood, nails, large needles (one with a head, one without).

She learned to throw salt into the coals of the fire to make them spit and jump. The hearth was of course another powerful site for magic. She knew that any potions must be cooked in a new pan on that hearth, and that pan must be purchased in the name of the Devil or her intended victim. To conjure up pain, live eels could be put under the coals with needles in the head and heart. She learned to shake an egg to check if it clicked; such enchanted eggs might be buried with a prayer, and prove powerful. She learned the power of measuring things – cords, babies, other things: anything measured was in some way contained and possessed by she who had the knowledge of its dimensions and such knowledge could be put to good use or bad.

She learned to whip a hearth chain against the wall to make a lover's heart beat harder, painfully if necessary.

She learned the formula for potent little letters, the *carte di voler bene*, refining and repeating the words to herself until she was word perfect.

She learned to comb her hair on Thursday nights and how to extract single strands from others' heads without their noticing it, for such hairs were vital ingredients in the most potent of spells.

When she was ready, and had written two practice exercises, she penned the words on a sheet of parchment, which she quietly dropped in the outlet of the *necessario* of the house where Sosia lived. Walking swiftly away she noticed the shoes airing on the windowsill and smiled to herself.

I declare by this contract, Gentilia had written on the parchment,
that I make myself the bondswoman of Lucifer and all the princes of Hell. I name him my lord, signed for on the flesh of my body, and I hold myself as his slave under the condition that he serves me in this way:

Let the nobleman Malipiero himself become inflamed with love for me. So much so that he will have no peace, no repose of spirit or body unless he's with me. Neither shall he be able to take his place in the senate of the city nor control the impulses of his own body so shall he be distracted in every second by burning thoughts of me.

I cast a spell on him, binding his love by all Devils who are within and outside of Hell. I bind all his members, his hair, his head, his eyes, his nose, his mouth, his heart and above all his phallus to me.

If he does not come to me then he shall suffer the pain of the Crown of Thorns, of the evil and vinagrous drink, the sweat of blood on the forehead and the tearing of his liver from his belly.

For I hold the measurements of his phallus and of all his vital parts, for he has eaten with me of my own powdered blood.

In return I promise my body and soul at death to the prince Lucifer and his devilish companions. In the meantime may all the hounds of Hell bear me attendance from this day forth.

Signed, Sosia Simeon.

Gentilia knew that the large sheet of paper, protected by a parchment pouch, would soon be spotted floating along the canal, and be fished out by curious neighbours. She knew that it would be taken to the local priest and then to the authorities.

Then the trouble would start. How much trouble even she could not guess though she turned the possibilities over in her mind as she sat on the boat going back to Sant' Angelo.

Certainly it would destroy the unknown Malipiero, whom Gentilia begrudged, strangely, just what Bruno begrudged him. But more than that it would destroy Sosia, and Bruno would be left in peace, and then at last be free to show the devotion to her, Gentilia, that she was now ready to accept.

On the same day that she sent the letter swimming through a cloudy little eddy of filth, she posted a signed denunciation, echoing the contents, through the mouth of the lion at the Doges' Palace and made a journey to Murano where she left an anonymous missive for the attention of Fra Filippo de Strata.

'*An Account of the Printers' Whore*,' it began.

That night, at Sant' Angelo di Contorta, she undressed in her cell until she was completely nude, by the light of a candle which she had bought in the name of the Devil, whispering the name under her breath as she handed over the money. She turned her face to the shadow she had created against the candlelit wall of her cell, and said, 'I have undressed myself and you dress yourself, good evening, my shadow, my sister, I beg you to go to the heart of Sosia Simeon and strike her a blow.'

Then she lifted the candle and said to it, 'Now I understand that I must pay my dues to the Devil.'

It was Gentilia's shadow sister, created by her alliance with the candle and the Devil, who arose the next day. This shadow was more powerful than Gentilia, empowered to go out into the public world, for she was dressed to go forth and do the business of the Devil. When Gentilia looked in the mirror, she could not see her: just the camouflaging skin of her former self. But she knew what she had inside. Gentilia reasoned with herself that a witch was a kind of fairy, and fairies were always beautiful and never more than nineteen years old, and always light on their feet and irresistible in their whimsical ways.

She took the boat to Venice. As if privy to her intentions the boat that day behaved strangely. It lurched like a drunk and righted itself precariously with each wave. Gentilia was not a superstitious person – her witchcraft was purely practical – so she merely folded her hands in her lap and observed the queasy faces of her fellow passengers.

~*There's no danger*, she told herself. *There are boats*, she added, *which have a shoddy gait, and this is one of them.*

A man leaned over to her, confidentially, gesturing at the beams of the boat. 'See, it's been badly put together and will never give a sweet voyage, like some women.'

He winked at her. She winked back, and laid her hand on his arm, as she had seen nuns do with the men who visited the convent. The man turned away from her, disgusted. He'd caught a whiff of her breath, with its strong smell of cabbage. Her digestion was exceedingly slow and the cabbage soup of one day swilled from the pores of her skin the whole of the next.

Once landed, she briskly made her way past her whey-faced fellow-passengers and took a gondola to the shop that sold holy oil and linen for shrouds, taking two small detours. One was to the witch who had instructed her, to collect a small vial of foul-smelling liquid. The other was to daub it on a pair of shoes airing on the windowsill of a certain house in San Trovaso.

Chapter Nine

What can I do?
What is there left to trust?
You asked me for my soul
as if I had nothing to fear by giving it.
Wasn't that what you said,
in so, so many words?

Since the roach bit me, there's been silence in our house at night.

Alone in the kitchen I salved and wrapped the wound, trembling and weeping. The bite was not big, and throbbed rather than burned me. But the poison of that moment lingered in the air, reminding me with every pulse of the times when I used to have his love and my man would do anything to save me from the creatures who creep and crawl.

When we tiffed before it was like reading of perilous wars from the safe comfort of a deep soft chair. A little adventure in the imagination only. But since the roach there is no more fantasy about it. The conflict is real, the walls have melted away, the armchair disappeared, the pages are gone and we stand on a real battlefield, with real arms to do actual harm.

It has come to this: although I hate and fear sorcery with all my heart, I think I really shall go to see a wise woman. I've heard of a white kind of witch who knows how to get a man back when his love has strayed off.

I used to laugh in my hand at such tales and look at my face in the glass – at my ripe soft mouth and the full curve of each lash, and the long nut-shape of my eyes and the way they turn up at the ends – and I used to think, 'Who needs a witch to keep a man?'

Not now. Not since he let the roach bite me and moved not a muscle to help me; my spirits are bruised black all over. This morning he failed to ask me how I felt, and left for work earlier than usual.

I've seen her in the street. She's an old lady with a three-point chin that pokes out from dark pink jowls with hairs on them. The lower lids of her eyes hang slack from the balls of her eyes. Can such a one help with love or lack of it?

I hear that this witch knows all kinds of things – how to make dogs chase the one you hate (this you do with a smear of juice from a bitch in heat on his shoes) or drugs to make a fire burn with no stop or render a man unable to take one scrap of food down his throat so he starves to death, slow but sure.

Then I think it may be that I can win him back if I make him one more son. So I've been back to the books and I'm mad with sad thoughts for it seems I may not ask him these days to do those things which would surely make a son. We do not speak aloud of such intimacies now, where once we laughed and talked with our hands. How can I ask, as the books tell, for him to tie up his left pouch when we make love, as it is seed from the right one that makes boys? I would blush now but to name this part that once I cupped in my hand each night. How can I tell him to leave off the *cortinelò* wine (whose deep red he loves, and which casts such voluptuous dreams) for it hardens the paunch and stops the making of male seed or sends the seed out cold and of no use. And all the foods we eat – prawns, fish, fruit, herbs – are moist and so make girl seeds. How can I ask him to change his diet? We are not so close that I can talk without a blush of what he puts in his mouth. It is too personal in these days when we are strange to one another. Sometimes I even try to speak to him in German now, stumbling over those break-teeth words, so he can forget I am a Venetian, whom he made the mistake of marrying.

Gone are those conversations and the laughter beneath the

sheet, that talk which some might say was lewd but for us was mouthfuls of joy. As those who love food water at the mouth when they talk of saucing the meat, or as Giovanni Bellini quivers a little when he talks of colour, so we used to talk of our acts of love. Not like love poets! We were not the pawns of our fine words, but they were our instruments, which we used to make more precise our pleasures. And worse, according to the books, when we make love, I should ask him to make sure his seed, when it comes forth, is sent straight to the right side of my womb. It is up to me to twist my hips and direct it where it must go. But now I never move beneath him. I lie still and quiet, as if he makes love to my corpse (which I do believe he would prefer). So if, during the act of love, I were to move to point the seed – what would he think? That I'm full of lust again, intent on my own pleasures, and scarce a chaste wife?

I go to the kitchen but the thought of food stirs in my belly a queasiness. I do not feel well. I know not what ails me, but I shake, hot and cold by turn. I feel all-overish with desire for something, as if I were with child. It seems not, from the other signs. My head hurts all the time. It is an especial kind of headache, arrowed in sharp throbs between my brows. It feels as if an invisible someone was sewing my brows together! I feel the needle stabbing in and out.

The clamour of the town singes my hot brain. The bells insult me, wringing their clappers and shouting faith in the love of man. Minstrels bleat their songs under my very window. When I walk past the convent of San Zaccaria I hear nuns praying for new admirers, suitors pledging eternal untruths in gondolas, thralls of lovers breathing kisses into each other's lungs like pairs of bellows. *Lies!* I want to scream. *Pin up your lying mouths and leave me in peace!*

The maid brings me a mess of cucumber boiled to pulp and the broth of a gourd, much gingered, to loose my belly. I see she's not well either. She says she has a fever and there's definitely a lump on her neck. I cannot taste or smell things now – I who used to love flavours and perfumes so much! I lie on the bed all day waiting for the night; all night I lie sleepless waiting for dawn. I'm sticky as a blade of grass at sunrise, and my arms itch. I scratch and scratch. It seems that all my fears have oozed out of my body and lie restless on my skin.

Wendelin found himself passing Ca' Dario yet again, on each of his nightly walks to the *Dogana*. Any trip to the promontory entailed passing the house, the old home of the cabinet, twice, coming and going. He did not know why he felt drawn to follow this itinerary, but it had come to feel that the *Dogana* was merely a coincidental stop en route and that his real journey was a forked one, leading both ways to Ca' Dario.

Knowing how his wife hated the house, he felt disloyal staring at it, but his footsteps slowed of their own accord as he approached it, and he stopped for long moments, gazing at its rear façade and into the thick bushes of its deserted garden. Each time he did so, he burned with shame, remembering the moment he had let the roach bite his wife and had made no move to help her. He had not yet found the moment to beg her forgiveness.

Other walks, to distant parts of Venice, seemed to lead to Ca' Dario.

Why? It was vacant, soundless.

Their marriage had become like that house, empty and haunted with the past, he thought. He missed the words that used to flow between them, a rich junket of two languages. Now his wife tried to speak to him with German words, which she pronounced badly, as if to confirm the distance between them.

What possessed me to be so cold to her? he asked himself. He was too ashamed to raise the dreadful subject, let alone apologise. She never mentioned it herself, hid her bandaged hand if he approached, so that he'd started to think that she had absorbed the offence. Motherhood seemed to make women capable of forgiving anything. Perhaps even the roach had finally brought her to her senses about the cabinet. Looking into the blank windows of Ca' Dario he wondered, for the hundredth time, which room it had once occupied inside the silent *palazzo*.

He found it the most beautiful in Venice. Others raved of the fairytale traceries of Ca' d'Oro or the Pisani Moretta, but for Wendelin, the simple straight lines of the old Dario house gave him more satisfaction than the fantastic creations of the celebrated new architects. It was, in his opinion, the most sensible-looking house in Venice, perhaps the only one. He hated the thought that it might be torn down to make way for a new *palazzo*, no doubt gaudy as the rest. Its present lack of ornamentation made it seem honest. A Ca' Dario jewelled with porphyry and serpentine would look like a good woman painted up as a courtesan.

One night, as he passed, he heard a high-pitched laugh, like that of a very old man or a very young girl. There was no light, no life to the house, but the voice continued, giggling and singing to itself, from somewhere within the ivy-encrusted walls. The happy snatches were punctuated with sharp thwacks followed by dragging groans in a deeper voice.

'Who's there?' called Wendelin. 'Are you lost? Are you trapped inside the walls? Is someone hurting you? Can I help you?'

A peal of laughter greeted his words and the sound of something rustling, like a birch broom being dragged through leaves.

Two small hands appeared above the wall, as if the little person were about to pull him or herself up. But they rested there, inanimate, like cuts of veal. From his distance Wendelin could not distinguish the age or the sex of the owner of the hands, any more than of the disembodied voice.

He pressed his head against the wall, hoping to hear at least rustling among the bushes. He heard nothing, except the throb of his own pulse.

Chapter Ten

O Gods, if pity be among your raiment . . .
Tear out from my heart this plague, this pestilence

Padre Pio, my dearest father,

I write to you because I must do something with my hands other than strangle one with the other.

She is sick, my wife, my fate, my little Venetian fish, my heart, my . . .

When I say 'sick' I mean to tell you that she lies at present on a bed from which I fear she may never rise. It started with a general weakness, and then a bad pain in the head. She became quite unlike herself in many ways . . . but it turns out that this was probably the early sign of her illness. She has contracted a plague they say was brought to Venice from Damascus. It takes a form that I shudder to describe to you. Our maid has already died of it.

My wife's face is perfect as a Madonna's and when she sleeps she is sweeter than little Bambino Gesù in his manger, but when I lift her linen there are buboes on her swanlike arms, her thighs. They're pointing out of her perfect skin like small red snouts, moist and hot. From her body, which normally smells of eggs and cream and vanilla, rises a stench of pestilence as if she were already rotting beneath the earth. When I reach for her hand, I find that the stem of a glass is less fragile than her wrists. She is moaning now. I must go to her.

I suddenly realise that I have started mourning her before she is even dead. At this, I'm struck cold with guilt. I had consigned her to oblivion while she yet lives. I did this selfishly, so as to put an end to my unbearable suspense, waiting for her to die. It was as if I had smothered her with a pillow before her time! I, who love her . . .

Now I know that I was wrong. That smell in fact proves that she still lives. The plague does not feast upon corpses, but on living beings. It may not even be the plague, but some lesser ailment! And while she still breathes I am not alone on earth. I shall not even think that she might go into the silent world. It is certain that I cannot bear the thought of her extinction and my own continued existence at the same time. Not even to protect our child, who squalls at the keyhole while I write. I love him but I would not care to live without her. (Our son loves her with an unthinking love, and scrabbles at the door for her just as a veal-calf brays for its mother. I mean, he is loving her without a soul, as yet. I am loving her with my whole soul.)

I want nothing to disturb her: I've ordered straw to be laid down in the street below so that the footsteps of the passers-by and the wheels of the carts are muffled.

I have summoned the Jewish physician Rabino Simeon to our home. I've heard good things of this man and now I watch him bend over her – a Jew in my house with his hands on my wife! But I shall not describe him to you, for I realise, and I am glad for it, that it means nothing – race, religion, caste, compared to the great singularity, the clear water, the nectarous feast of a true love between one man and one woman. That is, if it is love such as I bear for Lussièta and have with her, or used to, before she became unwell in spirit and body.

The doctor is mixing the herbs now and he has placed black stones on her wrists, belly and forehead. I wonder if this is legal. I almost pray that this is witchcraft if only it is omnipotent.

I close now; the doctor summons me, not with arrogance (as you and I were both told is the style and manner of his race) but with a gentle finger. What a good man he seems to me! My haunches have already risen from the chair as if my dream self is already at her side again. Whatever he says, I shall not hear it unless he tells me she will live.

I cannot wait for him to leave so I may lay my own hands upon her again. This time I shall not let go . . . I cannot contemplate the domestical darkness and the loneliness that shall befall me and our child if I should lose her.

Rabino had been in his apothecary studio when Wendelin's messenger arrived. Sosia was nowhere to be seen. Since the day he had come home to find the ashes of the *ketubbà* drifting over the kitchen table, the kettle boiling dry and the door in splinters with the lock hanging loosely off the wood, they had tacitly arranged things so that they were rarely at home at the same time. The house had looked as if vicious burglars had sacked it. Quietly, he cleaned and swept up the evidence of her anger. It had been expensive to replace the herbs and powders she had destroyed, but he bore it without reproach. He was not innocent in her regard.

When he opened the newly repaired door, he looked wearily at the boy outside. Rabino was suddenly brought low by the thought that no one ever came to his home with good tidings. It was merely a question of how grave the illness each knock betokened.

'Damascus Plague, the maid had it off a sailor,' the boy panted. '*She* said a bug bit her, but we all know she spends her nights at Arsenale. The mistress got it off the maid.'

Rabino raised an eyebrow.

'The maid coughed in the breakfast and took it straight upstairs.'

Rabino poured the gulping boy a glass of water. 'What happened to the maid?' he asked.

'All hell. Like she was got in the teeth of a great succubus. Retching and screaming and great boils bursting open and a stink you could smell downwind a mile . . .'

'But did she live?'

'Of course not, it was *Damascus* plague. But my master says to come in any case, at all costs,' he said. 'He thinks the stars shine out of her. Indeed, she's as soft as butter and I shall be sad to see her go out of the house in a box.'

The boy pulled a purse from his sleeve and settled it in the fine dust on Rabino's mixing table. Beside it he placed an exquisitely printed sheet of paper.

'Wendelin von Speyer,' Rabino read aloud, '*La prima stamperia di Venezia.*'

A German, he thought. *Only a German would pay a doctor in advance.* He saw that the man lived away from the *Fondaco dei Tedeschi*, so he must be married to a Venetian. Campo San Pantalon: just fifteen minutes' walk.

Damascus Plague was a picturesque rumour; at most a refinement of the old, deadly enemy. Rabino was exhausted at the prospect of witnessing yet another soul perish in agony that day. He knew no sure remedy for the disease, could offer just a few stones and herbs to lessen the suffering of those clawing their way towards survival or death. But he knew that the mere thought of his arrival would now be giving the wretched husband something to hope on . . . a husband who loved his wife like that . . . Then, Rabino knew that the moment he came into the room, the poor man would be distracted from his pains by the sight of him.

In all likelihood this German printer had never spoken to a Jew, believed that they ate their own sons' foreskins. He would barely know if Rabino's bodily design were the same as his own. He would be repulsed but at the same time unable to contain his curiosity. Politely, for the Germans were always correct, this von Speyer would regard him narrowly from the corner of his eyes and in them Rabino would be able to read plentiful misgivings at the thought of a Jew touching his beloved wife. Still, even such thoughts would give a few moments of relief to the husband while Rabino examined the woman. If she were in the final stages there would be nothing he could do. She would be beyond even pain. He would break the news; he would not be believed – 'Lying Jew!' – or he would be abused. He would retreat backwards, dodging thrown objects and insults to his forefathers.

But when Rabino came into Wendelin's bedroom, the printer – a tall fair man – barely raised his eyes from his wife's unconscious face. Nevertheless, he reached out and clasped Rabino's hand warmly, saying, 'Thank you, sir, thank you for coming; thank God for your skills and for your compassion. I leave you to your work, that you may do it better.' He stood up and went to the table, where he began to write feverishly.

Rabino suppressed his astonishment and turned his attention to the wife. He was filled with a sudden fervour to help this gentle man. Rabino touched the woman's forehead and her eyes fell open like a doll's. Her pupils swivelled towards her husband, who continued to write, his back turned to her, and in that moment a sigh of tinted air seemed to issue from her mouth and rush around the room, binding all three of them in a soft loop, palpable as muslin.

This is not the plague; this is love, thought Rabino. He could not help but pursue the thoughts this phenomenon raised in him. *Perhaps Sosia feels this for someone. All my life I longed for it myself.*

He opened up his bag and took out his stones.

He lifted the wife's coverlet and it seemed as if that pulverous current had found its way under the sheets, for her sores were visibly drying at an astounding rate. He saw a blister curl up like a dead leaf before his eyes. He felt the heat coming from her body.

She is trying to save herself, thought Rabino, *because she cannot bear the pain of her husband. She loves this man more than she loves her own beauty. For him, she has the will to live, disfigured, perhaps, and certainly weak, for years to come.*

Love like this, thought Rabino, *must be allowed to live on. If only it were in my power to make sure of that.*

You see, I thought I was dead. In my death I was white with red spots. I could see my own face for I seemed to float in a high space from which I could look down and see my man with what looked like real tears bent over to stare at me. It was strange that I could still see for I had watched him reach out and close my eyes after the doctor left.

In my ears was a noise of birds, a great pitying of pigeons and sparrows outside the window.

For a long time my man sat close by my head, just holding my hand. It seemed to me he wished me to live still in spite of what he had done. But a part of me said, 'No, he just feigns this grief for the sake of the new maid and the Jewish doctor. He wants them to see those tears.'

I could hear nothing of what went on inside the room but I saw the door shake. There was a pink thing in the hole of the lock: I could see all things from up high. So I knew it was my little son who thumped and thumped the door to come in. Sometimes he put his eye to the lock, sometimes it was his thumb, and sometimes he threw his whole self at the door.

But my man just sat there by my side, with his mouth in a big 'O' as though he howled for pain. I felt myself rise higher. From that moment on I could not hear a thing, just a blur like the roar of a fire in my ears, so I knew not if he made a noise.

Then at last he closed his mouth and let go of my hand. He went to the door and let in our son, who, it was clear, did not think to be allowed, and so fell into the room in a rush like a huge sigh.

My man looked down on him where he lay on the floor. The boy did not weep. He just looked up at his pa. Then they both turned to look at me and each of their mouths framed at the same time that same 'O'.

Then my man took our son in his arms and held him up to his own face. He carried him to the bed and sat close by me once more with our son on his lap turned to face him.

With his hand he touched my lips and then the lips of our son. It is true; we have the same lips, my son and I. Then my man touched my nose, and then our son's nose, and the swell of my cheek, and then his, and the curve of my ear, and then his, and so on till he'd laid his hand on my whole face and then my son's.

If I did not know what he does each dawn, I would say that his was an act of love. I would say that he made a map of my face on the face of our son. That he tried to make a print of his love for me and press it on our son's face, so that his love for me would not die, but live and grow in the eyes, nose and cheeks of our son – that my man might not once lose my face and that he might love our son all the more.

While I was watching these things I felt a call of light on my eyes and soon a white wind pulled me from the room. I saw my man and son no more and the next thing I heard was the wheel of a cart nosing through mud. I knew it should be cold out of doors at night, and yet I felt no chill on my skin. I felt I was flung on the cart and that I landed on top of a man who was green and frail with death. I heard a bone in his hip smash with my sudden weight. Face down now, I was blind and I could just hear the cart make its way through the town. Sometimes a new dead man or child was thrown on top of us. No one moved or talked so I felt I was the only one who was not dead. I learned to hear where the cart went for I know the count of steps from one bridge to the next in all parts of this town. It seemed to me that we did make a big curve, and then a turn, and that in a short time we would be back at the place where I lived with my man.

I thought of them, my man and child, and though I could not feel, I somehow felt less far-away than I had done. I heard the wheels turn round a street that I was sure was the one next to my own and then one more turn . . .

I had no strength but as we passed our house I wished, I wished with all my might to be back in that bed where it seemed perhaps, after all, that I had died. The fire in my ears was most, most loud then, as if it fought, flame by flame, to eat me. But I did not give up on my wish. I wished to lie there with them; I wished my son and my man to touch me, though I could feel it not.

Then it was all quiet in my head, and dark and I knew not a thing. It was as if I fell to sleep.

PART SIX

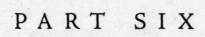

Prologue

You have forgotten.
But the Gods remember
and so does the Truth.
It's the Truth that will make you sorry
one day
for everything you did, and everything you do.

Lucius, my Lucius,

You are dead, my brother, of some nameless eastern fever.

The fact of your death is indigestible. Such an impossibility cannot wean me of my habit of writing to you. I defy your extinction with living words!

I was about to go to Baiae again when our father called me back to Verona with the unspeakable news.

Now I have executed all the expected acts. I took part in your funeral rites like a ghost, as if it were I myself who had died. In that mourning household, awash with grief for your loss, I went nearly mad. In every corner where I sought peace I stumbled on a slave weeping incontinently or an impromptu shrine set up in your memory.

I left indecently fast, kissing my father's closed, reproachful face without meeting his eyes.

'Why do you hurry away, son?' he asked me. 'Stay a while, and recover your health, and give me the pleasure of seeing you grow fat again. Rome has not been good for you.'

'It's been good for my poems,' I told him.

'Why may I not read them, then?'

I hung my head. It hurt to withhold them, but I did not want him to see why I was really going back.

I thought my grief for my darling brother would bring forth her tenderness, but Clodia had seemed absent-minded at my leave-taking. I smelled Clodius' musky hair-oil and wondered dully if he was hidden behind a curtain. There were two cameo glass chalices beside her divan and I leaned forward to see the wine-dregs in both of them.

I carried the scent of that stale wine in my nostrils all the way back to Verona. My heart was opened by your death; it made me more sensitive to everything. I was painfully aware that something was not right with Clodia, less right even than usual.

To confirm my fears, her 'welcome home' was less than enthusiastic. I'd been back in Rome two burning days before she summoned me. I devoured the road up to her house, but when I arrived, a certain dishevelment in the bedroom and a sharpness to her scent showed me, as all Rome had seen before me, that she was cheaper than I valued her.

While we made love, I calculated the comparisons that she must have been making. This had a deleterious effect on my performance.

'Got used to the goats again, country boy?' she asked, fanning herself, for our ineffectual exertions had been long and laborious.

Since then I've made it my business to know every foul detail of her infidelity, collecting incriminating statements from anyone who'll talk to me. Whenever I see the hairy pulp of a nobleman's armpit in the Baths, or the spit glistening on his lip at a banquet, I wonder when Clodia was there. Not if. *That*'s a certainty.

When I find a new instance of betrayal, I scourge us both with it in a new kind of poem, each a species of versified suicide note, uttered in a quiet, bitter voice.

Give up, I tell myself, and yet still the frail fire scuttles up in sparks and bonfires under my skin.

Sparrow-like consonants no longer fly around the page. Just

memories of them. I remember when I loved her as if her veins ran with family blood, when my altruism was as deep as my passion. I remember when I was almost happy to exist in a unilateral state of love, a state of qualified grace from which I'm now exiled. Now I celebrate a sick, sad love, which knows the horror of its condition.

Against Clodia's indolent indifference I launch verbs, packing eight of them into a two-line poem. Who needs adjectives to blur and simper round the edge of the action? Not I, who loves, hates, knows not why, and is crucified for it, all at the same time.

I fled Rome.

I went to Bithynia with the pompous governor, Gaius Memmius. Caesar and his hangers-on were feeding in a frenzy on Gallic loot. This provincial sojourn was supposed to be *my* chance to fatten my purse. Instead I spent my time hunting for your bones to take back to Sirmione. I could not bear that you should rest in exile.

No one among those iron-eyed bureaucrats could tell me your exact resting spot in Troad, though I searched for information without cease. Other men made themselves millionaires, scrabbling under the shadow of our chief Memmius for the few coins that were too small for his grasp. I just looked for you.

In the end I found an unmarked grave and appointed it yours, so that I might address you with the tears I'd saved for that moment.

My thoughts were these: Who closed your eyes at the last? It was my right — I who gave you so many mock-deaths as a child, pushing you in the lake and down haystacks and whispering ghost tales in your sleeping ears at midnight so you woke white and nibbled by the Shades.

Who covered their eyes, rack-throated, at the sight of your bundled corpse? It should have been me.

Who strewed your grave with wine, milk, honey and flowers? That was my right too, who stole so many apples with you and shared the warm juice of the cow from your cupped hands.

Who wept at the graveside? Those tears belonged to me. Who returned the day after to lie on the warm earth and embrace you, pressing his humid face to the place where yours lay just below?

Not I, alas.

And now what can I do? What can I give you? A poem? A little rustling stack of unfeelable caresses, untasteable tears. I come all these mazy ways simply to tell you that I love you, and I cannot bear to be deprived of your love.

I've come home empty-handed, poorer than I left, and without your remains. I travelled via the Black Sea, the Sea of Marmara, Thrace and the Cyclades, sailing on my own beloved yacht. Finally we sailed up the Adriatic, then down the Po and the Mincio. Finally, all the way to Sirmione, gratefully abandoning the slavering beaches of the ocean, with its waves that smote my aching prow like rocks.

Instead of your remains I've brought back the carcass of my love for Clodia. It's still more powerful than the bodies of living, lovely women. In Bithynia I took an interest in Cybele, for in her native land her cult is practised more violently than in Rome. More and more I saw the parallels between Cybele and Attis, and Clodia and myself. Standing on a cliff above the ocean, I sketched the outline of my poem, in which Attis comes to his senses, after castrating himself in the frenzy of his devotion, and walks to the sea, where he (now, poignantly, 'she' in the pronoun) laments his/her losses. Cybele, of course, will not spare any of her eunuchs, and soon sends her lion to drive poor Attis back into the thickets of Mount Ida.

And so my love for Clodia has driven me back to Rome. She has a lien on my *mentula*; like Attis, my condition is irreversible.

Still she calls me to her side, when she's bored with the others, or sometimes, I think, to monitor my pain. I still believe that it enriches her. What a vampire bat she is! How rapacious her appetite for the vital fluids and sentient parts of men! I pass other fellows in the street and wonder, *Is it your turn next? Or yours? Or have you already been there?*

The only thing that comforts me is a new rumour – that Caelius has given her the cold shoulder, the first time such a thing has happened. He has turned on her like a serpent, and bitten hard. We've all known for some time that Caelius was involved in some murderous Egyptian business; we knew he far surpassed us in his ambitions. But

I never thought he would be able to do what I could never do: pay Clodia in her own coin.

When Caelius abandoned her, Clodia went insane. This is the only way I can explain the terrible error of judgement that followed.

I saw with wonder that Clodia could not bear to be rejected. Whether she loved or not, it was her role to cast off lovers, not to be cast aside. All Rome now knew that Caelius had coolly sidestepped her. The personal humiliation was also a political one: it turned out he'd been working secretly with Pompey against the interests of her too-much-beloved brother.

Caelius flitted from the apartments at Clodius' house, leaving his rent contemptuously in arrears. He was out of Clodia's reach: she could not go after him in person. Even in her fury, she would not humiliate herself by hunting him around the town. Instead she went after his blood, accusing him of plotting to poison her, or defrauding her, conspiring to murder a diplomat and to provoke a riot at Naples. She launched a shoal of spears, sure that at least one of them would stick in him, and fatally.

But Clodia's case against Caelius has gone gravely wrong for her. Unluckily for Clodia, the accused poisoner went to Cicero for his defence. No one would have thought that the great man would take on the case, as Caelius, a former protégé of Cicero's, had already double-crossed him once in allying himself with the Clodian clan. But Cicero did, and probably just because of his bitter hatred of Clodius, who had him exiled from Rome last year and saw to it that his house was thoroughly pillaged in his absence.

The day she heard that Cicero had been appointed counsel, how Clodia must, for the first time in her life, have trembled.

I returned from Bithynia in the middle of the furore.

It did not escape my notice that the trial took place in the first days of the games devoted to the Magna Mater, Cybele.

Hidden at the back of the crowd, I watched the whole trial. I know it was less than dignified of me to show my face, but I could not resist. I stood twenty yards from Clodia and her counsel, seated in the front row of the circles that fanned out from the central area. It was a long time since I'd observed my mistress from such a distance, and I had never seen her with that defiant, fearful expression upon her face. She gave me no sign of recognition.

Caelius arrived, all oiled and plucked, with a sheen of sweat above those soft lips. Clodia averted her eyes and never once looked at him while five long prosecution speeches sought to paint him black.

Then, on the second day, Cicero took his place in front of the seventy-five judges and the presiding magistrate. The corona of bystanders drew a deep collective breath, awaiting the stab of his tongue. They were not disappointed.

But they were surprised.

Instead of Caelius, it was Clodia who was put in the dock. Cicero seized his chance. With deliciously skilful innuendo, well attuned to the absorbent ears and busy imaginations of the Romans, he vented his spleen against the whole corrupt Clodian clan. What a carve-up! What a fox in the chicken house was Cicero! With his jaws clamped on my lover and her brother!

How dare Clodia, the expert, accuse someone else of poison? thundered Cicero and all present sniggered behind their hands. I saw Clodia, knowing all eyes upon her, assume a futile smile.

I felt suddenly faint. I'd laughed at all those rumours that she poisoned her husband. This was the first time I'd heard them taken seriously. The fact that Cicero dared to allude to it so openly, without fear of retribution, gave me grievous cause for thought. Had I been making love to a murderess? I felt as if all the oily heads in the room had suddenly swivelled to look at foolish, gullible me. They had not: it was merely the entrance of another witness that drew their attention.

Even while these thoughts surged around my brain, Cicero was taking the drama in another direction.

Clodia was known for writing playlets, said Cicero, clever little after-dinner entertainments, he simpered, as if full of innocent admiration, his tone silkier than a Bithynian handkerchief. All Romans know that when Cicero seems to praise his victim must watch for his — or her — back. In this case the stab was not long in coming.

Cicero continued, smooth as cooked cream: How could Clodia, a lady-librettist (smile, wink) of some note in the circles where *private* entertainments rule, come up with a scenario so implausible, unless it was distilled from the pure bile of an older woman rejected by her handsome young lover? Caelius, of course, was to be excused for his lapse of taste in bedding her. Given the times, and his youth, it was an understandable fling — and, after all, what were such women for?

What were such women for? I thought to myself. Cicero had me under his spell like all the rest, and I was not capable of thinking for myself. I waited for Cicero to tell me.

Gradually, he did.

Cicero showed Clodia as a noblewoman with the habits of a prostitute; not just a whore but a whorehouse full of vices, a powerful woman gone to the bad, a one-woman morality play from which society could draw a severe lesson.

How he enjoyed himself! He harked back to disgraceful incidents in Clodia's past, using her hated nickname Quadrantaria, acquired after a young man sent her an ironic gift of forty copper coins in a jar, her supposed price. Clodia had sent two henchmen to rape the offender. Nevertheless, another angry young man had dared to despatch to her a perfume jar full of something more personal and more filthy. Cicero, merely by describing these gifts, made it clear that they defined the contents of Clodia's soul.

He piled on the innuendo, particularly to do with Sextus Cloelius, whom Clodia's powerful influence had recently delivered from justice in another criminal trial. Regarding Cloelius, Cicero constantly referred to his polluted mouth and tongue, which was, according to the lawyer, always to be found busily engaged in the business of pleasuring Clodia. Cicero managed to insert into his denunciation every 'licking' word in the Latin lexicon ... *lingere, ligurrire, lambere*, each already heavy with lascivious innuendo, and in Cicero's own deft mouth working overtime to create an impression of a woman who had men at her knees, busy between her thighs, a humiliating position for any blue-blooded Roman.

'Where will you find Cloelius these days?' asked Cicero, sly as a left hand. 'You'll find him over at Clodia's house, with his head down . . .'

The crowd roared and thumped their feet. All I could think of was this: I'd been there myself. Had I tasted Cloelius or Clodia?

Or even the hateful Clodius, her brother?

'Lady Ox-Eyes', Cicero called her, referring to the large-orbed Goddess Hera, who was both wife and sister to Zeus – who could miss the reference to her overly intimate relations with her brother? And in case the slur evaded its mark, Cicero continually faux-blundered, 'The Lady's husband,' he simpered, 'forgive me, I mean her brother. I always make that mistake.'

Cicero condemned Clodia and her whole class . . . degenerates with not a thought for the good of the world, lost in their luxury and lechery, simply addicted to *ludi e quae sequuntur* . . . 'dinner games and all that comes after them'.

He described Clodia's villa at Baiae as a palatial floating brothel. Her park on the banks of the Tiber was just a discreet place for picking up young men.

Whatever the result of the trial, Clodia has already lost. Caelius has won more than just his freedom.

Does she care?

Probably not. Her contempt embraces the whole of Rome. She can afford to scorn everyone. No one is more aristocratic than Clodia Metelli, even if no one is more debauched.

And who's going to stop her?

Certainly not I. Clodia's not going to listen to the whinings of an old lover, already gone stale. Although she still calls me to her bed, presumably when she craves a bout of *poetic* lovemaking, I know that she sends other servants to other men, to satisfy other needs.

I turn my little wax *devotio* around in my hand, making plans for her. I don't know why I keep her. It was my intention to burn her in the fire, to melt Clodia's pebble heart. Somehow I found I could not do that, so I keep her wrapped in a sheaf of linen in my bedchamber, and I sleep with her in between my fingers. I could not hold her in my naked hand or my warmth would distort her shape.

I'm pained to discover that I myself have become slightly ridiculous, somewhat tainted, in association with Clodia now. It does not make me love or hate her less. It's just a new edge to the pain of those things. Cicero has also made my *poems* ridiculous, those of a cuckold. I hate him! If I were stronger I would set upon him. But Cicero has too many enemies; he's well guarded.

And I am not well, these days, not even strong enough to thrash an old man. I'm troubled with a cough. I'm not yet thirty years old; I should be in the prime of my manhood. Instead my chest is hollow as an adolescent's and the bones of my face are pushing to the surface, stretching the skin. The flesh hangs loose on my upper arms, like ox skins on the rack at a tannery. All the asafoetida in Cyrene will not still the bubbling in my lungs. I even incubated a night in the temple of Serapis, hoping the God would send me healthful dreams. None came, just vivid nightmares of Clodia's unmistakable silhouette engaged in frantic acts with random men in back alleys.

My father sent a physician all the way from Verona to listen to my chest. For his sake I downed a bitter infusion of hellebore, a swift purge for insanity.

'And rest,' the doctor urged me, 'fewer late nights, more swimming. More fruit.'

So I have doubled my intake of squashed grapes, slightly fermented. Ha!

Chapter One

Listen to me now!
I scream my wrongs to the sterile sands.
I am scorched, ash-blind, brainless with pain.
My misery is clear: I scrape the dregs
inside me to show it to you,
So don't walk past me. Take it with you.

Sosia and Felice were in his room at the Locanda Sturion. She had taken to coming there without an invitation, as if that proved her claim to him. She faced down the beautiful landlady, who turned away without blushing from Sosia's impudent stare.

'Why does everyone say she's so peerless?' asked Sosia, flinging open Felice's door without a knock. 'Her nose is big, her mouth is crooked. She's thin. If Bellini painted her, and told the truth about her, the portrait would not be beautiful.'

Felice, at the window, did not turn to greet her, answered over his shoulder, 'It's true; she's not a conventional Venus. But her looks are yet more pleasing as a result. People enjoy thinking that in her they've discovered a rare beauty for themselves and that everyone else lacked the discrimination to distinguish it. They're always disappointed to hear someone else raving of her charms.'

'Do you find her beautiful?' Sosia edged closer, hoping for a welcoming embrace.

'I find her attractive. She attracts me.' Felice, finally turning, nodded a cool greeting.

'Does she know that?'

'I have given her certain incontrovertible proofs of it,' Felice said, casually.

Sosia shut her eyes, muttering through clenched teeth, 'I thought she was supposed to be above that kind of thing.'

'Ah, she lets me have her, but she's somehow not really contaminated by it. She simply rises above it.'

'Why does she let you, then?'

'I think she's biding her time, waiting for something better.'

'Better than you?'

Sosia turned away sharply, knocking a small quire of paper to the floor. She bent to pick it up but Felice pushed her aside briskly.

'Don't touch it. It's a proof copy.'

'Proof the editor's a drunkard. This is Squarzafico's work, isn't it? I heard he'd gone over to Jenson. You too, Felice? Poor Wendelin and Bruno, what hope do they have with friends like you? How could you, and with Wendelin's wife . . . ?'

She pointed to two mistakes on the first page and a little smudge in the bottom left-hand corner. Her learning constantly amazed Felice. It despoiled his theory that she was pure instinct, which permitted their couplings, intellectually, as a kind of experiment, in the uncluttered realm of the flesh.

'And what do you know of Squarzafico, Sosia? No, don't answer that. I shall forever interpret the stale dregs of wine in that interesting smell of yours. Still, I don't know how you could – or if he could, even given your provocation. It must be many years since he made love to anything but a bottle.'

'You think I'm so lacking in discrimination?'

'You're intelligent, Sosia, no, that's not it. You are *pantegana*-shrewd. You're a rat who runs round Venice, spreading filth.'

Sosia, hearing an unaccustomed acerbity in his smooth voice, looked up quickly and retreated to the back of the desk. She had achieved that rare thing: she'd made Felice angry. Instantly she guessed the cause. He was diseased, because of her, he who had always been so fastidious. He'd long since ceased to give her the rigorous examination he performed the first time they lay together. She knew he always checked his whores and casual lovers, so it could only be she herself who had infected him. Indeed, the discomfort in her genitals pricked her sharply just then, and she rubbed herself against the edge of the desk. She regretted not using the herbs Rabino had left her. He had not offered them again since she wrecked the apothecary studio. She had not felt inclined to ask, or to ask why some of her clients had fallen to the disease, while others, like Bruno, remained unaffected.

Felice said, 'Yes, scratch away, don't mind me! Who was it, Sosia? Which one of the six men? In fact, is six enough for you? I merely allow two each from the current columns in your ledger. If you can sleep with six, why not nine? Sosia, let me make some introductions – Sosia's left leg, meet Sosia's right leg. I know that you used to be acquainted but you've been apart so much now that it's as if you never met.'

He walked around the desk, took the corner of her sleeve between two fingers, and pulled her to the mirror.

'Sosia, look at your face. It has been plastered on the loins and lips of so many men that it's like a mask which has been passed around and around at *Carnevale*.

'That's right,' he said as she spat at the image in the mirror. 'You never swallow your own saliva if you can swallow someone else's. You only look pure because semen washes off. You must be rich as Croesus from all your paying customers. Do you even know who left you this little tribute you've kindly shared with me? By the way, you must remember to leave me an account when you leave. It seems I have neglected to settle my debts. What's the going rate? I'd reckon 40 *zecchini*, enough to fill a small chamber jar.'

Sosia said quietly: 'I only charge Venetians.'

'Why?'

Sosia looked at the floor. 'Why should I tell you that?'

'And so it's only because I'm from Verona that I get my service *gratis*? Bruno gets his for free because he's an orphan I suppose? Wait, of course, I remember, he's only half Venetian. So he gets half-service for *nothing*.'

'Bruno was something I picked out for myself. I thought it would be nice. I did not know he would become such a weight on me.'

'Poor Sosia! How you suffer about it! Bruno's pains are nothing to yours, I suppose?'

Sosia picked up a jug of milk from a tray in the windowsill. She walked slowly back to the desk, and poured the milk in a thick stream into an open drawer where a finished manuscript lay drying. The pink and yellow inks instantly marbled the milk in its little rectangular pool.

At first Felice spoke only to himself: 'The woman doesn't have the run of herself any more,' he said wonderingly. He had been angry before; instead of becoming more so he was now calm and detached. He picked up a book.

366

'Talk to *me*,' screamed Sosia.

'And what would the madwoman like to talk to me about?'

'About what I've just done, of course, *Bog te jebo*, God fuck you.'

'Well, there are a number of things I could say,' Felice murmured, smoothly. 'For example: you have stolen a year of my life by doing that, Sosia.'

'It's a worthless life. Letters of the alphabet. Not a life. Not a man's life.'

Felice failed to lose his temper. Instead, while she turned the empty jug round and round in her hands, he turned two pages of his book and started to read. She clutched the handle. Despite her worst play, she had not managed to pierce his feelings beyond irritation.

'Felice, are you not furious with me?'

He did not look up until she struck the jug against the wall for emphasis.

'It's hard to be angry with you because I find my feelings are not engaged in the matter. I can be bothered to explain this far: books are life, for those of us who love them. It's not a kind of love you would understand. It's a subtle, fragile kind of love, the kind parents have for children. The book is never perfect, never as perfect as the idea of it. Once it was crystalline and miraculous in the mind of the writer. In utterance, it came out imperfectly, only carrying a scent of the original thought . . .'

Sosia screamed, 'At a moment like this you talk about books! You are obscene in your love for books. A woman for you is like having a lover on the side. Something to be ashamed of!'

She threw the jug across the room. It exploded against the far wall. White tears, the dregs of the jug, were surprised out of the bottom of it, and ran down the red paint and slapped on the broken shards of the pottery. Felice looked away in distaste, remarking, 'You did not think so when you first came to my bed.'

'My coming to your bed should have proved to you that yours is a worthless life.'

'Sosia, I've no taste for this idea of you as a victim which gives you the right to hurt everyone in your path, as if it were self-defence.'

'Then why do the curs follow me?' She was panting, and tears hung from her eyelashes.

Felice sniffed fastidiously: 'Because you have the aroma of the fields, or is it the fish market, my dear? It's revoltingly attractive.'

It was true. Lately, dogs followed her everywhere, burying their snouts in her groin. Ugly dogs; dogs with skin conditions of unspeakable putridness; dogs who held their fourth leg up under their bellies and loped unevenly down the street after her; dogs with eyes like saints and dogs with eyes like devils . . .

She yelled at them in Serbian, '*Krvavu ti majku jebem*, Fuck your blood-splattered mother', or '*Otac ti je govno pojeo*, Your father ate shit.' They followed her anyway. She would scream at them, 'Let the owls carry you away and eat you.' Only then would they leave, for some reason, whimpering, as if she had somehow identified all their worst fears.

'Felice,' Sosia said suddenly and hoarsely. 'You know what I feel – for you—?'

Her voice trailed away. Felice laughed. Sosia, holding his unwilling hand, bore it as long as she could. Then she unbuttoned her dress and looked at him hopefully.

I awoke from my illness naked as a worm under soft clean linen, as if I'd been born quite clean and new again.

But I was not glad to find myself alive. A mange of sadness dines on all my days and I wish them over. I am tired of wrestling this melancholy that still ambushes me like an importuning blanket in the dead of a hot night.

I get more well, they tell me. The bite on my wrist has healed to a little pucker of pink. I can lift a hand or a leg, languid as seaweed. I can take a full spoon of broth in my mouth and let it wash down my throat. It takes nought from me. I do not care.

Nothing is right. The blooms are too dark a red in the pots on my sill. I think their sap is vile now. Sourness infects my nature, worse than the illness, makes my breath carrion, turns my pillow to gristle so it marks my face in the morning in long red lines. Who looks at my face anyway? I am shorn of all my seductions now.

My ma and pa come to look on me with eyes rimmed round with query. Their question is, what's the matter with me? I've grown far apart from them. I wish they would think of me as a daughter whom they lost long ago, that the owls carried me away, unravelling my insides over the rooftops, that . . .

My friends tell me I'm well, as if this will make it so. Sure, my body is improved, for I can walk, in slow steps, with a score of rests, to the southern shore of Dorsoduro, and I go there when the sun is at its worst as if to scorch off the plague sores and the pain in my heart which is worse than the sores. I live but I am not pleased to be alive. I am lonely as a soldier's grave by the edge of the sea.

The Jew saved me, they say. He came each day to sit with me. He gave me drugs and laid rolls of eggs on my breast. But most of all he looked at me, as if he wished that I might live. I think that is what called me back to life.

This was his strength, then, to wish me to live with his heart and mind. Not like my man who did not wish it at all, but just feigned it at times. Not like my son who would as soon have the teat of a wet-nurse as mine. Not like the cat who stayed in the sick room just to see what came in on my tray for he knew he would get it in the end.

No, the Jew came to save me because he had a wish to, and this wish must have been strong, for here I am still, despite the Damascus Plague.

I watch the waves jump round the three legs of the woodpiles accompanying them with small nods of my own head, like a mad wife. I knit my cares to each wave in the hilly water, sending them clambering and sliding to the horizon. But when I turn to leave, I know they will still be there, dog-craven at my feet, waiting to be taken home.

'Sun is good,' says the Jew when he hears of my hours on the shore. 'But take care. Do not burn the fluid from your skin. It's most unseasonably hot this autumn. I never saw weather like it.'

He does not know that this is just what I wish to do. If the one plague could not kill me, then I choose a plague of sun to lay waste to me, till I become just a straw wife.

My friend Caterina di Colonna told me, in confidence, that she has recently called the Jew in to attend to Felice Feliciano, who has caught a dose from one of his whores. That's the price of buying love! He was taken peculiarly when staying at the Sturion and did not even know who he was, so high was the heat of his fever.

I've never understood how Caterina could bear to touch him. With *her* looks, she could have anyone, a noble like Domenico Zorzi, yet she trifles with Felice. When I say so, she turns to me with her eyes wide open and says, 'Lussièta, most of us put some time in – in the gutter. Did you never do something beneath your idea of yourself? And yet you could not stop yourself?'

I think of how I hide the wax-lady, of how I murdered the poor printer Sicculus, how I dissembled with my man on our journey over the Alps, and I hang my head, unable to meet her beautiful eyes.

I wonder what the Jew thought of Felice? Of course I may not ask! It's hard to imagine the two of them together. From what Caterina says, Felice will not remember anything about it when he's well and on his usual courses again, flirting with himself and everyone else like a courtesan who has not yet lost the pleasure of her work. If he should know that the Jew visited him *in extremis*, that would deflate his crest somewhat!

And when he's well, he'll be round to my house again, to taunt me without seeming to do so. He has declared that the box from Ca' Dario is the most lovely piece of wood in Venice, and I'm sure he did it just to see the flash in my eye. My man no longer mentions it, or praises it to the skies since I was sick, but nor has he rid us of it.

I look at the woodpiles. They seem to me to be nailed in place with planks like a poor one's coffin, the kind which stand in front of the church till some kind soul puts coins on top to pay the man to dig the grave.

The big boats pass, full of gold or spice or some such stuff as folk think makes their life good. I think you must be glad of heart to love gold and silk, for I tell you that if you are wretched, then there's no thing that shines or twists which can bring back joy. Just the one you love. He brings worth to all things – or, to tell the truth – he just lends it. If he looks away, does not love you more, then gold is but yellow dust and silk only worm shrouds.

Some poor ones come to sit in front of me by the sea. Beggars, one of whom lacks legs. He wears empty hose with shoes sewn on the ends. They've brought him in a kind of stretcher. Despite that, there seems to be a woman who loves him. She reaches down to hold his hand, and kisses the top of his head. In that moment, I am jealous of them both.

If anyone passes, they all look pathetic as can be, and hold out their hands for alms. If the person looks to pass without paying them a small tax, then the legless man looks mean and shouts 'Miser!'

They trap one man, who turns around and says, 'How do you know I'm a miser?' He looks ashamed to be thought a niggard.

They laugh and say: 'Show us we're liars!'

The man, on fire with blushes, does not see what they're about and hands them coins that disappear into crevices in their clothes in an instant. This seems to buy them some peace, and for a while they desist from harassing those who pass by. They're on holiday for half an hour, it seems.

They point at the ships, chirp like seabirds that have heard of a whole loaf floating nearby. They move from the sun to the shade now, the heat is too fierce for them. I see that they wish to stay moist with love, even though they are poor.

I, in the meantime, accept the full malice of the sun on my back, feel the sweat pooling in the crooks of my elbows and the backs of my knees.

I let the sun hate me.

I walk to the edge of the sea, where the seaweed dances under the water like blood spreading from a wound. I stand there and burn.

Chapter Two

What fears she endured in her fainting heart!
How often did she grow more wan than the white sheen of gold?

Wendelin's joy was short-lived. His wife did not die but nor did she thrive. She roused herself from her bed and resumed her duties but she did not return to the flower of her confidence. Her fever had not cleansed her mind of doubt. She never mentioned the cabinet now and he assumed that the reality of her illness had cured her fantastical obsession with it.

When she was out at the market, Wendelin went to their room and stood at her dressing table. He handled her brush and comb with reverent fingers. He winced at the amount of hair woven into the teeth of the comb and the bristles of the brush. He noticed sorrowfully how the white-gold had darkened in the past few months. In more ways than this, she was losing the lightness of her youth.

For the first time, he began to regret the absence of anxiety at the beginning of their love. That sureness, the absence of rational thought then – he was paying for it now, it seemed. Their love had been unnatural in its naturalness; and an illusory rush of unearned happiness had deceived him. *We skidded into love. I was still dizzy with it when we married.*

He should have known that nothing truly good comes without work and integrity. *A love that drops into your lap will not stay there*, he thought.

His wife's illness had left her fragile in body and spirit. He could see the destruction of her self-belief in her new, jerky movements, her diminished substance, the lack of lustre in her eyes. He was torn with a tender compassion for her losses, quite separate from his own self-pity.

Since she was sick he had become more creative with his love letters. 'I want to gather up your feet in my hands with my fingers circling your toes,' he wrote. 'I wish to lift the hair from your neck with shivers.'

If he touched her feet though, that evening, he knew that she would flinch.

If he said, 'I love you,' she would look pointedly at the floor.

Shyly, he discussed the problems with Rabino Simeon.

'It's more usual that an experience so close to death leaves exhilaration in its wake,' the doctor explained kindly. 'But some poor souls grow melancholy, it's true. No doubt she fears for the loss of her beauty.' Rabino blushed, for he knew he had conjured the same image in his mind as Wendelin's, of the plague sores on Lussièta's shrunken abdomen, and that he was the only other man to have seen her thus.

'Will the scars not disappear?'

'Not entirely.'

'My poor darling! I believe she trusts they will. How can I tell her? Or not tell her now that I know. I hate to have secrets from her.'

Rabino took pity. 'I shall explain it to her as gently as possible.'

'Would you do that? You are too kind.'

His wife out of danger, Wendelin took to walking the streets again.

After many nights of aimless wandering, he found a pattern that seemed to comfort him. It was in this circuit, between San Samuele to San Vidal, that he started to feel each night the hot breath of someone following him and hear footsteps echoing his own. He would spin around, and could swear that he saw the shadow of something slipping from the corner of the *calle*. But he never saw anything tangible. In deserted courtyards he heard things, suppressed laughter and whispered screams, words in a dialect that he did not understand, but seemed familiar, like the archaic words of an old nursery rhyme his wife sang to their son.

Twice he saw the pupil of an eye pressed against the keyhole of a gate as he passed. Too unnerved to stare, he had hurried away. Afterwards he wondered at how he could have seen such an eye when there was no body visible through the iron palings.

One night, walking near the Grand Canal, he began to feel dizzy with an inexplicable fear. His breath constricted in his throat. Venice loomed around him, a sudden wind banging the shutters and loosening the petals of window-box flowers that swirled like blood-tinted snow. Morsels of strangely formed clouds roamed restlessly across the sky, moonlight pouring through them or suddenly blacked out by them. In gardens hidden behind walls, he heard trees jangling. Taking a deep breath, he found himself choking on tiny feathers wrenched from windswept birds.

Beneath all these noises beat the slow steady drumming, like a funeral procession, of unseen footsteps, which seemed without hurrying every second to draw closer to Wendelin. With neither a body nor a shadow to endow them with substance, they throbbed like a fever in his head.

Absurdly, heavily, he started to run. The footsteps quickened. Wendelin lumbered on, lurching right and left into unknown alleys, praying that none should prove a dead end. At last the footsteps ceased.

Wendelin felt he had gained a few dozen yards on his pursuer at last. He leant back in an alcove, feeling his heart smash to and fro against his ribcage. He waited for the footsteps to pass by, but the silence remained unbroken. He sagged his haunches to the ground, and covered his head, awaiting blows.

Nothing happened.

After some moments, he raised himself up and looked around. He emerged back into the street, and continued blindly on his way. He had no idea where he was.

There was no mistaking the immediate resumption of stealthy footsteps behind him. Wendelin, faint with terror, felt the hairs rise on the backs of his hands. Dark spots, livid as bruises, invaded his vision, and he was no longer sure if he was fully conscious. He gagged as a noose was slipped around his neck and a damp blanket over his head. He was dragged into the shadows, winded, unable to see his assailant. He could smell him, though. An overwhelming stench of putrefaction assaulted his nose and belly.

Inside the pall of the blanket he retched and coughed. Through its coarse weave he could make out dreamlike details. It seemed that the hand he was

374

fighting off was gloved but he could see that an emaciated wrist protruded from it, marked and striated around the bone as if long buried. He realised that his attacker was much smaller than himself, and yet controlled him easily with a strength that was far superior.

Wendelin fought until he felt himself losing the will to continue. He had made no impression on his gaoler who merely gripped him calmly in the gloved hands. Finally, numb with hopelessness, Wendelin was forced to relax in the arms of his assailant. Barely conscious, he fell back into the hollowness of the attacker's breast. He thought vaguely of what would happen next, as he was sure to die. His mind filled up with beautiful images of his wife, of how she might learn to love him again after his death. He called out her name. In his mind a couplet from Catullus repeated itself over and over again: 'No woman was ever loved as I loved her, no woman . . .'

Then, as if Wendelin had spoken aloud, the stranger snarled hotly in his ear, dampening the blanket with his breath: 'Leave off the filthy poetry, barbarian!'

Wendelin tore himself out of his attacker's arms and turned to face him. Giddy and gasping for air, swigging drunkenly on its black moisture, his vision only gradually returned to him. By then there was nothing there, in the corner where he had been held, just a shadow through which he passed his hands again and again, grasping at nothing.

'Lack of sleep,' he muttered. 'This is what it does to you along with a surfeit of this town's noxious vapours. I begin to have nightmares while I yet walk around.'

Why dead? Why not just harmed in some way? In what way did I cause this?

Is it because, as the doctor tells me, the scars shall not leave my body? I did not much care about that until the thought struck me: does my man know? I could not forfend from asking and the Jew told me that he did. So he's keeping it a secret from me. Along with what other dark secrets?

The itch of those scars roams my skin on clawed feet, even where there are no scars. No place on my body is suffered to lie at peace, for the scars have signed my skin like a document that pledges: 'This marriage is dissolved.'

Is this why he stays out all night and creeps back to do that bad thing at dawn? When he has emptied his gland of poison into that drawer he leaves promptly and I am stupefied by a tiredness that strikes between the blades of my shoulders and fells me like a split sapling. I lie weak upon the bed, tears pumping from my limp eyes until they are trenched all round with water.

I try to think on hopeful things. Lately I've been wondering about Paola and her mean words to me. Whore that she is (the red-haired man!), and much as I hate her, I own she has a point. Now that my own happy life is over I want to do some real thing to help people. No more rumours, no more secret whispers. I would like to see someone happy. It has occurred to me that the unhappiest person I know, outside myself, is poor young Bruno Uguccione.

Bruno has become caw-pawed these days. I do not remember him dropping things before, and now he spills his beer on the table and stumbles on our doorstep. He's developing the wrong way round, not from a great clunch of a fellow to a fine young man, but a fine young man to a sorry sort of creature. He used to be a skilled archer, he tells me, but I wonder if he could bend a bow now? He's fuzzled with bad love, as bad as if he'd drunk bad wine and too much of it.

The only cure for a bad love is a new love. This is a solution forbidden to me, for I could never love anyone but my man. However, in the case of Bruno, I can see a different ending. When I think of the two most attractive people in Venice, the faces that come to my mind straight away are his and that of Caterina di Colonna, my friend at the Sturion. Everyone loves her, just as they love Bruno, and yet she wastes the flower of her years taking care of strangers and consorting with the likes of Felice Feliciano. What if she were to have a young man of her own to cherish and rescue? She's a few years older than him, but it seems he prefers women more mature than himself, perhaps because he was orphaned at a tender age.

There are certain things I can do to put those two together, and it's my feeling that this is all it would take, that their two sweet natures would most naturally graft. Their two shy needs might meet and breed a desire! As yet, they do not even know one another, and I aim to confect a meeting.

Thoughts like this take me out of my sad self. But I return to my brooding soon enough. Since the plague left me I am given to imaginings. It takes nothing to feel myself back on the death cart. When I close my eyes I hear the rumble of the wheels.

And why do I see rope? All shops, it seems, are full of it. It hangs and swings and coils in front of my eyes no matter where I look. I did not know before how much rope there is in this town. To hold the beasts, to drag the carts, to tie the boats. The town swarms with rope. All these things, I know, have no harm to them. I say out loud: 'There's no harm in rope,' and then from the edge of my eye I see a thing move like a bad worm and I feel pricks in my hands and cold in the bones of my back.

When I went to the shop this day, I asked for all the things I needed, but then when the man asked: '*Basta così?* That's all?' a voice came from my mouth which said, 'And a coil of strong rope, please.'

I went to my purse to pay for the rope we did not need and there was no more coin in it.

It has been like that for some time now.

'Take it anyway, *Signora*,' urged the shopkeeper. 'Pay next week. Times like these, you never know when you will need a fine piece of rope.'

Bruno took a copy of Catullus to the Locanda Sturion.

Wendelin had never forgotten the kindness of the landlady when he and Johann first arrived in the city. So, when Lussièta had recovered and he could think on other things, Wendelin asked Bruno to take Caterina di Colonna her presentation volume. It was not from the most expensive vellum quires; nor one of the costly ones printed on heavy paper. It was a good paper, crisp and translucent as the bone of a wren, from the first flower of the main run (before the ink began to smear a little). Wendelin had asked the most dexterous of the nuns he employed to rubricate it, and the cover was tooled in calfskin dyed with real lapis tints and studded with three semi-precious stones. This work had taken two months and by the time it arrived on his desk, Wendelin had almost forgotten why he'd commissioned it.

It was his wife's suggestion that Bruno should deliver it. She had roused herself from her listlessness long enough to say that Caterina and Bruno should become acquainted. Wendelin had not questioned her: it was such a pleasure to be able to accede to a simple wish of hers. A discretion born of shyness stopped him from explaining his wife's motive to his editor.

'Take it to the Sturion,' he requested Bruno. 'You look pale, a little walk would do you good in this long-lived sunshine.'

Tales of Caterina di Colonna's loveliness had, of course, reached Bruno, though he had never seen her himself. He was curious to see her face, rumoured to give a strange illumination – though he expected little effect. Her eyes were said to be no less blue than the cover of the book he was carrying, yet he found himself interested only in the specification of their colouring, not in the effect that they might have on him. His love for Sosia had drained his ability to enjoy the beauty of other women. He could watch a pretty girl tie her sandal or bend low over her bucket so that the shadows reached down between her breasts – and feel nothing but regret that she was not Sosia.

Walking towards the bridge, Bruno noticed Wendelin's sister-in-law Paola talking intently to a pale red-haired man in front of the church of San Salvador. Her elegance did not attract him at all: he'd always wondered why Johann von Speyer had chosen her. Bruno found her somewhat overbearing, as did all the men at the *stamperia*, where she was frequently to be found, dispensing advice and, he had to admit, extremely useful information. No one knew how she could find out what she did.

He put Paola and her mysterious errands out of his mind and descended the wooden steps, turning left into a boiling haze of sunlight and taking the few steps to the Sturion.

At first glance, the landlady did not appear to match her legend. He came across her in the parlour, where she was bent over a ledger, writing. She was standing with her back to him, one leg a little forward, while she pored over the entries. Her neck was awkwardly inclined, her nose over-large in silhouette. But when she turned to face him, he saw that it was all true: the lamplight of her complexion, the honeyed golds of her hair, and the perfect arc of her cheeks. He saw from her self-possession that she was educated in her own effect, conscious of the eyes of men and women constantly upon her. She countered them, as she met Bruno's now, with a general and vague smile.

She moved towards him gracefully.

'Can I help you?'

He did not stammer as he explained his errand, and perhaps it was at this – for she was accustomed to waiting patiently for coherent speech when her beauty had addled the tongues of men who first beheld her – that caused her to widen her own eyes and look at Bruno.

He did not blush, but met her eyes as he handed over the book; perceiving simplicity and truth in her gaze, he lingered in the contact, not flirtatiously, and without embarrassment.

He took his leave soon enough, and slipped out into the street. Finding his foot sliding through mud, for the tide had risen high that morning, he was soon already lost again in thoughts of Sosia.

Felice asked: 'And what did you make of Caterina?'

Bruno blushed, 'She was pleased with the book.'

'And pleased with you, too, I hear.'

'In what way should she be pleased with me? We barely spoke at all. It's a beautiful inn, Felice; I see why you like to live there. I would love to go there with Sosia, to sit in the dining room that faces the canal, eat good foods, and not be ashamed to be there . . .'

Felice was irritated. The trouble was that this naïvety on Bruno's part was absolutely genuine, which made his obsession with Sosia tedious as well as incomprehensible.

He changed the subject deftly.

When he was next at the Locanda Sturion, Felice remarked to Caterina, 'So you've met young Bruno Uguccione?'

Caterina said nothing. She nodded and smiled a little, as if he had offered her a compliment. But from the expression on her face – in that moment she *looked* like Bruno, the same grace of contour in the cheek, the same mauve shadow above the eye – Felice knew that she was thinking of the boy, as he had suspected she would, when he suggested to Wendelin that he send Bruno over to her with the book. Wendelin had smiled, asking, intriguingly, 'You too? Lussièta also . . .' But Felice had decided the matter too delicate to pursue with questions.

Caterina turned away from him as soon as she could, on the pretext of stilling a shutter that flapped in the hot wind. But Felice knew that this slight motion indicated the end of all but respectable commerce between them. He watched her transformation, enchanted by its subtlety: now finger-tipping a butterfly out of the window, now farewelling a traveller, now nodding politely to Felice himself, Caterina was renewing her purity.

Chapter Three

Yes, the white-heat of the sun pulsed for you once.
But today she doesn't want you.
And, stripped of your power, you must not want her either.
Don't keep chasing her escaping shadow.
Don't live in desperation like the poor and the damned.
Be a survivor, be brave, don't melt.
Goodbye, girl. From now on unmelting Catullus
will not ask for you, will not look for what doesn't want him.

Rabino, making his way through the streets, marvelled at the misery on the early-morning faces. He noted to himself, *It's always the unhappiest person in the house who rises earliest. As I do.*

His thoughts were on the printer's melancholy wife.

He wondered if she would be cheered by the news, which he heard everywhere, that Fra Filippo's sermons on Catullus were beginning to have the opposite effect to the one the priest had intended.

Fra Filippo should have known, Rabino reflected, that in Venice there was no better way to make a book irresistible than to condemn it. The more Fra Filippo ranted against Catullus, the louder he condemned its noxious obscenity and its salacious syntax, the more he now seemed to arouse the appetite of the public. The flavour of proscribed fruit is ever more delectable than that which is praised: after the initial swell of revulsion, Catullus had thus become the very thing in Venice.

Men with barrows were selling Catullus on street corners. They came to the *stamperia* and paid in cash for the stock. At dawn, they started crying their wares with small phrases translated into Venetian dialect.

'Give me a thousand kisses,' rasped the hoary barrowmen, winking at the housewives. 'Come, my sweet . . .'

Catullus made no impression on the impassive faces of the scurriers-by. The hour of poetry had not yet come.

During the mornings, the barrowfuls of Catullus remained unsold. But later in the day, at that needy time of evening when the dusk started to rot the crisp busyness in the air and the colours became languid, then people would begin to think of love, and think of Catullus. In the meantime, the barrowmen cried the books anyway, inscribing the audible memory of the poems upon the ears of passers-by, ready for that moment.

Rabino picked up a copy as he passed and looked through it. His eyes caught on loving phrases and he thought of his friends Smuel and Benvenuta. *What can be wrong with this?* he thought. *I can see that this book can satisfy the dumb wants and the secret yearnings of every man for tenderness.* Then he strayed into the darker parts of the book, and his eyes fell on the lines,

> . . . *He's married a green girl*
> *who's not even come into bud.*

Rabino snapped it shut and walked swiftly away, ignoring the affronted cries of the bookseller.

In the time of this Catullus, the Romans, Rabino knew, had believed above all in the efficacy of cabbage, to treat dimness of the eyes, heartaches, and cancerous sores. A sprained ankle, according to the Romans, should be held in cabbage steam.

Even in these modern times, Rabino fought against the local superstitions, picturesque but deadly. Gently, he insisted that placing a dead dove on the chest would *not* cure pneumonia, nor would eagle marrow make an effective contraceptive, and carrying the heart and right foot of an owl under the left armpit would never remedy the bite of a mad dog. Goose grease mixed with turpentine, he insisted quietly, would *not* cure rheumatism and earache.

'No,' he would say quietly. 'It's not true that eating a nightingale gives pleasant dreams.' He denied that larks must be driven away because if that bird should stare at a sick person it meant that he would never recover, but if it averted its eyes then the victim would die. 'It's simpler than that,' he insisted, but in vain.

Rabino trod the streets, tending to his patients. Most were poor or *borghesi* but some were nobles, disillusioned with the tinkering and simpering of the Venetian surgeons, and wanting the mystery of Levantine eyes and hands to cure or at least pay attention to their often imaginary ills. The rich Venetians adored to learn about new diseases and would soon be mimicking the symptoms with gusto.

Boredom had lately forced them back to town from their cool retreats on the Brenta. The prolonged summer suited them ill. They were always tired, teased by their irritable libidos, their bowels disordered by eating only the most refined and richest of foods. Even the truffles must be grated for them and nothing tougher than a shimmering goat's cheese might be served to them after supper. There were such quick shifts between their deep apathy and their shallow passions – quite often Rabino thought he'd been called in merely to consult on their boredom, as if his attendance on them, waiting for him and talking about him afterwards, gave them something to do.

Their fatigue was incredible. They were always living under the threat of enthusiastic appointments made for social activities, but tiredness almost inevitably intervened at the last moment; sudden and dramatic onsets of extreme and potentially life-threatening tiredness. It was all very comical to Rabino at times, if it were not for that other vision in his head, of children dying for the want of a mouthful of milk such as the noble ladies fed their cats from their dainty fingertips while he examined a sore toe. The summons would have been urgent but more often than not the affliction of the toe turned out to be a dancing injury.

Yet he loved them, his noble patients. They were held together, like the city, by a splendid idea of themselves. The lagoon yielded naturally only cockles, crabs and a few fish: Venice had fashioned herself entirely out of her imagination, and in that she had allowed every excess. As she was such an imaginary city it was small wonder that she succumbed so readily to imaginary illnesses, not to mention the vast number of her citizens who considered themselves cursed or bewitched!

And he would depart almost regretfully into the darker, narrower streets where the women rarely sat if they could stand, and rarely stood still if they could be running somewhere, the better to forage for food to nurture their spindly children and their pale, overworked husbands.

Rabino knew all kinds of women in Venice, rich and poor, and he'd come to judge them not on their wealth but their proximity to his ideal of womanhood. There was none quite like the wife of Wendelin von Speyer, a woman so transparent with love that she might be a window into Paradise.

She seemed so dispirited. He could not understand her pessimism when he had seen in her all the best things in life, those that were denied to him.

The sky teases us with early morning mist, as if it intends to bless us with a little rain. But by the eighth hour the soft wet air is scorched away and we know ourselves cursed with the fires of hell for yet another day. At eventide, sometimes, a few doubtful raindrops puncture the arid sky, but they soon change their minds and the night comes on dry as ashes.

Through all this heat, the kind Jew comes back to see me. I am well by all the signs, but he still comes each day. Not at the same time, at a set hour, but when he passes our way on his rounds. It's always when my man is gone from the house and from this I see that the Jew does not wish to be paid. He comes and looks on me with brown eyes all moist with what he feels. I know not exactly what he feels, for he is yet strange to me, but I know he feels it strongly when he sees me.

When I talk to the Jew about my state, I try to keep my voice steady but it goes tottering off into the high notes. He has this way of baring my feelings. With him, there's no defence: there's no need of any. Still, it's bizarre to have him reach inside my soul like this, to make himself at home with all the most secret and tense things I hold inside. Not all, of course, for I do not tell him about my fears or about the cabinet and what it holds. Instead we talk of polite things, like my man's work. He observes that Catullus seems a great success in the town, and I tell him that yes, at last the folk of this town are taking those poems to their hearts.

'So this is good news for you and your husband?' He smiles. I nod.

My heart is torn, very quietly.

It could be that it's wrong for the Jew to come here so much and for me to let him. It could be that folk talk ill of us. But I find I do not care now. Since I was sick and went on that cart (I still know not if this was in my head or in my life) I feel bound by no rule save that which spares me pain.

The hours when the Jew comes are times with less pain, you see. We sit close but not so close as to touch and we say very little. The new maid leaves us and for once she thinks to close the door so we are there, just our two selves, with just our breath in the blistered air.

Sometimes I tell him the tale of my life, of my man, of our journey over the Alps. When at last the talk fades to nothing I look in his eyes and he in mine for a long time. I lose my sense of myself, of this house, of my place in the world.

I feel that all is black like the world beneath the sea, as if someone ate all the words. When he rises to go I am calmer than before.

When he leaves my house I hear the bad calls that follow him in the street. 'Dirty owl' they yell as he makes to pass. I hate to hear it. They call him 'owl' for that bird wakes in the night. The bird of the dark is like the man who does not know the truth of God – in other words, the Jews, who deny Jesus.

But when their young ones fall ill or the plague comes to call, then they forget their bad words. Then it's 'Send for the Jew! Fast as you can!'

Sometimes he went away to the mainland on a tour of duty with some other Jewish physicians. But these days the roads that took him away from Venice always seemed to have an adverse camber. Carriages veered with their doors hanging open like the broken wing of a pigeon. Rabino found the landlocked cities stagnant and their people but half-alive.

He remembered the words of the printer's wife, recalled her hatred of the land and her homesickness for Venice on that terrible pilgrimage to the North.

Her words were so fervent they had perhaps infected his own perceptions. He smiled fondly, remembering her vehemence. 'Land! – Floor for cows, the French say,' she'd declared. 'Give me marble and stone, say I, floating on water!'

Outside Venice Rabino too now suffered crises at certain times of the day. As the light faded in the evening, he felt a crawling under his flesh and an unbearable sense of sadness. It was painful for his nerves to hear orchards shuffling in the wind and to see the clouds roaming the sky as if looking for somewhere to rest. Seeing a long shadow cast down a bush-furred hill, arched like a body in *rigor mortis*, he longed for home, though not for the home he really had, the comfortless house he shared with Sosia . . . he longed for the home of his imagination, a wife who ran to greet him and kissed him decently on the cheek in front of their children, who crowded around their knees and leapt up like puppies for their own embrace.

In his fantasy, which he embroidered a little on every journey, he looked up at her – she was as blond and small as Sosia was dark and tall – and intercepted her Madonna-gaze upon their baby. His imagined wife bestowed a little of that gaze on him, too, and he drank it in like a warm *tisana* on a cold morning, feeling it fill his lungs and stomach with goodness and a nourishment for which he'd been starving since he could remember. Before Sosia had come to despoil his celibacy, he had always been alone.

Then he remembered by what unwholesome means he'd obtained the wife he had, and bowed his head.

I do not deserve what I desire.

Lately he had succumbed to a strange ailment of his own. It would start in the last days he spent in Venice, with blurred sight and headaches that intensified when he arrived on the mainland. Since the start of his hours of dark seclusion with the printer's wife he'd grown hypersensitive to light and sound. The red exclamations of the poppy fields stabbed his eyes. Worst of all, his vision faded as a layer of skin formed over his pupils so that he could not bear to open his lids during the hours of daylight. He performed his duties by touch, like a blind man, listening more carefully than he had before. He returned to Venice half-blind and weak in his limbs.

The only cure was to live a murky hermit existence in the house at San Trovaso. He rationed himself to an hour or so in the light of a veiled lamp with patients every day until the surfaces of his eyes healed and the dead skin dropped off in tiny little flakes. Only the printer's wife, who seemed to need it so much, received his attention as before.

They say we are made of four things – wet, dry, hot, cold, and when we are sick, it is because one of these is out of tilt.

Men are born hot and arid, but wives are too wet by nature, they say, unless their men keep them warm and dry with acts of love. If not, we grow bad and warped, which we show by teasing, nagging and arguing.

But if this is true, why is this town so wet, and yet so good?

This town is more wet than all things.

Of course the men do their best to dry the town. Each year they pull more land from the sea – to do this they send down in the mud long poles so tight-packed that there is no air at all down there. And more than this, they build in all parts. Huge *palazzi* and towers, each more grand than the next. It used to be that we heard the song of larks all day, now it's the smash of hammers and the flirt and grunt of the workmen with their barrows and back-loads of stone. Venice grows more beautiful, I less so.

This town was always fine but now it looks like a rich maid all decked out to wed, in lace of stone.

Dry, wet, hot, cold.

I was all these things, when I wed my man.

I think of the Jew, who wants to help me, but no one ever cured a torn heart with physician's healing. And the poor Jew is in need of help himself. His eyes have glassed over and he does not see well these days. He still comes to me to ask me how I am, and to talk awhile. He gazes vaguely in the distance, but sits a little closer to me, as without the clear sight of his eyes he finds he does not hear so well.

I even gave him some of my salve which I make for the eyes of my man, that are often pink when he returns late at night after many hours of squinting at the proofs. Each fresh mixing contains a drop of the oil that flows from the remarkable fountain of Zorzania in Armenia. The merchant at Rialto assured me that it would cure even the most scabrous cutaneous distempers.

I spread the salve on the Jew's lids myself. At first I felt a sudden flush of shame that I had touched the private skin of a man to whom I was not wed. That he's a Jew worried me not at all, for I feel he is closer to me than many of my own race. Men like Felice Feliciano, for example! Boh!

I could not help but notice that the doctor's lids are more delicate than my man's; they are soft and yellow like vellum.

The Jew says my salve has done him good. I'm glad to be of this tiny service to him, who has helped me so much, even though I do not tell him the whole tale of what ails me. That is confidential to my man and myself, and I shall not betray him by talking of it.

I have lately trusted the Jew with one secret, though. I'm still troubled by the wax-woman so I showed her to him.

He turned her over in his hand. I saw that he jumped a little inside his skin when he saw the 'S' or '5' marked on her back with nails and hair. I guessed from this they must be very evil symbols.

'What do you think she is?' I asked, though I'd divined it all too well.

'You found her at Sirmione, you say? I think she's very old, from the look of her, perhaps from Roman times.'

'So they had witches, even then? Who made such things?'

'It was a little different, I believe. I've read somewhere that figures like this were love charms. The person who loved and was not loved' – and here he stopped and looked at me with such great feeling I feared he'd guessed my secret – 'would put the figure in the fire to make it dissolve to liquid. This was supposed to melt the heart of their desire's object. Some people hold that ancient figures like this one have more power than the ones made today. Certainly she's more finely crafted than anything I've seen before.'

'How do you know of these things? Have you studied witchcraft? Do you believe . . . ?'

I was most surprised to think that the Jew might believe in witches.

He sighed: 'For myself, no. Too many of my patients think such things work wonders, and spend their money on them, when a good meal of wholesome food would help them so much more. I've had to learn about them only to make myself credible in refuting them. I've been presented with amulets and figures like this so many times, as an excuse for why they haven't been to the apothecary for the herbs they really need. It's quite dispiriting.'

He handed her back to me quite hastily, as if he found the feel of her unpleasant. This reminded me of something else. I led him up the stairs to my man's room, and showed him the box, studying his face.

'What do you think of that?' I asked him, in a careful neutral voice.

'The piece of furniture?' he asked, and it seemed that he was still distracted with thoughts of the wax-woman.

'Yes,' I replied.

'It's unusual,' he said, and I could see he struggled to know what to say.

'Not evil?' I persisted. I stroked my nose hard to push the tears back into my eyes.

'Only humans are evil, or their acts. Or their thoughts,' he said. I found this a shallow, avoiding sort of answer. Then I feared he thought me tainted in the wits for asking what I did. Soon after he left, I realised then that he had not helped me as I wished to find a way to rid myself of the little figure.

I put her safely back in the cat's boudoir under some silk scarves and considered what I'd heard. I did not want to put her in the fire. That would make her magic alive again after all these years. Then what things might happen? Who knows whose love was nailed inside the kidneys, liver, spleen and heart of that lady from Roman times, and why? If I burned her, why, she might come back to haunt *me*!

'And what is she to do with me?' I asked aloud.

Now I am more afraid than ever of the wax-woman, and know I must think of some way to turn her into nothing, without making her powerful again. It's too hard for me to work out, like a toy puzzle for a child who has not all the pieces.

In the end, it's easier to think on my usual problems, sad as they are.

I comb my hair while I read the notes my man has written and left inside the box for me.

One rake through my scalp and there are thick tendrils of gold on the ivory. Dark gold. My hair is more dark each day. It used to be white-blonde, sun-blonde, cream-blonde. Now it's ash-blonde, dirty-blonde and if it goes on like this, soon it will scarce be fair at all. In this heat my curls should grow white as lambswool. Instead, each day, they darken like my hopes. I pluck them off my comb, and wrap them in a rag each night, for we believe in this town that every person has one hair on their head, which, if a swallow plucks it, dooms him to eternal perdition. I hide the loose hairs away from greedy birds.

My man writes, 'Your skin is like milk, pale as a feathered angel from heaven, as if you were too good for this world.'

Chapter Four

When that schemestress Venus had me under thumb,
this is how she set fire to my heart,
made it boil like the bowels of Etna or
the hot springs of Malis,
blurred my eyes with spaceless tears,
washed my cheeks with heart-rain.

There is love that needs tending like a rare plant in an arboretum, where the merest cool breath of air can render it extinct. There is love that thrives on hard rock like a cactus, and the more difficult it is to find the moisture of affection, the deeper that kind sends its roots down. There is love that thrives best on nothing but its own imaginative constructs. And those are far more delectable than anything on offer in the real world. That kind of love is the most hardy, and that is what Bruno bore for Sosia.

Felice urged him to leave Venice for a while.

'Let's get out of this heat. Come, let's shoot some birds, like the old days,' the scribe urged, unable to resist a soft caress down Bruno's thin face.

But Bruno always shook his head. He could not imagine himself outside the city now. He walked obsessively, often in circles, though always tethered to the places where he and Sosia had been together.

Bruno, making his way to the church of San Giovanni e Paolo, found a service was in progress. The white-robed priest swayed his musical censer like a very serious child with a rattle.

This was where he was to meet her this evening, not at his apartments. No physical intimacy was to be allowed then, he noted bitterly. She could do without that, from him, today. No doubt that meant she had plans to refresh herself elsewhere, or had come from someone else.

The steps were occupied by the haunches of a foreign legless beggar who trapped the worshippers with his empty hose. He flung the slack tubes upwards and when the wooden pattens sewn into the ends of his stockings dragged them to the ground, they tangled up the legs and shoes of his victims. Bruno gave the man a coin, and was permitted to pass. When Sosia finally arrived, he was standing just outside the church, gazing in.

He said to her, by way of greeting, to show her how little he had noticed the hour she'd kept him waiting, 'Have you heard about the new Ca' Dario that is to be built?' This was a good opening; it caught her by surprise.

'Hello, Bruno,' she smiled, acknowledging his advantage. 'I hear your Catullus is the cheese in the town now.'

They stood together in the doorway, like the lesser shepherds at the nativity scene, looking upwards at the cupolas where cadaverous painted saints unfurled gold scrolls and at the dark angels of mosaic in the gold architraves; at the terracotta and cream marble chessboard floor, the patinated silver chandelier like the tendril of an exotic fern growing downwards, its candles splayed out at awkward angles from it like the pistils of a stamen. Priests were chanting the liturgy, old voices stained with faith like dark teak wood.

The legless beggar crawled over to them and grabbed at Sosia's feet, gibbering at her.

'Filthy Croatian,' she spat.

Bruno caught her hand, and remonstrated, 'The poor man only wants to speak to you.' He imagined some elaborate flattery in the mouth of the beggar.

'To prdio, to govorio, njemu sve jedno, whether he farts or speaks, it's all the same to him.'

'You know him?' Bruno asked.

'I know his accent.' She raised her voice so the beggar could hear her every word. 'Da moè zavukao bi mu se u dupem, he's a slimy character – if only he could, he would climb into the arsehole.'

She kicked him and he moaned. Bruno saw that she had slit the old man's cheek with the edge of her heel. He leant forward with concern, his arm on Sosia's wrist. She did not resist. The beggar's wound was not deep but it filled vividly with blood. He spat at Sosia: 'Poljubi mičelo kurca!'

Sosia laughed, 'That's a good one!'

'What did it mean? Is that Serbian?' Bruno asked, anxiously.

'Yes, it's Serbian. And it means *"Kiss my prick's forehead."*'

Bruno smacked his hands together at the beggar, to make him desist, as if he were a cat or a small child. The beggar replied with a crude motion of his thumb.

'Ever the master of the ineffectual hand-gesture!' Sosia sneered at Bruno. She turned on the beggar and asked him, in a neutral tone, where he came from. When he answered, she spat. Bruno, interpreting the exchange although not understanding one word, turned to Sosia.

'But I thought you came from—?'

'Yes, I do, but nowhere is safe from his kind of scum, they come everywhere. Did you never hear of the war in Dalmatia here? Is no one interested in what happened to us?'

'We hear very little; the merchants at Rialto know most of what happens, but only really talk about what is of interest to them. You could explain it to me, what happened to you and your family; tell me about it, Sosia—'

'No.'

To his surprise, she had taken his elbow and was steering him down the street towards his apartments.

It was what he'd wished most of all, but there was too much pain pent up inside him. Instead of trotting obediently at her side, he turned on her.

'You always terrorise me into hiding what I feel.'

In the silence that followed, they walked towards his rooms. Bruno counted their paces to distract himself from his painful thoughts. By the time they arrived at the doorstep, however, his indignation had escaped that containment. He opened his mouth to speak and she broke away from him, running up the stairs, tearing at the ribbon of her cloak.

'You want too much. Won't this do?' she asked.

Her clothes were discarded in a moment and she stood before him naked. Her face distorted with anger, she turned on him, a finger stabbing the air.

'What would you do for me, then? Would you die for me? Would you kill me if that was the better path?'

'What kind of questions are those, Sosia?'

'I feel as if you make some kind of emblem of this love you say you have for me.

It's all about your feelings, nothing about mine, that's why I feel it so heavily. I want you to think of me, for once, about how I feel. It would do you good.'

'That's so unfair. I think of nothing else but you. I build my life around you.'

'I never asked you to do that.'

'Sosia, can you not feel how much it hurts to be just a fragment of your life?'

She looked thoughtful.

'It feels just a fraction of alive.'

He turned away from her, his head filled with hurtful images. He pictured her looking up from some embroidery when Rabino came home, or filleting a fish for him and lifting the humid shiny flesh onto her husband's plate. He imagined her, in the black of night, rolling against Rabino's back in the bed they shared and staying there in the indentation she had made in his slack elderly flesh, as if she were the missing rib trying to push its way back inside Adam. This was what marriage was about. No matter how evilly she spoke about Rabino, or how often she betrayed him, Sosia stayed married to him: this was the proof of the contract's binding power.

He followed her into the room, made love to her in miserable silence. She left without a word. He whispered to the empty room: 'Goodbye, Sosia.'

He heard her footsteps down the stairs and then the street door click closed. She had not even bothered to slam it.

Outside lightning scratched feebly at the sky, trying to release the moisture. Darkness inserted itself surreptitiously, as if ashamed over itself. It ambushed the sky by degrees, only clapping its black hand over the light at the last moment, when the *palazzi*, like bone-white sponges dipped in ink, crumbled their colours away.

I saw a most disgusting thing today at Rialto. It was one of those merbabies that the fisher folk are always talking about. At last one has been brought in for us to see and judge. It turned my belly to look on it: a tiny creature with the head and torso of a human baby and the rear end of a fish.

It lay on the salt at a fish stall, and next to it was another thing found in the same net. This was a large rat that had been sewn, with the most exquisite stitching, into a baby's shroud. These two horrors were found in the usual place of the dead babies, near Sant' Angelo di Contorta.

The sweaty crowd gazed on them, fascinated, full of theories. The most obvious is that this is the work of a foreign witch. Others were insisting that this merbaby had been washed in from a distant ocean after some accident to its mother. An old fisherman, prodding the horror with salt-crusted fingers, insisted it was just an ordinary baby. He said a fish had tried to eat it, swallowed half and choked on it.

I turned away, sickened, myself, and walked home sad and slow as a gathering teardrop. Ghost tales are one thing, but such evil things, real and visible, have no charm for me.

On the way I passed Paola – what an outrage! – talking to the red-haired man so anyone might see her. She saw me from the corner of her eye and did not even blush, so brazen is she. With a flash of some base metal under the hoods of those falcon eyes, she even motioned with her hand that I should come and be presented to her lover. I could see from her finger pointing at me that she was telling him who I was. I pursed my lips and marched on, pretending I had not seen her. I would not give a glass of salt water to know who he is.

As usual, I went to sit in front of my mirror and look at myself. I look like a child who has aged too fast from hearing too many monstrous fairytales. I turn my neck in fear from this ghost-face but when I steal one more look it's still there, full of whiteness.

I ask the Jew what has happened to my hair. He says that he has not seen anything like this before. It's not natural, he says, and I can see he longs to reach out and touch it, just for a moment, as if the good feelings in the tips of his fingers might bleach it back to its old beauty.

'It could be something you are eating,' says the Jew. 'Try to remember what you've eaten, and tell me next time I come. Some foods have naturally darkening pigments in them.'

It's not the food; it's the misery that blackens my hair. I remember how my man used to watch me brush it. After a while he could not bear it any more and would come up behind me and enfold me in his big arms, hold me so tight my bones ached and I snuffled for breath. He would do a great damage to my misery if he would just once do that to me again.

Then I would be blonde again, naturally, no matter what I put in my mouth.

'Not natural,' I say over and over to myself.

It was not long before I started to think that this new dark hair was the first sign that my man was trying to do me ill.

Chapter Five

What have I done, or what have I said,
that you sent so many scurvy poets to destroy me?

A t last, the weather broke. Ice storms and snow suddenly replaced the sear-
ing heat, as if autumn had been forsworn entirely.

At first the Venetians stood in the freezing rain, mouths open, letting the
large drops crack like quails' eggs on their heads, and the water run down their
throats. But the cold quickly grew unbearable and they bustled into the taverns,
enjoyably lamenting the unspeakable weather, taking out all the old complaints
from last winter, dusting them down, and finding them almost inadequate to
describe the infidel clouds, gusts, showers and treacherous crusts of ice on the
streets. Soon a robe of frozen ermine clad the town in a silence crisped with
nostalgia for the former blue-and-white damask skies.

Back on Murano Fra Filippo was still fulminating like an abandoned pot of
oil on the fire.

Hunched over his desk, he dipped his pen to scrawl another tract against
Catullus, but let the ink drop in useless spots upon the page. Outrage had not
served him well lately. Nor had sending out his thugs on to the streets at
night.

The Venetians had heard all he had to say about printed books and were
looking for entertainment in other places. Only a few members of his congregation, nuns mostly, had stayed faithful to him. When he could number his

parishioners on his hands one morning, Fra Filippo knew it was time to change direction.

He did not like the look of his reduced flock: he performed better to a large and anonymous crowd. The intimacy of the tiny congregation embarrassed him. One woman in particular made a point of sitting under his nose and looking up into his nostrils as he spoke. A shiny little sow of a woman, she sat heavily in her chair, and never moved a limb while he spoke. But she followed each word of his raptly, whispering them to herself under her breath.

He made enquiries of the piglet, as he thought of her. Ianno came back with the intelligence that she arrived by boat from Sant' Angelo di Contorta. None of the other parishioners knew her name, but it seemed she was a nun.

'So they're not all whores then?' asked Fra Filippo.

'It would seem not,' Ianno replied. 'This one's pure as the snow, I'll warrant.'

'And likely to stay that way.'

'Well, I wouldn't mind—' Ianno began, with a slap-beseeching smirk, but quailed, as his *capo* loomed over him, hand raised. Stunted little Ianno was strong as three normal men, but he would not dare retaliate against Fra Filippo de Strata.

Fra Filippo penned some experimental sermons. He was trying out a pungent distillation of mockery and threats. The new formula, ironic and scathing, brought people crawling back to his sermons and saw them leaving the church, fired with just the passions Fra Filippo most wished to rouse. The ferryboats to Murano were full again despite the dramatic break in the warm weather. Fra Filippo's congregation huddled in the pews, welcoming each arriving member for his animal warmth.

Fra Filippo started gently, his breath frosting the air.

Let us picture the world the way these so-called 'scholars', these lovers of antiquity, want it.

When these oh-so-refined nobles are lying in their fake antique bowers, reclining on their replica Roman divans, writing poems to grapes of the past while turning like spoilt children from the real grapes of the present – what will happen?

They will come to despise the honest trade and hardworking commerce that has made Venice great. Their morale and their morals will decline at the same time, together, dying the same death as their dignity.

Look at these pathetic creatures! Talking to themselves in their affected accents! Unable to fulfil their real-life roles as husbands and fathers.

Then Fra Filippo's voice changed. He lowered his head and seemed to whisper to himself.

This clutch of the past on our throats is fatal as the grip of an evil giant round the fragile stem of a daisy. For even in the flower of our success we Venetians are the most pluckable, we droop imperceptibly with the heavy opulence of our petals, we are too vain to see the moment of perfection is already past, and we are heading down a steep incline straight into the rapacious mouth of Lucifer himself.

And who is behind us, pushing with all their might? The printers. These men, love-slaves of prostitutes and equally slaves of the bottle. Now if printing were controlled by the Church, instead of perverted by this conspiracy of the so-called scholars and the Germans, what an organ of rectitude it could be . . .

Take these instruments from the hands of the barbarians and give them to God, and if you cannot do that, then destroy them in his name. Burn the printing presses! Burn the heretics who turn them! Burn! Burn!

The enemy of our State is no longer the Ottoman. We've made monsters of them – but the Turks are mere flesh and blood. The real monster lives among us and it cranks out every day more pages that eat our souls, that murder our innocence in our beds, that soak up our consciences like blood in winding cloths on a battlefield.

You see how books are destroying this city. It's now impossible to find a groom or a cook because everyone is infected with the vile and arrogant ambition to read books. Then they get above themselves and want to teach others to read, to glorify their own achievement. This is the printers' work, the reason why the horses go unshod and the tavern kitchens are empty.

Venetians, I tell you, go to the printers and destroy them! Destroy those muses of the printers: the whores and editors! Arise; the day of salvation is at hand!

Then Fra Filippo rolled up the text of his sermon and brandished it at his people like a torch.

They raised their arms in echoing motions. Except one pale horse-faced woman, impeccably dressed, who sat in the third row. She rose from her pew and turned to face the congregation, gesturing back at Fra Filippo.

'The man's a lunatic,' she said in a firm clear voice. 'Printer's whore! There's no such woman. He invented her from his own rabid imaginings. I'll admit he gives the best entertainment in Venice on a Sunday morning, but I hope none of you takes this ordure seriously.'

She pointed to the plump nun in the front row: 'Unless you're patently mad, like that one.'

Silence fell in the church as Paola di Colonia, formerly Paola von Speyer, née Paola di Messina, gathered her elegant furs and strode belligerently from the church into the cold white air.

A dozen people rose and followed her, their heads held high.

Fra Filippo, stunned to muteness, quickly recovered himself. When Paola was safely out of the church, he pointed a finger at where she had gone.

'And that, my children, is how the printers like their women. Would you like to be married to one such as her? Viragos and whores and editors and printers . . .'

He was annoyed to see that the ugly nun from Sant' Angelo was still among the worshippers, mouthing something to herself. He leaned over the pulpit to see if he could catch her words. But they were only his own, repeated under her breath like a chant.

The ugly nun whispered, 'Whores and editors, whores and editors.'

By day, Ianno was kept busy running around under stacks of pamphlets against Catullus and the printers. He bore bruises from scuffles with men selling barrow-loads of books, men with baskets thrusting books into the faces of passers-by.

'You drive yourself hard, my son,' said Fra Filippo, trying not to look at the little brain throbbing in different shades of pink and grey. Ianno was not well; his exertions had taken too much out of him. His muscles were hardening; his wrists were knotted.

'It's not the pamphlets. It's the cursed book itself. Somehow the verses have imprinted themselves on my memory and I keep hearing them. Oh please hear my confession, Father! I am bursting with vice. I take the pamphlets hither and thither to try to exhaust myself and to punish myself for what I've done and thought.'

'You don't need to tell me . . . really, your own confessor is more appropriate to this . . .'

'Ah, but he would not understand as you do, for you've read this Catullus and you know it in the heart of your loins as well as I do.'

'But, please don't . . .'

'You see, I have palpated my organ with unnecessary tenderness this morning, and thereafter, when scourging myself, I found that the effect was pleasing, and I've committed . . .'

'Ianno! Do not pollute this chamber with a narration of this kind. You scaly scab-witted . . .'

'Why are you so full of spleen? You would have me abandoned in my sin?'

'I would have you leave me.'

Ianno swept a low bow and departed.

Over his shoulder he said, defiantly, 'The nun from Sant' Angelo agrees with me.'

Now he had won back his audience, Fra Filippo allowed himself the luxury of a little more brimstone. His sermons took a darker turn. He was gratified to see the red robes and sable furs of senators in the crowded pews, and for them he fashioned the words of warning that were most likely to strike fear into their ambitious hearts. One morning he noted that both Domenico Zorzi and Nicolò Malipiero, known patrons of both the printers and the whores of Venice, had made the journey to Murano to hear him. He dismissed from his mind any thought that they might have come to laugh at him, these sophisticated aristocrats, who thought nothing of buying whole libraries of printed books.

He also tried not to think of the piglet nun who sat below him. He spoke faster than normal in an attempt to lose her shadowing whispers.

Mark you how this work of the Devil, printing, has coincided with the destruction of the Venetian empire? When did this Gutenberg commence his vile trade? 1453, need I remind you? – the year we lost Constantinople to the Turk! When did the barbarian von Speyers start printing in Venice? 1470! The year we lost Negroponte! And now we've the heathen invading our very churches . . . that so-called architect Codussi is building a baptistry on San Michele, which looks ungodly as a harem of the infidel . . . Even our own painter, Giovanni Bellini, is stooping to disgusting allegories, using foreign women as his models, polluting his studio with visitations from his friends who are, of course, printers.

Gentilia, sitting in the front row, mouthed each of his words a second after he said them, her teeth chattering with the cold.

Behind her sat a woman of exceptional beauty, whose blonde hair caught the cool stream of daylight and converted it to fire. Caterina di Colonna gazed coolly at Fra Filippo and appeared to manage without blinking at all. Next to her sat a tall, handsome man, equally fair. Fra Filippo felt vaguely enhanced by the presence of two such beauteous Venetians in his church. But the blue eyes of the woman were fixed on him with an unmistakable frank hostility.

'What graceless lies you speak,' said her gaze, clear as sunlight. 'Why do you not simply desist?'

For the first time, he faltered and began to stammer, hypnotised by the disdainful lapis of the blonde woman's eyes. He tottered lamely to a finish without the usual flourish.

When he looked up from his text, he saw, with nightmare clarity, the piglet nun staring at Caterina's luminous beauty as if at a comet, and at her good-looking companion with unmistakable cupidity.

Instead of accepting the usual congratulations on the doorstep of the church,

Fra Filippo scuttled back to his cell as soon as he could, where he sat for many minutes breathing fast and shallowly, unable to lift a pen.

'Ianno!' called Fra Filippo, 'Where are you?'

Ianno appeared, brandishing a large bone.

'I've been reading about the English Saint Alphege. He was beaten to death by the Danes. They used ox bones. Or a stone . . . like Saint Jerome. He beat himself with a stone. I could not find a good stone, there're just miserable little ones in this town, not even sharp enough for Attis, so then I thought about an ox bone again and the butcher at Santa Maria del Giglio gave me . . .'

'Enough, enough of that, I have work for you.'

Ianno drew near, which made Fra Filippo draw back. He had caught a whiff of his assistant's hair pomade.

Ianno's hair was strangely curly on one side and not on the other . . . whole hanks hung languidly over his right ear, while the one with the deformity was bare: the hair around it curled up frizzily, as if recoiling from the ugly little brain.

'Go to Rialto. I want to know about that blonde woman who was here this morning. Is she a courtesan? Was that her husband or her pimp with her? You know which one. And tell me what they're saying about the Dalmatian Jewess. It seems she really is mixed up with the printers, somehow. I received a letter . . .'

Fra Filippo leant forward a little with each word, arching his neck and snapping his jaws as if spitting out stones.

Ianno met Gentilia coming in as he left. He did not meet her eyes and she averted hers. He could not tell how long she'd been waiting at the door, but it seemed likely she had heard their entire conversation.

'There's someone to see you,' he called back, maliciously, to his *capo* as he left.

'No, I'm not receiving today,' Fra Filippo called through the door, 'I have urgent correspondence.'

Gentilia stopped, uncertain, on the threshold. The shadow of her profile fell across his desk, and a hazy recognition of it stopped the priest from looking up. He continued to scribble, pretending to be unaware of her.

Eventually she sighed and moved off towards the jetty where the boats left for the other islands. Fra Filippo leapt up to bolt the door. As he did so, he noticed a small figure following the nun: Ianno. He shook his head. Ianno caught up with her, and placed his hand on her elbow. Instead of jumping away in alarm, she slowly turned to gaze at him. Even from a distance Fra Filippo could see that she was looking intently at the little brain above Ianno's ear as he capered in front of her. The faint buzz of Ianno's words floated over the path back to Fra Filippo, but he could not make out a word of it.

He wondered what this nun might have wished to tell him, but it was not worth the trouble of making her acquaintance. Ugly women always had a grievance of some kind or another, usually against their prettier sisters. If she knew anything worthwhile to denounce then she was probably thrilling Ianno with her tale right now. And then, he reflected, she should go to the stone lions and deliver the requisite letters into their mouths, and save him the trouble. He, Fra Filippo, was destined for greater things than malicious female tittle-tattle.

It occurred to him that the system of anonymous letters and spies worked most effectively for the state of Venice. There were always means at her disposal to rid herself of unwanted men and women. If letters failed to arrive in the mouths of the lions spontaneously, then such letters could be written. Or paid for. Who was to know the difference?

Wendelin wrote again to Padre Pio:

My dearest Padre,
Yes, Catullus is at last a success, but he has not saved us. It's probably too late. Fra Filippo has not wasted his breath. My spirit has broken, along with the weather.

I took it upon myself to attend one of his dogfights, his sermons. (My poor wife is not well enough to accompany me so I went with her friend Caterina di Colonna of the Sturion.) I wanted to see my enemy in his lair. I was not disappointed. I got the show I went to see.

He ends each of his sermons with a chant, 'Save our souls, burn the books, save our souls, burn the books.' Instead of Our Lord's Prayer, the parishioners stream out of the churches, chanting 'Save our souls, burn the books,' and my blood runs cold. How long before they change it to 'Save our souls, burn the printers'? They've already had a taste of our blood.

Gentilia went to San Trovaso to await her quarry. She'd already been to the butchers in San Vio to choose a pork fillet three days off the bone. Blood and fat were swarming at its surface.

She knew, from Bruno, that Sosia left the house early in the morning for her marketing and sometimes less respectable activities.

Gentilia waited, hunched in her cloak. The damp cold soon penetrated the wool, but she would not relinquish her post.

Still, it was not until the eleventh hour that she saw the low door swing open and a woman lope out. *It must be Sosia, that is without doubt the house, and she walks impudently, like a whore,* Gentilia thought.

Is this what all the fuss is about, she wondered briefly, *this woman who swings her hips like a monkey and dresses like a mouse? She has a cheap way of wearing her clothes. Her hair is thin and straight, swarthy as a dirty shoe: I thought it would hang down in those follow-me kind of curls. She moves a lot, a sack of small shifts with each big move. I suppose this means the smells rise from her. From one quick look at her I can tell this: she has too much brain. She reads too much. She has the look that Bruno gets after hours at his desk. Ah, now she passes a group of gondoliers and we see her true profession. She moves through the men like a snake through grass. Each one turns to look at her, rubbing his thigh. How does she do that?*

And Bruno thought her worst crime was to destroy a painting of Bellini's. Some Madonna or other! My poor innocent brother, he has not the smallest idea, she thought tenderly.

Gentilia started forward, manoeuvring to the left so that she would pass Sosia on her right-hand side. As she did so, she pulled her little pork fillet out of her pocket.

It was done in an instant. As Sosia walked past, Gentilia smeared her arm and dress with the moist meat and quickly pushed it back in her pocket. At the same moment she nipped a single strand of Sosia's hair and wrapped it round her finger.

Then she brushed past Sosia's door, reaching out a deft hand to throw the contents of a vial against the aged wood. It splashed against the handle, running down in rivulets. No one saw a thing, but everyone, for the rest of the day, hurried past, grimacing.

For Gentilia had anointed the entrance to Sosia's home with the most powerful magical solution she knew: wolf fat, the *faeces* of dogs, powder from the bones of the dead taken from San Giovan di Furlani, stinking fennel root, the water of San Alberto, and a handful of dust taken from the ground between the columns in San Marco where all public executions and tortures took place. She mouthed the necessary incantation under her breath and hurried away.

Sosia felt a moist coolness on her wrist, and turning around, noted an ungainly nun waddling fast away from her, muttering. She seemed to be carrying something, no doubt some holy relic. The city had a passion for them. Sosia often mocked the Venetian craving for toes and elbows of saints, which they loved as if these scrags and bones marked the city out in the eyes of God for his particular joy.

Sosia's wrist was sticky. She wiped the slime against her dress, noting the greasy stain. Never mind. Where she was going that dress would soon be discarded. She continued on her way to San Giobbe, where Nicolò Malipiero would be waiting. The distant doorstep, she could see, was already blackening with the shadows of the young men she'd commissioned for the afternoon.

She had known all along what Nicolò really wanted, and today he would have it.

'*Jede govna kao Grk alvu*, he'll enjoy eating shit, like a Greek eating halva,' she smiled.

She did not notice the dwarf loping unevenly from doorway to archway behind her, or see when he followed her into the church and disposed himself behind a column. She did not hear him gasp as she commenced her work.

'But I am pure,' protested Ianno.

'You are not.'

'I have not indulged in any of the seven mortal sins. No one can say so.'

'But you've been seen indulging – in very disgusting peccadilloes.'

'Of what sort? I deny it!'

Fra Filippo waved a sheaf of beer-stained notes, the reports of his informers, who had drunk their wages while earning them.

'It says here that you've been seen in The Three Stars, The Four Dragons, respectively, looking at lewd pictures, talking dishonestly with women, fondling and kissing commercial women, singing unspeakable songs.

'And there's more. A nun has sent me a letter to tell me that you expressed yourself uncleanly before her. A nun from Sant' Angelo, it is true, but a *nun* all the same.'

Ianno was groaning, holding himself in his own arms, whispering to himself.

'You must desist.'

'But how? When my mission is to find out the whore of the printers, how am I to find her without consorting with whores? You get the freshest information in . . .'

'You must take the advice of Gregory the Great and Isidore of Seville. If you feel desire for a woman, you must conjure in your mind a picture of how her body will look laid out in death.'

Ianno moaned softly. Fra Filippo realised to his horror that his assistant was yet more stimulated by that idea. Hastily he added: 'You must think about the miry fluid in her nostrils and the phlegm in her throat.'

Ianno grew silent, considering this in the light of mental images that were hideously transparent to his superior. Sitting at his desk, Fra Filippo looked up at him with loathing, noting the stalactites of dried mucus in Ianno's own nostrils and the stains on his hose.

'Then you must also think of your own pure guardian angel, watching you at your lewdness, disgusted and laid low at the sights and sounds and smells even, of you at such horrid play. Imagine him forced to watch your virile member in a shameful state, see exposed the dishonest part of a woman, see the Act of Venus in all its horrifying bestiality.'

Ianno challenged him: 'But what am I to do when I'm forced, in your service, to listen to endless libidinous confessions? I grow humid and taut . . . and when I hear those of women I cannot bear it. After this, no matter how heavily I eat and drink, I wake from my stupor to find that I have committed nocturnal pollution!'

His voice rose to a whine. It was more than Fra Filippo could bear.

'Leave me,' he ordered. 'I do not need so much information. I shall think on your fate. In the meantime you are dismissed from my service.'

'How am I to eat then? It's bitter cold . . .'

'Do you think I care?'

Ianno flushed red and bowed. He said in a low voice, 'I have lately committed many acts in your name that I would not have done in the name of our Lord.'

'Is that a threat? Do you think to blackmail me?'

'That's not my way of doing things,' replied Ianno.

The balance of power in the room had suddenly shifted. Fra Filippo grimaced with the realisation of what damage might be done by such a masterless beast of burden. Ianno bowed low and strutted out, his narrow buttocks stiff with dignity.

Chapter Six

I'll have you upstairs and downstairs
Aurelius and Furius, you infamous sluts,
who deduce from my verses,
because they are a little filthy
that I am filthy too.
A true poet must be pure
but his works have no need to be so.
On the contrary,
the very thing which gives them wit and zest
is that little spark of filth . . .

Sosia lay on her bed at San Trovaso, unaware of her surroundings. She moaned as Rabino raised the damp coverlet gingerly. Sosia suffered not from plague, Damascus or any other kind. He had treated the symptoms of advanced venereal disease too many times not to know what he would find. He saw her fingernails orange as a pigeon's eye; her skin flushed red.

When he moved her arms away from her chest, he found a book in the crook of her left elbow, wedged so tightly that its corners had gouged deep grooves in her skin.

His first thought was: *She has started another diary of her sordid life.*

He lifted it up and opened the cover grimly, holding it away from him. But instead of Sosia's records he found a printed book, the production of the German printer Wendelin von Speyer, whose wife he tended. He was astonished to discover it was the Catullus book, the love poems, which were so convulsing Venice.

What could Sosia be doing with such a book? A bitter voice inside him asked too, *If they are, as it's said, true poems about deep love, then what use would they be to her?*

He laid the book at the side of the bed, and listened to her heart, noting the familiar irregular beat. Her heart had always beaten sluggishly, in tugging rhythms, like a reptile's. *No change there, then.*

He noticed a row of pink pearls hanging off her neck, the clasp wrenched apart. He had never seen them before. *A gift, no doubt, from one of her lovers,* he thought with disgust. The pearls were irregular and slightly pocked, like a row of nipples.

He forced himself to examine her, to begin the normal repertoire of responses of a doctor to illness. Venice had no pity for foreigners with the pox. The fate that awaited Sosia, without his attention, was to be thrown in a cart and paraded through the city as an unchaste wife and whore. If the city cared to make an example of her, she might be crowned in infamy at San Marco (with a painted wooden ring rudely made for the occasion) before being dumped at the Hospital of the Incurables, to die slowly in her own filth.

He bathed her with warmed plantain water, removing her chemise at the last moment and trying to avert his eyes. When the front part of her body was clean, he made to turn her over. Then he saw the dark blood on the mattress underneath her. *It's not her time of the month,* he thought. The relevant days were still imprinted on his memory.

She has miscarried an ill-gotten child, he shuddered. *It cannot be mine.*

He turned away for a moment, in pain and disgust. This was somehow a more brutal proof of her infidelities than even the venereal disease had been. He stared at the wall, not wishing to look at Sosia again, but knowing that his calling required him to calculate the age of the foetus and find whether it had been expelled from her womb by illegal means; whether infection had set in which might yet be stopped to save her reproductive parts from a painful gangrene.

He took up a fresh rag and dipped it in the basin of warm water and went to put it at the mouth of what he told himself to call, for comfort, *the birth canal.* He had not approached that part of Sosia as a husband does for so many years that it seemed more natural to touch it as a doctor. *She is one of God's creatures,* he told himself; *my vocation is to ameliorate her suffering, no more and no less.* The rag came back to the basin untinted with blood. He jumped to his feet and stood over her again, paler even than before. *No, it cannot be true. I deserve to be branded for such obscene thoughts.*

He took her shoulders and gently twisted first the top half and then the lower half of her body around.

It was true.

He dropped her and she rolled on to her back, moaning slightly.

Sosia then whispered. It broke from a bubble at the corner of her mouth.

'Malipiero,' she said. 'The boys,' and one hand stole backwards to cup where she was hurt.

Gentilia signed the last letter with a clumsy flourish. It was her masterpiece, she thought, for in it she had combined all the elements most likely to bring down the forces of the state upon the she-dog from Dalmatia.

The hair she had snatched from Sosia's head was already wrapped around a living scorpion she'd buried in a pot of sand. As the insect slowly died, so would Sosia meet her fate.

Having posted her letter through the mouth of the lion at the Doges' Palace, she made her way to the quay to find a boat that would take her to Murano. Letters were all very well, but she wanted personal congratulations too.

All the way there she hugged her pleasure to herself.

On arriving at Murano she walked quickly past the church and to the door of Fra Filippo's cell.

This time, she knew, her entrance would not be barred. She had made sure that the repulsive little assistant would no longer get in her way. She'd already had the satisfaction of seeing him in his new employment as a porter on the Riva degli Schiavoni. She had made certain he saw her too: her gloating smile had informed him that she was the author of his humiliation. He had shaken his scarred fist at her, his birthmark glowing vermilion and white.

Now she rapped firmly on Fra Filippo's door and raised an expectant face.

Fra Filippo started up eagerly at the knock. He had laid down his pen already, and was about to finish his work for the day. The distracting aroma of fried fish was wafting from the kitchens and into his thoughts; he hoped that the knock was that of the servant coming to announce dinner. So he walked quickly to the door, and opened it without enquiring as to the identity of his visitor. When he saw the piglet nun in front of him, he stopped short, suddenly alert.

Before she could say anything, he had bustled past her.

'It's good of you to come to see me, sister,' he announced over his shoulder, 'but I am urgently called to administer the last rites to one of our brethren.'

God forgive me for the lie, he whispered under his breath. *Indeed perhaps I spare her the greater sin of speaking ill and unjustly about a fellow nun.*

But Gentilia could move surprisingly fast. Fra Filippo was mystified to see his feet made no progress though he moved his legs vigorously. The heavy little nun had stepped deliberately on the hem of his robe and held him tethered to the ground.

'I have great news for you, father,' she said, smirking behind a modest hand. 'I have ruined the printer's whore. Ruined her. Driven her down to hell. Made sure she'll burn.'

'What are you talking about, my child?'

'The Jewess. I have purged her, as you said to.'

Fra Filippo smiled nervously. 'I myself did not ask any of God's servants to commit evil acts such as harming another person. That would be a sin.'

'Yes, you did,' said Gentilia. 'Anyway, I wanted you to know.'

'When you say "purged" do you mean that she is actually dead?'

'She will shortly be removed from this earth.'

'At your instigation?'

'Yes.'

'And yours alone?'

'Except in that you always . . .'

'Ah yes, I see.' Fra Filippo looked down on her craftily. 'Does anyone else know of this, my dear?'

'Well, soon all Venice shall know.'

'But not yet?'

'Not quite yet.'

'Then go in peace to your convent, my child, and await my further instructions.'

She did not move. He realised that she was waiting for something.

'Ah yes, you have done well my child. You are a good girl. An exceptionally good girl. God will reward you.'

Gentilia nodded serenely, and shuffled away.

Fra Filippo hurried back into his cell and pulled a new sheet of paper towards him. In minutes he had filled it with words. He called his new assistant, a colourless little boy.

'Deliver this to the Mother Superior at Sant' Angelo. Immediately. Allow no one else to see it. You may take our own boat and two strong rowers. It is imperative that you arrive there before the ferryboat from San Marco.'

Murano glass is supposed to shiver when poison is put into it.

Rabino poured the deadly green herb *tisana* from the crucible to the goblet and looked at it dully, waiting for the rim to tremble or the stem to sway, just a little. He normally disliked the idle mischief of Venetian proverbs, but on this occasion, it would provide a moment's comfort or distraction to see the picturesque adage proved right.

Nothing happened. The green liquid rested still as an emerald inside the goblet.

He had poured it almost without thinking.

Now he must decide if the poison was for himself or for Sosia or for both of them. In his mind it was clear: someone must be sacrificed to his sordid discovery this night. It was not possible that he and Sosia could continue to live now as they'd done for these past years. It was a relief, in a way, time to throw aside the suffocating curtain of dishonesty and confront the truth. Of course, it was a far worse truth than he had imagined.

He sat heavily on a chair, and raked through his mind for all the legal information at his disposal. As a doctor, and leader of the itinerant Jewish community, he had been brought to tribunal after tribunal to give characters for Jews on trial and even Christians with medical disorders of a sexual nature.

He knew that in 1425 a *parte* had been passed by the Council of Forty forbidding Jews from having intercourse with Christian women, but there was no law stopping Christian men from copulating with Jewesses. The fate for a nobleman accused of indulging in intercourse with a lowborn Jewess would not be so devastating. The Malipieros were powerful. Whichever one of the clan had committed this indiscretion would know and be warned exactly what moment would be judicious to leave the city for a while; perhaps he'd departed already. Maybe he was already at Mestre, thinking of Sosia and cupping his own hands over the soreness between his legs.

'Was it worth it, my Lord?' Rabino asked aloud, bitterly.

I must not think that way.

Rabino returned to other considerations. It was not for moral reasons that the nobles were discouraged from intercourse with their inferiors or servants; it was for practical ones. The *Signori di Notte* were obliged to investigate such matters actively because women favoured that way too often became arrogant, inefficient or pregnant, and being the mother of a nobleman's bastard rendered them disagreeably ambiguous in social position. But women slaves were sold at a premium for their beauty, so it was obvious what was going on. It was well known, for example, that the forthcoming Doge Mocenigo, though seventy years old, kept two young Turkish slaves as concubines in his house.

Rabino recalled that, under Venetian law, men were considered responsible for the purity of their wives. Even Jews would be bound to this convention, in the eyes of the Council of Forty. The chastity of wives, the virginity of daughters reflected on the men who kept them. A woman's sexual honour did not belong to herself. It belonged to her family, and a lack of it could put the whole family in danger of prosecution.

Rabino's thoughts hurtled on. The problem was Sosia's injury. The penalty for sodomy or unnatural congress, for noble or commoner, was to be burnt alive. This punishment was carried out between the pillars in the *Piazzetta*.

The rulers of Venice suffered paranoia about sodomy. This was not just moral, but political, he knew. Venetians feared secret societies. The crime of sodomy seemed to unite so many in secrecy for the sake of their perverse pleasures. There was a horror of any secret cabal, but one based on illicit physical passion was more to be feared than anything else.

Only five years ago, Rabino had shaken his head over a new law requiring surgeons to report evidence of sodomy to the authorities. He remembered more: the penalty for sodomy with your wife was to have your head cut off and your remains burned.

I could be accused of this, he realised. *If Sosia dies and is examined, I could be accused. Who is to know it was not I myself who inflicted this upon her?*

He thought of the noblemen to whom he might turn for help. So many children saved; so many wives safely brought to bed of heirs. But his friendships with the noblemen were necessarily discreet. He knew of no one who would advertise his or her debt to him. There were still too many influential men whose hatred of the Jews overcame even their desire for life. No, Rabino would not find any help for himself or for Sosia among the patricians.

The glass started to chatter fretfully on the tray, like women waiting in a surgery.

Poison! thought Rabino. Then he realised that the tray was shaking in sympathy with the door, which vibrated as if assailed by the beating of a dozen brutal hands. It took Rabino a moment to realise that the noise was in fact just that. He leapt to his feet as the hinges gave way and the street door crashed to the floor.

Three officers of the *Signori di Notte* ran up the stairs and swept into the room, looking down on Sosia and her grey-haired husband.

'We've come for Sosia Simeon. She's to be tried for witchcraft.'

'She's ill, possibly dying.'

'Then she can die in prison, cuckold.'

'Let me prepare her. Please leave me alone with her for a moment.'

The soldiers looked at the livid body of Sosia, one breast exposed above the coverlet, her hair wild against the sheet.

'Let the old boy say his goodbyes.'

They marched outside, slamming the door. Rabino thought: *Witchcraft? Three officers? Sodomy must be the least of her crimes.*

Rabino rushed to her body and cleaned it as best he could.

Sosia opened one eye, and said in the clearest of voices: 'So the poison – was it for you or for me?' As Rabino's face drained of colour she added, 'I despise you, Mister Doctor. *Pas ti majku jebao*, a dog fucked your mother.'

And she shouted over his shoulder, 'I'm ready!' She reached down and grabbed for the book.

It was still in her hands when the soldiers, tying her arms with rope, carried her from the room.

PART SEVEN

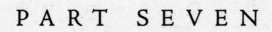

Prologue

Why, Catullus, are you delaying to die . . . ?

December 54 BC

I think, sometimes, about the future, Lucius-who-has-none, alas.

For whom, after all, do I continue to spew out these poems? Not for Clodia: she can barely be bothered to read what I write about her, unless she sees it scrawled on the wall of a bathhouse somewhere, as she passes on her way to another assignation. Then she's forced to look, though she doesn't know how to blush.

I'm sure she thinks to herself, 'Catullus? Oh yes, the young writer-fellow from Verona, what's he good at? Haven't seen much of him lately.'

And she will cast her mind back to me through that pile of autumn leaves in her head — for so I see her historical love affairs, dry, rotting, withered, wispy, interminable, uncountable — and then I think of all the leaves still to come, still to fall fresh and sappy on the soft pile . . . and perhaps she will send her servant round to me again. But perhaps she won't. Perhaps she'll leave me hanging as usual, one of those bats in her cave, archived for possible use later.

I never told you that when Caelius left her I went to see him.

'I helped you out over the sparrow,' I said to him bluntly, 'now you tell me how you cured yourself of her.'

He looked at me pityingly. 'I don't write about her any more. I don't think you are ready to make that sacrifice, my friend.'

He's right. I've been so in love with her it's hard to feel anything else. It's like fighting my way out of an egg: my strength is nearly gone in making the first small hole, from which I peer, hopelessly, at freedom, while the breath ebbs out of me.

I think that perhaps there will always be Clodias, just as there will always be mothers. The poor men will run from the breast of one to the other. They may invent new machines to change our lives, so we can run faster from one to the other, but what good is *speed* to a man who's forsaken the gentle breast of his mother to become ensnared by the bitter nipple of a Clodia? Nothing at all.

Better to write slowly, one word in front of the last. By writing you can use up a whole passage of the moon, and face the new day too frail to feel the pain except as a blurred kind of hatred for yourself.

I write now because I can do nothing else. I work and rework the old poems tirelessly, changing them into new ones. In the end it's just one. A poem about a man in love and a woman who's incapable of it, a picturesque and futile little prayer, endlessly chanted.

By its recital I have acquired the honour of being the most talked-about poet of my day.

Not for long, though. Rome lacks the concentration for poetry. I know this even as I write. From the moment I got my immortality, the day my book was presented to the world, I've been aware that fame itself is highly perishable.

Our empire is expanding, but the minds of our populace are contracting. The city's now in the grip of an obsession with *ludi* — gross entertainments; at the most innocent, chariot racing and beast-hunts; at worst, we've the glamorous obscenity of our gladiators who compete for the goriest kills. Caesar's up north invading some ungainly island of primitives, pitchforking those shaggy Britons out of their long-haired forests, to bring back more human fodder for our arenas. Assassins, not writers, are the real heroes in this town.

In my poetry, there's a breast laid too bare, shown too soft for a populace that lives on a diet of viscera.

Worse still, there are too many books, too many cheap productions by too many booksellers for a tiny market of readers. The scribes are working long hours to make copies of books better left unwritten. But even the good ones are implicated in the general over-production.

I know all too well the way these things go. Ignominious destinies meet some of the best books . . . after languishing over-long in the storerooms of the booksellers they're sold off by weight to the grocers and bakers to wrap pastries and spices or to line barrels in which cereals are stored, or they're sent to the butchers where they're wadded around sanguineous cuts of veal and the lolling heads of tiny songbirds impaled upon sticks.

There are so many ways for a poet and his poems to lose their immortality – even while he's still alive! I walk past the butchers and bakers, whistling, but in my heart I dread to see my own work embrace their wares one day. Yesterday I saw one of Caelius' poems flapping like a tunic round a fine mackerel, and smiled for the first time in weeks.

Meanwhile I'm still singing my poems. The publication of my book did not silence me; it's drawn more out of me. Perhaps I've over-exposed myself. I have lived too much, as if afraid of running out of material; I've used up my life too fast. I have always been too delicate for this world of Lesbias, or should we say Clodias.

You might ask me why I have written so much, why I've been writing, it seems, instead of actually living. I wrote when I could have been out looking for a better woman to love, when I might have been forgetting – getting drunk with men friends who had not (yet) slept with Clodia. There are so many things I could have done which would have served my happiness better than writing.

I myself have come to think of it less as an art and more as a way of breathing. I take a deep swig on her latest lie, and out come these songs, fluent as blood.

Just as with the birds, the instinct to sing is alike manifested by heaven-born musicians and the carrion-gnawers of life: the lark and the crow both make their music when they want to make love. The crow plainly thinks his caws and splutters are as eloquent as I believe mine to be. Or used to. Perhaps the crow is more effective. It is said the crow-wife maintains the highest monogamous standards throughout their married life. In the case of Clodia and myself, only one of us attempted monogamy, the one who sings.

Sometimes I fear I've grown stale; that, like the crow, my vocabulary is stunted. I know too much about love now to write about it properly. I would like a pristine voice, with wonder still alive in it, instead of this plaintive one, dirtied by too much experience on the darker shores of love.

I sit here during these slippery hours when the sun stops beating and no one else can mark what no one else can see. I wonder what Clodia is doing now. It's winter again. She's here in Rome, filling the nights with groans of one kind or another; milking the milk-herds, bearing down on the orange-squeezer, kneading the exhausted dough of the baker, screwing the pimp for money.

I know better than anyone how easy it is, by night, to insert half-hours of secret pleasure. The night bulges a little, pats its black paunch and belches stars. That is how it is with me, when I have my turn with her, as I still do, when the thought of me takes her fancy and she sends out her servant to summon me.

Meanwhile I walk round the town, watching my own feet fall in front of me. It's cold and I cough a lot, despite my furs. Our father's money cannot keep out the ills of the soul that tax my health. He asks me to come back to Sirmione, to the beautiful house on the lake where it's never too cold and where even the winter air is scented with health-giving herbs.

But I cannot leave; she might change her mind again. She's done it before. Eighteen times, to be precise. That is how often I've possessed her since she first rejected me. The nineteenth time might be tonight. That's what keeps me here.

In my walks I see all the other rich people piled up in furs — we seem like a shambling breed of badly clipped beasts. I laugh at the thought: the more fur we show on our backs, the more superior — the more above the beasts and slaves — we think we are!

Except perhaps Clodia. She's different. She's above us all. She has the power of the kingdom. She knows how not to love.

In the mists of the gull-squalling river, I think I see her eyes under every hood. I nurse a memory of her yawning with her arms hooked up over her head like the handles of an amphora. Her nipples are laughing at me, and she rubs her belly in satisfaction at all the seed I've planted in there. Gods! How I desire her! There's no cure for the lust she inspires in me.

I take my friends' advice — I try to think of that smile in her grave a hundred years from now — a twist of teeth and black bone. For a moment I can envision it. Then the moment passes, like a glimpse at infinity. I am back in her thrall again.

Even if she called me to her tonight, I could not be sure of satisfying her. The periods of calm between the violent fits of coughing have become shorter. My lungs are hungry as a pair of cupped hands, but the charity of a little air is not forthcoming.

I keep walking, contesting each breath. The ovens of the town are alight. Women are cooking for the men they love. I choke on the ghosts of ashes, my stomach tightening with envy at the thought of husbands and wives sharing simple pleasures, with no fear of poison in the pot.

The night is coming. Leaning on the rail to catch my breath, from the Pons Aemilius I see a pale lavender sky pricked by tree skeletons. The darting tongues of evening light, swift and sweet as ideas, have vanished and soon this town will be dark as the grave. Who says that dawn must come? A gland of satisfaction swells somewhere inside me at this thought. If I must die, why not the city too?

And all those who live in her.

It grows yet darker. The moon rises. I am hunched around my own chest trying to protect it from the cold fumes of the river. Furtive figures move about the edges of the streets, dumping the waste of the day. Someone rolls the corpse of an overworked ass into the street and runs off. Other men come to empty the public urinals, and carry the contents off to the tanners. Out of noxious liquid, supple leather. Out of pain, poetry. It's that bad time, that vulnerable stretch of time, the time when it is essential for lovers to be together. Those who cannot be with their lovers call for drink, violence or fornication, or all three. The needy cluster round the portico of Pompey, where even a hunchback may pick up a girl for nothing.

Now it's time for me to go to my room and write, if only this cough will let go of me for an hour. Wine will soon perfume my ink and rock my brain till it clicks to attention, and I will start to write. I shall bend like a shroud-maker over my work, sewing the corpses of my feelings into neat little poems . . .

Who knows, her servant might be waiting for me at my door.

Since I returned from our lake house at Sirmione this last time, I have been waiting.

I'm calmer now. Burying the wax doll in the earth there seems to have laid to rest at least a part of my pain. When all seems unbearable, I remember what I did and what I said then, and it has the power of a prayer to calm me.

Beloved Sirmione! Delicately bubble-floating on the lake, so unlike Rome, who has bolted herself into the land with great stone latchets. Perhaps I did wrong to desecrate the sweet ground of my birthplace with my wax doll and my curse?

On the last day before I left for Rome, I went down to the lake with the doll and unrolled her from her linen sheath. I drove five little nails into her shapely back, one each for the two kidneys, the liver, the spleen and the heart. Around these I wound the last strands I have stolen of Clodia's hair. (I noticed that this formed a shape like the letter 'S'.)

Then I dug a small hole with my hands, and bent down to smell the sweet earth. With my mouth to the hole, I whispered to the Gods of the Underworld: 'I am here, can you hear me?'

I listened, and heard the quiet breathing of the soil. The shades are said to be kindly folk, and I was not afraid of them, even though my mission was dark.

'I consign to this earth this *devotio*,' I whispered, in a quavering childlike voice, 'this image of the lady Clodia Metelli. It is made in her likeness, and so I invoke homoeopathic magic to bind her soul to it. It is made using her hair, and I so invoke contagious magic, conferred by this substance that intimately belonged to her. I invoke these things to carry my curse.'

At this point I heard a noise like the crunch of a light footstep on a twig, and I jerked up my head in alarm, for such curses are outside the law. But it was just a brave and curious sparrow, hopping close to see if I would feed him. Sirmione is so kind a place that even the beasts are optimistic in their spirits. I thought about Clodia's dead sparrow then, and considered this little bird a good omen: perhaps it was the soul of her bird, come to help me bind my curse.

So I lowered my head to the mouth of my hole again, and continued.

'My curse is this. Clodia shall not die. At least, her body may die; that is, the body she wears now. But I curse her spirit to wander the earth unsleeping, borrowing other bodies if needs be, both male and female. She will wander the earth like that, until she learns to love someone as I have loved her. Until then she will burn in all the seats of love, in her kidneys, her liver, her spleen, her heart, and she will roam the world, unrequited. And her pain will be inscribed on her back, as it is on this *devotio*'s.'

Then I put her in the ground, and covered her with soil, as if I planted the seed of a malignant flower. While I did so, I hissed: 'May this curse fracture and splinter and go off in all different directions like the scintilla of sparks when a hot ember explodes. My hate's as deep as that.

'I swear by the feather of Clodia's sparrow, by the slant of her neck, by the planes of her cheekbones, by the groove of her sex, that this curse shall go beyond my life and beyond hers and into the future where everything shall repeat itself endlessly until my pain is expiated.'

My hands hovered over the earth as I delivered my last words.

'Anyone who knows how to love will help carry my curse from this world to the next, and the one after that.'

Back in Rome, now, I miss my little *devotio* sometimes. I used to sleep with her like a doll in my hand.

I don't even know if I believe in the curse. I suspect the power of any curse rests in the catharsis it offers the one who utters it. Certainly, I can say now: 'Yes, I have settled my accounts.'

What happens next? When you have settled your accounts?

Better to work on the poems and not ponder on the wax figure any more.

I've heard they say in Egypt that this world is an egg and the image of it cracking insists on entering my poetry somewhere, I know not where to insert it. Clodia's sparrow never laid an egg. Like all her loves, it was barren. Perhaps the little figure, laid into the ground, is a kind of egg, which must gestate until her time is come. Perhaps she is my last poem.

I feel a pressing of time on my shoulders, as if it were a more precious commodity than even a look of love on Clodia's face. The river mutters filth at me, and my own lips are restless as a moth, tasting phrases for . . .

Chapter One

My lover's sparrow is dead.
My darling's darling sparrow is dead,
whom she loved more than her own eyes.
He was honey in her hands, as intimate
with her as a girl with her own mother.
That sparrow seldom left her lap,
but pranced on the air around her, here and there,
forever making music for his mistress alone.
Now he takes the path of shadows,
whence neither bird nor man returns.

Why do I see rope in all parts where I go? Why not chains? They last longer and are stronger. Rope grows slippery, frays and rots. Is that why I see it – for it's like the love of a man for his wife?

Then there's this new thing in the house. When I serve the wine there's such a shake in the glasswares that I fear each one will shatter. I do not know if it's the trembling of my own hands (for they do this now each time he's in the house) that has caused this. I try to think so, but I cannot.

There is one more thought which comes and comes to me, no mind how I try to fight it off.

It is this: the glass of this town is known to shiver when a poison is poured inside it. If there's a bad illness corked up inside a bottle, it will burst forth. I do not wish to say out loud the thing with which a man may rid himself of his wife if he no more loves her.

I think you can guess what thing it is.

I see it in the letters now. He writes to me of the pleasure he takes when I sup at my glass. 'I love to see your lips wet,' he has written, 'with some sweet thing I've fed you.'

Late in the frostbound night the *Signori di Notte* came to Wendelin von Speyer, still lingering at the *stamperia*, with an urgent commission. Quick, secret and on a grand scale. This was unusual. The *Signori* had no need to deal with printers on a normal basis. Wendelin sent a servant to rouse the apprentices and set them to work. He told them to wake him with a proof copy. He was only half awake and he would wait to look at the scrawled text when it was rendered in his own lustrous type. He set off on his nocturnal wanderings, returning home in the early hours.

Soon after came a knock at his door. Stumbling downstairs, Wendelin opened the door and took the proof copy Morto handed him. The cold breath of the lagoon swept into the hall.

'It's *her*,' Morto croaked in a broken voice, 'the one Bruno loves.'

Half a dozen grim realisations fell on Wendelin at once.

'She came to the *stamperia*? She's Bruno's *innamorata*? It's for this woman – this Sosia Simeon – the doctor's wife? – that he walks around like a ghost?'

'Him and a couple of hundred others it seems, sir.'

'What's she like, this woman? You've met her?'

'Bruno was robbed, sir, in my opinion.'

'Shall you go and tell him, Morto?'

'I cannot bear it. I think it should come from you, sir.'

Wendelin started at a slight noise upstairs. Had Morto's knock woken his wife? He awaited her footsteps, her call. None came. She must have fallen back to sleep. He burned with anxiety for her. She would be painfully sorry for the Jewish doctor, who had been so humiliated by this dreadful woman. Privately he feared for himself and the *stamperia* in the aftermath of her crimes: he had seen, with a pang of dread, that a copy of his own Catullus book, found with her, was named in the denunciation.

Two hours later, Bruno arrived at work, his face twisted and translucent with suffering. Wendelin gratefully assumed someone else had told him on his way to work. He put his arm around the young man, and pressed the document into his hands, that were mottled with cold.

'So we've been asked to print it. I wanted you to see it first. Bruno, if the horrors in here should spread to envelop you then I shall support you before the *Avogadori*, should my opinion count for anything in this town.'

Bruno stared, ucomprehending.

'Take it home and read it. You need not work today, my son.'

In his little apartments at Dorsoduro, Bruno lit a candle and balanced it, barely, on his pallet. He lay there with the pages of the proofs spread over his body. He did not care if the flame took the sheets of his bed. His thoughts, metallic and cold, ran in vicious circles between his sister and his lover.

Until that morning he had been preoccupied with Gentilia.

A messenger had arrived the previous evening with a letter from the Mother Superior at Sant' Angelo di Contorta. His sister Gentilia, he read, had been found to be suffering from a riotous imbalance of the brain, and they'd been obliged to confine her in a hospital administered by the priests on Murano. She had been taken there that very night, for her own safety. He might not visit her until her mind had settled somewhat. He was not to worry unduly about her, and on no account to try to make contact with her as in her present condition any communication would exacerbate her suffering.

'Poor Gentilia,' he said aloud. 'She doesn't even know that Sosia has been disgraced, just as she predicted.'

He thought of his sister as he'd last seen her, muttering to herself, a dark skein of someone's hair wrapped so tight around her finger that its tip had grown blue. He'd tried to detach the hair but she fought him, vicious as a polecat, and he had backed away, called for nuns to help her and slipped out of the convent.

As the morning light fortified the shadows of his room, he noticed disturbances. Sosia had been there, he realised. She must have come the previous day, before he came home from work to the dire news about Gentilia. There were signs of her everywhere, and a chemise he recognised on the floor beside the bed.

'She's used her key; brought another lover here!' he cried out. 'Perhaps whoever it was who gave her that copy of Catullus!'

Then he noticed the strange silence of the room. In the blank shock that followed the news about Gentilia he had forgotten about his sparrows. They were not singing. He rose from the bed pallet and walked to their cage. The birds lay among the seeds, their necks awkwardly ranged, their eyes glassy, their beaks open as if in one last desperate song.

She had not bothered to close the door to the cage. He reached in and took the little corpses out, one in each hand. He went back to the pallet and lay there, with the birds placed delicately on his breast.

Last night there were knocks on the door in the dead of night and whispering. This morning he came back just briefly and left tight-lipped for work. I pretended to be sleeping when he came to kiss me goodbye, but I leapt out of bed to watch his stiff walk down the icy *calle*. No time to leave a letter, thank God. No doubt the bad business in the night explains the hunch in his shoulders – perhaps he's called in help for his plan to do me harm. Now I have a new thought.

What will he do to our son? Will it be the same thing? A slow death by soft hate, hid as love? Or does he love our son more than me because the babe has his own blood in him, the sap and marrow of the North?

Our son lies at present in his crib with a thumb in his mouth and four pink fingertips splayed up with one on top of his nose. His eyes are shut, his lids blaze like pearls in the waxlight and the shadows of his each lash stretch like arrows to his cheek. He sucks on his fingers and mumbles some miserable little whines in his sleep. I think he feels what goes on here, poor babe, though he cannot understand it yet.

I raised my voice against him this morning, for which I am

most sorry. He'd crawled into the *boudoir* of the cat and taken from the heap of scarves the little wax-woman from Sirmione the thieving beast had hidden there.

I was sewing at the table, with my back to him. I heard him coo and cry with pleasure. I did not turn around. I thought he was playing some happy game with the cat, who will oblige in this way if he's in the mood for it. Then I realised that the cat was in fact out of the house on some private business of his own. So I jumped up at the same moment my son began to choke.

A piece of the wax-woman had stuck in his throat. I turned him upside down and beat on his back till the small wet gobbet shot out on the floor. It was only then I saw that he'd not tried to eat her, but had crumbled her to tiny pieces on the floor. Just one piece had gone inside his mouth.

Little crumbs of white wax lay all around me, none bigger than a fly. The nails that had pierced her kidneys, liver, spleen and stomach lay at odd angles, like a beggar's crutches thrown down in the snow.

Well, I thought when I stopped shaking, *so long as the baby is safe, this is perhaps the best ending for the wax-woman. My son, in his innocence, has turned her to dust, and not unleashed her magic upon us. It was the only way to rid me of her. Bless him!*

With my son still clinging at my side, like a monkey's child, I cleaned up all the wax and nails, brushing them into an old linen bag. I walked out of the house to the canal and emptied the bag into the water that was grey and dimpled with sleet. The wax scattered like tiny blossoms in all directions, the fragments torn away from one another by the waves. A swoop of gangster sparrows, thinking them breadcrumbs, hovered over the pieces for a moment, and a couple tried their savour, but, finding it unpalatable, disappeared. Meanwhile the crumbs of wax spread out so I could not hold them all in my eyesight and suddenly they were so diffused that they were invisible, gone to do goodness knows what to goodness knows whom, or to sink without trace.

Throwing something in the water is just like publishing it, I suppose.

The baby still sobbed quietly, so I kissed and kissed and kissed the smile back on his face and carried him upstairs to the loft, for there are many things up there for him to look at.

Most times, all I need to do to make him laugh is open the top of a chest or a drawer and say '*Eccolaqua!* Look what's in here!'

It might be just a spoon or a sheet, but the surprise of its sighting and the wonder in my voice is enough to catch his imagination and make him joyous again.

Now I spend some part of each day in the room in this roof where I keep my old quilts and sheets. I go up there and sit among the pretty dresses I used to wear when I was a loved wife, the shimmering sky-blue Bombazine cotton from Armenia and the pink silk stole from Milan. The smell of lavender comes up my nose and makes me want to drowse and dream on those prodigiously fine days before the paint was dry on our marriage, before we took it on that dolorous journey north.

Outside it blusters so the snow grows wings and flies around, and the waves bay in an ugly way at the *riva*.

My man never comes up here. Except at the centre, the roof is too low for his head. I am safe. That makes me so happy, as does the scent of dried lavender, so that I feel light as a child in the head. In the sifted ruins of our marriage, of our life together now gnawn with fear and doubt, this is what remains: a son, a cat, one quiet, sweet-smelling room with strong dark beams above it.

He has stayed later even than usual at the *stamperia* tonight. What business keeps him there I have no idea. All day I've felt the air more charged with fear and strain than ever before. And mystery. I brood on more things as the time drags on my hands.

Domenico Zorzi was in the *Broglio* by the Doges' Palace when he heard the news in passing. He was conducting a supple piece of business with two merchants who had come, as they all did, to petition the red-robed senators for their patronage in various wise and unwise enterprises. As Domenico shook hands over a land acquisition on the mainland, he heard out of the corner of his ears a whispered phrase, 'And she's a doctor's wife, a Jewess, of course. The lions have been talking about her for ages. I think they'll burn her, because it's a nobleman she did it with.'

Domenico felt his bowels lurch inside him. He stumbled against a column. 'Forgive me,' he said to his clients, 'I have not eaten today.'

'Go, eat!' they urged him. 'You must eat! Pasta with butter and white bread first, and nothing cold, it does such damage to the stomach. Then a little sleep.'

Domenico slipped through the gates of the Doges' Palace and did not quite run to the office of the *Avogadori*. He told the smirking clerk: 'I believe that there's a case against the Jewess Sosia Simeon. I would like my copy.'

As he suspected, the *Avogadori* had anticipated a certain amount of interest in this case. The accusations had been printed a hundred times on good paper. He put his hand out of his red sleeve to grasp the thick sheaf, recognising Wendelin von Speyer's typeface.

'Thank you,' he said smoothly.

He opened the pages, searching for his own name, his eye snagging on words like 'bestiality' and 'diabolical will'. With his lawyer's eyes, and his lover's heart, he started to read in detail. With this scrutiny came calmness and a cold, penetrative anger. The tumult of his feelings for Sosia stilled to a single beat, a heavy heartbeat, of hatred.

How cretinous he had been! First, to think that he himself might be the victim-nobleman of the accusations. Of course, in that case, he would already have been taken by the *Signori di Notte*, and not walking around freely. But also, of course, how vain of him to think that he might be Sosia's only noble lover!

Bitterness swarmed inside him. *She may be damned*, he thought, *for all I care.*

How generous he had been with her: clothes, money, books – even a first edition of the Catullus poems.

'My God!' he whispered. 'It's that book they found with her. It's mentioned in the charges. Will they trace it to me?'

433

The document had ruined him. He placed his finger in his navel and pushed. He wanted Sosia and now he also wanted her badly hurt. The pain that had begun to haunt his genitals in the last few days was nothing to the agonies he wished on her.

And if she were first to run the gamut of the toys in the torturers' arsenal, he shrugged, *what of it? I know her; she won't tell them where the book came from.* He lay on his bed, staring at the ceiling, and running through their grim repertoire in his head. For Sosia, he imagined, in order, subtraction of the tongue, blinding in one eye, breaking on the wheel.

It did not occur to him to intervene on her behalf.

When her body was mangled he might finally learn not to want it any more.

Felice Feliciano heard about it at the *stamperia*, where the workers were huddled together over the news like a group of seagulls around a fresh loaf dropped from the baker's boat. They'd taken possession of the story and were worrying it between their teeth. They'd claimed it for their own, for they had the glamour of knowing the lady herself. At least by sight. For how many times had she come here looking for Bruno with that yellow light in her eyes?

'And sodomy too,' he heard hissed under someone's breath as the vivid account came to a close. It had not taken long to divulge the information, even embroidered with the private fantasies of each man. For months they'd nursed these thoughts inside them when she sauntered in and out of the studio, arrogant as a thin she-cat in season.

Felice's first interior thought was of Sosia's buttocks adorned with many practice circles in green ink, like the eyes of so many serpents.

Felice thought: *To write in green, first seek in the months of March and April the blooms of the Iris and pound the three pendant leaves well and draw off the juice. Add alum. Soak a strip of linen in this liquid and leave to dry. When you wish to draw off the green colour, take a cockle shell, together with some lye and the frothy white of an egg, and press the said cloth well until the green colour comes out, and write with it, and it will look well.*

'Felice,' stammered Morto, 'we must help Bruno.'

'What did you say?'

'Have you read the charges?'

Felice picked up the printed sheet and scanned it quickly. His brows met.

'But this is not about Sosia,' Felice muttered. 'What's going on?'

Chapter Two

It's because of you. My mind's gone,
reduced to what it does to serve you,
so that now I could neither love you
if you were to become good
nor stop loving you
no matter what you do.

Now I know what it was that disturbed our night.

I went to Rialto this day and all are at talk and sneak and sniff about the wife of the Jew, my Jew, the one who saved me.

They say she's been seized and taken away to the cells and the charge is one dread to tell, for she's a witch and a whore and has done things which no one can say out loud for fear to turn the air black and bring the crows to peck at you.

Who knows if it's true? She's not of this town and a Jewess, so anyone may exercise a grudge against her . . . still, there's no smoke without something roasting, is there?

How strange that my own Jew should have a whore for his wife. He seems so good, so pure, and yet he must have had his acts of love with her like all the rest. I think on how it must feel to grind grain with one whose private parts are known to all.

Then I think on those trips we used to make on summer nights, my man and I, by boat, when our son would not sleep. At those times, from the *rio*, we could catch a glimpse of courts and paths and doors – each place closed up to the world like a nun – save to us, who passed by in our boat in the quiet hours of night, from that point of view which a boat and nought else in this town has.

It could be that it's like that with the Jew and his wife. All others have seen the open parts – he alone is privy to a part of herself she kept closed and never rented out? And he feels safe to love her that way?

I know he has love in him, that he knows what it is, I'm sure of that.

But what did she feel with her wed man, when she did with him as with all the rest? Did she like those thick black hairs that curl on the top of his hand; did she watch them as he moved to touch her hand or cheek? Did she like to look up and see him above her, with those deep eyes fixed upon her? These thoughts whirl through my brain like dust in the waxlight.

The priests say it's wrong for a man to love his wife as if she were a whore – with full lust as if with a girl bought for just that. It may be that this is where we went wrong, my man and me.

We loved not like man and wife but with the fierce heat of *adultery*. We were beyond control, and now we are punished for it.

Our happiness was on loan. We could never have afforded such a luxury.

The word 'punished' reminds me that my sister-in-law Paola came to call on me today, a rare event indeed. She was up to no good, of course, and relishing it. She looked at me down the great length of her nose for a long moment and I was soused in her pity, as welcome to me as a shower of drain water.

'Hello Lussièta,' she said, in her patronising way and added immediately, lest I think she meant me well by it, 'I have to warn you that you spend too much time with the Jew doctor. It's not good for the business.'

I opened my mouth but nothing came out. She went on: 'The scandal with his wife taints him even more.'

Then the words broke free of my throat: 'But that's not the real problem, is it, for you? It's his race, is it not? You had rather lose your husband – one of them, of course husbands come in flocks for

437

you – than consult the Jew doctor who could have saved him. When you refused you might as well have killed Johann.'

In my mind I continued the sentence, And destroyed my life by sending me and my man back over the Alps from where we might never have returned, and where the first splinter of ice formed inside our love . . . and meanwhile you carry on without shame in dark alleys with some red-haired foreigner! There was no end to the crimes I was ready to lay at Paola's door in that moment.

Paola said coolly: 'Poor Johann would have died in any case. He had lesions on his lungs when I married him. I knew it would not be for long. You cannot hurt me with these intemperate accusations. I have mourned Johann and I've done what he would have wanted: tried to keep the business alive by allying myself with another printer to make the backbone of it stronger.'

'Do you not love your new husband?' I asked, thinking of the red-haired man.

'You're so naïve it hurts my teeth, Lussièta. You insist on being a child, yet you demand all the privileges of an adult. Wendelin says . . .'

'You mean you talk to my man when I'm not there . . . ?' My voice shrilled though I tried to cool its strident tone.

'About the *stamperia*. Yes, I attend meetings about the manuscripts they're considering and I make researches about the books that are wanted. I talk to other printers. I help the men to help themselves, not undermine their every day with notions and tales without the sense it takes to stuff a zucchini.'

I don't recall the rest of what she said. Perhaps I stopped listening. The only thing I could think about was this new fact that my man consulted Paola's opinion and talked to her of matters that he did not bring home to me. Dimly, I heard he had asked her thoughts even on Catullus! Why, he never even mentioned that she came to the *stamperia*! I hate the thought of her there, hanging round like a disease.

It has become his habit to keep secrets from me and to leave me in isolation. I dare not ventilate my opinions in his presence. I have only my friend Caterina and the kind Jew to talk to, and now Paola insists I cut myself off from *him*, because of things his wife did. In what way is this fair or right?

Paola and my man conspire to drive me mad. Until I'm under the *campo dei morti*, they will play with my tired brain, play . . . indeed something's already shaken loose, madly scampering round the hutch of my head.

Nicolò Malipiero heard about Sosia at the strangest of times. He was clambering his way up a pile of tables, arranged above the Bellini dressing table painted with her likeness. He was heading for the home-made scaffold where he had tied, after many attempts, an inexpert noose with the cord of his dressing gown. The cord was looped to the fixing of the chandelier, which he'd sheared of its heaviest drops with a large pair of scissors. The pieces of glass now lay smashed on the ground below him. The denuded chandelier swung wildly, its sparse flowers tinkling, while Nicolò threaded the cord through its branches to the sturdy hook in the ceiling.

For he had, that morning, by coincidence, received a packet from Sosia with a letter to tell him that he no longer existed for her. If he no longer existed for Sosia, then he no longer had any wish to exist in any context whatsoever.

He could not dwell in his memories, and in the things she had induced him to do. 'Be a man. If you don't do it, you won't see me again,' she had said that night, smiling in the hectic candlelight while the boys grinned like fish behind her.

When the envelope arrived, he felt the key to his studio in its wrapping. *So that's it*, he thought. *The key returned. I renounced my honour; I disgusted myself, for this.*

He slumped down in his chair, tucked his hands under his armpits. He could not lift his eyes. They seemed cast down like a Madonna's, unable to be raised to the piteous spectacle of the world. Occasionally he pulled one hot hand out from under his armpits and made a weak gesture of desperation. He looked at the floor of his apartments, at the space between his bed and the floor. He paced, as if there were a harness on his shoulders and breast, which dragged him from room to room. It was too painful to sit still, too frightening, as if the pain might catch up with him.

It had taken nearly all morning to build the pyramid of furniture. Unaccustomed to physical labour, he was now so tired, Venetian-tired, that he was already effectively a dead person. Unfortunately, he'd constructed his pyramid just slightly out of alignment with the noose, so the circle of cord hung behind him, grazing his neck as it thudded against him. He had to reach behind him and grope for it blindly. Then, with typical clumsiness, he'd tangled the tassel round his ear before dragging it over his face, burning the delicate skin to a rash with its coarse bristles of gold wire. He whimpered.

His servant knocked politely at the door and entered without waiting for a reply. With him were two *Signori di Notte*, who bowed low to the ground before looking up at Nicolò Malipiero standing high above them with his scarlet face in the noose and one foot dangling uselessly from his perch.

'With respect, sir,' the leader said to him, 'you are requested to accompany us to the Doges' Palace. There is a little matter that the *Avogadori* would like to discuss with you, should it please your Lordship.'

Chapter Three

... Fancy the rut of the lash to blush
your sweet flanks and soft buttocks?
You'll gyrate like a toy boat
caught out at sea in a wind grown wild with pain.

The prisoner will stand
    You are the Jewess Sosia Simeon of Dalmatia?
    Yes
    You are the wife of the physician Rabino Simeon, also a Jew, of
San Trovaso?
    Yes
    Sit
The other prisoner will stand
    You are the nobleman Nicolò Malipiero, of San Samuele?
    Yes
    You are the son of Alvise Malipiero, also of San Samuele?
    Yes
    On this day of our Lord, 15 December 1472, you both stand
accused of crimes against the Serene Republic of Venice. You are
accused of vile fornications, violations of the laws of race, and of
commerce with the Devil, this last in contravention of the law of
28 October 1422, which forbids sorcery of any kind.

The *Avogadori* of the *Comune* have considered the matter in the
light of information collected by the *Signori di Notte*. We have examined the diary of the prisoner, Nicolò Malipiero, and the account of
an eyewitness, one Ianno Spippoleti, who has beheld you at your

congress. We have also a witnessed denunciation on the part of one nun of Sant' Angelo di Contorta, *Suor* Gentilia Uguccione.

Sosia Simeon, it is alleged that with alluring speeches, gestures and looks, and by the help of *salvia* leaves, beans and consecrated oils, you created in the breast of Nicolò Malipiero a diabolical desire to know your body carnally on a bed, on a chest, against the trunk of a tree, in the *campi dei morti* of more than one church, in a gondola and in diverse other places.

It is alleged that, on the twentieth day of March this year, you, Sosia Simeon, prepared a potion made from the heart of a rooster, wine, water and your own menstrual blood, mixed with certain flowers whose esoteric properties are known only to witches. This potion you placed in an iron vessel and cooked until it formed a powdery cake. On that night, or one soon after, you induced Nicolò Malipiero to eat of this cake, and as a result he became insane with love for you. After this point, his copulations with you became both frequent and diligent.

It is further alleged that after one of these copulations you took the dust of his navel and mixed it with the dust of your own. Then you mixed these scrapings together in a goblet with red wine, and you caused Nicolò Malipiero to drink of it. You also drank. From that day his love, and the number of his copulations, already, as predicated, diligent, increased twofold.

If the state had not intervened in a timely manner to save him, it is clear that you would soon have induced him to adopt the monstrous resolve of leaving his noble wife and marrying you, by which means you planned to bring into the world scandalous, subversive bastards of ambiguous status.

It is alleged that you possess the Devil's secret repertoire of smells for the temptation of the flesh, and that this is signified by the large letter 'S' tattooed on your back. You required Nicolò Malipiero to humiliate himself at your feet in ways we do not care to name in this place, that whilst so doing you required him to whisper the words of Our Lord's Prayer continuously. In this way, too, you increased the madness of his lust for you and caused him to hold God and the Serene Republic of Venice in the most disgustful contempt.

The insane love of Nicolò Malipiero also caused him to commit further perverse and sad stupidities. For by your ministrations you were able to force him to abandon the dignity of a Venetian nobleman to indulge in acts of a wild bestiality, both with you and with young men whom you procured for these purposes at his expense. In these acts you yourself took part.

It is alleged that you, Sosia Simeon, also measured the *membrum virile* of Nicolò Malipiero against a candle that had been blessed in church. After you had inscribed certain notches in this candle, to show the measurements of the *membrum* in its quiescent and provoked states, you took this same candle to the Church of San Giobbe, to the funerary chapel of the Moro, and that you did deface that place of holiness created by the genius Lombardo, in that you lit that same candle and in its light you chanted obscene verses by the pagan Roman poets, most particularly the one known as Catullus, to celebrate your vile loves.

A copy of this book, printed by Wendelin von Speyer, was found in your personal possession on the day of your arrest. The officer of the court is holding it aloft now to show the members of the Council of Forty.

We take this moment to point out that your uncanny grasp of our language, given that you are a foreigner and a woman, is further proof of your occult tendencies, for the Devil himself is known to talk with facility in all tongues.

Sit

Rise, prisoner Nicolò Malipiero

Have you anything to say?

No

Sit

The Council of Forty has considered the case. We have reached our judgement.

Nicolò Malipiero, you are acquitted of the charges of fornication and blasphemy because we consider that you were acting, helpless and unconscious of your state, under the diabolical will of the foreign woman Sosia Simeon. We consider that your most egregious act has been to cast off your rationality, the precious treasure that distinguishes us from beasts, and succumb to such a woman. For this, your name will be excised from the *Libro d'oro*, the Golden Book of our patrician class.

The prisoner may stand down

Rise, prisoner Sosia Simeon

As a foreigner, you are not entitled to speak in this court

The Venetian Republic considers that the responsibility for evil deeds applies only to intentional acts. Nicolò Malipiero we regard, with compassion, as having suffered a period of temporary insanity, this being clearly demonstrated in that he was able to lose himself in such a creature as you. He surrendered his will to yours and so we hold you responsible for all the deeds he committed during the time you held sway over him.

You are convicted of all the charges brought against you, including blasphemy and fornication. Stimulated by sensual dissoluteness, you followed your appetites without reference to the law, forcing Nicolò Malipiero to break the sacred yoke of matrimony and betray his own noble wife. Unmoved by modesty, you caused him to know you in ways prohibited by godly and civil laws. In contempt of God and not holding in awe the State, you used your will to overcome his scruples and dishonour both himself and his family. You are guilty of corrupting a noble Venetian, a Venetian of the *Libro d'oro*.

You, being a foreigner, and a woman, have no honour to lose.

Your sentence is as follows: You will be paraded in a wicker cage from San Marco to Santa Croce, whilst being scourged in the back, along the points of your kidneys, liver, spleen and heart, with spurred whips made from the tails of horses. You will wear on your head the wooden crown of ignominy painted with the scenes of your debaucheries. A herald shall walk in front of you, proclaiming your crimes, particularly as you pass those places where you performed them. You shall perforce submit to the contumelies of the public and the substances they, in their righteous anger, shall throw at you. From Santa Croce you will be taken to the *Piazzetta* of San Marco, and between the columns you will be made to stand on the Platform of Justice. There you will be branded with an 'S' – for your vile trade of *stregoneria* – upon both of your cheeks and upon your upper lip. Thereafter you shall be exiled from Venice in perpetuity.

If you are ever found to have returned to Venice you shall suffer the following punishment: your nose shall be cut off and you shall be led through the streets bleeding. Your right hand, with which you have defiled our altars and our nobility, will be cut off and hung around your neck upon a chain. Then you will be taken to the *Piazzetta* of San Marco and hanged for three days upon that same chain.

Your book of the poems of Catullus is confiscated by the Republic and shall be burned at your feet while you endure your punishment.

All present repent upon their own sins, for none of us is without them. Remember always to hold in awe the Serene Republic of Venice and all her officers and laws.

All rise, and depart. Go with God.

Chapter Four

At least let's force a blush upon her iron dog's face.

'Rub your legs together if you want to start a fire and keep warm, bitch.'

'She does things with candles that wives don't do with their husbands.'

'Got down to your last man, bitch? Trying to fuck the rats now? They'd get lost inside your cavern, bitch.'

'There's no pricks in heaven, bitch. Where you're going, you'll be riding pitchforks.'

Sosia lay on the straw in her cell. The damp fibres had frozen into spikes of ice. Small rivulets of blood ran down her arms and legs where the ice had cut her. She was in one of the *inferiori*, the cells that ran along the quay at ground level. With grotesque humour the warders gave these cells the most pompous names, as if they were salons in a grand *palazzo*: the *Liona*, the *Morosina*, the *Mocenigo*, the *Forte*, the *Orba*, the *Frescagioia*, the *Vulcano*.

The guards bundled Sosia into the *Liona* after her trial. Somehow, it had got out that she was in one of the cells near the waterline, one that could be seen from the *riva*. Despite the intense cold, crowds awaited their turn to try to peer at the witch through her bars. Rotten vegetables wrapped in curses were thrown through the window. Pumpkins exploded like fire against the bars.

She picked up these offerings and devoured them, and ate the paper too. The guards did not believe that she would survive her sentence and so they no longer brought her food. The stench from her cell was dreadful, worse than other prisoners' somehow. It was as if the sentence had already been carried out, and her body had started to rot, and an angry, corporeal ghost now lurked down there afire with malice to take her revenge.

Her sentence was to be carried out on the Friday before Christmas. She looked at the shadow of her profile against the pale light that flowed into the cell. It was the last time she would see it without the ridges of her branding. For Sosia herself did not believe that she would die. She watched the sportive fleas in the moonlight and found it impossible to think that she would not see them again.

Rabino came to see her, with medicines in his sleeve. She turned her head away from him. He'd brought the Torah under his robes, and started to read aloud, thinking to comfort her. Like the guards, he did not think that she could live through the tortures that would be administered. Her disease was too far advanced. He alone knew of the small murmur in her heartbeat that could be dangerous *in extremis*. The shock of the branding, terrible enough for witnesses, would almost certainly be too much for a weakened victim. He could only hope that by the time she had been whipped from Santa Croce and back, she would already be unconscious, too far gone towards her death to be roused even by the smell of her own burning flesh. So each night he read from the Torah, of the martyrdom of the Jews, and tried to see Sosia as one in that tradition. He saw himself visiting her grave in the Jewish cemetery on the Lido, laying small flowers there the following spring.

But when he went to see her, the living Sosia spat at him. She would not share his gentle fantasies.

She said nothing to him, but as he left, she murmured quietly behind him: 'The only thing I regret is that I've been charged with some crimes I did not yet have time to commit. By the way, don't look so guilty. It's not your fault, Mister Doctor, *prodati muda za bubrege.*'

'What does that mean?'

447

'My parents sold you testicles instead of kidneys.'

He did not turn around. Rabino did not wish this ghastly death on her, but he could not staunch a welling resentment about the legend she had attached to herself and hence to him, too. He was ashamed of his own self-ish thoughts but they piled up inside him, and they would not be stilled. He would be the widower whom no woman would ever want to touch, who would lack the confidence to touch another woman again. He'd been where every man had been. He, more even than Malipiero, alone of all Sosia's other men, must bear her sins on his reputation. He would go to his own grave starved of tenderness. Sharply, he reminded himself, 'I deserve this. I am among her violators.'

He had worried that Sosia might try to compound her sins by wishing to take her life, but he realised now that she was still fighting. She did not care to die well. She detested posterity already. She would go snarling and kicking out of this life. He, Rabino, was trying to feel for her as if she was already dead, in a state of renewed innocence.

God be good, he prayed, *take her from us as quickly and cleanly as possible.*

Outside the cell, the crowd roared.

'Listen to them,' she said to Rabino's retreating back. 'You'd think they'd all had me.'

He turned back to her with sudden bitterness. 'Yes, plenty of them did, but you won't find *them* outside howling like animals. They've abandoned you. Where are they now, those men who said they loved you? The noblemen? The rest?'

While his words still hung in the air Rabino was filled with shame. 'I apologise, Sosia. You do not deserve my unkindness now.'

'Yes, I do.'

'Perhaps you loved those men. You never cared for me so I cannot identify the symptoms of love in you. At least I'll be honest with you, and tell you what perhaps you wish to know. I'm afraid Nicolò Malipiero has left the city and he's not tried to intervene on your behalf. It's being said that he was trying to hang himself when they came to get him. I'm sorry if this hurts you.'

'The idiot! He could never do anything right,' Sosia muttered. '*Da padne na ledja, slomio bi kurac*, if he fell on his back he'd break his prick.'

'You didn't love him either, then?'

Sosia laughed.

'Did you love any of them? If it helps you to talk about it, I can listen. Don't worry about my feelings. I just want to help you.'

Sosia did not answer.

Rabino asked again: 'Didn't you love anyone?'

'Go away,' she hissed. 'As if I would tell you.'

They say the Jew's wife was found guilty, that she did things . . .

It's a shame, for he's a good man, the Jew.

The Jew's wife, they say, is beautiful. Just to see her stings the heart like a snake. They say she's so pale that waxlight faints when it sees her face. They tell me that she's a strange gold skin on her body and big golden eyes like an owl. It would take days to count her eyelashes, so lustrous are they. She speaks and reads in all tongues, they say, like the Devil. Yet she swears like a porter and smells like a dog!

As always, I go to my friend Caterina for the truth. She's seen this Sosia Simeon a sack of times. She alone tells me: 'That woman is beautiful only to those who want to see her that way.'

This made me wonder that perhaps I'd passed her in the street many times, even brushed against her arm or caught her eye, but I did not notice her for I was not in love with her?

Caterina said: 'Oh no, you would notice her.'

And how did Caterina know this? It turns out that the Jew's wife came to the Sturion to do what she does – with Felice Feliciano! This makes me think she's lovely after all. He's not known for choosing ugly playmates for his bed.

Now the Jew, he touched this wife of his and he touches me. In different ways of course, yet he has the taste and feel of our two skins on the tips of his hands. How does that feel to him? I wonder.

Despite his problems, he still comes to me. (Paola may go to hell, if the Devil will have her.) We do not mention the brutal matter of his wife.

Instead we talk of a terrible story at Rialto, that some owls have come to Venice who carry off the dogs. They take them away in their talons, nipping their necks. No dog is safe, if he's small, and the loved ones usually are, so the town is full of noble-women, clutching these little balls of fluff to their breasts and looking fearfully at the sky.

They say dogs constantly attend the Jew's wife. Now, when I go about the town, I think of her each time I hear a dog bark.

Suddenly I'm bilious with hate for dogs and wish the owls to take them all. They remind me of men, of husbands. Dogs and husbands wear their sex and their conscience on the outside; women keep theirs within.

Except this Sosia Simeon.

There's trouble in the town about her. You feel it in the drains first, for the small pools of wet (which have oozed out of them) are stirred with dizzy ripples. You know that the pools, like a magic ball, show events far off. In this case it's human steps, two, three score steps at once. It is not a good sign. We of this town go by choice in ones or twos. Except at *Carnevale* (when we go masked and are not ourselves) we are not ones for great parties or groups of friends. Only for badness and conspiracy do we join in force. When there is someone or something to fear or to fight.

You know there is trouble, too, by what floats on the sea. In the good times the spits of men come in ones like gell-fish, like one good thought on a page. But when they mass in groups, the men's spits come in fleets.

Now you see the fleets of spit wash up from the bad parts of town and you know they brood on dreadful matters. Other things float past, too – a bloodied kerchief, short pieces of rope with knots in them.

My man does not see it, for he's not of this town. He does not know spit from the spume of the waves, and just now he's too distracted to look close.

The first night, as Sosia lay in her cell, a very small man, it seemed to her a monk of some kind, came to the bars. He had brought a box with him to stand on so that he might look down on her. She could not see his face beneath his hooded cloak; just the glitter of his eyes, which met her yellow ones and held them.

As she watched, he produced a bundle of birch twigs from his cloak and began to scourge himself. He beat and slashed at his skin, never taking his eyes from hers. Eventually the little man groaned sweet and low down in his lungs and slumped against the wall.

His exertions swelled the hood of his cloak with air. She glimpsed a repulsive deformity, just like a little brain, pulsing above his left ear.

'See you again, little man,' said Sosia to his departing shadow.

Wendelin von Speyer was but dimly aware of what was happening to Sosia Simeon. He knew that the poor doctor must suffer for his reputation but he found it hard to believe that the Jew had loved her, as Wendelin himself loved his own wife, with all the heat of heart and loins, with all that was good and rich in his brain.

When Wendelin passed the crowds of the *riva*, he wondered how many of them were literate. And of those, he tried to calculate, how many would prefer to read the lurid pamphlets of Fra Filippo's, rather than the books that had provoked these paper storms of abuse. Copies of Catullus were still selling, but fitfully now. He'd almost exhausted the first edition. He could not bring himself to commit to another printing, not while things stood as they did.

The town had its teeth round the scandal of the doctor's wife, and while the thought of her obsessed everyone, they would not think of buying love poetry.

Crowds of men and women passed to and fro, over the bridge near the cell that housed Sosia Simeon. Wendelin felt no urge to look on her, to have the memory of her face watermarked on his memory. There were sufficient sadnesses to render his world piteous already. He watched the crowds craning their necks for a glimpse of Sosia and then quickly walking on.

The Venetians always ripple down the steps, he noticed. *I still plod. But they ripple, like snakes. How do they do that when I cannot?* he thought, thwarted and unhelpable as a child who tries to calculate the reality of angels.

He crushed the pages of his latest letter to Padre Pio between his fingers.

My dear Padre, Wendelin had written,

Women spit at me in the streets. Why? They think me ungodly! I am in the mood to find it bitterly amusing that the greatest ferocity of the Church has been pitted against the best book and the greatest writer I have put through my press. Fra Filippo has reserved the very nut of his hatred for the most wondrous poet of love.

I never used to ask, 'Why publish books?'

I used to laugh at my wife when she decried words and books. Now I see her point so much more clearly.

With our pitiful little words, can we hope to do anything more than trap a hollow echo of the truth? Worse, these faint echoes become fixed as a dead butterfly on a pin. People who read books will all have the same things to say and will soon lose the capacity to use their own imaginations. They will begin to believe that all the knowledge that is available is only that which is printed. And what a pathetic small sample of human intellect that is!

The truth does not come in words. It comes only when you hold someone's hand and look deeply into her eyes, or when lovers speak silently and voluminously to each other with their fingers. Remember, I have known a happy marriage, and I know these things from life, not just from books.

Why compare Jenson's typefaces to mine? What use is it to compare the egg-like cavities of the Roman letters to the fabulous fairytale spires of the Gothic ones? In what way is this relevant to life or truth or anything that matters?

I have lost the faith, my dear Padre. I confess it to you, but to no one else. I think of Johannes Sicculus (the executed printer) and his head falling in the basket, and I feel a great weight falling from myself. That weight was the heaviness of my honest, German sincerity, a useless commodity in Venice.

Johann and I ventured here because it's a great commercial metropolis. We did not come here as parasites. We came here bursting with faith and energy. With our daring and our industry, we made Venice the centre of literary activity in all Europe. We have printed more law texts, more Bibles, more classics, more books on philology, medicine, geography and astrology than anyone else. Our books go abroad, to Germany, France and Spain and the Low Countries and even England, making money and jobs for a whole dynasty of Venetians. And what gratitude has Venice shown us for this . . . !

What is the lagoon but a wet grave for all our hopes?

Why should I waste my time on the Venetians? They care nothing for what's inside their books. They buy them for the beautiful bindings. Lately, to my shame, I've even been experimenting with scented inks to see if I can tempt the jaded palates of the Venetians. I am dressing up my books like peacocks, like harlots.

The fondaco, *as I now see it, is just a big birdcage for Germans. We crow, a golden egg rolls down the stairs, and into the hand of some grasping Venetian.*

They say our letters are opened and read, and if this one is then shall I face even worse trouble than before. I find that I'm not caring very much.

You ask of my wife. I no longer know what to tell you. Please do not ask. Just pray for her.

Wendelin refolded the crumpled letter and tucked it into his sleeve. As always, his thoughts returned to his wife, to the rustle of her hair as she unwound it, to the dark pupils of her brown eyes fixed upon him as she lay on their bed, awaiting him. Of course those days were gone: now he understood that she did not wish him in their bed. She was too frail from her disease, needed to sleep undisturbed by the clumsy movements of his big body. And she no doubt feared his lust these days, thinking that with one thrust he might break her thin hips apart.

He shook his head, to dislodge these thoughts. Into the cavity came a vision of young Bruno Uguccione, who had also loved this Sosia. Poor Bruno, another ghost who haunted him, like his wife. Between them, Wendelin's wife and his favourite employee had lost enough substance to create another being entirely.

He reflected how two of the loveliest forms he had known – curved and plump inside lustrous skin – had lately wasted to almost spiritual thinness, and that it seemed that the lost flesh had taken their happiness with it. Both had seemed so rich in all the body promised; now they looked as starved as beggars.

Worst of all, his wife seemed to think that . . . She seemed to think she was unpalatable to him. How could she?

The legless beggar with the slack hose came to Sosia. He had shuffled on his buttocks all the way from Zannipolo to see the whore from Dalmatia who was to get her just deserts. He could not raise himself to see inside the cell. So he contented himself with a litany of the worst insults of their common language until he tired, muttering the words like a prayer under her window.

'*Poljubi mi čelo kurca!* – kiss my prick's forehead,' he told her. 'You liked that one, last time. How do you like it now, Missis? Seems from what they say that you kiss any part of a man if he only puts it close to you.'

She turned her back on his voice, only the drumming of her fingers betraying that she was conscious of him at all.

'You'll never be a martyr,' he called to her finally, 'if that's what you're after. *Ne pravi se pita od govana* – you can't make a pie out of shit.'

There were rich pickings for him there; so many tourists came to see the prisoner, presenting so many opportunities to snare them in his empty hose. He decided to take up residence there, as if he were her personal custodian. He performed his little dances for the crowds, waving his arms about like a ballerina, manipulating his ribbon legs like a pair of frenzied marionettes. He stayed for three days, until the *Signori* moved him along. There had been complaints that he barred the way to the most interesting sight in Venice.

I know my man thinks of the Jew's wife. Don't ask me how I know. I just know and it makes me sick, even iller than I was.

I know he walks past her cell and that he thinks of her. The clever woman, who loves books, unlike me. I think he pays the Jew to come to me, and each time he puts gold in that pale palm he must think of it on the Jew's wife's skin, as his used to be on mine.

I heard she had men by the score, that she scarce knew who was

454

on top of her or at her rear, that she did it with no love, just for the feel of it, any time she felt the need of it, like a beast in a field.

A vile thought has come in my mind, that my man was one such of hers and that is why he changed. If she's a witch, then her spell could have reached me this way. It might have been she who wrote those so-called love letters to me; her hand could have been the guide for his.

I cannot bear this thought of my man with her. I feel a scream swelling in my throat but I must not let it out lest he hears and comes up to look for me. Then he'll stand with his hand on the door, and not come close, but just stare at me, with that face of his, which I thought I knew but I know not.

When he comes here again I shall sniff him for her scent, to see if he has been with her.

I think I cannot bear it, that I must die of this pain, and then my next breath comes and I am still living, though I do not want to.

There's a kind of luxury in how bad I feel. It has grandness to it. Now I begin to wonder: did the love we had, my man and me, take us to the same high peak in Paradise; did it match, in reverse, the low point we have now? I cannot remember.

I think on this whole world of bad loves. Bruno, my man's nice young man, loves the witch, Sosia. She, I'm told by Caterina, loves Felice, who loves no one but himself and beauty and prefers to cut the fat around the town rather than settle with one woman. I love my man who may want Sosia too. And now, I think, the Jew loves me.

Chapter Five

I've come at last to know you for what you are.
Yet I spend my love on you still more lavishly
now I know you vile and cheap.
How is it possible, you ask –
it's because I know you.
It's that hateful kind of love:
the less you love, the more you love.

Bruno came to the bars of her cell every night. He waited until Rabino left, watching the slight shadow melt into the lightless pathway. He had thought he would be curious to see Sosia's husband, the object of so many wretched fantasies. Now Rabino seemed irrelevant, just another man who'd taken his turn with Sosia.

And for Rabino, Bruno thought, this is just one more deathbed vigil. He's used to saying farewell to people. I am not; I'm not accustomed to losing people in such a public way. I did not even say goodbye to my parents when they died.

An image of them, wrapped in each other's arms, laughing, rose fresh and kind in his mind. Perhaps, he thought now, it was the very absence of goodbyes that had preserved their memory.

He peered into the cell. Sosia would not even look at him.

He talked to her anyway, as if she were in a swoon and the sound of his voice might bring her back to life. He told her what he'd learned in the years that he had known her. Looking out at the water that rippled like the greased fur of a cat, he spoke to her of whatever came into his head.

'Listen to the waves, Sosia. The waves are good for the soul. They pace out your pain; they regulate the rhythms of it. Whatever is raging inside you is forced to slow down to accommodate their roll and retreat. Let them help you, my darling, listen, breathing in and out.'

She turned her head slightly towards the water, and seemed to be listening. He continued.

'What is happening now means nothing to our love. Between us, it's not even real. We two are so bound to each other by so many strands, all inter-woven; you cannot simply snap a braided rope of love. You must cut each filament separately and even then the love will hold out to the last thread before it snaps. That is how I love you. To the last thread.'

Fra Filippo came to see her. He brought a little party of Murano nuns whose dreams he had enlivened with detailed accounts of Sosia's malfeasances. Unlike those of Sant' Angelo di Contorta, his own nuns were rigorously pure.

To their rigid care he had consigned the piglet nun. He'd had the satisfaction of inspecting her, swaddled in a confining garment and gagged with an iron bit.

As a reward for their efforts he had invited her guards to come to Venice with him for an education in the evils of witchcraft.

'Look at her. Living proof of the existence of she-devils.' He gestured proudly as if he himself had conjured Sosia as a perfect example for them.

The nuns tittered like dry leaves underfoot, and covered their mouths with their hands.

Sosia rolled in her straw and opened her legs to their view. The nuns fled, dropping scarves, sweet cakes and small vials of water and wine.

Sosia herself made a rare foray to the bars of her window. She looked out, scanning the street, her eyes alert for just one silhouette: Felice Feliciano.

I smelled something in his hair.

Late home from work, he dipped his head over his food and I sneaked up behind him. I nosed up the back of his head – all the while he saw nothing – till I hit that *stink*.

Confounded, I began to blink so fast my lashes snipped up the light. My lips all through supper snapped open and shut like travelling clams. While he chewed like a penitent on the scorched food, I ate bile, and talked of all things but what ailed me: that perfumed drop of sweat from that musk-cat whore, that she-dog from Dalmatia, and still he presented his pink eye for salve, stained no doubt from his evening nuzzling her through the bars of Her cell. Couldn't keep away from Her.

'It's all used up,' I told him, 'squeezed dry.'

He looked down, embarrassed.

I was thinking: *Perhaps She's not the only one – that stink maybe compounds some several flavours of harlot! I have been blind to this all along!*

Meanwhile he tried to be too nice to me, asked me if I had any new ghost stories from Rialto. I cut him short with green-tinged raspberries and a stack of letters from our creditors.

'Let's go to bed,' he said, as if it were not desecrated.

We made married love. Other kinds are what I thought of.

All night I smothered in the fume-cocoon of Her smell, my eyes jammed open as if they could sniff too. I raged when I thought he shammed sleep, worse when I saw he really did. He had the gall to snore the way I like it, soft ruffled growls. His morning kiss slimed like a peddler's voice.

Was our love not extraordinary enough for him? Of all shabby acts this is the most threadbare; of all dirty ones the stalest. Better to beat me with a letterform, print on me an S-shaped bruise – that's her name, 'Sosia', isn't it?

There's no end to the torture my brain treats me to when I think of him with her. I crave detail. She sells him her flesh – how? By the hour, by the minute, by the kiss?

Every time I think my curiosity is worn out, something new comes to make it ripe and testy again. Even now, I wonder, is he at the *stamperia*? Or is he fumbling with some dank whore in a slippery alley?

Whether you are a modest wife or one who flutters the fringes of her thighs all over town, it all ends the same way.

Sosia's trial had inflamed the populace. On the tenth night a crowd seethed up around her cell as suddenly and silently as if it had seeped from the stones of the Piazza like *acqua alta*. What they wanted with the witch-Jewess no one seemed to know; just to be near her seemed to be their object. The atmosphere around her cell was dry and feverish. They crowded round the entrance to the portico of the prison, pinching and kicking to gain an advantageous position.

This was no ordinary swelling of the crowd. This time they'd brought their wives and children. It seemed that Sosia's crimes had united them in communal antipathy and outrage.

Every night, for three nights, they'd gathered there, watching and waiting, as if for a signal. Those closest to Sosia's cell reported on every moment inside. Their accounts were whispered backwards into the crowd so the news spread like a wave to a far shore. When they heard a new thing, 'She's turned on her pallet so her back is to us,' the crowd seemed satisfied for a while, folding its arms and nodding its collective heads. Each night the tension rose and the numbers increased.

The weather conspired in the atmosphere of suppressed horror. Night after night, lightning seared the air without releasing any moisture from the hard sky.

Felice Feliciano looked down from his window at the Sturion on the crowds amassing there by evening, on their way to San Marco. All night he watched, unable to go to bed.

Sosia's fate did not pain him, but he carried it heavily. It had affected him in ways he'd not thought possible. The thing was, it had devastated Bruno, and that he found difficult to bear.

Why, thought Sosia, a thousand yards away, *can they not leave me alone? This is what I wanted. They should all just go away and die. Except Felice. Why doesn't he come to me?*

The little man with the extraneous brain came back. In the dead of night, she heard his breathing misting the bars of her cell. He started his rasping motions inside his cloak almost immediately, at the sight of her.

'Hey little man,' said Sosia, 'you're a priest or kind of priest, is it not right? Or the whoreson slave of some priest? Yes?'

He flinched, but he was too far lost in himself to stop now.

'Mister Priest-boy, I have something to tell you,' said Sosia, sitting up in her straw. 'Confession time, it is. Listen or leave.'

'Aaah,' said Ianno indistinctly, but he did not leave.

'You know, friend, it's very interesting in here. I suppose suspense is always interesting. Suspense . . . your eyes focus on ridiculous details. Arbitrary positioning of objects seems to take on a character that is a threat. A stranger walking past seems authoritative. You become hypercritical of things – why *three* notices stuck on the wall about my sentence? Nicely printed, but badly spelled. See, there are four mistakes . . . I've come to the conclusion that this irritation and one's instinct to criticise is the little bit of power one has left.'

Ianno stopped what he was doing, and crept closer. He'd not expected her to talk, let alone to be so articulate. No one had ever said of her, 'clever Jewess' – only 'dirty Jewess'. He was not sure what use to make of this new insight into the woman, but certainly it had a detumescing effect on himself. He looked down to his groin, disappointed.

Sosia continued.

'Time elongates, reshapes itself into discrete periods. When you don't know what will happen next, each moment becomes the beginning of a new period of suspense. Solitary confinement is so wearing; you need the corroboration of periods of time passing to know you are still alive.'

Ianno sniffed. He could sympathise with this, thinking on his former hours of thankless labour, distributing leaflets for Fra Filippo, copying endless passages from offensive books for his master, and for what gratitude?

'I tell myself stories, true ones, to pass the time.'

Her voice had become lower and softer, as she seemed to disappear into her own reflections.

He craned towards the cell, grasping a bar. Sosia looked up at the powerful sinews of his fingers hooked around the metal.

'Would you like to hear?'

'Mmhn.'

'I choose you, then, to tell. Some of the men who fucked me have begged me for this story. They thought that if I told them I would be cured of all the hate inside me. They thought I'd been abused. Some said that by describing my pains I would be released from them. I did not tell them, any of them. I let them wonder. I did not want to be cured of the hate, for that would make me weak. Nor do I now, but I have a wish to talk about it.

'That all right with you, Mister Priest-boy?'

Ianno nodded.

And so Sosia told him a story. She told him about her birth in Dalmatia, what it was like to live in a far-off province governed loosely by Venice. The Venetians swept in and out, demanding tribute, taking anything beautiful from the churches and houses, hardly curious about the population they had gathered into their empire for mere strategic reasons.

Sosia told Ianno about small and bloody civil wars, of little interest to Venice, that sprang up from nowhere and subsided quickly, filling the graveyards. She told him of the soldiers who had killed her grandparents, tortured and rejected her, and the bereavement of her mother's adoring gaze.

'That was the worst part,' reflected Sosia. 'So then my family thought I was dirty, beneath contempt. The soldiers, they said I was not good enough to serve the bed of a Venetian, so they would not have anything to do with me either: then my family acted as though they felt the same way. Even my mother, my mother would not look at me. That killed my heart inside me, more than anything else. It has never come back to life, except that there is one man . . . but he doesn't see me, any more than my mother did.'

Ianno grunted. He knew something about being ostracised, too. He had always known that people preferred not to look at him.

Sosia continued, describing the flight of her family, the silent journey to Zara, the sordid boat to Mestre. Sparing no detail, she told of how she had seduced and acquired her husband.

'A Venetian, even though he's a Jew,' she pronounced.

Ianno grunted interrogatively.

Sosia said: 'You see, I have always thought about it, what they said. The soldiers. That the Venetians wouldn't touch a scrawny piece like me. The lowest pieces of pigs, those soldiers, could tell me that I was not good enough for *Venetians*. My family obviously thought the same way after that:

I was not good enough for Venetians and so I wasn't good enough for them either.

'Well, they were all wrong, weren't they? I was plenty good enough, for plenty of Venetians. Plenty good. I sometimes wonder what my mother would have thought, if she knew that I shared the beds of Venetian *noblemen*, not dirty soldiers from the provinces. Would she have taken me in her arms if she knew how far I've come?

'I've had more Venetians than I can count. I've cost them plenty, which is how you make men know you're worth something, by the way, little man.

'So the soldiers were wrong. Venetians have run after me, implored me, gone down on their knees to me, wept for me, abased themselves in all kinds of ways you would find most interesting, little man.

'Not one of them has said I wasn't good enough. Many of them have wondered if they were good enough for *me*.'

The bitterness in Sosia's voice curdled to a whisper and then silence.

Ianno strained his neck to hear but no further words came from the cell. He slid down from the bars and scuttled away. Sosia had detained him for hours. Already the fingers of dawn were illuminating the pale manuscript of the sky, and it was not safe to linger.

By the twelfth night, the senators had seen enough of the silent, milling crowd. They feared that the situation was building to something grave. They did not like the emphasis given to the life of one worthless foreigner; they did not like the cult of any individual at all.

A decision was made to clear the *riva*. In the courtyard of the Doges' Palace, the guards armed themselves and assembled silently at the huge doors. The moonlight beat down on their helmeted heads.

At the signal of the quiet bell, the doors opened and they coursed out in two forks, cleaving the crowd in half. They did not waste their breath on yells; they had been instructed to disperse the crowd, to hurt those who would not flee.

The first blows smote on the tallest heads and certainly a few fell then and there. Those who ran felt the bones of small hands and feet cracking under them for the children died first, of course. A mother fell backwards, her child sprawled back upon her chest at right angles so they formed a crucifix of flesh and blood.

Within minutes the *riva* was cleared, except of those who could no longer move. The dying exchanged intimate glances. Dogs careered everywhere, barking at the dead to wake them up, and at the living beseeching instructions.

Soon even the dogs stopped whimpering and there was only the creak of trolleys come to bear the fallen back to their family homes. By dawn all was silent; the *sestiere* of the town had opened up to accept their sorrowing, battered sons and closed around them again like the mouths of two great fish. The disorder was over and it would not come again.

The Senate now made sure of this. Acting on the information of his former assistant, the Council of Forty had sent the *Signori* to take into custody one Fra Filippo de Strata on the island of Murano. They had learned from their highly authentic source that the priest had been responsible for stirring up the blood of the crowds; it was he who'd roused their anger against the printers and harnessed it to their hatred of the witch from Dalmatia.

There were no official charges against Fra Filippo, but it would do him no harm, the senators purred, to cool his heels on the mainland for a spell until he'd learned his lesson. At least until the State had punished Sosia Simeon with all pomp and ceremony. The Venetian State would not have its thunder stolen by a hysterical priest with aspirations to be a demagogue.

'He hates books?' remarked one of the senators. 'Rovigo hates books too. Let us send him there.'

There was always a vacancy for a priest in the ugly town of Rovigo, anathematised throughout the Veneto for its brutish ways.

'How big is the congregation there of a Sunday?' asked another senator.

'Three, perhaps, if you count the verger's widow and the mice.'

The night before Sosia's sentence was due to be carried out, Wendelin walked along, talking to his own feet. He wondered if he could have shared his problems with his brother Johann. It had not been their habit to talk of intimate things but these years in Venice and those happy times with his wife had taught

Wendelin to open his heart like a child who weeps. It was not easy to become self-contained again.

The one person he longed to turn to was closed to him now. She would not look at him, except for strange moments when her eyes locked on his and sent an almost palpable comet of pain straight into his heart. He understood that this was her sadness, which he had somehow caused, and that she was mutely asking him to taste it. If he concentrated, he could do so, and it tasted strangely like his own. But he could not understand what made her feel that way.

The other night, for example, when he arrived home not much before midnight, she'd looked almost frightened to see him. She laid his food in front of him with such a crafty expression on her face that he wondered if she had poisoned it. He felt her breath behind his neck as he bent over his plate.

She talked more than usual, but of disconnected, strange things. She did not even enquire as to the problems that kept him so late at work. His experiment with scented inks had gone disastrously wrong. He himself had seized the ladle to stop the emulsification that spelled the ruin of all his expensive ingredients. He stirred so hard he'd splashed his hair and face, cried out with the pain of the hot fluid in his eyes. They still hurt sorely.

Wendelin asked himself now: 'But did I get sympathy? Did I get salve?'

She loved ghost stories; to smooth things down he'd even asked for one of those, and all he got was sour berries, no honey, a tirade and a sheaf of bills.

Pins and needles bit his hands when she looked at him like that.

At dawn he fled the house and walked swiftly towards the *stamperia*. He had no time to wash. The perfume still stung his eyes and clung to his hair. In the silent courtyard, he splashed himself furtively with icy water from the well, humiliated and wretched. Now anyone could see how he was exiled from his own home.

The plague had deranged her, he tried to tell himself. The early symptoms of her distressed state were probably warnings of the disease taking its grip. Yet now that she was well, she derived no apparent pleasure from her continued existence. She had isolated herself from all other creatures, even sent a maid to Rialto, and was as indifferent to the bloom of each grape or plum as she had previously been raptly attentive.

He remembered how she had once, during their courtship, seized his finger and run it delicately along the fuzzy contour of an apricot. He remembered sharing that same apricot with her, and her laughter, '*Ecco*, my darling, we each have a mouthful of sunshine!'

Wendelin remembered how he had loved to hear the swish of her dress as she glided up the stairs and the clink of her bracelet against the table as she laid down her fork. Lussièta used to have the most amazing sense of scent, a historical sense of it! With her tiny nose, she could sniff old smells and guess what they were when they were young. Of course most of all, like all the Venetians, she liked the odours of fish, salt water and luxurious perfume . . . and the scent of his own neck each night when he had kissed her. Then she would bury her nose in the folds of his skin.

She had wished to live each day to the full. Her tiny frame had been robust with happiness. Her breasts had strained to escape her bodice. Her laugh was always exploding like a sneeze. Flocks of small joys flew up from her, like flicked gold dust, iridescent. Her lips had been full of mischief, forever imprinting quick kisses on his hand, his elbow, his mouth, declaring 'Aha! You are haunted by butterflies!' She would seize their son in one hand, scooping up the cat in the other and dance them both around the kitchen in a wild, poetic ballet. Their son had laughed his fat baby chuckle; even the cat had folded its paws and curled its tail, snuggling closer into the crook of her arm as if it, too, like Wendelin, wanted to be closer to the source of all that grace and all that energy. And then she would land great smacking kisses on the heads of the cat and the baby and fling them both into the air for a moment till they landed, a tangled ball of fur and soft pink skin, in her arms, and she would be dipping her head among paws and fat dimpled legs to land yet more kisses upon them.

The image faded in his mind, merging with the wife he had now, this wife of straw, damp as a wet rope, who slid from his arms, lay slackly in the bed or folded in a chair.

She doesn't wish to live now, she who was life itself before, he thought. A sudden, hideous thought struck him. He turned and ran, in the direction of their house.

Chapter Six

Love is all armed
even when he's naked.

Paola has come to taunt me again. Like a witch, she knows just which nerve to stab to make me writhe in front of her.

She brought fruit in a glass dish that she held in front of her like a battle-ram when I opened the door. I did not ask her in, but she walked in anyway and followed my listless steps to the kitchen. There she faced me squarely and said: 'Your man is not unfaithful to you, you know.'

What I know is that she means the opposite is true. She who spends her nights on the streets with a red-haired man. For all I know she rents out her body like . . .

I slammed my mouth shut and would say nought. I do not reach out for the fruit, for I do not want her to see that my hands show the light and dangle like loose threads.

When she had gone, I went back to the book about how to deal with wives.

The book says the little wife should go to the stool. It says the little wife should climb it.

I can no more bear it.

I read the last note from the box once more.

'I want to see the air beneath your dancing feet.'

There is no doubt what he wants. I do not fight more, neither his cold heart nor my mid-fall madness.

It was only a little love story, I suppose, in its way. But it was mine.

My bracelets are so heavy I can hardly raise my arms.

How easily may a love story turn into a ghost story.

Once I predicted that the *fondaco* would get its own ghost. Now I think it will be mine.

Bruno sat in the somnambulant *Piazzetta*, looking at the columns.

He rehearsed his agony, and hers. It was on a platform here that Sosia would be lashed to the wicker frame before she was beaten and branded. The mark of the witch would be burnt into her cheeks. There would be the smell of her own burning meat loud above her screams.

He had seen a branding before. He remembered the glow of the brand iron soaking up the red of the fire, and the white sparks which leapt from it as the executioner pulled it from the flames. The crowd had drawn breath then, looking from the red metal to the cheeks of the man, a seller of spells, who was to bear its imprint. Bruno looked away at the last moment, but he remembered the unbearably sweet roasting aroma and the pig-like shrieks of the man as the metal approached his flesh. Then silence, for a long time, before another inhuman cry pierced the air like a bird of prey. It had come much too late, when they all believed him far beyond pain. This was the worst horror, for then in their minds they were forced to re-live the last unspeakable seconds of his silent agony.

Sosia never cried, but she would shriek, he knew, at *that* moment, when it came to her.

He listened to the *campanile*. Each of its five bells had its own task. The littlest, the *Maleficiò*, announced death sentences, tinkling down like little drops of blood. It would not toll Sosia's death today, but that was pure hypocrisy. Sosia could not survive that treatment.

An owl hooted among the houses. Bruno recalled the old superstition – a girl somewhere near had just lost her virginity. He sat huddled in the moonlight, remembering how that had felt for him, in Sosia's arms.

A plan began to stir in his head, almost too hideous to contemplate.

At dawn, Bruno went to work. Emerging from the shadows, Felice Feliciano greeted him at the door, taking Bruno into his arms and stroking his back.

'But why?' whimpered Bruno.

Felice answered: 'Sosia's case has shown what the senators always suspected . . . a low foreigner might use sensuality to bring down a noble Venetian, who is after all a piece of the state.'

Bruno muttered: 'But why do we do nothing? Why do we stand around and allow her to be killed slowly?'

'We've no power compared to what is ranged against her now. The crowds are disposed to hate her already. They blame her for the massacre. She must bear the full fury of the State and the wrath of the populace between those slender thighs, and upon the scar on her back . . .'

At this intimate description of Sosia, Bruno had looked at him, and suddenly understood, as Felice wanted him to do. He knew that this stripping of discretion was Felice's gift, a way of helping him to hate Sosia, liberating him a little from the pain of her demise. Felice had offered to sacrifice their friendship in order to help Bruno bear his burden a little better. Bruno could understand Felice, and appreciate all this, but he could not bear to be with him.

'I see,' he said, white-lipped. 'You too, Felice?'

'Hate me if you must, but, please, my dearest Bruno, you must know that I love you,' said Felice, 'and such hopeless love is grievously hard to bear.'

Wendelin was rushing back to the house, up the stairs towards their bedroom past his study, past the cabinet, *no, stop*, there was something sticking out of a drawer. It was his own paper, but pocked with little holes, like insect bites. Had she taken to storing things in there? In the cabinet she hated so much?

Wendelin opened the drawer, and pulled out the document.

It was folded in a packet, as were all his love letters to his wife. He opened it and read, scrawled in his own hand, 'I bind you with the ropes of love, tight, tight.'

Wendelin felt nauseous. How clumsy was his imagery! How primitive his Italian! He suddenly saw a threat hidden in his own words of love. Perhaps Lussièta too had chosen to read his letter like that, had extracted only what could be malevolent from it.

He opened another drawer. Another parchment packet lay inside. He read: 'I want to see your lovely eyes wide open as when rope tightens.'

He wrenched open other drawers.

His letters were to be found in every drawer, each one, in this new sinister light, terrifyingly ambiguous.

Her failure to thrive, her illness, he saw it all now, understood where it had come from.

But the letters, how? It seemed to him that the drawers of the cabinet had been secreting them, like poison from a gland. More and more letters he pulled out. The cabinet was a veritable manufactory, more productive than the *stamperia*. But all the letters were written in Wendelin's own hand.

'I want to possess you in this life – and the next.'

'I won't be happy till you're beyond all this pain.'

Wendelin shivered, stuffed the letters back in the drawers and slammed them shut.

It's an evil thing, this cabinet, his thoughts raced. *I have let its beauty distort my heart. Lussièta was right,* he reflected. *I should have listened to her. She is sensible of far more things than I, though she scorns most books. She believes and apprehends things at a level that is far deeper than my own perceptions. I merely read and nod my head to the facts that enter. The transaction is shallow. Lussièta's convictions run in her blood.*

Where is she? he thought suddenly. *My poor, sweet, abused darling? I have so many apologies to make her.*

And then he heard a noise upstairs in the attic, a swinging, creaking noise.

Bruno bought a single arrow in the *frezzeria*. Alone in his apartment, he practised until he could barely hold the bow, until he had to make an effort to miss the target.

At two in the morning, he approached the cell, stumbling across the unpaved

Piazza. He walked through the vines and trees in one corner, past the small stonecutters' yard in the shadow of the *campanile*. He automatically turned his head to avoid the stench of the humble latrine that served the populace. Even by night, when the moonlit basilica was at its most gorgeous, the ripe odour of human manure reminded Bruno of the oddly combined magnificence and earthiness of the Piazza, like a noble lady rusticating at her country villa. By day there were flesh and fruit markets, bakers, dentists and barbers and notaries. There were little shops encumbering the very columns of the Doges' Palace and a hospital. Disgraced clerics clung to the bars of their cages under the *campanile*.

All life and death, he thought, *and now Sosia was here among it, not hiding away in San Trovaso for once, but on display for everyone.*

Not that there was anyone to watch her at this dead hour.

He peered down. Sosia lay asleep, attended by drowsing rats. How could she sleep? Knowing the long torture that awaited her in the morning?

He knelt down to look more closely. She was half turned away from him and seemed to be in deep slumber. He could see the outline of one eyelid, dark red in the faint moonlight. Her dark hair looked cleaner and more lustrous than he remembered it, as if she were growing to a kind of sainthood. She lay softer in sleep than he had ever seen her, in the brief moments he had watched her at rest in his rooms. She had hooked her hands round her back, with her torso curved and her knees drawn up. From behind, she looked as if she was lying in someone else's arms.

I was selfish, thought Bruno, *I wanted her to be good. She had no instincts for it. It was like forcing a dog to fly or a cow to swim.*

They were also selfish, he added, *those other men. They wanted her to be more bad than she is. And what did her husband want with her? Is he happy with this result?*

How marginal he had been to her life; he had no idea what Rabino Simeon thought of his wife and her apparent crimes, whether he knew or cared that Sosia was not guilty of witchcraft.

Still on his knees, Bruno drew the bow from his cloak, positioned the arrow. He hesitated for a second, not unsure of his task, but seeking the best angle for the trajectory of his arrow.

He whispered softly: 'I love you. I'm sparing you a fate you would despise, my darling. I'm saving you from unbearable pain.'

In the moment the arrow left the bow, perhaps roused by the singing whir of its flight, Sosia awoke. She looked straight at Bruno, and her lips opened. The arrow went directly to her throat, piercing the vein. It shot through her neck: suddenly its tip glinted at the other side.

Bruno remembered running his finger along that soft throat. He recalled the moments he'd looked on it with hatred, as lies about her activities emerged from it through her mouth.

She was trying to claw the arrow from her throat but succeeded only in snapping off the stem, widening the wound from which her blood now pulsed in thick spouts.

Bruno watched as the rats woke, and surrounded her. He saw her head fall back, the wing of the arrow fall from her hand.

He did not weep or tremble as he had supposed he would. Instead Bruno felt a sensation of heat in his hands and a burning blush on his cheeks. He'd forgotten to breathe for many seconds; now he fought for air.

Then he felt a tender hand caress his shoulder, and Felice's smooth confidential voice in his ear. 'I thought I might find you here.'

For a moment, Bruno roused himself to bitterness. 'Couldn't keep away from her, then?' he shot at Felice.

The scribe closed his eyes briefly, acknowledging the taunt. 'It's not that, Bruno. It's you I was looking for.'

Bruno was feeling faint. His features were fast decomposing into a grimace, his profile blurring with a slick of tears. Felice peered into his face, reading it. Shocked, he took a step backwards.

For the first time, Felice looked down into the cell and then back at the bow in Bruno's hand. Then he brushed Bruno's hair back from his pale forehead and kissed him there. Swiftly, he took the bow from Bruno's hand and dropped it in the canal. He came back to Bruno and put an arm around his shoulder, gently uprooting his feet from the paving in front of Sosia's cell.

Bruno spun around to look at Sosia but Felice, taking his chin, turned it in the direction of the sea, gently but firmly.

'Quick! We must be quick now, Bruno. We must get away from here.'

Bruno felt the pads of his feet rise one after another. He looked down on them – yes, he was really walking away. It was possible then, simply to leave. No footsteps followed them. The rasp of their two breaths rose and fell in unison.

When they were five hundred paces from the cell, in a square where life still rousted on in the taverns, they stopped and faced one another.

Neither spoke of what had just happened. They stood in silence, each searching the eyes of the other. They waited for the sounds of discovery from San Marco, for shouts and running feet. None came.

'Gentilia has sent word to me from Murano. She begs you to go to her,' said Felice, at last. 'But first there are some things I have to tell you about your sister.'

He handed Bruno a piece of paper. Gentilia's careful script covered it. Bruno held it to the light of the tavern door. It was a draft of the letter that cast a spell on the soul of Nicolò Malipiero.

'Gentilia did this?' Bruno asked, 'not Sosia?'

'Not Sosia.'

Bruno lurched where he stood. With one hand, Felice steadied his shoulder.

'Then I shall not go to her, not now and not ever. Better to go to Sosia. She was honest with it. Innocent, even.'

Felice said: 'Sosia was not innocent.'

'She must have been once.'

Bruno tried to imagine her, not contorted in death but in love and passion, with him, on his pallet. Nothing came to him. The memory of her face had dispersed from his mind like condensation from a mirror.

Felice was guiding him along the stones, and he did not, for many minutes, ask where they were proceeding with such speed and intent. Only when they reached Rialto and started to climb the wooden steps of the bridge did Bruno pause to ask, 'Where?'

'To the Locanda Sturion, to Caterina,' said Felice, 'she's asked me to bring you to her.'

'At this time? I – I'm not ready—'

'And nor is she, but it's good that you go there now, and talk to her a little. It will be good for both of you,' said Felice. 'You think love is all about losing. Let me tell you that winning is more beautiful,' he added, with a smile.

He was surprised to find that this smile cost him something, and that he was still prepared to give it.

472

After Wendelin cut her down, his wife smiled at him before she passed out.

Though she lay unconscious, by the second she grew more fresh and lively in complexion. Her eyelids twitched and more small smiles came and went from her lips.

The plague sores, too, seemed to grow fainter and he unwrapped her from her outer clothes and laid her on the bed. The bruising on her neck had not yet become livid. In the candlelight she looked as unmarked as she had the day they married.

While he gazed down on her, panting, she stirred and raised her head a little, offering her lips to him. She tugged at the ribbon of her chemise and reached for his hand, which she brushed over her lips.

Come to bed, she told him silently. *We must find each other again.*

He bent over her, kissing her softly on her nose, her lips, her forehead. She sniffed at his neck, and smiled with pleasure. Then she sniffed again, burying her nose in the skin.

Before he joined her, but explaining his intentions in sign language first – he wished to follow her example and so avoided words just yet – Wendelin went to the room with the cabinet and smashed it with an iron stool.

When it was buckled and splintered, he heaved the corpse of it to an open window and pushed it into the ink-black canal. He did not look to see if it floated against the tide, as its eggs had done before it.

Chapter Seven

*No woman can say that she was loved
as Lesbia is loved by me, and not lie.
No bond was ever struck like the one that binds me to her.*

It seems so long since I heard the box smash and fall in the water. Yet just one year has passed since that day, a year of prodigies.

We have both learned, now, to give and take on the matter of the box. My man has learned to admit that it was wrong to buy it and bring it to our house. I have learned to admit that there was nothing wrong with the letters he wrote me. From the moment he saved me I knew that the missives I'd thought so deadly were merely misunderstood, deformed by the mistaken thoughts that had grown up between us. The box, I mean the cabinet, had not poisoned them, my own mind did that.

My man has learned to respect the ghosts of Venice. I have learned to laugh at them, under certain circumstances. We have both learned that instinct is not the converse of reason, nor ghosts the opposite of life.

We have also learned to open our world and love our friends better. It's not healthy for the soul to be sealed up in a bubble of just two people, no matter what rainbows appear inside. Fondle secrets in your breast and they will cut your heart. When things go wrong, as they do, one needs friends to reach in and explain the truth from the outside.

Bruno and Caterina come to us often, and Bruno is teaching our son the poems of Catullus. Little Johann lisps them out and they are so sweet on his tongue. I love to hear him tell the sparrow poems. Bruno has started to write poetry himself! He's too shy to present it in public as yet, but Caterina, blushing, tells me it is beautiful.

It was at our house that Bruno first came face to face with my dear Rabino, the husband of his old lover, and I thought the moment would be sore. In fact both men stared for a moment, and an identical tear came to the corner of each of their right eyes. Then they silently embraced, while Caterina and I wept, she gracefully, I noisily.

Now Bruno helps Rabino to record the plagues that sweep the city from time to time, in the hope that one day something may be learned from the pattern of the outbreaks. Rabino in turn goes to visit Gentilia in the place on Murano where they keep her, and it is he who tells Bruno of the progress of her treatment, which is slow, but there is hope of a good outcome in the end. She will never live a normal life, but it may come to a point where she's not a danger to anyone else. Kind care will stop her from following any more of her gruesome enthusiasms to so evil an end again. When Bruno swears Gentilia did not know what she had really set in motion I believe him. The merbabies, the rats sewn in shrouds, the witchery . . . I think she was absorbed in her strange passions and her mind was distorted at the same time with guilt. I know how these things discolour the world.

And Rabino has also helped the unfortunate dwarf who used to assist the vanished priest on Murano. It proved a swift and simple matter to cut off the dreadful birthmark that had blighted his looks, and with its removal such a torrent of sweetness and gratitude has flowed out of the man, that he has become devoted to Rabino and serves him with the loyalty of a disciple and Ianno has become obsessed with doing good where once he committed only badness.

And in this regard I think of Felice Feliciano who has become obsessed with the colour of gold. He has set himself up as an alchemist, which will surely ruin and disgrace him. He has drifted away from Venice and we see him but rarely, and then he has the blasted look of one cursed by a ghastly spell, like a man who has fallen in love with someone who returns his passion with cruelty. I cannot say I feel sorry at the thought of any misfortune falling on him. For Felice I have as much pity as there is milk inside a pigeon. I hate to think that he comes near Caterina and Bruno, for his corruptions might still cast a shadow between them.

I would like to say that I've softened with regard to my sister-in-law, that matrimonial phoenix Paola. I have not. Best not to dwell on it, but I still fail to see the point of such a woman. I suppose I wish her well. Johann di Colonia seems hale enough, so it will be some time before she's fitted out with a new husband. I hope the red-haired man does not lack patience.

Speaking of matrimony, our cat has found a wife who is not impressed with his thievery. He has hung up his swag and sneak. Since he got married, he looks embarrassed all the time. He even looks after the kittens when she goes out on business. Without his profession, he has grown somewhat portly.

Padre Pio from Speyer comes to visit us this autumn and I hope he shall arrive in time to baptise our new baby. For yes, it seems I am with child again. A daughter, this time, I've made sure.

But something else is growing inside me.

It is a love of words.

Now, each day I write a love letter to my man and wrap it around the good bread I prepare for him to eat mid-morning when he first lifts his head from his work at the *stamperia* and the hunger strikes him.

As the light falls I wait for him with as much joy as I used to dread his return. I picture him hurrying back to me, the loitering sun poppying his upturned face with its last drops. I see him pass the gondoliers churning fishes. I glimpse him through the wooden masts tiptoeing like drunks and above the waves gasping their last

476

on the pea-green steps. And everywhere he goes there springs up a smile, a confidential arm on his elbow. I see approving nods in his wake, heads drawn together. 'There goes our *Tedeschino*, our little German,' Venetians say to one another. 'Bless his gentle ways.' I see him stop a moment and wipe his eyes, glazed wet with gratitude for these sweet ways our town shows him its love.

And he in turn comes home with presents for me. Wherever he goes, to the *cartolai*, to the leather merchants, to the *Broglio* to talk to the senators, he always asks them, 'And have you heard any good ghost stories lately?' and when there is a good one, a ripe one with virgins and beasts and shivers down the back, then he takes me to bed early that night, and recounts it with his arms around me.

Postscript

You want something so desperately.
You long for it
without hope.
Imagine the species of joy
when it comes to you,
after all.
Is anyone happier than me?
Is there anything more to want?

He was a small man, it turned out, not tall and dark as some had styled him. No earring swung on his lobe. He sprouted no twirling moustachios. He did not swagger, and nor did he mince in the French manner.

He was red-haired in the sandy way, not with the auburn tints admired in Venice. His face was freckled; his eyes small and pale, his bearing modest. He carried a faint fragrance of rabbit-glue.

Wendelin was sitting at his desk, absorbed in a proof, a small roll of bread broken in fragrant pieces in front of him. No one else took notice of the red-haired man who stood hesitating on the threshold. He looked like a clerk of the State or a prosperous peddler.

Finally Morto called kindly to him: 'The *sensale*'s office is on the ground floor. We do not buy here.'

The red-haired man almost whispered, so modest was his speech: 'Ah no, that's not it. That's not . . . I am Nicolas Jenson and I have come to meet with Wendelin von Speyer.'

The *stamperia* fell silent. Each man stood rigid, watching the small man walk uncertainly across the floor towards Wendelin.

Jenson did not hold out his hand, but a small smile on his face betokened a strong and subtle inner warmth, like that at the core of the earth.

Wendelin had risen.

Jenson spoke softly but clearly: 'I have wished you no harm, you know.'

Wendelin nodded. He could see that now, looking at Jenson.

'Nor your wife, nor your son, nor all these men. I've been talking with Paola, your sister-in-law, and she has encouraged me to think that what I wish with all my heart may – may not be repulsive to you.'

Wendelin found his voice at last.

'Will you sit?' he asked, courteously. But Jenson took small steps closer to him till he stood at Johann's old chair. He put his hand on the back of it, seemingly exhausted by the effort of reaching it under the eyes of all Wendelin's men.

He stammered: 'I congratulate you. You published Catullus. I could never dare to do it.

'Yet if I had helped you . . .'

He drooped and wiped his brow. 'I'm losing my way. I am not much used to such . . .'

Wendelin murmured gently, 'There's no hurry.'

Jenson made a visible effort to rally himself. Finally, he said: 'It's simple as this. I admire your work. You are the only printer in Venice I respect. I would wish to be partners with you. Will you think on it, at least?'

There was silence in the room.

Jenson repeated. 'Will you think on it, at least?'

Author's note

The characters who are invented in this story are Sosia, Rabino, Bruno, Morto, Gentilia, Ianno, Padre Pio; also this particular Nicolò Malipiero.

The following characters really existed: Gaius Valerius Catullus and his brother Lucius, Gaius Julius Caesar, Clodia Metelli (Lesbia), and her brother Publius Clodius Pulcher, Felice Feliciano, Johann and Wendelin Heynrici von Speyer (though their actual surname is open to doubt), Paola di Messina and her father, Domenico Zorzi, Caterina di Colonna at the Sturion, Giovanni Dario, Gerolamo Squarzafico, Giovanni Bellini, Fra Filippo de Strata and his campaign against the printers (though not specifically against Catullus), Nicolas Jenson.

It is known that Wendelin married a Venetian girl, but the identity and personality of Lussièta are invented.

The poems of Catullus were indeed recovered from a corn or wine measure in Verona. From that point onwards the trail forks many ways. From that first manuscript, known as the Veronensis, the local scribe made a single copy, known to the scholars as *A*. Immediately thereafter the original Veronensis disappeared. Two more copies were made from *A*, the manuscripts now known as *O* and *X*. But as soon as *A* had been reproduced, it too became lost. *X* came into the hands of Gasparo dei Broaspini, of Verona, who lent it to the

Florentine scholar Coluccio Salutati. In this way *X* bred the copy *R*, which is to be found at the Vatican, and, in 1375, the copy *G* which is now in Paris. Many Renaissance scribes were given access to them. From the Vatican *R* and the Parisian *G* came a hundred manuscripts, and it is one of these I have attributed to Domenico Zorzi.

The first modern edition of Catullus was printed in Venice in 1472 by Wendelin von Speyer. He included in the book Tibullus, Propertius and Statius, though I have assumed his motive for doing so. This *editio princeps* does not appear to have been reprinted. The second edition of Catullus, including hundreds of needful corrections made by Francesco Puteolano, was printed in Parma by Stefano Corallo. Many more refinements were made to the text over the next thirty years, with poems that had run together separated and missing lines restored.

The Catullus poems are my own translations, made with the invaluable help of Nikiforos Doxiadis Mardas. Where possible, I take on trust that the emotional truth of poetry reflects the poet's personality and preoccupations. Scholars continue to debate the true identity of his Lesbia: there are several contenders. I have styled Catullus' brother Lucius a soldier, but he might equally have followed the family tradition of provincial tax farming. Troad was a peaceable outpost of the empire at that time. Lucius' death could be dated as late as 56 BC. His grave, as a prosperous Roman citizen, would probably not have been lost.

The wax *devotio* figure described in the book is of a type known in ancient Rome. Clodia's virtual trial by Cicero is as recorded in his *Pro Caelio*. Catullus may have attended, but it's also possible he was still in Bithynia at the time. The date of his death is probably 54 BC. I have supposed that he died of tuberculosis, which was rife in ancient Rome. In its prolonged state this disease causes a mind-wandering fever with diurnal peaks, common at dusk, hence the frequent alleged association with eroticism. One of his bitterly humorous poems refers to a severe cough.

Wendelin and Johann von Speyer were the first German printers to come to Venice (though not to Italy: Sweynheim and Pannartz went to Subiaco first, in 1465, then Rome in 1468).

It is not known exactly when and where the Speyers set up their printing works. A document relating to the betrothal of Johann's daughter in 1477 opens the possibility that they arrived in Venice well before 1468. Certainly they would have been involved with the *Fondaco dei Tedeschi* at Rialto (now Venice's main Post Office). The original building was burnt down in 1505 and quickly rebuilt as it stands today, although in its early days the façade of the new structure was decorated with frescoes by Giorgione and Titian, alas long since eaten away by the moist breath of the Grand Canal.

De Strata's sermons are based on several known ones and his poem against the printers (in fact written after the date of this story). His fate in Rovigo is imagined. In 1492 Filippo de Strata sent what he called 'a hundred and thirty-four verses in heroic metre' to the newly elected patriarch Tomaso Donato, and asked him 'to spread many copies of my words abroad through the printers, so that Your Grace will enjoy the fame you deserve'.

The currency crisis and persecution of the printers reflect real events in Venice in 1472. The tomb of Doge Nicolò Tron at the Frari bears an inscription paying tribute to his actions at that time.

The trial of Sosia Simeon is based on an actual case brought before the Venetian *Avogadori* in the 1480s: that of a Greek woman, Gratiosa, accused of seducing a Venetian nobleman with witchcraft. The judgement of the court and the punishment were as those handed down to Sosia in this book.

Jews, apart from doctors, were expelled from Venice from 1397 until the early sixteenth century, though the Jewish population in Mestre is thought to have been large, and a chronicle of 1483 records the presence of a fine synagogue there. Businessmen might enter Venice herself on two-week permits, were obliged to wear yellow circles sewn on their cloaks and possibly also yellow skullcaps, and their activities were limited to dealing in used clothes and money lending. Jews were occasionally accused of ritual murders, requiring the drinking of children's blood. Two cases of infanticide in the Veneto were blamed on the Jews for this reason. However, there was probably no more discrimination against the Jews than any other foreign race or religion in Venice. Sosia's maltreatment at the hands of the Venetian state is therefore as much to do with her foreign birth and low status as her race.

Jews were known to live in Serbia and Macedonia since early times but they were not recognised as a community there until 1492, after the mass exodus from Spain. The perception of Sosia as a Serbian Jew therefore reflects a purely Venetian point of view.

Giovanni Dario, born in Crete in 1414, was sent on diplomatic missions to the court of the Ottoman Sultan, and is thought to have arranged the 1479–80 residence of Gentile Bellini in Constantinople. Dario started rebuilding his house on the Grand Canal in 1486, between sojourns in the East. The new *palazzo* incorporated part of the original Gothic foundations. His daughter Marietta did marry a member of the illustrious Barbaro family but not till 1493. It is in fact to the new building that the famous curse still clings. Dario's daughter was the first victim, dying of a broken heart after her father and husband were ruined. Financial scandals, murders and suicides have continued up until the present day. The building, near the Salute end, remains unoccupied and still anathematised by most Venetians at the time of writing. But photographs of the interior show a house of exquisite beauty with a heavy oriental influence. The cabinet is invented, as are the roach and Damascus Plague.

The Sturion was there in those times, though known as the Sturgeon. An inn called the Sturion still offers accommodation at Rialto.

The nunnery of Sant' Angelo di Contorta really existed. The Pope closed it down in 1474 after too many cases of fornication by its nuns – fifty-two in the fifteenth century alone. The nunnery was to be absorbed by the more virtuous establishment of Santa Croce on the nearby island of Guidecca. But the noblemen who had sent their daughters to Sant' Angelo and endowed it with gifts, were unhappy with this edict, and a typically Venetian compromise was reached. The nuns who still lived in Sant' Angelo were permitted to stay there until their deaths, though no new nuns were to be admitted. Thus prosecutions for sex crimes continued even until 1518, only decreasing gradually as the inhabitants presumably grew too old to be sexually attractive to their former patrons. Finally the last nun died and the convent closed its doors in 1555, when it was turned into a powder magazine. One day in 1589 the powder was accidentally ignited and the convent was destroyed completely in a vast explosion, leaving no trace whatsoever apart from the stain of its reputation in the legal annals of Venice.

Pero Tafur, a Spanish traveller in Venice, recorded the plague of baby corpses in the lagoon when he visited in 1436.

The spells and talismans researched by Gentilia reflect evidence presented in contemporary witchcraft trials. The ghosts described by Lussièta are still said to haunt Venice today. The *triaca* was indeed the drug of choice for Venetians, a picturesque concoction of amber, herbs and eastern spices, probably as harmless as it was useless. The free-ranging Tantony pigs were in fact deprived of their freedom in Venice by special decree in 1409.

Wendelin and Lussièta's journey back to Germany is imagined, though based as much as possible on early accounts of such travels. The cat-headed dragon of the Alps is cited and delightfully illustrated in several early guidebooks. Wheeled traffic did not come to the Alps until 1775. The Inn of the Red Bears still offers hospitality in Freiburg. Evidence of early Renaissance life in Speyer is fragmentary: the French systematically torched Speyer in 1689, and Napoleon later looted what was left of the town archives, carrying off 160 boxes of precious papers that were never seen again. However, it remains a handsome and comfortable little town, still dominated by its immense cathedral, very close to Little Heavens Alley and not far from the well-preserved Jewish bath.

Whatever sexually transmitted disease Sosia contracted and spread, it is unlikely to have been modern syphilis. The arrival of the 'mal franzoso/napoletano' is usually associated with the return of Columbus' sailors from the New World. Certainly most authorities cite the mid-1490s as the moment from which western Europe became infected. However, many venereal diseases, including gonorrhoea, were already rife at the time this book is set.

The words of Lussièta's mock-*Sposalizio* are based on Giovanni Gabrieli's madrigal *Udite, chiari e generosi figli*.

The accounts of early printing techniques are as accurate as I could make them. Watermarks on the papers used by Wendelin von Speyer include scissors, scales, winged lion, bull's head with a crown, lily, dragon and castle. Jenson was indeed interested in small formats very early. His chosen title was the *Officiettum*, a little service book usually of the prayers to the Madonna. Three versions are recorded, the earliest in 1474, later than I have portrayed here. They were printed in *sedecimo*, and they were hardly cheap, priced between half a lira and a lira. But they were aimed at both priests and laymen, and they really would have fitted into a sleeve.

Giovanni Bellini's allegories painted on wood, including the painting I have suggested as a likeness of Sosia, are sometimes dated around 1480 but scholars have differing views. These tiny, exquisite paintings have recently been restored to their original colours and may be seen at the Accademia Gallery in Venice.

Felice Feliciano, born in 1433, was the link between the printers and the painters of Venice. The scribe's personality does appear to have been an extraordinary one. Martin Lowry, in his marvellous biography of Nicolas Jenson, sees in Felice's style 'a contrived perversity that carries a distant whiff of Beardsley and Baudelaire'.

Felice was a frequent visitor to Venice, and a close friend of Andrea Mantegna, the brother-in-law and intimate of the Bellini brothers. Lussièta's description of Catullus's lakeside home in Sirmione is based on Felice's account of the romantic excursion he and Andrea Mantegna made there in 1464. Several of his beautiful manuscripts have survived, including some letters to Domenico Zorzi, one of which amusingly describes his dream about a floating egg and an angry devil who warns him to desist from eating beans. Felice tried to set up a printing works of his own in 1475–6 but it appears to have failed. He died in 1479, having bankrupted himself with experiments in alchemy.

The Bellini brothers were definitely involved with the German community in Venice. Both brothers served as *sensali* in the *Fondaco dei Tedeschi*, as did Titian some time later. It is my belief that it is more than coincidence that the techniques of oil painting and printing came to flower in Venice at exactly the same time. It is tempting to imagine, as I have done, a shy friendship between Bellini and Wendelin, their worlds of art and ink linked through marriage (Johann and Paola) and Felice Feliciano. Giovanni Bellini's affinity with the northern sensibility is clearly evident in his work. Moreover, he was the only Venetian painter to develop an amicable relationship with Albrecht Dürer when the great German artist came to Venice in 1505. Perhaps his friendly contact with the early printers predisposed him to be more tolerant than his fellow-Venetians?

After the events of 1472, the Speyer–Colonia–Manthen partnership continued to battle out the Venetian market with Jenson. After Johann di Colonia died, Paola di Messina soon married again. Husband number four was Reynaldus of Nymegen, also a master printer, in September 1480.

But Wendelin himself gradually disappeared from view. By 1475 it seems that his entire editorial team was at Jenson's disposal. In 1476 Wendelin appeared to try to set up again but the enterprise lasted only a few months. He was last heard of in 1477 and afterwards there is silence. It is even possible that he returned to Speyer at this point.

Some writers have theorised that Nicolas Jenson worked for Wendelin and

Johann von Speyer until the latter's death, when he seized his opportunity to strike out alone, but I believe that he arrived in Venice with fully-formed ambitions of his own.

Venetian printing was changed for ever by a particularly virulent plague in 1478. Of the twenty-two firms active at the outset of that year only eleven remained when the disease slackened its grip. At that point some of the old rivals amalgamated . . . Jenson and Johann di Colonia (Paola von Speyer's third husband) fused as a single company. But Johann di Colonia died in 1480 and Jenson soon afterwards. My final scene, in which Jenson visits the *stamperia* von Speyer, is wishfully imagined.

Wendelin was right: Jenson did indeed become something of a cult, not unlike his indirect heir Aldus Manutius, whose Aldine Press would become the most famous of the Renaissance period. (The first Aldine edition of Catullus, incidentally, was printed in 1502, and the run was an astonishing 3000 copies.)

But modern scholarship has restored to the Speyer brothers the historical honour of being the first printers to set to type and print a book in Venice.

And there is no doubt at all that it was Wendelin von Speyer who first published the poems of Gaius Valerius Catullus.

Acknowledgements

I would like to express my most affectionate thanks to my editor Jill Foulston, and my admiration for her deft and graceful way of unlocking what was imprisoned inside the original manuscript. Warm thanks in this regard, and in so many other ways, are also very much due to my agent, Victoria Hobbs at A.M. Heath.

I'm grateful to Simon P. Oakes, for his invaluable advice with background to the German community in Venice. I would like to thank Alan Morrison for translating archival records of the *Fondaco dei Tedeschi*; Jelena Brayovic and my father Vladimir Albert Lovric for their help with the Serbo-Croatian proverbs and curses. For examining various historical details in my manuscript, I thank Rabbi Paul Roberts, Howard Fitzpatrick of Venice Art, and most particularly Martin Lowry, who was astonishingly generous with his time and own research archives. For help with the typographical history, I thank Peter Fraterdeus, Laurence Penney and Lilian Armstrong; for checking my accounts of Catullus and ancient Rome, Peter Wiseman and Llewelyn Morgan.

I am grateful to Ornella Tarantola for checking my Italian translations and the *Italianness* of my characters, and to Wendy Oliver and Susannah Rickards for their help in refining the text.

With thanks also to the staff at the British and the London Libraries and the Marciana Library in Venice and the National Gallery in London.

This book was written with the help of a research grant from London Arts for which I am most grateful.

I also acknowledge the extraordinary generosity of the academics and curators in Germany who gave freely of their time and expertise to help me track down what precious little is known about Wendelin and Johann von Speyer. I was able to reconstruct part of Wendelin's life and work with the help of Hannelore Müller at the Gutenberg Museum in Mainz, Hartmut Harthausen of the Pfälzische Landesbibliothek in Speyer, Cornelia Ewigleben of the Historischen Museum der Pfälz, and particularly Katrin Hopstock of the Stadtarchiv Speyer. Above all, the fondest thanks to the superb town guide, Irmtrud Dorweiler, who showed me all the sights of Speyer, and cheerfully submitted to all my strange inquisitions. It was only when she checked the last draft of the novel that I felt confident that I had, with her vital help, recreated in Wendelin a real citizen of Speyer in the late Middle Ages.

And in Venice warmest thanks again to Sergio and Roberta Grandesso, this time for all the *prosecco*, and to Graziella, Emilio and Valentina Scarpa, for many more 6 a.m. *ottimi cappucci poca schiuma* ('*tipo Michelle*') at the bar da Gino at San Vio, without which this book would never have met its deadlines; speaking of which, by the time *The Floating Book* is published Valentina will have given birth to twins who were not dreamt of when this book was conceived.